ANOTHER DAY

BY
JEFFERY FARNOL

LONDON
SAMPSON LOW, MARSTON & CO., LTD.

MADE AND PRINTED IN GREAT BRITAIN BY PURNELL AND SONS
PAULTON (SOMERSET) AND LONDON

CONTENTS

v

ANOTHER DAY

CHAPTER I

DESCRIBES A MEETING OF IMPORT

THIS narrative should begin with the death-sob of
Red Rory as the murderous bullet smote him from
life; it should continue with the sick awaking of
young Keith, Dallas, Chisholm in a certain evil haunt
of Hell's Kitchen, New York City, to find himself
staring into a hated face, seen as it were through
a swirling mist, a ghastly face—grey, dead, blood-
smeared, and beneath his own lax fingers a revolver,
while with throbbing brain and mind a very chaos
of horror he strove desperately to think back . . .
dispel this dreadful mist that benumbed his every
faculty . . . to remember. . . .

But:

This narrative really opens with song of a lark
carolling joyously in the sunny air high over a certain noble swell of the Sussex Downs whereon lay
young Keith, Dallas, Chisholm flat on his back, a dusty,
travel-worn figure, gazing up at the soaring bird with
such wistful, haggard eyes. Sitting up wearily at
last, he glanced down at the crumpled letter in his
fingers, a large sheet of thick notepaper bearing neither
date nor address but these words in bold, hasty scrawl:

"There are sins I can forgive and have forgiven
you, but murder is not one of them. Your allowance

shall be paid as usual so long as you keep clear of the States and forget you were ever the son of

"WILBUR I. CHISHOLM."

"And that's—that!" sighed the outcast. "It's rough on the poor old dad, yes—it's certainly mighty tough . . . !" And presently, crumpling the letter in quivering fingers, he struck a match, lighted the paper and, sighing dismally, watched it burn.

"Ooh—a bun-fire!" cried a gleeful voice, and glancing swiftly up and around, he saw a very small damsel scrambling towards him down the grassy slope. Mutely he stared at this child with his troublous, long-lashed grey eyes and she at him with eyes very wide, brown, and critical.

"Good afternoon, man!" said she, demurely.

"Hello—girlie!" he answered, gently.

"But aren't you going to make a bun-fire, please?"

"Why no," he replied, almost apologetically and smiled, whereat she smiled also and in manner so friendly that he felt strangely comforted, and reached out as if to touch her bright hair, then hesitated, stared at his hand with dilating eyes, clenched it suddenly and let it fall. The child came nearer.

"Yesterday," she announced, "our cat 'Blinda found three teeny-weeny kittens in our Sarah's workbox!"

"You don't say?"

"Yes I do, man. And Sarah was dreffly cross, an' said drattem, she'd drownem. So I said she was a beast, an' so she is. Sometimes I can't 'bide our Sarah. Then Aunt Jemima, that isn't our real aunt, you know, sent me to bed and no tea—not a scrinch only my sister Jo brought me some an' jam too, an' kissed me. Jo's nice though she is all growed up. An' she's going to let me have one of the weeny kittens for my ownself—you see she likes me, Jo does though I am troublesome—a bit."

"Sure she does, girlie. But what are you doing out here all alone?"

"Well," she answered, sitting down beside him and arranging the somewhat shaggy bunch of cowslips she had gathered, "I'm looking about for a rich husbant."

"Gee-whiz!" he murmured, staring into the demure, little face. "You've sure started mighty early!"

"Oh yes," she sighed, "hours an' hours ago, but I haven't found any yet, there don't seem many about on the Downs to-day, though I've looked an' looked."

"Well, well!" said he, opening his grey eyes a little wider. "Now what d'you know about that!"

"Only what our Aunt Jemima said this morning—she said: 'Someday we must find Patience a rich husbant,' an' I'm Patience so I came out to find one for my ownself. You see I'm nearly growed into eight."

"And—are you named Patience, really and truly?"

"I are, man. Though our Sarah says mother should have put an 'im' in front, 'cause I'se so impatient."

"And what does your mother say?"

"She can't say anything now, man, 'cause she's a holy angel."

"Oh!" he murmured, "So is mine," and he turned to stare down and away across the wide valley where village and hamlet nestled amid the green of bowery trees.

"An' now, man, please what's your name?"

"Well folks call me . . . you can call me . . . Dallas, Dal, for short."

"But you're awful' long, you know!" she answered, pointing at his dusty legs. "But I like your face, 'specially when you smile."

"Do you, Honey, do you?" he inquired with a strange eagerness. "Honest and true, Hon, do you?"

"Oh yes," she nodded. "Are you a rich man?"

"Why no . . . no I'm afraid not——"

"No, I was 'fraid not," she sighed, glancing at his shabby person. "Your hat's not a rich man's hat—nor your boots. But if you could only grow yourself rich you'd do an' then I'd marry you an' have a motor-car like Mr. Meredith, an' give Jo a ride in it if she 'haved herself an' was p'lite to me."

"Jo?" he repeated. "That sounds a kind of pretty name to me, Honey."

"Well her reel name's Josepha an' she's quite growed up, with red hair—bobbed you know, and keeps bees an' they stung me once oh triffic! But I love honey, only she sells it nearly all. And Aunt Jemima says bees are spiteful beasts, an' so they are. An' she keeps chickens too—lots an' lots, only it's been such a drefful bad season for eggs."

"Josepha!" he murmured. "That sure is a dandy name, Honey, as pretty as your own. And where do you live?"

"Oh miles an' miles—triffic!" answered the Small Damsel stabbing slim finger towards the wide valley below. "There, behind those trees, the thatched cottage. You can't see it, but it's there. And nobody ever called me 'Honey' before. Why do you call me honey, please?"

"Well it's just an American love-name."

"Well, I like it better than Patience or Pat or Patty, an' I simply 'dore honey!"

"Then won't you please call me 'Dal'—just once?" he pleaded, with look and tone so wistful that she edged nearer, and proffered him three wilting cowslips.

"Why do your eyes look so big an'—weepy?" she demanded.

"Do they, Hon?" said he, glancing down at the flowers in his hand.

"Yes—jest like Jo's when she hasn't got quite 'nough to pay Mr. Jessam—he's a great beast, he is an' with a beard. I hate beards, don't you, Dal?"

"Sure thing, Hon. But who's Mr. Jessam?"

"A large man that comes in a car an' lives on our rent. You see our cottage b'longs to him reely, an' he won't mend the sitting-room chimbley though it smokes dreffly awful sometimes."

Now listening to this sweet, childish voice, looking into these clear, childish eyes, there rushed upon him the blasting memory of those latter discreditable months in New York with their final culminating horror, and, knowing himself for what he was become —a fugitive from Justice, an outlaw branded by stain indelible, he bowed his head while the soul within him grew sick. . . .

"Now you look weepy again!" sighed little Patience suddenly. "Haven't you any friends—is that why?"

"Yes I . . . I guess that's why, Honey," he answered, keeping his eyes averted. . . . Out to him came a little hand, somewhat grubby, but full of cowslips.

"Ne-ver mind!" said she consolingly. "Here's more flowers what I picked for my angel, but she's got heaps of flowers in heaven an' you're a lone, lorn soul like Jesse Blee, the shepherd, only he's old with whiskers."

So the hand of Innocence took and clasped the hand of Guilt wherefore Dallas spoke, below his breath:

"God bless you, Honey!"

"Thank you!" said she, demurely.

"But, say now why do you thank me?"

"'Cause you prayed for me, an' our Sarah says I need sech a lot of praying for——"

At this moment, above a tussock of grass, a few yards away, rose a weather-beaten old hat shading a weather-beaten old face, yet a ruddy face lit by shrewd, bright eyes and framed in wiry whisker.

"Lordy!" exclaimed this head, and up from steep, grassy hollow rose a somewhat bowed figure yet all vigorous strength from stooping shoulders to lean, gaitered legs. "Lordy!" repeated the new-comer, and leaning upon the crook he carried, stared very hard at Dallas who, meeting this sharp scrutiny, immediately blenched with sense of guilt and extreme unworthiness.

"Good afternoon, Jesse!" quoth the Small Damsel in dignified yet kindly greeting. "He's a shepherd, Dal, an' his name's Jesse Blee," she explained. "How's your rheumatics, Jesse, an' where's your Roger?"

"Whoy Roger 'e be down-along Deepdene way arter them ewes, Mis' Pat, an' me rheumatics be naun so bad 'cept for me back, an' me feet, an' me 'ands, an' the j'ints o' me knees an' elbers, an' a crick in me back as ketches me crool noo an' then, otherwise I be purty chig. But Lordy, Mis' Patience, wot be doin' up 'ere arl b'yeself—an' 'long of a stranger tu?"

"Oh—but this isn't a stranger any more, Jesse," she answered, pointing small finger at Dallas's despondent figure. "You see I know him now, an' his name's Dal-for-short, an' he's a lone, lorn soul—jest the same as you, Jesse."

"Then 'e didn't ought to be!" retorted the old shepherd, frowning at the silent Dallas and shaking his head. "No 'e didn't nowise ought to be—nohow."

"But you're a lorn soul, Jesse, you tell everybody you are——"

"Sure-ly, Mis' Patience. But 'tis nat'ral in me for I be a old un. But 'e be a young un, and to be young an' lorn beant nat'ral—and yon come them ewes!"

Sheep were bleating, lambs were wailing and up from grassy steeps below a dog came bounding, a

large, very shaggy, tailless dog who leapt towards
Patience, red tongue a-flutter in joyous welcome,
then turned to survey Dallas with a pair of light-
grey, inquiring eyes, his shaggy coat seeming slightly
more shaggy than usual.

"This," explained the Small Damsel, "is Roger
an' he only bites beasts, doesn't he Jesse?"

"Ar!" nodded the shepherd, glancing at Dallas,
his dusty garments, somewhat askance. "Roger don't
like strangers—specially tramps an' sich."

Dallas smiled and reached out a large, well-cared
for and perfectly assured hand.

"Come, Roger!" said he gently. The dog cocked
an ear, tilted his head to the right, tilted it to the
left, snuffed, stepped forward and butted shaggy
crest to Dallas' caressing fingers.

"So—Roger's took to ee, then!" quoth the shepherd gloomily.

"Why sure," nodded Dallas, pulling the dog's ear,
"I like all animals, especially dogs and horses, and
I guess they know it."

"That theer dog knows a sight more 'n you'd think?"
quoth his master. "Got more sense nor a good many
huming beinks. My Roger's full of instink an' that's
better nor reason, leastways 'tis surer."

"And that's right, too!" nodded Dallas.

"Ar!" quoth old Jesse, nodding also. "My Roger
ain't to be took in by nothink nor nobody on four
legs or two, 'e knows 'is friends and 'is henemies an'
ax accordin'. An' theer aren't a better ship-dog in
Sussex, nor nowheres else an' wots more——"

Roger growled suddenly and sat up, shaggy coat
bristling, whereupon the old shepherd glanced round
about and pointed triumphantly with his crook.

"Theer, wot did I tell ee neow?" he demanded,
"Roger knowed."

"Knew what?"

"Why yonder comes young Ben Lomax—theer 'e be a-comin' over Windover 'long by ' the Giant '."

"Eh, Giant?" questioned Dallas.

"Ay, sure-ly! Doant ee know ' the Giant ', young feller?"

"Jesse means the 'Long Man'," Patience explained. "Haven't you seed him, Dal?"

"Why no, Honey."

"Then I'll 'duce you to him prensly——"

"And theer comes Ben, dannel 'im!" quoth the shepherd, pointing at a distant figure with his crook. "A bad un be Ben, allus usin' his fistes on folkses an' knockin' folkses down. Ye see 'e were a puggilist-chap up to Lonnon an' 'e can't nowise forget it."

"Meanin' he's fought in the ring?" inquired Dallas sitting up.

"Ar!" growled the old shepherd, "an' moighty ready to fight out of it tu—at any time."

"What's he doing down here?"

"'E be in Lord Withymore's stables. They du say as 'im an' 'is ludship punches each other regular —wi' them boxin'-gloves."

"Aha!" murmured Dallas, and turned to survey the approaching figure with a new interest, while Roger rumbled and growled in such uneasy fashion that the old shepherd thrust crook into his collar and bade him 'lie down!'

"So Mr. Ben Lomax kind of loves to fight, does he?" inquired Dallas, musingly.

"Ar! But theer aren't nobody left as dare stand up to 'im 'ereabouts," sighed Jesse, mournfully.

"Our Tom did last week, though!" said the Small Person. "Tom's our gardener, Dal!" she explained, "an' helps Jo with the chickens——"

"Ar, so 'e did, Miss Patty," answered the old shepherd sighing deeper than ever, "and got 'isself knocked down for 'is pains!"

"'Cause our Tom's only a little man, you see, Dal."

"Why then, bully for him!" nodded Dallas, still eyeing the approaching Ben, who showed as a smartish, fresh-complexioned, burly young fellow, small as to eye and nose but large as to chin and thick of neck and shoulders.

"Looks pretty hefty!" murmured Dallas.

"But only a Londoner!" quoth Jesse. "'E aren't Sussex 'e aren't, no—an' never can be!"

"Though a trifle heavyish about the pins!" murmured Dallas. Then the legs in question halted within a few yards of them and their owner spoke in voice aggressive as his looks:

"Hey, shepherd—you Jess, look arter that dawg o' yourn. I thrashed 'im once mind. One o' these days I'll take a gun to 'im——"

"Will ee so—will ee so?" cried old Jesse fiercely. "Then b' the pyx I'll tak' a gun to ee, sure-ly I will!"

"Shurrup!" cried Lomax, flourishing the stout ash-plant he carried. "Gimme any o' your lip an' I'll thrash 'im again——"

"You tech my dog an' I'll jag ee wi' me crook! Ar—jab yer eye out I will!" So saying the old shepherd turned and strode away, dragging the snarling Roger with him. Ben Lomax made to follow but meeting the unswerving gaze of Dallas, paused to eye him truculently.

"Well?" he demanded. "Wot are you starin' at?"

"I'm sure wondering," murmured Dallas.

"Well—wot abaht it? You'll know me again, praps?"

"No, sir-ree, not unless I have to."

"Wot d'ye mean, eh?"

"Into the discard for yours——"

"Eh?" demanded Lomax, seeming all jaw and chin.

"You sure pack some grouch——"

"Garn! You sounds like one o' them blarsted Ameri——"

"Hush-up!" said Dallas, admonishing finger upraised. "Remember the child!"

"Lumme! I bleeve you are a perishin' Yank——"

"And you," nodded Dallas, "fought in the States and were beaten by Gunshot Gragson in the third——"

"On a foul!" cried Lomax hoarsely. "On a foul as weren't a foul——"

"I saw the blow!" quoth Dallas.

"You'll see some more in a minute!" snorted Lomax. "Ah, an' feel 'em too—unless you're one o' them Yanks as is too proud to fight an' collared all our gold species—one o' them cursed Americans as we're payin' for keepin' out o' the war when it was a war—one o' them damned——"

"Bottle it—can the rough stuff!" quoth Dallas, reverting to the vernacular. "The girlie's piping us, so cut it out right now—pronto!" And his voice was soft as ever, but his eyes glittered suddenly beneath their long lashes. Ben Lomax's answer was an oath as, clenching his fists, he stepped forward eager for strife, in which same instant Dallas was on his feet and his smile, like the glint in his eyes, was a menace; then, even as they fronted each other thus, the Small Person was between them:

"Oh, Ben!" she exclaimed, little chin aloft, brown eyes serene, bearing herself like the small, great lady she was, "I'm s'prised at you! What'll ever our Sarah say? An' she won't let you kiss her any more —I know!"

Ben's fierce gaze wavered, his fists dropped and he scowled round about at the far-flung landscape like one at sudden loss, while the Small Person, pointing slim finger at him, continued inexorably:

"Sarah'll hate an' 'spise you worser an' worser—
an' so shall I too!"

"Miss Pat," said Ben, his gaze still afar, "get out
o' my way, like a good, little gal."

Patience merely wagged her small finger at him,
quoth she:

"Sarah told my sister Jo she'll never let you be
her husband—never. 'Drattim!' she said—I heard
her—'drattim, I'd rayther marry Farmer Jordan's
prize pig ' . . . an' then she said you was a blood-
thirsty hoger . . . and Oh Ben, what'll she say if
you knock down Dal like you did our Tom? She'll
say something drefful—triffically awful!"

Ben quailed anew, gurgled hoarsely in bull throat,
and shook his bullet head:

"You don't 'ave to go tellin' Sairey nothing, Missy,"
he growled (albeit pleadingly). "Sairey knows an'
says a sight too much——"

"Then you'll please not to knock Dal down."

"Right O, Miss Patty," sighed Mr. Lomax heavily,
"only don't ye say nothin' about me to Sairey—
promise now! See this wet—see this dry——"

"'Cross my heart I hope to die!" added Patience
as per the formula. "I promise, Ben."

"Right y'are, Missy!" he nodded and turned to be
gone but, so doing, scowled at Dallas across broad
shoulder and silently mouthed the words: "Next
time!" And so, away he strode.

"Ben's a beast!" said the Small Person, gazing
after him, "but sometimes almost a nice beast—to
me. An' his heart b'longs to our Sarah, he gave it
to her one evening by the big chicken-coop. I heard
him tell her so, an' she said she'd rather have a wrist-
watch. An' so should I—a teeny-weeny one, you
know, all real gold with di'monds onto it like Jo's,
only she had to sell hers to pay Mr. Jessam an' buy
some new brooders only they died, the chickens in

the brooders I mean—the rain an' the damp, you
know, chickens all hate rain an' so do I. Now hold
my hand and I'll take and 'duce you to the 'Giant'."

So Dallas took the small hand she proffered and off
they tramped together; she led him up steep, grassy
slopes upon whose velvety ling the foot trod unwearied,
up and up and so at last to a noble eminence upreared
in a gentle grandeur, whence he might look down across
this wide Sussex country—sunny meadows, darkling
woods, winding roads, sparkling streams, with grey
church-towers peeping here and there amid the green
of ancient trees—a smiling, rural landscape stretching
away mile on mile to where a far sea seemed to meet
sky in a vague, blue mystery.

She brought him at last to a narrow grassy path
bound on the one hand by a swelling, green upland
and on the other by precipitous green slope whereon,
deep cut into the soft turf was the colossal figure of a
man who stood, mighty arms outstretched, grasping
a staff or spear in either vasty fist.

"There he is!" cried Patience, flourishing her posy
of cowslips as if in greeting. "There's the giant,
isn't he triffic?"

"My, yes, he's certainly some monster!" answered
Dallas, gazing down upon the thing of wonder.

"Yes," nodded Patience, "and a long, long time
ago when I was young I used to be 'fraid of him 'cause
he is so 'normous big, but now that I'm growder-up
I know that big men are kind—an' you're awful'
big you know, Dal. An' now let me please 'troduce
you. Dear Giant," she called in soft, caressing voice,
"I've brought you a friend 'cause you must be so
lonely sometimes, 'specially at night in the rain an'
wind. Dear Giant this is Dal-for-short that I've
found for a husbant, so I want you to like him a lot
please. . . . Dal this is Mr. Giant Long-Man an'
whenever you see him you must 'member me 'cause

we'se all friends now for ever an' ever. And now, Dal, what do you say to him?"

Very gravely Dallas took off his shabby hat and bowed:

"Mighty pleased to meet you, Mr. Giant," said he, "and whenever I see you I'll sure remember our Honey—well, I guess yes!"

So they presently rambled on together again; and listening to the Small Person's artless chatter concerning Jo, her chickens, her ducks and her other worries in regard to proper feeding, bills, eggs, rent, broody hens, Mr. Jessam, murderous rats and divers other inconsequent items, Dallas began to understand how very hard and difficult life may be for one, especially a woman, young and spirited, whose father did not happen to be a multi-millionaire.

"So your sister Jo's all alone in the world, eh, Hon?"

"Oh no, she's got me, an' Sarah, an' B'lindy—that's the cat that found the teeny kittens——"

"I mean she hasn't a mother or father?"

"Well, I haven't either, you know, that's why she cries over me sometimes when she's very tired."

"Cries, does she, Honey?"

"Yes, an' calls me a norphan. The other night when I was saying my prayers she cried all over me —such watery tears, an' said 'however am I going to bring you up properly if things get any worser?' I s'pose she meant the chickens, they've gone off laying again—the beasts! So then a course I kissed her an' told her she must marry Mr. Meredith like he wants her to 'cause he's rich with a great, big house —oh fine! What's your house like, Dal?"

"Like nothing on earth, Hon,—you see I haven't got one."

"Oh but everybody has a house of some kind, else where do they go at night? Everybody must have a home, Dal, so where's yours?"

"Here and there, Hon, anywhere under my hat."

"Oh! An' your hat's so drefful old, Dal!"

"It sure is, girlie."

After this they went awhile in silence until at last she paused, sighing heavily.

"Tired, Honey?" he inquired tenderly.

"Not very—only I do wish you were rich, Dal, an' I want my tea."

"A great idea!" he nodded. "Where can we get some?"

"I'll show you, come 'long with me."

So down went they and down, across a chalky, flinty road, down a narrow, winding lane, past a small, bleak-seeming inn, along a shady path, through a small wicket-gate and then—Dallas halted suddenly, opened his long-lashed, sleepy-looking eyes, drew in his breath and stood staring.

CHAPTER II

SHE wore a faded jumper, a short, plaid skirt (also faded) and a pair of enormous rubber-boots . . . moreover she was scowling. . . .

But what o' that? The eyes of Keith, Dallas, Chisholm saw but the lissom beauty of that shapely body —nay, in puckered brow, deep eyes and jut of resolute chin he sensed something of the strong, brave soul of her . . . and instantly recognizing her for the Goddess of his Destiny, he stood mute and awed, drinking in (as it were) her every motion as she stood on the muddy verge of miry, little pool vainly endeavouring to drive a supremely nobby stake with a too-ponderous hammer grasped close beneath the head; once she smote—the stake wobbled; twice she smote —the stake fell into the pool with a splash.

"Oh—dash the thing!" panted the Goddess. . . . And then the Small Person spoke:

"Jo dear, I've been and found myself a husbant —here he is."

The Goddess turned swiftly, dropped the hammer into the mud, and, meeting Dallas' rapt gaze, flushed, glanced down instinctively at her tremendous boots and bit her rosy under-lip.

"Do you s'pose he'll do?" queried the Small Person, "I mean if he grows nice and rich. Please look at him, Jo."

The Goddess looked again and saw a tall, slim, shabby young man with eyes vaguely troubled and a general shrinking air that seemed somehow in odd contrast to the square set of his jaw. He saw a face deep-eyed, vivid of mouth and framed in bronze-gold hair cut close, sleek and shining like a golden helmet. And in this fateful moment she forgot even her vasty rubber boots and he, forgetting his diffidence and the dark and dreadful cause of it, stepped forward, took up the muddy hammer and drove the stake deep and firm.

"Will that do?" he inquired.

"Splendidly!" she answered.

"An' his name's Dal!" explained the Small Personage. "An' he's a lone, lorn soul like old Jesse Blee. And we bofe want our tea, please." Here, glancing from the child to the man, our Goddess flushed for no reason in the world and, aware of this, blushed furiously and stamped her foot petulantly, therefore, became aware of her rubber-boots and, glancing askance at Dallas, found him regarding them also . . . and then a bell tinkled faintly.

"That's tea!" cried the Small Person joyously.

"And I . . . I bid you . . . good afternoon!" said Dallas with a remarkable awkwardness, and his gaze still abased to the rubber-boots.

"They . . . they belong to Tom Merry!" explained the Goddess.

"I . . . er . . . beg pardon?"

"These—atrocities!"

"Oh yes . . . the gum-boots, of course!" he nodded. "They . . . don't seem to fit——"

"Of course they don't!"

"Yes I . . . I kind of noticed they didn't," he stammered.

"How frightfully clever of you!" she retorted.

"That means you think I'm a sure-enough gump,"
he sighed, "and I guess you're right. . . . Good-
bye——"

"Oh!" cried the Small Person. "But you can't
go and no tea! Now can he, Jo? 'Sides he hasn't
got any home to go to, he told me so his very own
self. So make him stay to tea, Jodear—jest to please
me, please!"

Hat in hand Dallas turned to be gone while Josepha,
this Goddess of his Destiny, stood mute and, for once,
completely at a loss. . . . But . . . glancing down
again at the "atrocities," these so detestable rubber-
boots, she remembered a certain pair of dainty shoes
carefully treed within doors, and her capable mind
was made up forthwith:

"Of course you will stay to tea—if you care to,
Mr. . . . Mr. . . . ?"

"My name is . . . Dallas," he answered in his
halting fashion, "Dallas Keith and . . . and I . . .
I'd better go . . . hadn't I?" he inquired, voice
and eyes at their wistfulest.

"Well," answered Josepha, smiling suddenly, "tea
won't take long and . . . there are lots more stakes
I want driven——"

"Tea, miss!" cried a voice at this moment. "Tea
be brewed an' a-gettin' cold an' my scones is growin'
like lead—rapid. Tea, Miss Josepha!"

"We're coming, Sarah," called her mistress in
sweet rich contralto. "Set another cup and saucer,
please. . . . And Mr. Dallas, my name is Josepha
Dare."

"That sure sounds too good to be true!" said
he.

"What does?"

"Your name."

"Oh, you mean 'Josepha'—it doesn't suit me a little
bit. I'm too matter-of-fact."

"Are you?" he questioned.

"Yes indeed," she answered—but here, meeting his grave and wistful regard, she blushed, and sped into the cottage, there to kick off those hateful rubber enormities.

CHAPTER III

WHICH CONCERNS ITSELF WITH TEA AND TALK

"AND how do you like England, Mr. Dallas?"

"Fine!" he answered, stirring pertinaciously at his empty cup. "Great! A beautiful country and beautiful . . . weather——"

"Another cup of tea, Mr. Dallas?"

"Thank you!"

"That's three, Dal!" nodded the Small Person.

"Hush, Patience, I'm surprised at you——"

"But, Jodear, he drinks such an awful lot—gollops it down so triffic quick, an' stares an' stares at you as if——"

"Patience!"

"But he does, you know. Don't you, Dal?"

"I . . . I'm afraid I did," he admitted, staring hard at his plate.

"Oh you needn't be 'fraid, Dal, she's uster being stared at, 'specially by Mr——"

"Patience!"

"Oh, Jo, I do wish you'd call me 'Honey' like Dal does. An' please I'd like some."

"I've a great mind you should never taste honey again, Miss!"

"Then I 'specks if I died you'd grieve an' grieve, an' cry worser 'n you do when you haven't 'nuff to pay——"

"Oh—here's the honey!" cried Josepha, a little breathlessly. "And now for goodness' sake—eat, child!"

"Well, I am so fast as I can, only I must talk a bit now an' then——"

"But not all the time, my dear."

"Well, then Jo, you talk an' Dal an' I'll listen. Go on, please." But instead of ' going on,' Josepha, suddenly bereft of words, frowned, flushed, bit her lip, peeped into the tea-pot and busied herself with the hot-water jug while the Small Personage, demurely aloof, munched solemnly and glanced from her sister's rosy loveliness to the abstracted Dallas who was carefully tracing out the pattern of the table-cloth with the handle of his tea-spoon; thus, having munched and nibbled daintily, sipped her tea delicately, the Small Person set down her cup softly and with extremest care, and spoke in hushed and awesome whisper:

"If you please, Josepha, may I speak one question?"

"Yes, dear, of course you may."

"Then please, why are you so awful red—in the face, you know?" Josepha glanced at her small questioner speechlessly, glanced at Dallas and laughed:

"Did you ever——?" cried she.

"Never in my life!" he answered.

"An' I'd like another piece of sugar, please!" sighed Patience.

The Goddess took up the sugar-tongs and pausing, sighed also:

"Mr. Dallas," said she, "for heavens' sake don't notice my hands, they're awful!"

"But quite clean, Jo!" nodded the Small Person consolingly.

"And—pretty!" Dallas added impulsively, and yet with such obvious sincerity that she smiled, though a little wistfully, and shook her head at the hands in question.

"Oh, they're all right to work with," said she, "but so coarse, so brown, two broken finger-nails—and getting frightfully horny. But then I'm my own labourer—Tom Merry comes to help me sometimes, but he can't work for nothing and—well, money is money!"

"That's so!" said Dallas, watching the graceful motions of those slim, brown hands with a new interest.

"An' please I'm waiting for my sugar!" sighed Patience.

"What with my garden," continued the Goddess, busied with the sugar-tongs, "and my bees, and chickens and ducks, I ought to do well enough but . . . things have been rather frightful lately."

"That's the chickens, Dal!" explained the Small Person. "The more she does for them the less they lay! Chickens are great beasts—ours are, but old Mrs. Hubbles' chickens go on laying and laying eggs all over the place."

"Some day," murmured the Goddess staring towards the open lattice, her beautiful eyes brim-full of dreamful yearning, "some day, I hope to afford a pig!"

"I—I beg pardon?" said Dallas starting.

"A pig!" she murmured. "There's money in pigs."

"And I 'dore them!" nodded Patience. "'Specially when they're teeny an' pink. Don't you, Dal?"

"Sure thing, Honey."

"There, Jo!" cried the Small Person flourishing her tea-spoon, "he said 'Honey,' an' that's a 'Merican love-name. An' please I'd like a weeny bit more—jest a scrinch!"

"But," demurred Josepha, helping her sister to more honey, yet viewing Dallas with her direct gaze, "are you really an American?"

"Well, I was born in li'l old N'York, Miss Dare."

"Then you aren't my idea of an American."

"Oh, now why not?"

"Well, you don't drawl, or speak down your nose, or chew gum, and you haven't said 'Howdy stranger,' or 'Wal, I calklate.'"

"Wal, then, Miss Josepha mam," said he, smiling but sighing also, "I calklate you'll be reckoning it's sure about time I beat it. But before I hike I—I'd like you to know I'm . . . mighty grateful, indeed I sure am. It seems just wonderful to be sitting right here—so . . . so very kind of you to . . . to take me on trust like this. Why I might have been some rough-neck, a thug or even a——" He stopped suddenly, for his glance had lighted upon his own right hand . . . ! Now staring upon these sinewy fingers he saw them (as it were) horribly stained and smeared as he had seen them in dreadful verity once before and, uttering a gasp, he clenched that hand, hiding it beneath the table. . . . But as he sat thus whelmed again in the awful shadow of past evil, he heard Josepha's smooth, soft voice:

"No, Patience! Too much honey is bad for little girls."

"But I'll soon be as old as you, Jodear, only I'll have a nice rich husbant 'stead of a pig like you want!"

"Goodness me, child!" exclaimed Josepha, and laughed. "Anyhow a good pig is better than some husbands, Miss!"

"Well, I'd rather have Dal than a pig—even a teeny pink one! You know I would, don't you, Dal?"

"Eh? Oh yes," he answered, starting. "I—I think that's real sweet of you, Honey. Though I guess Miss Josepha's right—a pig may be a much better proposition than some men. And now I . . . I'd best be on my way."

"Are you on a walking tour, Mr. Dallas?"

"Well . . . kind of. I'm just rambling around . . . looking for a job of work."

"What sort of work?"

"Any old sort."

"Do you understand farming?"

"Not a whole lot—but I can learn."

"What about horses?"

"Ace high!" he nodded. "Horses are my long suit. I mean——"

"That you can ride?"

"Why, yes. Oh yes, I can ride."

"But can you groom them, vet them?"

"Well, I once fed a pony a ball, but——"

"Do you know anything about cows?"

"I learned to rope steers—out West."

"Can you milk?"

"Why no, but I might——"

"Do you know anything about poultry—chickens?"

"I can tell a hen from a rooster any old time."

Josepha laughed, grew solemn and shook her head at him:

"Heavens!" she exclaimed, "you don't sound very promising."

"Miss Josepha," he answered gravely. "I would sure promise you anything."

"Don't be rash!" she retorted. "Because if you weren't such a rambling sort of person I might ask you——"

"No!" cried the Small Person suddenly. "You can't ask him to be your husbant, Jodear, 'cause I went an' found him for my ownself. 'Sides, he's got no money, he's not a bit rich—yet."

"Oh . . . Patience!" The Goddess gasped, 'tis true, yet frowned as Minerva might have done, then she laughed; but seeing how painfully she was flushing Dallas rose to the occasion and from his chair.

"Gee—whiz!" he exclaimed. "If I'm no farmer there is one thing I can do, Miss Josepha . . . I'll go hammer in those stakes for you if you will show me just where."

"That would be awfully kind of you," she answered with swift look of gratitude, not altogether for his offer, perhaps. "But it must be strictly business, please. I usually pay Tom Merry sixpence an hour, but then he charges me less than the proper rate, so if——"

"Miss Dare," said Dallas, smiling but resolute, " you fed me tea and cakes and what not and I'll pay for it with chores."

"Chores?" she repeated, knitting puzzled brows.

"That's American and means a job for a meal. I'll make my first job in Sussex fixing that fence for you and you don't pay me a cent. So that's—that!"

"Was them scones middlin' fair, Miss Jo?" inquired a pleasant voice, and glancing round Dallas beheld a tall, buxom, rosy creature who stared at him, his face, his hands, his every garment from collar to boots with a pair of handsome brown eyes.

"Oh quite, Sarah."

"An' did the gentleman like 'em, Miss?"

"They were mighty good!" murmured Dallas, smiling.

"Which, is the gen'leman stayin' in these parts, Miss?"

"I really don't know, Sarah."

"Yes," answered Dallas decidedly, " he is."

"Which might I ax wheer, Miss?"

"Any old place," smiled Dallas. "The nearest hotel."

"Which, Miss, you knows as there beant no sich things 'ereabouts, there be only inns an' taverns."

"Well, then, the nearest of 'em," said Dallas, meeting Sarah's wide stare unflinchingly.

"Which, that be the 'Duck i' the Pond,' Miss."

"Sounds kind of moist," answered Dallas, "but it'll suit me fine."

"But Mary Weldon don't like strangers at ' The Duck ' an' won't tak' the gen'leman in, p'raps."

"Well I'll try, anyway."

"Which, Miss, you ain't told me the gen'leman's name, which me, bein' one as have served the fambly an' you so long an' faithful, Miss, I rackon I oughter be told."

"Keith!" he answered, "Dallas Keith, and I sure hope you——"

"Which, his boots, Miss, beant a gen'leman's boots!"

"And that's right, too!" he admitted, shaking his head at the articles in question. "But what about me . . . my dial—I mean this thing that does for my face?" And here he smiled with flash of white teeth, a smile that was in his eyes also, indeed a smile so boyish, so frank and winning that Sarah's grim yet rosy mouth quivered and she nodded slightly.

"Strange gen'lemen beant welcome round 'ereabouts," said she, "but, Miss, I thinks if I was to say a word Mary Weldon might tak' 'im in—so by your leave I'll step over an' say it." With which Sarah vanished as suddenly as she had appeared.

"Holy smoke!" quoth Dallas, drawing a deep breath, "next to the Third Degree that was sure some experience!"

"Sarah's very sharp and terribly cautious, Mr. Dallas, but I think she has decided you are respectable —in spite of your boots!"

"I . . . wonder?" he stammered and she was struck anew by his troubled, shrinking air. "I guess it's up to me to make good."

"An' here's my teeny kitty!" cried Patience, running in from the kitchen with a small, furry bundle in her arms. "And she's opened one eye at me—look, Dal!"

"I hope she's a he!" said the Goddess.

"Sarah isn't quite sure, Jodear, but she says if 'tisn't a her it's bound to be a him, an' you can stroke it if you wish, Dal."

So, having touched the little, furry creature with one caressing finger, Dallas went forth to his labour

in the garden; and here, tossing aside hat and coat
and with a goddess to direct him, he took up the hammer
and fell to work. And he worked well, yet with a
certain deliberation, almost as if he feared ending this,
his first job, too soon; thus when dusk fell, he noted
with a lively satisfaction that much remained to do.
The which fact seemed to impress her also for she
sighed, rather despondently.

"It will be more of an undertaking than I
thought!"

"Oh, I don't know," he answered, reassuringly,
"if we stick to it all day to-morrow we will have the
posts fixed by evening."

"But," she answered dubiously, "I can't expect
you to work for me without——"

"Next day," said he, a little hastily, "we'll fix the
wire."

"Oh, that's a dreadful job," she sighed, "wire is so
beastly to manage—so scratchy and springy. I was
going to leave that for Tom Merry."

"Then we'll count him out of this, for, Miss Dare,
sticking up wire is where I shine,"

"I'm wondering!" said she, glancing at his care-
fully-tended hands. "Have you ever tried nailing up
wire?"

"And that dog-kennel," he went on, gesturing towards an odd-shaped structure that stood a little
crookedly beneath an adjacent tree, "that dog-kennel
would do with a nail or so."

"Mr. Dallas," said she, frowning at him, "that
'dog-kennel' is a chicken-coop, or meant to be. I
. . . I made it myself."

"Sure!" he nodded, "my mistake," but she saw his
mouth quiver.

"Is it so awful?" she inquired, suddenly wistful.

"Miss Dare," he answered gravely, "it just makes
me yearn to be a chicken."

At this she laughed a little ruefully, and approaching her handiwork, stood to frown at it.

"I suppose it does look rather queer," she sighed, "but it answers well enough, and then I had to make it out of odd pieces of wood; you see timber is so fearfully expensive! And I smashed the end of my poor finger doing it . . . you can still see the mark——"

"Can I?" said he gently. "Thanks!" and, almost before she was aware, had taken her hand, firmly yet reverently and lifting it, bowed his head; to be sure the light was growing dim, and yet——

"Ooh!" cried a voice unexpectedly near, "what's Dal kissing your hand for Jodear?"

"He isn't!" answered the Goddess tranquilly. "And it's time you were in bed, my Patience."

"Yes, I know," sighed the Small Personage regretfully, "that's why I came to wish Dal good-night, an' mind you come an' tuck me up."

"Of course I will—do I ever forget, dear?"

"Well no, but you might, and then if I died in my sleep you'd be awful' sorry—an' so should I. . . . Good night, Dal, an' please do grow rich soon."

"I'll do my best, Honey. Good night and sweet dreams——" Then Dallas caught his breath as up towards him reached two small, imperious arms.

"Well, aren't you going to kiss me good night?" she demanded. So down he sank on one knee to fold the child in tender arms, to feel the touch of her little hands upon his neck, his bowed head.

"God bless you, Honey!" he murmured and, loosing her suddenly, rose.

"God bless you, too, Dal," she nodded and, waving her hand, sped away bedwards.

"She's a sweet . . . a wonderful . . . kiddy!" he murmured, gazing after her. "She's sure my little good-angel!"

"Oh—why?"

B

"Well, for one thing she brought me to . . . my first job."

"Which isn't finished, Mr. Dallas."

"True enough!" he said with sudden cheeriness. "There's always to-morrow, isn't there?"

"Yes," she answered softly, "and to-morrow is always going to be better than to-day. To-morrow is always going to bless us—somehow! Yes, there is always another day."

"Now that's certainly a great thought!" he exclaimed. "Another day—I'll sure remember that!" Here he crossed to the little wicket gate that opened upon the narrow, shady lane. "Good night, Miss Dare, and believe me I'm mighty grateful."

"Good night, Mr. Dallas. And what for?"

Here he stepped into the lane, closing the gate with the utmost care.

"Well," he answered, making sure the gate was latched, "for . . . for . . ."

"Tea?" she inquired, gently.

"And taking me on trust. . . . What time shall I come round to-morrow?"

"Well," she answered, leaning gracefully upon the gate, "it's quite light these mornings at—four o'clock."

"Four?" he repeated. "Four o'clock? Why sure, I'll be here."

"Though nine o'clock will be quite early enough and—but where are you going to stay to-night?"

"Well, say now, I'd clean forgotten. But any old place will do for me, a——" But, at this moment Sarah loomed upon them through the fragrant dusk; quoth she:

"Which, Miss, I've been a-wonderin' if he'd remember. . . . And that motherless child waitin' to be tucked up!" Then as her young mistress turned and sped away Sarah addressed herself directly to Dallas for the first time, staring at him very hard the while.

"Which, Mary Weldon says, young man, as if you don't mind the little room over the bar, she'll tak' you in."

"The little room'll suit me fine," he answered heartily. "And Sarah I—I'm glad, I'm mighty glad she's got you to . . . to look after her."

"Meanin' Mary Weldon, young man?"

"No no, Miss Dare . . . and the child, of course. She seems lonesome, kind of——"

"Well, she beant, not nohow. And she can take care of herself, I rackon—'specially wi' me to look arter her."

"That's what I meant," he answered, with his quick, bright smile. "Good night, Sarah, and thank you."

"Good night," she answered, peering into his comely face with her fine, sharp eyes. "Good-night young . . . sir."

And even as he smiled, so smiled she, and nodded buxom head as she watched his tall, lithe figure stride away down the darkening lane.

CHAPTER IV

WHICH DESCRIBETH A SMITING OF FISTS

THOUGH the shadows of evening were all about him yet his own particular shadow of stark horror and bitter remorse had left him—for the time being, since in his mind, just now, was no thought of self, for Dallas was dreaming of better things:

Not of her deep, grave eyes; nor her freckled nose that, being neither Greek nor Roman, was yet of shape the exact perfection or (as he phrased it) absolutely "It"; nor of her ruddy lips whose habitual wistful droop seemed but to enhance the wonder of her smile. He had duly noted each and all of these, to be sure, but just now he was pondering her hands—those slim, brave, capable hands scarred by ceaseless labour and "getting frightfully horny!" . . . He had known other hands but how vastly different—smooth, soft, white, pink of palm and finger-tip, with nails like coral, daintily polished, hands to be fondled, kissed and forgotten. But those other hands, despite scars and broken finger-nails, glorified by work, might surely be some man's comfort, raise him perhaps to nobler living and lift him at last as high as heaven.

. . . A beam of yellow light falling athwart his way roused him and, glancing up, he saw a small, lonely inn, or rather tavern, shaped like the letter L and set back from the lane upon a small, raised green.

So thither turned he, and thus saw two doors, one directly before him, whence came the growl and mutter of voices, the other upon his right, from whose glass panels the warm light beamed, and upon this he knocked.

After some delay this door opened and he beheld a placid, smiling, comfortable woman.

"Good evening, sir," said she in placid yet kindly greeting. "You'll be the gen'leman as Sairey telled me of, I rackon?"

"Yes, Mrs. Weldon," he answered, taking off the shabby hat.

"Then if ye'll please to step upstairs, sir, I'll show the room." Candle in hand she led the way aloft to a small bed-chamber exquisitely clean, its walls adorned with sundry pictures one of which, an aged German lithograph framed and glassed against possible injury, was entitled "The Festive Cake," and portrayed two stiff and extremely pallid kittens, with three whiskers apiece and legs and tails like well-stuffed sausages, coquetting heavily with something between an over-ripe Stilton cheese and the distant aspect of a blotched and mildewed hay-rick.

"This is certainly a home from home!" sighed Dallas, his gaze riveted on the picture. "And I sure like those dingoes."

"Dingoes, sir?" repeated Mrs. Weldon, glancing about in placid surprise. "Oh, them? Them's kittens, sir, I bleeve. Yes, sir, I've took them for kittens this forty year an' more."

"Well, anyway, I like 'em, Mrs. Weldon."

"Why yes, sir," she answered with a passionless complacency, "there's others has admired 'em afore now."

"And no wonder, mam, those cats are the cutest creatures in a frame or out. And this room was just made for me. I'll take it right now."

"Well, sir, if you eats out it'll be seven an' six a week, if you eats in I can do it for twenty-five."

"Anything you say, Mrs. Weldon, I mean——"

Dallas paused as from the nether regions swelled a sudden clamour of harsh voices, rising to an angry uproar.

"'Tis only that Ben Lomax again," sighed Mrs. Weldon, shaking her placid head.

"Aha?" murmured Dallas. "Ben seems rather a sore-head. I guess I'll just step downstairs."

"Well, sir," murmured Mrs. Weldon, gently cautionary, "I don't think I should if I was you."

"But then, very fortunately for yourself, mam, you aren't me, and so, being myself I'll just have a look-see."

Accordingly Dallas descended forthwith and, guided by the angry clamour, stepped into the tap-room.

A smallish, dim-lit room, misty with tobacco smoke and furnished with a penny-in-the-slot piano just now happily dumb, and one table, large and wide, flanked by two benches, long and unpleasantly narrow set against each opposite wall; upon the table were mugs and glasses, and upon the benches eight or nine men in noisy disputation and loudest of all—Ben Lomax, whose brow lowered and whose brawny fist flourished:

"Shurrup, will ye!" he was roaring.

"No, I wunt!" piped old Jesse Blee. "Shut up ye'self for I tell ye—tech that dog o' mine an' I'll lay my gulley-knife t' your wicked 'eart, so I will!"

"That's enough, Shepherd!" cried Ben, head viciously out-thrust. "Get out ô' this—clear out quick! No man ain't goin' to threaten my life and drink beer in the same room wi' me—out ye go!"

But old Jesse Blee, pale to the quivering lips, shook grizzled head and sat back in his corner defiantly resolute.

"No!" he piped valiantly. "I beant a-goin' to leave me beer undrank for nobody and no man, pugglist or no—not me! And I beant feared o' no Lonnon Cockney, I be Sussex-barn, I be!"

"Get out o' this!" roared Ben, rising.

"Easy now, easy!" cried a rosy-faced, good-humoured looking fellow in corduroy and gaiters. "Jesse be a old un—shame on ee, Ben!"

"What?" snarled Lomax, turning on the speaker. "You shut your trap, John, or you'll be the next! Now old 'un—out ye go!" and he shot forth a powerful hand towards the old shepherd—but—a long arm interposed and Ben's clutching hand was seized and shaken heartily by another hand which, if less sunburned, seemed quite as powerful as his own.

"Howdy, Ben!" said a cheery voice, and Ben, his hand still gripped in those strong, white fingers, found himself staring into Dallas' smiling face.

Ben growled and wrenched at his hand; Dallas, still smiling, gripped the tighter.

"Say, Grouchy," he inquired, "what's eating you?"

Ben, struggling, cursed him savagely, whereupon Dallas, laughing, threw his hand away so violently that the ex-pugilist staggered. Steadying himself instantly Ben clenched fist to smite—but something in the other's pose, the sudden glare in those long-lashed, sleepy-seeming eyes gave him pause:

"So it's you again is it, Yank?" he demanded.

"Surest thing ye know, Ben," answered that other in the same cheery tone, "and I'm here in a spirit of friendship, good-fellowship and what-not. So cut out the beefing, Ben, and sit down like a regular lad. . . . Mr. Blee and everybody how-do—landlord fill up the glasses the drinks are on me." But:

"You blarsted American!" snarled Ben, unbuttoning his coat.

"You doggone sore-head!" retorted Dallas, unbuttoning his.

"I'm a-going," quoth Ben, putting off coat and waistcoat, "to rub your blarsted face in the grass outside, and I'm a-going to rub it till you squeals!"

"You sure can't think all that?" inquired Dallas, also putting off coat and waistcoat.

"Ah, but I do!" growled Ben, rolling up shirt-sleeves.

"Well then, I'll tell you what," nodded Dallas, folding his garments with extremest care, "take a deep breath, swallow hard and think again."

"Outside!" growled Ben. "Bring a couple o' lanterns somebody, I want see where to 'it 'im."

"Yankee-American or no, I'm for ee, sir!" piped old Jesse. "And if ye can only manage to give un jest one good un, or say a couple, afore Ben finishes of ee I'll be right j'yful—ah, so I will, sure-ly. A murdersome raskell be Ben!"

"Oh, I don't know," answered Dallas cheerily, "Ben's all right, I guess—he only needs a hammering."

"Ah, does 'e?" sneered Ben.

"Sure!" nodded Dallas. "That's why I'll do my damndest to lick you, Ben, I reckon you're worth while."

"Come on an' do it!" quoth Ben.

And so, without more ado, forth went they one and all out into the cool, fragrant dusk, and there upon the little green, lighted by the flickering beam of the lanterns and ringed about by pale, tense faces, the combatants fronted each other.

For a moment they feinted and dodged warily, then, spying an opening, in leapt fiery Ben, brawny arms a-swing, eager for close action, was stopped by a jabbing left, rocked by a stinging right, and ducked out of danger, hard-breathing and more ferocious than ever, while Dallas shook admonishing head:

"Shucks, Ben!" said he with contemptuous grin, "I guess you kinda forgot I've a couple of fists, the way you ran into 'em."

"Blarsted ammytoor!" snapped Ben, and was in again and fighting like a whirlwind, landed a glancing

left, missed with his right and reeled back from a
heavy cross-counter—back and back until he was stayed
by the house wall and leaned there a breathing space
what time Dallas, reading the psychology of his man,
taunted him anew:

"You're too hot-tempered for a sure-enough champ,
Ben! Get a hold on yourself or this fight'll be through
with before it's really begun."

Ben spake not; his great chest heaved, down went
his bull head and, laughing, Dallas poised himself
to meet the expected rush. . . . And now the flickering lanterns swung to and fro in nervous hands; the
watchers surged and swayed while the combatants
smote, clenched, reeled and broke away only to close
again with the thud and smack of rapid blows, the
quick trampling of feet, the hiss and gasp of labouring
breath as, to and fro, up and down the fight raged
close and ever fiercer; for now, scornful and heedless
of punishment, Ben Lomax bored in. Night had
fallen, and in its gloom these desperate fighters seemed
no more than writhing shadows until the uncertain
lantern-rays lit by chance upon a vicious fist, whirling
arms, the flash of swift-moving faces; showed Dallas
wide-eyed, fierce and grimly determined, showed
Ben snarling and savage, blood-spattered, smitten
three to one—shaken, staggering but dauntless as
ever striving to fight through Dallas's guard. . . .
A whirl of arms, a stamp of feet, the sound of a heavy
blow and, Dallas reeled back, to fall and lie gasping;
then, as he struggled to rise, came old Jesse Blee's
shrill voice upraised in piping ecstasy:

"Look . . . Oh, look at Ben! Oho—bless ee,
young sir, Yankee or no, blessin's on ee fur a rare
plucked 'un! 'Ere be I to lend ee an 'elping 'and!"

"Lorrim . . . be!" groaned Ben.

"Le'me . . . alone!" gasped Dallas, and scrambled
awkwardly to his knees and, rising thence slowly to

B I

unsteady feet, turned to front the rush that was
to end him—but, ducking a terrible right swing, he
clenched and held on desperately while lanterns and
faces blurred and wavered on his reeling senses . . .
fists battered him, his head, his back, his labouring
ribs . . . but the cool night air was sweet and heart-
ening . . . the wobbling lanterns steadied. And now
he was away, with Ben hard after him, but a Ben who
gasped painfully and lumbered heavily as he reeled
in to end the fight; perceiving which, Dallas laughed,
a hoarse croak, dropped his guard and, as Ben struck,
eluded the blow and in that same moment drove
in his right with arm and shoulder behind it and
—smitten upon the jaw, Ben spun round and fell
inert.

A moment's breathless hush and then, feeling arms
that squeezed and hugged, Dallas turned weary head
to find old Jesse Blee propping him.

"Lordy—Lord!" cried the old shepherd, his voice
cracking with jubilation. "You beat un, lad—you
beat Ben Lomax—licked un proper! B'the pyx you've
knocked Ben out! Oh glory be—I could kiss ee!"

With the old shepherd's long arm still about him,
Dallas came where he might look down on his fallen
adversary, and saw him a-sprawl upon the trampled
grass, his livid face smeared hideously with blood.
Now, beholding this dreadful stain, Dallas covered his
face with bruised hands, and recoiled so violently that
old Jesse cried out in wonder—back shrank Dallas,
and back to the wall, and leaned there as though
suddenly faint and sick—for just so had he seen
another man lie, livid, blood-bedabbled but horribly
dead. . . .

Against this wall stood a weatherworn bench and
sinking upon this, Dallas crouched, chin on labouring
breast, and watched them bear Ben's inanimate form
into the ale-house while the balmy night about him

seemed foul with horror, his own bruised, aching body became a thing detestable, and he writhed in a very agony of remorse. . . . A man-slayer, a guilty creature outlawed and beyond forgiveness. He was a man-slayer!

But presently, as he cowered there in the misery of self-hatred, he became aware of a voice hard-by:

"Chum!" said the voice, "Old cock! . . . Sir? Why—lumme you ain't hurted so bad, are ye?"

Then, looking up, he saw the bruised and battered visage of Ben Lomax bent above him in the light of the open doorway.

"No, Ben . . . not hurt . . . no!" he answered in his nervous, halting manner. "Only I thought . . . it seemed . . . you looked like—like . . ."

"Like a dead un, eh?" inquired Ben with gruff, short laugh. "Well, b'cripes I felt like it, chum. That was a—no, it was the most perishin' wallop as ever I took!"

"I didn't mean to strike so hard, Ben, but——"

"Sir, you couldn't help it—no man could. You measured me off and timed it very beautiful—ah—pretty as ever was. And as for 'ard 'itting, well I fancy I got in one or two benders, eh?"

"You sure had me going, Ben."

"Why then, sir—wot abaht it?"

"I . . . I don't quite get you. . . ."

"Sir, you're abaht the only man in Sussex as could get me and put me to sleep so sound. So wot I says is —wot abaht it?"

"Well, but what, Ben?"

"Well, sir, I ain't finished me ale and I thought p'raps—seein' as 'ow——?" He paused and Dallas lifted heavy head suddenly.

"Say now, friend, just what do you mean?" he inquired. Ben's swollen features expanded in a slow, somewhat sheepish smile and in shy, hesitating fashion

he held forth his hand, much as if it were an object
of which he was deeply ashamed.

"Just that, sir—'friend' says you and friend it is
says I if so be you—feel as 'ow——?"

Dallas was on his feet, and even as he grasped this
outstretched hand the heaviness was lifted from him,
horror fled awhile, his eye brightened, his lips curved
in their pleasant, boyish smile:

"Why, Ben," said he, "sure thing, old sport! And
the drinks are on me!"

Then, side by side, they entered the inn and, having
washed off the grime of battle, side by side they sat
down upon narrow and discomfortable bench while
the company stared, nodded, chuckled and finally
fell a-singing of old Sussex songs for pure good-fellowship.

So time sped cheerily until, the yellow-faced clock
above the mantel chiming ten, the company arose and
each man, more or less diffidently, offered Dallas his
hand and so away.

Then bidding his beaming host and placid landlady
a cheery good night, Dallas lighted his candle and be-
took himself (a trifle stiffly, to be sure) upstairs to his
cosy chamber; and here in company with "The Festive
Cake," the livid kittens and divers grim photographs
that stared on him from the walls, he undressed, thus
discovering certain bruises that bore witness to the
power of Ben Lomax, his knuckles.

The clock downstairs was striking the half-hour
(and making no small to-do about it) as, sighing gratefully, he slid between the cool sheets.

"Half-past ten!" he murmured drowsily. "Now in
little, old N'York it is just about half-past five in the
afternoon and the Dad will be ringing for Sanders . . .
the old Dad. . . ." Moved by sudden impulse he
got out of bed, opened his knapsack, took thence notepaper and fountain-pen and indited the following letter.

"Dear Sir (and of them all the dearest),

"Since I accept your fiat and am no longer son of yours, neither can I accept your bounty. Henceforth being fatherless, I will subsist by my own exertions. For your past generosity and care I am now and always shall be sincerely grateful. I could write more, so much more indeed that, under the circumstances, it were best to end. So then, here is the end of all relations between us, for never will I return to trouble you again unless, by some miracle, I may do so as

"Your son,
"KEITH."

CHAPTER V

MR. CHISHOLM rang the electric bell at his elbow and frowned.

Wilbur Chisholm, fifty years of age, vigorous, imperious, a potent factor in the world of men and things, whose power reached across continents and seas, scowled grimly at the marble head of the Emperor Vespasian that scowled as grimly back at him from its pedestal beside his great desk; and it was to be remarked (and duly noted) that the marble head of this long-dead Roman was strangely like the head of the modern, very much alive American citizen, for both had the same mighty spread of brow, dominant nose and massive jaw; both faces held the same look of power and relentless will, but the stern ruthlessness of each was tempered by the mouth, for about these firm lips lurked the ghost of a smile, humour was there and something more—these super-men it seemed might be human after all.

So Wilbur Chisholm, sitting lonely in his great house within this mighty city of New York, stared at the sculptured head of this long-dead, mighty Roman (that might have passed for his own), and apostrophised it, as was customary with him in solitary moments of crisis or distress:

"Well, Old-timer, history tells me you had your troubles too, and out-faced 'em like a man and Roman. But then . . . your boy was a son to you . . . of

sorts. Leastways he kept himself decently honourable
. . . clean. . . . And he won battles and carried
on after you . . . yes, became a mighty good ruler
too! But . . . my son . . . my boy, Old-timer
. . . I . . . have no son. Well, thank God his
mother's dead . . . this at least I can be thankful
for—now. . . . Ha, is that you, Sanders?"

"Myself, sir," answered a discreetly modulated voice,
"myself, sir, as per usual with your pick-me-up and——"

"Then I don't want it—take it away!"

"Not want it, sir? But you rang!"

"Sheer force of habit. You can go."

"Excuse me, sir, but——"

"What is it?"

Tenderly setting down the antique silver tray, with
its very modern shaker and glasses, Sanders approached
the great man deferentially; an imposing personage
was Sanders, whose pate, slightly bald, rose pink and
domelike through an aureole of carefully-brushed hair,
whose chubby, smooth-shaven face was void of line,
wrinkle and all expression save a solemn deference
that just now almost amounted to awe:

"Sir," said he, bowing, "permit me to inform you
that my lord the Earl of Withymore is waiting to——"

"Look at that!" said Wilbur Chisholm, gesturing towards the marble Roman. "They say I'm like
him."

"I have frequently remarked the resemblance, sir,
but——"

"Well anyway he was a man, Sanders. D'ye know
who he is?"

"When dusting him sir—which I do frequent, I
have gleaned the hinformation that the gentleman's
name was Vesp. Imp."

"Sure, his name's carved on him—Vesparianus
Imperator, Emperor of Rome. He began life as a
poor soldier under the eagles and ended it as ruler of

a great empire. . . . And he was the first of 'em
who died a natural death!"

"Highly commendable, sir! Very inter-esting! But
might I venture to remind you——"

"He called his ministers sponges, Sanders, and
treated 'em so,—for says he, 'I wet 'em when they're
dry and squeeze 'em when they're wet.'"

"Very facetious, sir, a re-markable character, which
reminds me that his lordship the Earl of Withymore
desires——"

"It's all of ten years since I yanked you out of gaol
and made an honest man of you, isn't it, Sanders?"

"Nearly eleven, sir."

"You are—reasonably honest, I suppose?"

"I hope so, sir."

"In your unregenerate days you never killed a man,
eh, Sanders?"

"Heavens forbid, sir."

"I'm asking—did you?"

"No, sir, positively—no never!"

"Murder's a pretty serious proposition to-day—
even in New York, eh, Sanders?"

"Undoubtedly, sir—unless one is blessed with
immense wealth."

"Ha—what'n hell d'you mean?"

Sanders recoiled before the sudden ferocity of his
master's tone and aspect:

"N-nothing, sir!" he stammered and, though his
triple chins quivered, his prominent blue eyes met
the piercing glare of the deep-set grey and faltered
not.

"I believe you!" said Wilbur Chisholm with sudden
nod. "Now you can show him in."

"Eh, sir . . . I . . . I beg pardon——?"

"That sprig of nobility, young Withymore."

"Certainly, sir—immediately!" So saying, Sanders
vanished much quicker than he had appeared, where-

upon Wilbur Chisholm leaned back in his chair with something very like a sigh and frowned at Vespasian, that old-timer, harder than ever.   Then the door opened and a pleasant, drawling voice hailed him:

"How do, sir? Hope y'haven't forgotten me?" Saying which, a pleasant young man entered, golden-haired, ruddy, blue-eyed and despite its drawl, his voice was deep, and contrived to sound hearty, and though his air was languid, his blue eyes were remarkably clear and bright, a well-set-up young man, as neatly turned out and groomed as any of his beloved horses.

"Met you at the polo-match, sir; Keith introduced us if you remember?"

"Why yes," said Wilbur Chisholm rising to shake hands. "Sit down, what'll you drink?"

"Nothing thanks!" answered his lordship shaking curly head. "Keeping a bit fit, the track, boxing and what not, just at present. I dropped in about Keith."

Wilbur Chisholm merely nodded his great head and murmured:

"About him—yes?"

"Yes, t'remind him of his promise; y'see we've arranged a bit of a do, what I mean t'say is, I suggested he should teedle over to England with me, if y'know what I mean, and give me a leg-up with my new gees. Y'see, sir, Keith's such an all-round sportsman, very sound pippin indeed, and as for polo and judgment of a pony, well, what I mean t'say is—there you are?"

"Ah, indeed?" murmured Keith's father, rubbing massive chin and knitting puzzled brows.

"Now, I'm trotting over with a string, next week, and——"

"A string, my lord? What of—beads?"

"Well no, sir, no not exactly, if y'know what I mean; fact is they're polo-ponies, six of the very toppingest—absolute birds! Keith helped me t'choose 'em, and Keith is about the top-holest judge in——"

"He is—a friend of yours, Lord Withymore?"

"About the best of 'em, sir. Keith's an absolute sportsman, absolutely——"

"When did you see him last?"

"'Bout month ago. I'm only just back from Palm Beach, and dropped in to see Keith, but your butler-man says he's out——"

"He is: in Europe, I believe."

His lordship opened his blue eyes very wide but (be it noted) shut his firm mouth very tight; then:

"'Stounding!" he exclaimed. "When did he leave, sir?"

"Nearly three weeks ago."

"Aha—gone to my place, perhaps, sir!"

"Where is your place, my lord?"

"Well, they're a bit scattered, if you know what I mean, sir—what I mean t'say is they're here and there—London and the country, but my stables are in Sussex. Perhaps he's nipped off there—I hope so. There's a cove in my stables, bit of a bruiser, call him bash-full Ben! Now your son's very hot with the gloves and if he is there, well—I hope he is, that's all!"

"But why should—he go to your stables?"

"Well, it's just a thought—a hunch y'know! What I mean is, I've a horse there, a devil—a mankiller that nobody can ride, and Keith bet me he'd ride it if ever he had the chance, bet me a monkey he'd tame it, and if anyone can he can, and if he's in old England the betting is that he makes for my place on the run to have a go."

"You seem to rate his prowess over-highly, my lord."

"Oh no, sir, y'see I know Keith pretty well. But that horse is a perfect demon, killed one man and savaged another. I only hope he doesn't break

Keith's neck—what I mean is, Keith's a bit reck-less."

"He might come to a worse end!" quoth Wilbur Chisholm, glancing at Vespasian and nodding a little grimly. "Yes, there are worse deaths!"

Here his lordship opened his eyes again, but this time, his mouth also, glanced from the grimmer face of flesh and blood to the grim face of marble, breathed hard and spoke:

"Cert'nly sir, of course, oh quite! But of course, if you understand what I mean, death's never a very cheery business—what I mean is, a bit coldish, clammy and what not, y'know! And now if y'll excuse me I'll be popping. No end of business so must toddle —Goo'bye, sir!" Saying which, his lordship rose, shook hands heartily, smiled cheerily, crossed lightly to the door and was gone.

And now, looking after this singularly pleasing young man, and contrasting him with another as young and once as bright and promising, Wilbur Chisholm sighed heavily and unmistakably and, doubt-less forgetting that marble Roman, drooped in his chair, bowing head upon hands like one faint and weary beneath some grievous burden. Thus, he was quite unaware that the door had opened softly a few inches to admit a very small, extremely slim man who, closing the door as softly, leaned against it, fanning himself with a broad-brimmed Stetson hat. A person this of uncertain age, for whereas his eyes were remarkably keen and, like his move-ments, quick with vigorous life, his brow was deep-furrowed by years and experience and his hair was snow-white, a silvery mane that curled almost to his thin but wiry shoulders. Motionless stood he, save for the gentle swaying of his large hat and his eyes that, beholding Wilbur Chisholm in his so uncharac-teristic and highly un-Roman attitude, instantly averted themselves, darting their bright glance about this noble book-lined room, with its handsome railed gallery and two flights of stairs, its costly rugs and luxurious appointments; at last he spoke in voice sudden yet soft:

"Jee—hoshophat, quite some books you got here Wilb—I guesso!" Wilbur Chisholm stared, raised his head and was on his feet, all in a moment:

"Jed!" he exclaimed joyously, and with hands outstretched. "Jed Wollet . . . old Jedidiah . . . well, well!"

"'S me!" nodded the little man, peering up glad-eyed at the big man who smiled down on him while their hands clasped and wrung each other. "'S me, Wilb—how are ya?"

"Well . . . for heaven's sake!" murmured Wilbur Chisholm, still shaking that small, bony fist up and down, and to and fro. "You old son-of-a-gun, I'm everlasting glad to see you! What's brought you so far from the ranges?"

"What's brought me? Say now ef that ain't a fool question, Bud! What should bring me but th' kid, yessir, our lad! In trouble kinda, ain't he? Well 's nuff for old Jed—that's why I come pirootin' east, heeled for what's a-goin', yessir—I guesso! Well, what's a-doin'? Where is he?"

Wilbur Chisholm's smile faded, the kindly light died from his eyes and he became as stonily Roman as Vespasian himself.

"I guess you mean . . . Keith?" he inquired in tone as altered as his look.

"I betcha! Where is he?"

"Away, Jed."

"Gol darn it—where to?"

"Europe."

"Eh—Eu-rope? An' ye let him go?"

"I sent him, Jed."

"Hells bells!" exclaimed Jedidiah, his bright eyes snapping fiercely. "You sent him—you? An' he should be right here in N'York to face them mean coyotes as framed him!"

"Jed, what d'you know of this dirty business, and how?"

"Only what I read outa his letter——"

"Eh—letter? What did he write?"

"Oh he jest 'fessed-up to bein' a murderer——"

"Ah, he—he wrote you a—confession?"

"Sure! He writes me some fool con-stuff o' that kind,—but it ain't good 'nuff for me t'swaller, no, sir —not Jed!"

"May I see this letter, Jed?"

"Shore! But first I'll read it ya—listen, Wilb!"

From the bosom of his rough coat Jedidiah drew a much-worn leather wallet whence he extracted a letter which he opened and read aloud, slowly and deliberately:

"'Oh Jed—' that's how he begins, Bud,—jest 'Oh Jed—you're the only creature that counts with me now that the dad'—that's all scratched out, Bud— 'and I am unworthy of yuh. An awful thing has happened, a man is dead and to the best, or worst of my belief, I murdered him. And yet, Uncle Jed, if I did I was sure mad, for I remembered nothing of it when I came to—only the gun in my hand when I woke, and the blood. So I'm going to bury myself, God knows where, but I shall try to act up to your teaching and the Dad's'—that's scratched out again, Bud—'I mean to live it down if possible, if not . . . I am always in my heart . . . just your . . . Boy Keith.'" Here for a moment was silence, for neither of them spoke nor moved; then with quick, sudden gesture Jedidiah thrust the letter into his companion's hand who read it through very carefully, refolded and handed it back without a word.

"Well?" demanded the little man sharply. "Whatcha gotta say of it, Wilb?"

"What do you think, Jed?"

"I say the boy was framed, yessir! An' I don't only think it, I'm almighty sure, well I guess!"

"But, old friend, what do you—know?"

"Well I know' nuff t'stand pat on our boy, yessir! To be everlastin' shore as he never commit no murder——"

"Sit down, Jed, and let us talk."

"Heck no—you doubt the lad, I'd rayther stand!"

"Sit down and listen to me, I say!" With which, Wilbur Chisholm set mighty arm about the fierce, little man and, leading him across the spacious library, seated him in his own elbow-chair.

"First of all, Jed, this was no frame-up——"

"Hey? An' you believe that, you doubt your own son——"

"Listen, Jed. Of late he had got in with a mighty ugly crowd, bootleggers and worse, and chief among them was Red Rory, the murdered man. Well it seems Keith quarrelled with him about some woman, thrashed him and threatened to kill him and . . . well . . . he kept his word, it seems——"

"Wilb," quoth the little man, glaring, "whatcha tellin' me?"

"The truth, old partner."

"Then I don't believe ya—no sir, not me, not Jed Wollet! Why, hain't I knowed Keith sence he wur foaled? Didn't I larn him to straddle his first hoss? Arter his blessed mother went aloft, didn't I help nuss him, feed him, hear him say his prayers agin me knee? Hain't I watched him grow and don't I know him outside an' in? Well, I guesso! Yessir, I sure do—an' nobody hain't agoin' to feed me slush o' that kind. Keith a murderer? Blah!"

"You were always a loyal friend, Jed, but——"

"'S me, Wilb, loyalty's me middle name, I guess, 'special as regards you an' the boy."

"Don't I know it, Jed? Those old days in the West, just you and me against Fortune and the World—full of hope, of confidence in each other and empty of all else! And because of this I'd hate like hell to hurt you, but truth is truth and——"

"No it ain't, Wilb—not always it ain't. Sometimes Truth gets so sot on itself kinda, an' wears so many gol-darn frills onto it that it looks more like a dam lie, yessir!"

"Well, Jed, here's the truth anyway. Keith admitted the fact to me more fully than he does to you in that letter—confessed himself guilty——"

"And you bleeved him?"

"Why, sure I believed him!"

"And let on to the boy that you bleeved him?"

"Well, naturally. Certainly I did."

The little man lay back in the big chair, looking up at the speaker, his thin-lipped mouth curled; and in eyes, nose and mouth was such withering, blasting contempt as might have shaken any man—even the mighty Vespasian himself at the head of his victorious cohorts; as for Wilbur Chisholm this Colossus of business, this man of destiny whose nod was law to so many thousand of his fellow creatures, he stared down at this small, fierce, silent accuser at first serenely, then he frowned, presently he fidgeted, and finally spoke as he might have done long years ago:

"Doggone it, Jed—what now?"

Jedidiah ran a small, claw-like hand through his silky, white thatch of hair and snorted:

"Now," quoth he, "now, Buddy, yore jest like what you was back in them old, wild days in Montanny when we first hitched-up—the day as I found ye by yore dead cayuse all shot up 'count 'o yore plumb bull-headedness. . . . Heck, don't interrupt

me! . . . You was a bull-head then, yessir—allus
a-jumpin' wi' both yore big feet, up to yore years
into troubla some sort as I has to shoot or yank ye
out of, I guesso! An' to-day yore the same—a bull-
head, yessir, a great, big bull-head——"

"Jed, now hold on thar!" cried Wilbur Chisholm,
reverting back to those other days and becoming
altogether Western. "What'n hell d'you mean?"

"Shucks!" snarled the little man, ferociously. "I
know you're the big noise now, from here to Californy
an' further, an' I'm still only a doggone cattle-man
but, by heck, I got 'nuff sense to reckon up two an'
two, I guesso! I got eyes an' know black from white,
yessir."

"Hold on, Jedidiah. If you mean——"

"Mean? Hell an' a hook-worm! It ain't what
I mean it's what does the boy mean! What does
he say in his letter? Why he says this: ' I remembered nothin' when I came to, only the gun in my
hand when I woke.' Well now, what's that mean?
I tell ya it means he was doped, framed, yessir! Anyways I know as there hain't no sure-'nuff vice in Keith
an' I know as he never murdered this fella. Now
mind, I'm tellin' ya, Wilb, an' me bein' myself—an'
a marshal, I sure knows dirt when I sees it, well I
guesso!"

"And I'm telling you, Jed, that he confessed to
the crime!"

"Shore he did, an' why? Because he was either
doped, or crazy with bum booch or—is shieldin' someone else. Anyways I know he ain't guilty!"

"But how, man, how d'you know? How in God's
name can you be so sure?"

"Well, think, Bud, think! Ain't he Lucy's child.
. . . Lucy, as come purty nigh bein' an angel on
earth? Could her son be so mean—a murderer?
Lucy's boy? No, sir—never, not him, not Keith—no!"

"True! . . . True enough, Jed!" sighed the big man in changed voice. "It all seems . . . utterly impossible . . . and yet——"

"Shore it's impossible, Wilb! And then again, ain't he your son, too, and ain't you always acted white . . . on the square, you blamed old maverick, doggone ye!"

Wilbur Chisholm strode to the nearest window and stood there awhile, staring down at the superior bustle of Fifth Avenue and seeing it not at all; but presently, turning thence, he came face to face with Vespasian and stifling a sigh, frowned instead.

"And yet," said he, squaring his big chin, and speaking in tone deep and utterly passionless, "one must be governed by reason, and as to . . . the boy, well . . . of late, as I say, he's been running around—consorting with a bad crowd . . . degenerating daily, Jed. Indeed he is not the clean, bright lad that left your ranch four years ago."

"Well, anyway, Wilb, he's shore in trouble to-day, and whatever you do I ain't agoin' to leave him flat, no, sir—not me, not Jed Wollet!" Here both men turned quickly as, with perfunctory knock, Sanders made his appearance:

He was the same Sanders and yet not the same, for his chubby face seemed almost pinched, his triple chins were agitated, his prominent eyes stared fish-like though his voice sounded as discreetly modulated as ever.

"Excuse me, sir," he began, "but——"

"What is it?" his master demanded irritably, without turning.

"A Mr. . . . Ryerson to see you, sir—a Mr. Derek Ryerson."

"Show him in when I ring."

"Very good, sir!" And with dignified obeisance he departed.

"See here, Jed, this Ryerson, it seems, was a friend of my—of Keith's, and is here to tell me the truth . . . further details of this black business."

"The truth, eh? What's he know of it?"

"He was there it appears."

"Ya mean a witness to the shootin'?"

"He was there immediately after, I understand, and saw Keith with . . . the gun in his hand. Now I'd like you to hear all he has to tell."

"Shore I will."

"Yet if he sees you he'll maybe not open up, so I'll ask you to step——"

"Betcha life!" quoth Jedidiah, and catching up his large Stetson hat, he scurried up the gallery-stairs and vanished in a moment. Then, sinking into his favourite elbow-chair, Wilbur Chisholm rang the bell.

CHAPTER VI

IN WHICH JEDIDIAH TAKES A HAND

ENTERED now Derek Ryerson, so elegantly slim that he seemed either extremely young for his age or much older than he looked; an altogether superlative creature in that he was too handsome as to face, form, and garments; whose dreamy glance was gentle and whose voice was a caress.

Mr. Ryerson smiled and bowed, Wilbur Chisholm did neither, he merely pointed at a chair into which his visitor sank, crossing his immaculate legs:

"I think," murmured Derek Ryerson softly, "yes, I'm pretty sure you know what I'm here for?"

"Let's hear!" answered Wilbur Chisholm, shortly.

"Well," answered the other, smiling down at his own perfectly shod foot, "it concerns your son——"

"You mean Keith, Dallas, Chisholm."

"Exactly. I mean your son, Keith."

"Well?"

"Well, Mr. Chisholm, how much is his life and reputation worth to you?"

Wilbur Chisholm selected a cigar from a box on the table, pinched the end gently, lit it carefully and spoke:

"Nothing!" said he.

Mr. Derek Ryerson drew a thin gold case from waistcoat pocket, extracted thence a cigarette, tapped it delicately, lighted it and laughed gently.

"We estimate it at precisely one million dollars!" he murmured.

53

"We?" inquired Chisholm, his keen, grey eyes staring into eyes of soft, velvety blackness.

"I allude, sir, to his . . . well-wishers, let us call them. You see, poor Keith is terribly involved —in Dutch, shall we say?"

"What d'you know?"

"On the contrary, Mr. Chisholm, it's what you don't know."

"For instance?"

"For instance then, you think you got him safe away, you imagine your money, your almighty power and influence did the trick. Now I'm here to assure you that it was we who permitted his get-away— shall we say, connived at it and helped you fool the police."

"Prove it."

"Well, we know just where your son's hiding, just where Keith's lying doggo."

"I'm listening."

"He's in Europe."

"Well?"

"In England, at a place called Sussex."

"Well?"

"And we can get on to him whenever it suits our book."

"For what?"

"The murder of Red Rory M'Guire on the night of the third, last month, at Hetzel's on Tenth Avenue and Thirty-fourth street."

"A friend of yours, this M'Guire?"

Derek Ryerson laughed silently, at least his white teeth gleamed:

"Why no," he murmured, "hardly that, not a friend of mine, no—he was more your son's friend than mine, certainly—until they quarrelled and fought over little Olive Lemay. You know about her, perhaps?"

"Go on."

"Well, sir, Olive was the Cause, the Reason, the Wherefore and the Why—*cherchez la femme*, d'ye see, Mr. Chisholm—and she was good, at least your son said she was and I guess . . . well, she was near-good, all things considered, and Red Rory was a—he was just Rory and pretty 'red' in every way, and so your son licked him, thrashed, pounded and lambasted the—well, he certainly made a butcher's shop of Rory that time, yes, sir, he made Red Rory redder than ever—blood, d'you see? But that was all of six months ago——"

"And now you're wasting my time!"

"After that," continued Ryerson, licking his smiling, shapely mouth with rosy tongue, "Rory quit chasing little Olive, and kept away altogether because your son Keith had threatened to shoot."

"I'll give you another five minutes!"

Derek Ryerson shook his sleek, black head gently, showed his perfect teeth again in pleasant, sleepy smile and went on, more deliberately than ever:

"And so, Mr. Chisholm, as I was saying, Rory quit chasing little Olive Lemay and made himself mighty scarce because your son Keith swore to shoot him if he didn't—yes, sir, he swore to put Rory's light out if he didn't leave the girl alone. I heard him and so did others. Well, one night Rory, being full, came back! It was over at Hetzel's, and we were sitting in a little game, just the four of us—your son, Keith, Whitey Neeves, Tosh Jennings and myself when, as I say, in walks Rory. Now, Mr. Chisholm, your son Keith had been acting kind of queer all night,—I'll admit it had been a wet session, and when Rory walks in on us so sudden, Keith got mad, went in off the deep end right away, he slanged Rory and Rory, being lit-up, as I tell you, Rory argued back, and guessing there'd be trouble, we left them to it. But just as I reached the door I saw Whitey slip his gun to your son Keith. . . . And presently, sure enough, we heard a shot. . . . Well, sir, when we opened the door—there's Rory stone dead, your son Keith laying across him and both smothered in blood—Rory's blood!" Here Derek Ryerson touched rosy lip with rosy tongue again and sighed gently: "Yes, sir, Rory certainly—bled! And there lay your son Keith kind of dazed and with Whitey's gun in his hand."

"Dazed, you say?"

"Why yes, he seemed that way, perhaps it was horror, perhaps Rory had landed him one, but I guess it was merely booze! And he kept on saying, over and over: 'Blood! I'm all blood!' And, Mr. Chisholm, he certainly was!"

"Have you done?" inquired Wilbur Chisholm, glancing at his watch.

"No," answered Ryerson gently, "no, not quite, but we're getting there. . . . I'm telling you M'Guire was very dead and—bleeding! Now murder, even here in N'York, may be pretty serious for some folks, —but if the guilty party happens to be the only son of a Money King like Wilbur Chisholm, it can be got away with if the matter is properly handled. Now here's your son Keith kills his man and——"

"Though," mumbled Wilbur Chisholm from behind his cigar, "according to you, nobody actually saw the shot fired!"

"I didn't say so," smiled Mr. Ryerson. "Oh no no, because, as a matter of fact, I—that is—'we', of course, have an unimpeachable witness whose evidence will surely send poor Keith to the Chair unless you close that witness's mouth."

"Ah, blackmail, of course!"

"An ugly word!" sighed Derek Ryerson, shaking his handsome head in gentle reproof. "Yes, a most unlovely word, to my thinking, but I suppose——"

"You?" growled the big man, square chin out-thrust,

mighty shoulders squared, deep-set eyes ablaze with scorn, "you're a Britisher—eh?"

"Well, no, Mr. Chisholm, no emphatically, for though my folks had the misfortune to be born somewhere over there, I am an American——"

"And a renegade also——"

"I count myself an American citizen, Mr. Chisholm."

"Then God help America! You are the sort of thing a decent man treads on—hard."

"Such a man is apt to get stung,—sir. Oh quite unpleasantly. But business, Mr. Chisholm, business! What about your son?"

"Nothing!"

"Well, I guess a million will be nothing to you, and your son's life won't be dear at the figure, anyway."

"Now see here," quoth the big man with his most Roman look and gesture, "once and for all, I have no son, d'ye hear? I have absolutely and finally disowned him. So do what you will, his future is no concern of mine—none, d'ye hear? You and your blackmailing gang get nothing out of me—not one cent! Now—go! The door's behind you."

"Oh but think again, sir!" murmured Ryerson, gently blowing cigarette ash from his neat person. "You tell me you've no son—well, you can say so but I know differently, and the daily papers won't believe you, dear me no! The day poor Keith is executed they'll come out with: Millionaire Chisholm's son expiates crime in electric chair—or some such squib——"

"And the door's behind you!" repeated Wilbur Chisholm, and the Emperor Vespasian grimed with battle surely never looked grimmer. But this very modern, extremely bland young exquisite merely smiled, tapped another cigarette, and nodded:

"I remember just where the door is, oh quite!" said he, brightly. "But nothing shall prevent me

sitting here and permitting you another chance of
saving poor Keith's life. . . . Think of it—your only
son—a miserable million dollars! What truly natural
parent could hesitate? Come, sir, what's to prevent
you signing a cheque and giving your son another
chance of becoming your son . . . of getting straight
with himself and you, of——"

"And what," demanded Wilbur Chisholm, reaching
out his long arm towards the electric bell, "what is
to prevent my ringing up the police and charging you
with attempted blackmail?"

"Well, Mr. Chisholm, first—this!"

A white hand flashed, and Wilbur Chisholm was
looking into the muzzle of an automatic pistol.

"And secondly," murmured Ryerson smiling, "all
the police in New York State wouldn't hold me, they
couldn't because of—let us say, political reasons. All
the same I don't want the police dragged into this—
just at present. . . . And now, Mr. Chisholm, seeing
I've got you set, what's to prevent me demanding
that cheque right now or, well—plugging you for an
unnatural father? Say now—do tell!"

Wilbur Chisholm shifted his gaze from that deadly
muzzle to the eyes behind it and read in their velvety
blackness a threat equally deadly. . . . And then—
from somewhere in the air above was a metallic "plop"
. . . the weapon spun from Ryerson's grasp and,
uttering an inarticulate cry he lurched forward in his
chair, hugging numbed fore-arm and shocked wrist.

"Purty fair, seein' I has t'use a silencer in this gol-
darned town!"

Glancing round and up towards the speaker, Derek
Ryerson beheld one descending the gallery stairs, a
small, white-haired, fierce-eyed person who, stabbing
at him with small, bony finger, pronounced the single
word:

"Git!"

Now in this person's right hand was a heavy revolver known as a Colt's forty-four, and in this person's eyes a glare not to be mistaken; wherefore, speaking not, Derek Ryerson struggled to his feet, took up his eminently modish straw-hat and crossing to the door with uneven steps, was gone.

For a long, long moment after the door had closed was an irksome silence, for Jedidiah was staring hard at the nearest book-case with the glare still in his eyes, perceiving which, Wilbur glanced out of the window; quoth he at last and a little huskily:

"You . . . you're as sure as ever with a gun, Jed."

"Ibetcha!" snarled Jedidiah. "But see here, Mister Chisholm, you can cut out the 'Jed'—I'm Wollet t'yuh, yessir—Mister Wollet, d'ya get me?"

"Eh? Why . . . why, Jed, what——"

"An' see here again, Mister Chisholm, sir, ef you've disowned ya own son, turned ya damned back on Lucy's boy, why lemme tellya I 'dopt him, yessir, here an' now—I guesso!"

"But . . . but, Jed, listen here——"

"Listen nothin'! Aw hell, I'm done wi' ya. You stick t'ya railroads, an' ships, an' money, an' when I've found Boy Keith—my boy, mindya—an' proved him innocent, don't yuh come monkeyin' an' nosein' around or I'll be apt to shoot ya up some, yessir—I guesso!"

So saying he turned his back, stumped to the door, swung it wide open and strode away, his large Stetson hat cocked at ferocious angle.

c

CHAPTER VII

CONCERNING A LABOURER, HIS HIRE

THOUGH he was a full hour before the appointed time and all her attention was apparently centred upon the battered old silver coffee-pot, you may be reasonably sure that she (goddess-like) espied him the very moment he opened the little wicket gate; and a goodly sight was Dallas for the eyes of any person feminine—his clean-cut hawk face, the lithe vigour of him as he went striding towards that remote and leafy corner of the garden where lay the miry duck-pond.

"I s'pose," sighed the Small Personage who chanced to sit with her back towards the window, "I 'specks when I'm growder-up you won't drownd all my coffee with milk."

"You should say 'drown' not 'drownd,' dear," murmured our goddess, glancing down in swift disparagement at the workaday garment that shrouded her loveliness.

"An' please, Jodear, aren't you going to give me any sugar this morning?"

"Have patience, child!"

"Oh there you go, Jo!" sighed the Small Person, wearily. "Aunt Mary is always saying it, too!"

"Saying what, pray?"

"Things you knew, like—'patience Patience, and 'Patience be patient.' Oh mine's a nawful name, mine is. I do wish you'd call me 'Honey' like he does."

"Who?"

"Oh you know—Dal does. I think it's such a nice name and——"

"Lauk, Miss Jo!" exclaimed Sarah bustling in with well-laden tray. "Wotever do you think? Such noos as never was, mam!" And she set down the tray with a jingle. "This mornin', Miss, when I goes down the lane for the milk, I sees Mary Weldon an' she telled me as he give Ben a turble bastin' las' night—give Ben wot-for, 'e did, so Mary says, an' I says to Mary, 'Mary,' I says 'it serves 'im right! I says. But next time Ben shows 'is face, wunt I tell 'im a thing or two! To go an' fight and get beat by any man, let alone one so young an' quiet-like as 'im, mam!"

"Who?" inquired Josepha again, but this time opening her blue eyes rather wide. "Who, Sarah, who beat Ben?"

"Oo, Miss, why—'im!" answered Sarah, pointing; and following that directing finger Josepha once more beheld a certain shapely figure.

"Why it's Dal!" cried Patience, clapping her hands.

"Well, eat your breakfast, dear," said her sister, knitting classic brows, for Dallas, all unwitting the six several eyes that watched him, was standing before the chicken-coop (that lop-sided result of her so determined and painful labours which he had dared mistake for a dog-kennel), and now seemed to be studying it profoundly, its every nail and timber ; and remembering the ill-fit of its planking here and there, and how very many nails had gone in bent, Josepha flushed and her level brows knit closer.

"How—how dared he?" she demanded.

"Dared wot, Miss Jo?"

"Eh—oh, beat Ben, of course, Sarah."

"Why, that's just it, Miss Jo—'ow did he? But 'e did sure-ly, 'cording to Mary Weldon 'e give Ben a turble wallopin'."

"Ooh!" cried the Small Personage, bounding ecstatic on her chair. "I'm triffickly glad—please let me go an' kiss him, Jo."

"Eat your breakfast, child—do! What did they fight about, Sarah?"

"Well, 'twere on account o' Mr. Blee, Mary says."

"Oh yes," nodded Patience. "Ben said he'd shoot Roger—Jesse's dog, you know. I think somebody ought to go out and kiss him, don't you, Jodear?"

"I'll wear the tweed!" murmured Josepha, glancing down at her print frock again.

"Tweed, Miss—lauk, why?"

"Well this looks so—I must ride over to Lewes, Sarah, this morning."

"Ah, t' see Mus' Jessam?"

"Yes, I've been intending to ask him for more time and put it off and off—I do hate asking favours especially from him, and yet I must, Sarah, I must. If he'll only wait another six months——"

"Why not a year, Miss?"

"I think I could just about manage if things only go a little better with us. If only he'll give me time!"

"'E wunt, Miss Jo! 'E wunt give nobody nothink, no, not Jessam."

"Well, I can ask him, Sarah—plead if I must."

"'T'wunt be no good, Miss Jo—not a mite. Jessam ain't got no 'eart, only a money-bag."

"But, Sarah, if he forecloses and I have to lose the dear old house after all . . . Oh Sarah . . .!"

"But, mam, 'tis only a old ruin."

"It was the house of my people, Sarah, as you know, back and back through the years it has belonged to the Dares, and if Jessam gets it away from me he . . . means to pull it down——"

"Old Jessam's a frightful beast!" sighed the Small Personage.

"Hush, Patience dear, it's rude to call people names."

"Well, but you called him worse last week, Jo, you said he was a blood——"

"Never mind—it was very wrong of me. I want you to be a little lady, Patience dear, much better than I am, very gentle and sweet and polite to everyone."

"But I don't like being p'lite to beasts!"

"Then you'll never be a true lady."

"Oh, all right, Jodear. An' please is my mouth eggy?"

"No—not very."

"Then please may I be p'lite now?"

"Why, of course—but what do you mean?"

"Well, I've had 'nuff breakfast, so now I thought I'd jest walk out very p'litely an' kiss Dal 'Good-morning', like a lady should."

"Oh?" murmured Josepha. "But ladies don't kiss strange gentlemen."

"Well, I do sometimes, Jodear, if they're like Dal, an' he isn't a bit strange—an' so does Sarah, I seen her kissing Ben once and——"

"Lorks!" gasped Sarah. "Oh, Miss Jo—that child! The very idea!" and she vanished into her kitchen forthwith.

Thus presently Dallas, bare-armed and busy, hearing a shrill and joyous hail, paused with lifted hammer and turned to see Patience flying to meet him.

"Oh, Dal," she cried, "I'm so triffickly glad you beat him—no, first I must 'member to be p'lite! Good-morning, Dal, how are you?"

"Fine, Honey!" he answered, smiling. "How are you?"

"Well I'm not very well," she sighed. "You see the sun's so sunny and . . . and the bees so droney an' buzzy, an' the birds all so singy this morning—an' I've got to go to my lessons."

"Hard luck, Hon!"

"Yes, isn't it? But she makes me do it—Jo, you know! She simply—makes me!"

"But everybody has to do lessons some time, Hon."

"Well I'm 'triffickly glad you beat Ben; Sarah says you walloped him awful. An' now you may kiss me Good-morning."

So Dallas swung her joyously aloft, kissed her rosy lips, and, perching her upon his shoulder, bore her across the sunny garden.

"And how . . . how's your sister, Honey?" he inquired, glancing expectantly towards the cottage.

"Quite well, thank you. Only she says I'll never be a lady 'cause I called somebody a beast—but last week she called him a . . . bloodsucker! Now that's a frightful bad name isn't it, Dal?"

"Well, I guess so, but——"

"An' now she says p'raps I'll never be a true lady, but I shall a course, and always wear gloves an' a sunshade an' then if you get quite a rich man you shall be my husband an' I'll have heaps of children —mostly girls, only I'll never send them off to lessons when they're sad like me. Do you s'pose a lady should sit on a gentleman's shoulder, Dal?"

"Why sure she should, if it's my shoulder and the lady happens to be you, Honey."

"'Fraid my Jo wouldn't think so."

"Where is she this morning, Hon?"

"Changing to her tweed tailor-made. You see she's got to ride her bicycle to Lewes."

"That's a goodish ride from here."

"Oh, but my Jo can ride heaps further 'n that—she's triffickly strong. She's going to see a frightful beast!"

"Eh?" inquired Dallas, glancing up into the piquant little face bent over him.

"Yes, Mr. Jessam, he's the beast, to ask him for some time."

"Time? What for, Honey?"

"Well, I specks money, it always is you know. And there's Sarah coming to fetch me—Oh dear!"

Now in this goodly world there are tweeds and tailor-mades innumerable—but, never did one or other or both together shadow forth (as it were) more beauty of line, more symmetry of form than this tailor-made of Josepha, a costume this, begun and perfected by a face of such allure (despite its freckles) and ending gloriously in legs, ankles and feet so exactly what such necessaries should be. . . . At least thus thought Dallas when, at last, Josepha dawned upon his sight; but then (as hath been said) he already had visioned her as the Goddess of his Destiny, a being remote and sacred, high above his reach or hope of attainment and therefore to be worshipped; in her he saw the stately pride of Juno, the glowing beauty of Venus, the aloof serenity of Minerva; the creature she of his loftiest dreams, clothed in divinity at whose advent the sun brightened in glory and the earth grew wholly radiant.

While, as a matter of fact, a mere, modern young woman habited for exercise more or less violent, stepped out of a somewhat ageworn cottage, smiled, wished him a Good-morning and gave him her hand.

Was it matter for wonder that the poor, dazzled, abject fellow, flushed, stammered, squeezed her fingers too hard, held them too long, dropped them too suddenly?

"Heavens, Mr. Dallas, what a lot you've done!" she exclaimed in glad surprise—just as if she had not been watching his powerful hammer-strokes with such singular interest.

"Yes, worse luck!" he sighed, scowling at the long line of newly-driven stakes. "I mean this job will very soon be finished."

"And," said Josepha, finger to chin, "I'm wondering how much I . . . what remuneration——"

"Now, please," he suggested, "shall we talk of something else?"

"No!" she answered, serenely resolute. "We must come to some arrangement. Your work must be paid for, of course . . . but how much? What do you suggest?"

"Well," he answered, staring hard at the hammer in his hand, "suppose you just stand around now and then to supervise—I guess that will make us quits."

"Perfectly ridiculous, Mr. Dallas! Now I pay Tom Merry sixpence an hour, which is little enough these days—though he doesn't work so—tremendously hard as you do, so——"

"And then," continued Dallas, gently persuasive, "if you'd please cut out the 'Mr.'—my front name's Keith, or you might call me Dal."

"But you can't and mustn't work for nothing, it's not right—the labourer is worthy of his hire, you know!"

"Sure!" he said, smiling. "And when I'm through with the wiring, I'd like to get busy on the old summer-house yonder, then the toolshed needs repairing, the hedges want trimming and——"

"Oh, for heavens sake—stop!" she cried.

"Why yes," he nodded, "that's just what I want —to stop and work for you."

"I know the place is frightfully neglected," she sighed, glancing round about distressfully, "but I'm always so busy, and it needs so much hard work!"

"Yes," he agreed, glancing about also. "It needs a man! And I need a job—work and plenty of it, and . . . friendship . . . I sure do! So, Miss Josepha, won't you please call it a deal and let it go at that? Do now."

"You mean let you come here and slave—for nothing?" she demanded, viewing him with the austere serenity of a Minerva.

"I mean allow me to come here and help you as —as a—friend," said he, with sudden diffidence.

"A . . . friend?" she repeated, dubiously; and now he sensed in her the stately pride of a Juno. "But I don't make friends easily, Mr. Dallas."

"No," he stammered, "no, I . . . I guess not."

"And I know nothing about you—who you are, what you are, where you have been, what you have done, why you are here—I know nothing of all this, do I?"

"Not a thing!" he answered in strange, muffled tone; the heavy hammer thudded to earth and he turned from her with swift, almost shrinking motion. "I see what you mean," he muttered, "and you . . . you are surely right. I guess I'll be on my way." So saying, he crossed to where lay his hat and coat, caught them up and had reached the little wicket-gate before Josepha could find voice; then:

"Stop!" she cried.

Without so much as a backward glance, Dallas opened the gate; whereupon she frowned down at the fallen hammer and from this to him, his bowed shoulders, his drooping head; then, acting on swift impulse, she sprang nimbly in pursuit.

Dallas stepped into the lane, took a step and paused —for her hand was upon his bare arm, a hand whose firm, vital grasp checked him instantly though he neither turned nor raised his head.

"Good-bye!" he muttered.

"Wait!" she commanded, and her fingers tightened their clasp. "I didn't mean to—to be unkind . . . hurt you——"

"No," he mumbled. "No—that's all right. Only you'd best let me go. Good-bye and—thank you——"

"Won't you—come back?"

"I . . . guess not," he answered, keeping his bowed head always averted.

"Won't you finish the wiring?"

"I . . . I'd best go."

"Won't you please stay and . . . help me, Dallas . . . Keith?"

Then he turned and looked at her and she, quick to read the pain and haunted misery in his eyes, caught her breath—and in that moment cold Minerva, stately Juno merged and changed to Venus, all tender allure.

"Come!" said she softly, and opened the wicket-gate.

"On . . . my own terms?" he demanded.

"Yes,—if you mean——"

"No mention of money between us ever."

"Not a word!" she murmured with very unwonted humility.

So back strode Dallas forthwith and catching up the hammer, fell to work again right joyously while Josepha, seated near-by, watched him with a new interest.

CHAPTER VIII

OF A PLOT MATRIMONIAL

"MISS JOSEPHA," said he, pausing suddenly to look at her, "are we going to be . . . real friends?"

"Yes," she answered, in her decided manner, "I'm sure we are."

"Why then," quoth Dallas, setting by the hammer and squaring his shoulders as for some mighty effort, "I . . . I guess it's up to me to tell you all about myself."

"No, I'd rather you didn't——"

"Well now—why not?" inquired he opening his grey eyes at her.

"Because it would be rather like forcing your confidence. And besides there's really no need, I think I know all about you that is necessary."

"But what can you know of me, Miss Josepha?"

"That you are a . . . a gentleman—I mean honourable and all that."

"If this means you trust me," said he, looking down at her with eager eyes, "well—you certainly can, through and through, always and for ever. But"—here he averted his gaze and drew a deep breath—"there is something I . . . I ought to tell you, something I must tell you if we are to be friends, something that I hate——"

"Heavens!" she exclaimed lightly. "You sound frightfully tragic!"

"Tragic?" he repeated softly. "Why yes, I . . . I guess you'll think so when you hear—and then if

you can still be . . . if you can still feel any friendship for me . . . if you can respect or . . . or trust
me any, why then I'll surely believe that angels——"

Dallas stopped, as from the lane a motor-horn hooted
blatantly, whereat Josepha glanced round; then he
saw her colour deepen as the gate swung open to admit
a tall, comely man, pink and white as to complexion,
yet of powerful build and extremely spick and span
from brown boots and neatly-gaitered legs to jaunty
hat which he flourished in assured greeting.

"Good morning, Miss Jo!" cried he, ignoring shirt-
sleeved Dallas and viewing Josepha with a smiling,
possessive look. "I'm running over to Lewes in my
car and stopped to see if you had any commissions
for me or, better still, by Jove—can I give you a lift?"

"Mr. Meredith, this is Mr. Dallas!"

The exuberantly cheerful newcomer glanced at Dallas,
nodded and turned back to Josepha with a certain
jovial eagerness.

"How about it, Miss Josy, will you come? Say
yes, do now, the ride will do you a power o' good!"
Josepha glanced towards the toolshed where stood her
dusty bicycle, round about at the hot, sunny morning
and nodded:

"Thanks!" said she. "On condition you get me
back before one o'clock."

"Whenever you like!" answered Meredith with
expression of such triumphant satisfaction that Dallas
turned away and, catching up his hammer, frowned
at it, and went back to his labours. Frowning yet,
he listened, between fierce hammer-strokes, to Mr.
Meredith's loud, full-throated laughter and Josepha's
soft, clear tones; he heard the motor start, roar and
die away. Dallas swore.

So the bees droned, butterflies hovered, birds chirped
drowsily and Dallas laboured until the sun was high.
It was as he paused to survey his work that he heard

a dismal sniff close behind him and, turning about, beheld a small, dismal man leaning mournfully upon a rake and who, meeting his surprised stare, sniffed louder than ever; a small, bony man who seemed verily clothed in despond, for his garments, all too roomy, hung upon him dejectedly, his age-worn hat sagged upon his ears, his frayed coat hung in melancholy folds, his baggy trousers, drooping dejectedly, shaped themselves concertina-wise upon his large and sorry boots.

And when Dallas had stared and the man had sniffed awhile, he emitted a kind of strangled groan and spoke:

"So you be the chap, eh?"

"Oh?" murmured Dallas. "Am I?"

"Ar—so they do tell me. But now as I sees ee I can't nowise bleeve it."

"Can't you?" murmured Dallas, still lost in wonder.

"No, I can't! You be a sight too young!"

"Am I?" said Dallas again.

"Ar!" nodded the little man, sniffing. "Though y'be purty big!"

"Fairly hefty!" Dallas admitted.

"But Lord—wot's size? Size beant nothink—look at I!"

"I am!" nodded Dallas.

"Well, I beant no giant, be I? No, I beant and wot's more don't want t'be. 'Little an' good'—that's me motter, an' that's me. Arl Sussex beef an' bone, I be, an' afeard o' nobody nor nothink—no, not even Ben! I've stood up to 'e afore now an' should ha' beat un proper if I'd been your size—so don't crow!"

"Why should I?"

"Ye beat Ben, didn't ye?"

"Well—I was lucky."

"Eh?" moaned the little man, opening his eyes very wide. "But John Croft telled me as ye knocked Ben out?"

"Well, it was a lucky blow."

"Dog bite me! And they telled me you was a American!"

"So I am."

"But Americans crow and blow and——"

"Not all Americans, I guess."

"Sting me!" sighed the little man, shaking mournful head, "Then seein' as you'm a American as beats Ben an' yet don't blow nor yet crow, I dunno as we wunt shake 'ands." The which they did forthwith; whereafter the little man sniffed, moaned and inquired:

"You've 'eard o' me, I rackon?"

"Have I?"

"Ar. I be Tom Merry."

"Why sure!" nodded Dallas. "Though you're some different from what I expected."

"Oh? 'Ow so?" demanded Tom, instantly truculent.

"Well, you don't act up to it."

"Up to what?"

"Your name. You may be Tom Merry but you're not merry, Tom."

"Not me. Wot should I be merry for—eh?"

"Well . . . the sun shines . . . birds sing——"

"Let 'em! Don't do me no manner o' good. I'm 'appier when it rains. An' as for the birds, they don't sing nothink like wot they done when I were a lad— no. The sun ain't s'warm and veggytables ain't wot they wos in my young days. I tell ee the world's gettin' wore out, an' me along wi' it—ah, an' 'er along wi' us—warin' 'erself t'perishin' skin an' bone, she be!"

"Who?"

"Why—she."

"What she?"

"She as you'm a-working for—or s'posed to be."

"Ah, you mean Miss Dare. You work for her too, don't you?"

"No—I 'elps 'er, occasional. But she wunt last
long, I rackon—and you'll be out of a job."

"Eh? What's that you say?"

"Workin' an' slavin' 'er life out, she be—and arl
for a dead man!"

"Say now, Tom, let me get this right—just what
do you mean?"

"I means 'er feyther, 'er pa—Squire Dare as died
five year ago—that's oo I mean."

"But if he's dead, well—I guess he's dead?"

"Ar—but 'is debts ain't, leastways she wunt let
'em die, and Jessam 'e be glad to 'ave 'em alive, 'e
is. Paid everybody off 'cept Jessam she 'as, and wot's
she got for it? Nothink, no, not even this here
cottage!"

"Anyway she's got her pride, Tom—her self-respect."

Tom Merry sniffed so loudly that Dallas glanced
at him in some consternation.

"Pride?" repeated Tom. "Pride don't fill no
stomachs, and no more you can't pay no rent wi' self
respect, an' if ye don't bleeve me, ask Jessam. And
now seein' as you licked Ben I'll buy ee a pint . . .
someday . . . if us should ever 'appen t'meet again
which beant nowise likely in this here world o' change
and death where folks be a-dyin' every perishin' minute,
but if ever we do meet again—a pint it be!" So
saying, this very mournful Mr. Merry, sighing dolefully trudged despondently away.

So Dallas got to work again, yet was presently
interrupted once again, this time by a voice very
loud, harsh and imperious:

"Hey you—you there!"

Dallas finished driving the stake he was engaged
upon and, looking up, beheld a face projected at him
across the hedge, a visage plump, fiery and adorned
with short black whiskers.

"Hey there, what are you a-doing?"

"Say now," drawled Dallas, wiping moist brow on brawny arm, "if you watch real careful you'll notice I'm in the cellar chasing spiders."

"That'll do, my lad, no impertinence! Answer me! what are you driving them stakes into my land for?"

"Your land?"

"Yes, my land—mine!"

"This is Miss Dare's land."

"I tell ye 'tis my land—mine d'ye hear?"

"Well, but she rents it——"

"That don't matter, I own it."

"While she pays rent, the place is hers——"

"Ah—while she does—p'raps, maybe! Anyhow I own it."

"Oh fudge!" murmured Dallas and took up another stake.

"Stop it!" shouted the plump man and hurrying to the wicket-gate, threw it open, but there Dallas confronted him.

"Keep out!" said he pleasantly. "No trespassing if you please."

"Eh—eh? Who's trespassing?"

"Nobody at present but if you do it'll be outside again for yours—mighty quick."

"D'ye dare threaten me?" roared the plump man, flourishing plump fists. "D'ye know who I am?"

"Why sure!" nodded Dallas sleepily. "By the moss on your map, the facial fluff, the alfalfa or spinach around the old dial you should be Jessam. How do and Good-bye!"

"Why you—you feller!" gasped Mr. Jessam, "you ignorant——"

"Beat it!" murmured Dallas.

"Beat what, you——"

"Ah, excuse me! I mean trot, hoof it, I'm busy."

"I'm a-going to see your mistress and by——"

"My what?"

"I'm a-going to see Miss Dare and if she don't get rid o' you, I'll——"

"But you're not!"

"Oh! Why not?"

"Well, I guess, because I say so."

Mr. Jessam actually swore; Dallas smiled. Mr. Jessam laid passionate hand on the gate; Dallas shook head in gentle warning. Mr. Jessam opened the gate; Dallas took a leisured step towards him. Mr. Jessam closed the gate and, his habitual pomposity overwhelmed in speechless indignation, gurgled throatily, shook plump fist and hasted off down the lane.

Dallas chuckled and hearing a joyous giggle, turned and beheld Sarah approaching; now in one hand she bore a plate whereon was a large slice of fruit cake and in the other a comfortable glass, wide-mouthed, deep and generous, a-brim with an opalescent fluid.

"F'you!" said she, smiling still. "Cake as I baked las' night an' a glass o' lemingade."

"Why that's mighty good of you!" said he gratefully. And when he had half-emptied the glass and bitten deep into the succulent cake, he perched himself upon one of Josepha's unique wooden structures that she had called a " brooder " and sighed ecstatic:

"Sarah," he murmured, glancing from the cake to its author, "you're a wonder!"

"Only I wish," said Sarah, leaning rounded shoulder against the gnarled old apple-tree, "ay I do wish as you'd give 'im a good, sound wallop—or say a couple —while you was about it."

"Eh?" inquired Dallas, glancing up wide-eyed over his hunch of cake.

"I means 'im—Jessam, that's oo!" answered Sarah, setting her dimpled chin aggressively. "I wish some un as can use his fist-es would punch Jessam—very 'ard! And, talkin' o' fistes an' punchin', wot about las' night—wot about you——"

"Sarah, I drink to your bright eyes," said Dallas, rather hurriedly.

"Go 'long now!" quoth Sarah, her fine eyes brighter than ever."

"Also," continued Dallas, lifting lemonade glass, "I drink to your good, kind heart and to the man who's sure worthy of it."

"Lork, sir! Wot man?"

"Well, I guess you know who, Sarah."

"Not me!" she answered, flushing and shaking comely head. "F'if you mean that Ben Lomax you'm wrong. Ben an' me has parted for ever—all, Mr. Dallas, all is o'er betwixt us."

"I sure hope not, Sarah."

"A nasty, guzzlin', quarrelsome, brutatious creetur," nodded Sarah fiercely, "as gets hisself beat!"

"No—no, you wrong him!" quoth Dallas, bolting a mouthful of cake in his extreme earnestness. "Ben's a white man and a sure-enough sport——"

"Which," retorted Sarah, scornfully, "you only says that becos you beat him!"

"I say it because he nearly beat me, Sarah—and then was man enough to shake hands—afterwards. Ben's a man!"

"Well, he beant man enough for I—a chap as drinks, and fights, and—gets beat, aren't fit for Sarah Chailey. Will I fetch ee some more lemonade or cake, now?"

"No thanks . . . And Sarah, I—was talking with Tom Merry——"

"Ar, I seen you! Which Tom Merry's a walking misery 'e is, allus grumblin' 'bout summat, Tom is. Wot were 'e a-grizzlin' about this time?"

"Well, among other things, he said Miss Josepha was slaving her life out for a dead man."

"Oh?" murmured Sarah, nodding. "Which then I rackon Tom weren't far wrong there. Y'see, years an' years ago Tom were one of 'er feyther's grooms, oh a great gen'leman were Mr. Dare!"

"Rich was he, Sarah?"

"Rich, sir? Why 'e were the Squire, an' Squire Dare owned the land pretty nigh from here to Battle an' the sea. Which, Miss Jo's pa were sich a very great gen'leman, in those days, 'e never worrited about sich things as money—not 'im!"

"Oh?" murmured Dallas.

"Ar!" nodded Sarah. "Mr. Dare left arl o' the worritin' to Miss Jo—an' 'er little more than a babe! And the end was, his money went, then his lands, then 'e died an' leaves Miss Jo a norphan with two farms, one ruin, this cottage, one baby sister an' a mighty lot o' debts. So she sells the farm, agin my advice, pays off most o' the debts, keep the ruin, agin my advice agin, raises money on this here cottage, an' now she's got to sell the ruin, arter all!"

"What's the ruin?"

"'Tis th' old Manor over to Southdene as nobody aren't lived in for years an' years."

"And she's got to sell it, you say? That's too bad!"

"Ar, unless she can find a hugeous, gert sum o' money for Jessam in a couple o' months."

"Just how much, Sarah?"

"Three . . . 'undred . . . and fifty—pound!"

"Oh!" murmured Dallas again. "Do you think she will find it?"

"No I don't!" answered Sarah positively. "So Jessam'll take 'er last bit o' property, pull th' old ruination down an' build a row o' cottages. Which'll be more useful-like than a ruin, only I don't like Jessam gettin' the place. But 'ave it 'e will sure-ly . . . unless . . ."

"Unless—what, Sarah?"

"Well, unless she marries Mr. Meredith."

Dallas very nearly dropped the plate.

"That," said he, setting it carefully on the grass out of harm's way, "that would be such a fool thing to do."

"Which I aren't so sure!" answered Sarah. "An' I'll thank ye for that plate . . . Mr. Meredith be a fine figure of a man, a gen'leman wi' plenty o' money, an' a friend o' this here lord or markiss as ha' just bought they stables over Alfriston way. She might do worse."

"But then, she might do much better, Sarah!"

"Oh?" inquired Sarah. "Meanin' 'ow, and oo?"

"Well . . . why not this Lord Withymore? She might marry him."

"Lork!" exclaimed Sarah a little breathlessly. "Wot an idea!"

"Well, think it over."

"Which to be sure Miss Jo's 'andsome enough to take any man's eye—when she ai'nt dressed anyhow."

"She certainly is!" sighed Dallas.

"An' she'm a lady . . . bloo-blooded from top to toe, she be—ah, well born as any in the land be Miss Jo."

"Sure thing!" nodded Dallas.

"And this here lord be expected in these parts purty soon, so Ben told me las' time I seen 'im which were nigh a week ago an' no less, says I, 'Now if this lord could meet Miss Jo an' 'er in 'er noo crape de Chine, and if 'e beant married a'ready——'"

"He isn't!" sighed Dallas.

"'Twould be the end of arl 'er troubles for my Miss Jo, God bless 'er!"

"Why then," sighed Dallas, rising and taking up his hammer, "you and I must work it somehow, Sarah."

CHAPTER IX

KEITH DALLAS—CHISHOLM

"THERE!" said Josepha, halting suddenly to point down into the little valley below them, a greeny sequestered hollow bosky with trees amid which rose the twisted Tudor chimneys and weather-worn gables of a once noble house.

"There!" sighed Josepha, a shapely creature poised thus against the blue, arm outstretched, head bowed, sad-eyed, a very grieving goddess . . .

. . . And how, how, how was he to tell her?

She so good, so purely sweet, a being so far removed from the shame and sordid evil of Hell's Kitchen.
. . . And yet, tell her he must! . . . Three days ago he could have spoken, should certainly have spoken but for the man Meredith's sudden interruption. So, in his thoughts Dallas anathematized Mr. Meredith, for now—now, try as he would, the words refused to shape themselves upon his lips: ' I am a killer . . . an outcast fleeing from justice!' . . . To read the sudden horror in her eyes, to see her shrink from him like thing accursed? No, speak the words he could not—dared not.

"There!" sighed Josepha for the third time and turning, found Dallas looking at her with eyes sombre and mournful as her own and, mistaking quite the reason of his sadness, reached out impulsively and touched his hand:

"Oh," she murmured, smiling wistfully, "it is good, it is so kind and friendly of you to sympathise with me, so truly understanding, because I suppose that really it is all a lot of silly sentimentality—most people would think so, I expect. . . . But there it is— the birthplace and home for generations of the Dares. . . . I was born there and lived there a little while. . . . Poor old house, so empty and desolate . . . and silent . . . no voices, no children's laughter— never again! It's falling into ruin now . . . crumbling away. But over the door, in spite of neglect and decay, you can still read the old legend, the motto of the Dares."

"What is it?" he inquired staring down at the ancient house, beneath puckered brows.

"'I dare!'" she answered, softly.

"That's fine!" he exclaimed. "That's a mighty inspiring sentiment, Miss Josepha."

"Yes," she sighed, "and yet its inspiration seems to have waned—for where are the Dares——"

"Why here!" he answered "and so long as you are you I guess you will live up to your motto."

"I've tried," she answered sadly. "God knows I've dared. I've ventured and striven and yet . . . the poor, old house! Sometimes I come just to . . . look at it . . . but . . . I shan't be able to do so much longer . . . you see it—it won't be here. . . . They mean to pull it down . . . and build . . . frightful little houses!"

"Why let them?"

"Oh, because I must. Do you think I wouldn't save it if I possibly could but I can't! Oh I can't!"

"And yet, I guess you might. There . . . there is a way," said Dallas, staring hard at a distant horseman who had set his powerful animal at the long ascent and was approaching them at an easy gallop.

"Yes, I guess you might save your old home—if you would."

"How—how?" she questioned eagerly. "Tell me, tell me—how?"

"Well, you might . . . marry . . . a wealthy man, Miss Josepha."

"What do you mean?" she exclaimed, looking at him in quick surprise; then she smiled a little sadly. "Ah, you're thinking of little Patience . . . her husband-hunting. You're joking."

"No," he answered, shaking sombre head, "I'm mighty serious." At this she viewed him in a deepening perplexity then, following the direction of his steadfast gaze, beheld the approaching horseman, much nearer now, a slim, shapely, very personable young man who rode like a light dragoon—an extremely pleasant-faced, bright-eyed young man who, being almost upon them, reined up suddenly, swept off his hat and spoke:

"Keith!" cried he joyously. "Keith, by all that's lucky! My dear old fellow. It is you, of course, it must be—and yet . . . what I mean t'say is—well! Well!"

"Myself, George," answered Dallas, lifting his shabby hat. "Miss Dare, permit me to present Lord Withymore." In a moment his lordship was out of his saddle, the better to bow.

"Charmed!" cried he. "Absolutely! It's all so perfectly merry and unexpected, if y'know what I mean, Miss Dare. What I mean to say is, meeting old Keith like this and with you who . . . who, well—I mean to say, might be the very Spirit of the Downs and . . . er . . . what not. Absolutely!"

"Thank you, Lord Withymore," she answered, smiling yet flushing a little beneath the pleasingly frank admiration of his blue eyes. "And so," she inquired, glancing from these same merry blue eyes to the sombre grey, "you are friends—old friends."

"Abso . . . lutely!" nodded his lordship. "Old Kay and I have soldiered together, read, ridden, boxed, travelled, shot, played and . . . er . . . what not —eh, Keith, old fellow?"

"Sure!" nodded Dallas.

"Which reminds me, m'doughty lad, to demand explanations and so forth—what I mean is, why the sudden flit, the hop, skip and jump across the herring-pond? When I saw your respected governor in New York and he told me you were over here already, you could have beaned me with a feather! What I mean to say is—why the hurry, the speed, the passionate haste and the like?"

Dallas shifted uneasily, opened his lips to reply but meeting Josepha's serene yet watchful gaze, was mute.

"You ride a splendid horse!" said she, turning to admire the animal in question with eyes of desire.

"Isn't he a topper!" cried his lordship enthusiastically, "y'know I love—what I mean is—admire a woman who really appreciates a good horse, most of 'em—women, I mean, regard a horse as an animal with a leg at each corner and so forth. Now a girl ʋith an eye for a horse's points is a *rara avis*, absolutely! What I mean is she's a—if you know what I mean—a rarity and—er—quite!"

"He's named ' The Don ' isn't he?" smiled Josepha, fondling the handsome creature's arched and glossy neck.

"Yes—blue blood y'know, pride o' birth and that, that's why I named him ' The Don.' I'm hoping to do something with him over the sticks, later on. . . But you know him?"

"Very well by sight. You see I live hereabouts."

"Oh, splendid! You ride of course?"

"I used to, but——"

"Topping absolutely! I can find you a mount whenever you will——"

"I'm afraid my riding days are over."

"No, no, y'know, once a rider always a rider—eh, Keith? What d'you say, old man?"

"It's up to you, George," answered Dallas, a little heavily. "I guess if you ride over some bright morning with one of those Blue-Grass mustangs——"

"It's a go!" quoth his lordship. "The true Spanish-American stock, Miss Dare, such pace, such sweet action! Keith helped me choose 'em. And that reminds me, old lad, when your revered sire informed me you had incontinent teedled as 'twere, quoth I to him, 'Mr. Chisholm, sir, it's even money that he,' meaning you, 'is off and away to win his bet and ride my four-legged demon "The Thunderbolt"'——"

"Thunderbolt?" repeated Josepha, quickly. "But Mr. Meredith says he's quite unrideable—dangerous!"

"That's it!" nodded his lordship. "That's exactly it! He's dangerous, an impossible, savaging, man-killing brute and quite unrideable—that's why Keith means to ride him—bet me a monkey—beg pardon, I mean t'say wagered certain monies on the event, and if anyone can ride the brute old Keith will, he's an absolute horse-master, y'know—Keith, I mean—the Woolly West, broncho-busting and so forth."

"And so," said Josepha, soft-voiced and serene as ever, "you told Mr. . . . Keith's father . . . Mr. . . . Mr. . . ."

"Chisholm, Mr. Chisholm," quoth his lordship. "I told Keith's Roman parent that I hoped my 'Thunderbolt' would break his neck before he had a chance of breaking Keith's. And 'pon my word I very nearly cabled Meredith to have the brute shot."

"Why didn't you?"

"Well, you see—I know Keith. I've seen him ride some pretty wild beasties and—well, I mean to say, I've never seen him thrown yet."

"But your 'Thunderbolt' is so frightfully vicious!"

"But then, Miss Dare, Keith's, well—just Keith, hot as mustard astride the pig-skin—I mean to say—well, look at his legs, if you know what I mean."

"I think I do!" nodded Josepha with a smile that came only to vanish. "And now, Lord Withymore, I must hurry back to tea and my small sister."

"Then au revoir, Miss Dare, I shall call for you with a mount pretty soon, if I may. No now, please don't refuse me, it will be a charity absolutely. I'm a pretty lonely soul, especially in the country, I mean t'say women—beg pardon—ladies, well I usually get on better without 'em—no, dash it what I mean is I'm no lady's man and you—you're such an absolute exception if y'know what I mean. So if you'll only be good enough to come for a gallop now and then I—we shall be charmed—eh, Keith, my dear old fellow?"

"Why certainly!" answered Dallas.

"As for you, Keith, m'lad, you'll trot over to the stables anon, I'll be expecting you. It's a go?"

"Sure!" said Dallas.

And so, having shaken hands heartily, his lordship mounted lightly, waved whip cheerily and cantered joyously away.

"A . . . real . . . splendid fellow!" said Dallas, staring after him.

"Yes," she answered, and, turning suddenly, walked on again.

"He's what you call a peer over here," Dallas continued, keeping his sombre gaze bent earthwards. "Also an earl and one of the . . . richest of them."

"Really!" murmured Josepha, glancing up at a lark that mounted above them in a carolling ecstasy.

"And what's more," persisted Dallas, "yes, and I guess the best of all, George is a . . . a man! White! A clean sportsman . . . through and through. He bears a grand, old name . . . historic . . . and is surely worthy of it."

"And what of you?" she demanded, turning upon him rather suddenly. "Your name is not Dallas, it seems."

"Why yes," he answered gently. "I'm Keith, Dallas, Chisholm."

"I see!" After this she kept her head averted and chin aloft while he watched her somewhat askance. And when they had gone thus no little distance, she spoke again, though without deigning to look at him:

"Pray, why didn't you tell me your full name—your surname when we met a week ago?"

. . . So then, here was his chance at last! Here the very opening he had sought these latter days—a question direct to which he should at once make answer: "Because I am a man-slayer, an outlaw and therefore utterly unworthy such sweet, confiding friendship as yours."

Thus should he answer if anything of honour were yet in him.

Dallas clenched quivering fists and strove to speak, glanced at her half-averted face and—was dumb . . .

They reached the leafy, winding lane at last and here he paused and took off his hat.

"Going?" she inquired with the utmost indifference.

"Why yes I . . . I think . . . yes," he stammered.

"Oh? Then Good-bye, Mr . . . Chisholm!" said Josepha lightly, and went her way, leaving him to stare after her very disconsolately indeed.

CHAPTER X

WHICH IS A CONSOLING CHAPTER

WHEN she had disappeared from his wistful gaze, Dallas turned, with some vague idea of finding his way to Lord Withymore's stables where, as he knew, the heartiest of welcomes awaited him; but presently he beheld a motor omnibus lurching and rumbling towards him and, acting on impulse, swung himself aboard, sank upon the nearest seat and relapsed into unhappy meditation, wholly oblivious of all else, even the uneasy jolts of the unwieldy vehicle.

"Whereto, mam?"

"I wants Loois, young man."

"That'll be fi'pence."

"Arl right, arl right, me lad, don't 'old out y'r 'and till I finds me purse. Go 'way. I aren't t'be 'urried at my time o' life, an' no more I wunt be!"

Glancing up, Dallas beheld a very small, wizen-featured, sharp-eyed old creature whose diminutive form was almost buried beneath a vasty bundle, two baskets and divers smaller parcels which, one by one with the greatest deliberation and complacency, she began to dispose on neighbouring laps or feet. Having thus unburied herself she opened a cloak, she pulled aside a snowy apron, she lifted a spotless print skirt, she felt and she fumbled amid the mysterious folds beneath and looking at Dallas—smiled, fumbling still.

"Now then, grandma, hurry up!" said the conductor.

86

"Not me!" retorted the old person, nodding brightly at Dallas. "Oh no! I don't 'urry up for nobody, too old I be!"

"Old lady," sighed the conductor wearily. "I'm waiting!"

"Well, young man, you wait an' I'll go on a-searchin'."

"And here's the fare!" said Dallas. "Give me two tickets for Lewes."

"Kind gentleman!" piped the old creature, instantly ceasing to fumble and adjusting her numerous garments. "I were a-wonderin' when you'd take the 'int." Here she nodded and smiled so roguishly that Dallas smiled also as he aided her to build herself in again.

The which done, he folded his long arms, bowed his comely head and became lost once more in his gloomy thoughts.

A hand twitching his sleeve aroused him suddenly to find the little, old womn peering at him with her remarkably sharp eyes.

"Never worrit, dearie!" said she, nodding at his surprised face. "Don't ee set there a-grievin' s' gloomsome, young gels be much of a muchness—if she frowns to-day, she'll mebbe smile t'morrer—ef she don't then jest try kissin' some other gel, that'll learn 'er, I rackon."

"Eh?" murmured Dallas, quite taken aback. "I . . . I guess I was——"

"You'm in love, that's sartin-sure an' plain as the nose on me face, it be!"

"I? No! Impossible!" he muttered, yet wincing beneath the old creature's shrewd gaze.

"Lordy, my dearie, why go for to deny it? Love's a fine thing for them as be young . . . sometimes. An' tidn't no manner o' good denyin' it to me. I knows a thing or two. . . . And now will ee kindly 'elp a pore, old soul off'n this here bus? Yon conductor man be gone to guzzle in the tap."

Up rose Dallas, forthwith, and having lifted out the large bundle, the baskets and the numerous parcels, lifted down their aged owner, also—whose feet had no sooner touched the pavement than she chuckled roguishly:

"Oh my, oh my! 'Tis a good many year sence any man 'ad me in 'is arms, oh my! A strong young man you be, an' wi' a face as I shan't nowise forget . . . Mother Parsloe, yarbs ab' simples, roots, barks an' berries—that's me, an' lives yonder agin the bridge, an' I knows a thing or two. S'if y'ever wants to ax any questions—past or to be, you'll know where to find me."

Then with a last nod and quick, bright smile, she caught up her burdens and trudged off.

Following the narrow High Street haphazard, Dallas climbed a steep hill and, coming where the road widened, saw before him the goodly and ancient inn of the "White Hart"; its hospitable door stood wide for it was past six o'clock and the bar was open, so thither went Dallas, forthwith.

And here, apart from the chattering and thirsty, glooming in corner remote, sat Ben Lomax, scowling and solitary.

"Hallo Ben!" said Dallas and held out his hand.

Ben lifted scowling, blood-shot eyes and nodded.

"What's your trouble, Ben?"

"Nothin'."

"What'll you drink?"

"W'isky."

"Why that's no sort of stuff for a fighting-man who'd keep fit."

"Well, I ain't. And I don't want."

"What aren't you?"

"A fightin'-man."

"Who says so?"

"She does!"

"Who—what she?"

"Sarah!" snarled Ben.

"Oh?" mumured Dallas. "So that's why you're at the whisky?"

"No, it ain't, it's only 'alf the reason. I've lost my job."

"You mean in Lord Withymore's stables?"

"Ar! I 'ad words wi' Meredith about 'Thunderbolt'—one o' the 'osses. Mr. Meredith's afraid of 'im and no wonder, but that ain't no reason to treat the beast so 'arsh as I told 'im, and 'e give me the sack. And 'is lordship's expected too!"

"Well but that's no reason for you to drink yourself blind on whisky, Ben."

"Oh, ain't it? Well, I think different. And, wot's more, I'm goin' to sit and drink w'isky so long as I blooming-well like—see?"

"Why sure, do as you like, but if you mean to get real soused why not do it with ale? A whisky-jag leaves such a hell of a hang-over. I've tried it, Ben, and I surely know."

"You lemme alone!" growled Ben, angrily. "I ain't blaming you, am I?"

"Why should you blame me?"

"Oh well—if I'd licked you that night when we— well, if I 'ad, I wouldn't be sittin' here like this, would I? And I'd ought to ha' licked ye—I'm pretty sure I could if I 'ad another chance at ye."

"You're welcome to try, Ben, whenever you like, only just now I'm thirsty and I find your English ale mighty good for it." So saying, Dallas crossed to the bar and presently came back bearing two foam-capped tankards, one of which he set before the morose and gloomy Ben.

"Drink it or leave it!" said Dallas, shortly. " Here's your health, anyway."

"It ain't," sighed Ben, dolefully, "no, it ain't as I mind so much takin' a lickin' from a real, good man, though that's bad enough, but it's wot Sairey says about it."

"And why do you suppose she troubles to say things?" inquired Dallas, eyeing his companion's troubled visage with the utmost sympathy. "I'll tell you why, Ben. It's because she thinks so highly of you, likes you so much, Ben, that she just hates to have anyone beat you—that's why."

Ben's troubled face became less doleful, his beetling brow smoothed somewhat, his craggy jaw became less salient, his deep-set eyes brightened.

"That sounds," quoth he, absently drawing the brimming tankard a little nearer, "yes, that sounds pretty reasonable, chum."

"Sure it's reasonable."

"But then," sighed he, pushing the untasted ale away again, "but then you don't know Sairey!"

"But I do know Sarah. I had a long talk with her to-day—about you."

"About me, chum? Why then——" here Ben reached for the tankard, grasped the handle, sighed and loosed it. "But Sairey's a fair, perishin' knock-out when she starts!" said he, shaking his head despondently.

"That I can believe," nodded Dallas. "But then, I guess she's mostly right about things and—anyway she's a mighty good looker, a real fine, handsome creature!"

"Don't I know it!" sighed Ben. "Nobody can't touch her for looks. . . . Wot did she say abaht me, chum?"

"Well," answered Dallas, choosing his words with care, "from the—way she said it, I'm pretty sure she likes you a whole lot more than she lets on. Yes, I'm pretty certain that if you act right, Ben, she'll

. . . she'll take you for better or worse someday.
And Ben, what a home she'd make you! What a wife!
What a—cook!"

"Yes, but chum," said Ben, hoarser than usual in
his extreme eagerness, "how should I act—ah, that's
the question, tell me 'ow!"

"Why, first—cut out the whisky!" Ben growled.
"Then wait your chance and tackle her like a man,
tell her all you want her to know——"

"Ah, but s'pose she won't listen?"

"Make her."

"Eh? Make Sairey?" said Ben, opening his eyes
in amazement, "Lor lumme—'ow?"

"Well, you've got arms, haven't you, Ben?"

"Wot? You . . . mean . . . ?"

"Sure I do! And you've got lips, haven't you,
friend?"

"Lips?" whispered Ben. "Oh crikey! You
mean——"

"Just what you're thinking, Ben."

"Blimy!" muttered Ben and—hid his blushes behind
the tankard.

And after some while, having finished their ale, they
arose and went forth into the evening; and Ben's eye
was bright and purposeful, his broad shoulders were
squared, his tread was springy.

"Now if," said he, halting suddenly to shake his
head in self-rebuke, "if only I 'adn't lost my
job——!"

"It was Mr. Meredith fired you, I think you said,
Ben?"

"Ar! Mr. Meredith's all right so long as 'e leaves
the w'isky alone——"

"Sure! Whisky's rotten bad stuff however you take
it. I guess we'd all be a heap better if it had never
been invented. . . . Meredith sacked you before
Lord Withymore arrived, didn't he?"

D

"Yes—that's the 'ard part of it! Ye see 'is lordship an' me got along oncommon well when we 'as the
stables at Newmarket."

"Why then, I guess I can fix this for you, Ben."

"You chum—you? 'Ow so?"

"Well, I happen to know his lordship. Which reminds me I promised to see him to-night! So if that
is our bus yonder—hop aboard, comrade."

CHAPTER XI

WHICH DESCRIBETH TWO FRIENDS

"AND now, old bean," said Lord Withymore, busy with glass and syphon, "if you won't drink—smoke! And enough o' the gees, tell me about yourself."

"Well—just what, George?"

"Why, everything. First, how many ponies did you bring over?"

"None," answered Dallas.

His lordship sat up in his chair so suddenly that he dropped his cigar.

"Wha—what?" he murmured faintly. "Why then —who's mounting you?"

"Nobody."

"But . . . man alive . . . the International polo match . . . Ranelagh . . . next month . . . ?"

"I'm not playing, George."

"This," exclaimed his lordship, stooping to retrieve his cigar. "This is some dashed, preposterous leg-pull!"

"No, I'm serious!"

His lordship merely stared awhile:

"But . . . but . . ." he stuttered, at last, "why are you over here then?"

"Well," answered Dallas, smiling, "for one reason to see you I guess, maybe."

"Who takes your place on the team?"

"I don't know, George."

"And what do they think—what are they saying about your dashed, sudden desertion?"

93

"I don't know that either, and I don't care, George."

"This," said his lordship, rising in his excitement and pacing to and fro, "this will probably lose America the cup, we've a dev'lish strong team this year."

"Not it!" answered Dallas, lightly. "Besides there are plenty to take my place, fellows as good or better."

"Rot!" quoth his lordship. "Ha, dash it—now I've bitten through my cigar! You're dev'lish queer bird, Kay!"

"I . . . I guess I am!" nodded Dallas. "And just at present I need some money."

"Well, you'll find my cheque-book in the drawer at your elbow, old lad."

"But I don't want to borrow, George."

"Why not?"

"Because I shouldn't be able to pay it back."

"Eh? What on earth? Not pay back? You? Why I mean to say what the——"

"You see, George, I'm at a loose end . . . on my own, very much so," explained Dallas, rather awkwardly. "I'm an outcast——"

"Eh? Outcast? But . . . your father——?"

"Why, George, I—I have no father."

"Good lord!" gasped his lordship. "You don't . . . can't mean . . . he isn't——"

"Dead, George? No, thank God! Only we've agreed just to drop all relationship."

"Well, I'm—— Dash it all, now I've spilt my whisky!"

"Consequently," pursued Dallas serenely, "I'm up against it, somewhat. My worldly assets amount to these clothes—look at 'em—and twenty-three pounds, seven shillings and tenpence ha'penny. And I need three hundred and fifty pounds, or say five hundred——"

"But this is simply dashed frightful!" quoth his lordship gravely, measuring himself another peg.

"I mean about you, Keith, and your old boy, your revered sire and what not. What's the trouble, Kay, the reason of the fuss, the family feud and so forth? Confide in me if you will, old bean, if not—here's the cheque-book—there's pen and ink, so—get on with 'em."

"No," answered Dallas, gently, "I can't borrow from you, old top, not now, not under the circumstances. What I want is the chance of winning the bet I laid you——"

"Ah, you mean about 'Thunderbolt'?"

"Sure!"

"No, Keith, old lad, what I mean t'say is—old bean, no——"

"But," Keith went on in his smooth, pleasant voice, "being penniless I propose, should I lose, to work for you—in the stables, George—help train those new polo ponies or any old thing you wish."

"By Gad!" exclaimed his lordship, joyously. "The ponies! Yet no!" said he, shaking his head, "not so, old lad, the idea of you having to work for me—having to, Kay, what I mean is—no, it wouldn't be right——"

"I'd rather work for you, George, than any other man in the world, I guess. And work I must—or win. So, old fellow—are you on?"

"It's a go!" said his lordship, grasping his friend's ready hand.

"When can I have a go at 'Thunderbolt', George?"

"Whenever you like."

"Fine!—To-morrow, then."

"That's dev'lish soon, Keith!"

"The sooner the better, George."

"So be it, then. And now, Kay, if you feel like explanations and so forth——?"

"Sure!" nodded Dallas. "If you want the reason of everything, sit down and listen."

"Then take a cigarette, old bean, fill your glass—
no? Then take a deep breath and fire away!"

So saying, his lordship cocked booted leg across
the arm of his deep, saddle-bag chair and disposed
himself to listen.

"About seven or eight months ago," said Dallas
slowly, "I shot a man, killed him, George, stone-
dead!"

"Good God!" exclaimed Lord Withymore, in voice
utterly changed, and, rising to his feet, stood gazing
down at his friend with looks as altered as his voice.
"Who . . . who was he, old fellow?"

"A very dirty dog, George—and deserved all he
got—and more. But it seems I—murdered him!"

"Never!" said his lordship with the utmost conviction. "I can understand you killing a scoundrel,
but—murdering him, you? No, never!"

"And yet, George, the bullet took him in the back,
and he was—unarmed! But . . . shot in the back,
that's what I can't understand and never shall."

"But surely, Keith, surely you must recollect the
. . . the actual shooting."

"No! And that's another queer thing! I remember nothing except the gun in my hand and myself
lying sprawled across him and . . . the blood,
George, it seemed all over me . . . ghastly! God
I . . . I seem to see it yet . . . to feel it . . .
warm . . . sticky——"

"Old bean drink this!" said his lordship with a
certain quiet authority and thrust his own whisky
glass into his friend's unready fingers. "Come—down
it, old lad—neck it!" he commanded.

"What I'm wondering is," said Dallas, setting by
the empty glass, "can anyone do murder unconsciously . . . or in a sort of sleep? I mean, having
threatened to shoot the man, could it be an act of
the sub-conscious mind and I know nothing, remem-

ber nothing of it? I've puzzled over this question, George, till sometimes I've been half crazy! The subconscious mind—it opens the door upon such terrible possibilities . . . the—the possibility, say, of committing some act in a sort of coma, a waking sleep. . . . Oh damn the sub-conscious mind!"

"Amen!" murmured his lordship fervently.

"Anyway, George, the whole thing is inexplicable, the more I think and try to reason it out and find some explanation, the more dazed I become."

"Why then, old man, tell me all you can remember."

"Well, he, Red Rory, was a pretty hard case, a real bad man, an Irish American which means he was neither. He was a thug, a rough-neck, the hanger-on of a boot-legging crowd and about as crooked as a dog's hind leg. Oh sure!" nodded Dallas meeting his friend's dismayed glance. "I was a crazy fool all right! But you see, George, after Myra Jessel threw me down, I kind of flew off the handle, got fed-up and went on a bat. Well, they were a mighty tough crowd but this fellow Rory M'Guire was the worst. . . . And there was a girl . . . young . . . the face of an angel . . . and good, George, good I'll swear, although she was mixed up with this ugly bunch. Yes, Olive was clean and sweet through and through, but this dog Red Rory had marked her down for his . . . hunted the poor kid . . . and nobody to protect her . . . nobody!"

"So you did—eh, Keith?"

"Why sure! I found him—well, molesting her so I pretty well hammered his beastly life out. And then, George, being right mad, I swore I'd shoot him if he ever troubled her again . . . there were plenty heard me and I . . . anyway, Rory's dead . . . !"

"Well, go on, old man! Tell me how, where— tell me everything you can remember."

"D'you know Hetzel's, George, on Tenth and Thirty-fourth? No, you wouldn't, I guess it would be after your time, its what they call a swell speak-easy. Well, I was there one night playing poker and——"

"Who with?"

"Some of the bunch—see now, let me think!" said Dallas, pressing hand to furrowed brow. "There was Ryerson, of course——"

"Who is he?"

"Why that's what I could never quite get on to, he didn't seem concerned in the boot-legging exactly and was no highjacker, of course, but he had a mighty big political pull somehow——"

"Who else was with you, old lad?"

"Well, there was a man called Dutch—no, Tosh Jennings, Whitey Neeves, a gun-man, and that's about all. The play was pretty steep, so was the drinking, and I guess I must have been pretty well lit-up, for right here things begin to grow hazy and I don't rightly remember, but I've a vague recollection that I'd just won a fair-sized jack-pot when the door opened and Rory came in and asked for . . . the girl. I remember the table crashing over, the chips and cards flying. I remember getting Rory by the throat and the lights spinning round us as we grappled . . . then comes a blank and then . . . the blood——"

"But what about the gun, Keith, the pistol?"

"Oh, it was in my hand all right—and warm from the discharge."

"Was it your gun?"

"No, it belonged to Whitey Neeves."

"How did you get it?"

"I . . . don't remember!"

"Think man—think!"

"I've tried to, George, over and over—and I don't remember, I can't. But they tell me Whitey slipped it to me just before the others left us alone to fight it out."

"Who tells you?"

"Neeves himself and Derek Ryerson."

"But you don't remember anyone giving it to you?"

"No. I've told you all I can remember, George. I guess I was too soused to know what I was doing—anyway it's clean forgotten now—utterly gone. . . . Ten minutes, George, five minutes or less—or, let's say drink and my own damn folly have ruined my life! And that's—that! So there's my confession, George, old top, there's the reason my father has . . . disowned me, and very rightly, I guess. And now," said Dallas rising, "now, George, if you don't feel like giving your hand any more to a——"

"Old bean," quoth his lordship, rising also, "pray don't be a goat . . . a silly ass—what I mean to say is, a blithering idiot, if you know what I mean. You may have blotched this bird and then again you may not, and anyhow this bird was a blighter and what not, a positive swine and so forth. Howbeit, you are no murderer, my poor chump, you never were and never will be, if you know what I mean. And so, my lad, excelsior! What I mean is, let us hoof it, forthwith, out to the yard and see those ponies bedded down," and tossing away all that remained of a very much gnawed cigar, my Lord Withymore took Dallas by the arm.

"But . . . George . . . get this, I . . . I'm an outlaw," said Dallas, somewhat unevenly. "I'm . . . liable to arrest . . . prison, the . . . police!"

"Quite!" said his lordship with odd-sounding laugh; but Dallas, looking into his friend's singularly pleasant face, sighed deeply, straightened his shoulders and gave the arm within his a sudden squeeze. Then forth they went together.

D I

CHAPTER XII

IN WHICH SARAH GIVES ADVICE

THE wiring had been finished days ago, the summer-house boasted a new roof, the tool-shed door languished no longer upon a single hinge. In their new territory ducks quacked in cheery content, hens clucked, chicks squeaked and Dallas surveyed the result of his labour with eyes wistful and gloomy. Now as he leaned, broad back against the old apple tree, his troubled mind busied upon a certain grievous problem, to him limped little Patience's pet hen, a speckled and somewhat scrawny creature to whom Fate and her fellows had proved exceeding hard, for she was lame, she lacked an eye, the majority of her feathers had been reft away and her name (according to Patience) was Catherine. This outcast of her kind then, limped up to Dallas, peered at him with her single, bright eye, petulantly scratched, found nothing, clucked irritably, limped nearer, and surveyed Dallas again very coldly with her quick bright eye; whereupon the mere human spoke:

"Well, old lady," said he, addressing the bird much as his father had often apostrophised the bust of Vespasian, "well Kate, old bird, do I or don't I? That's the question! Do I quit right now, clear out for good, which, under the circumstance I guess I ought, or do I hang around just because . . . well, let's say 'just because'—which, all things considered I surely ought not. . . . She and old George can fix things without

me around any more—well, I guess so! My job here's
practically done especially if George plays his cards
right. . . . You see, Kate, nobody really needs or
wants me. I'm not in this game any more, it's into
the discard for mine. . . . Besides even if she . . .
if things were the other way about, I could never tell
her, being what I am, never—'unworthy' 's my middle
name, so the sooner I beat it, the quicker I get on my
way the better. And yet to leave the kid . . . little
Patience, that'll come hard, old bird, damned hard!
She's sure jumped right into my heart that little honey
girl, my little good-angel! . . . Oh hell, Kate, it's pretty
hard sometimes to act on the square, it certainly is!
The question remains do I or don't I, eh, old lady?"

Catherine merely glanced at him, clucked, turned
scrawny tail and limped away, having no time to
waste upon futilities. So the mere human, thus deserted, gloomed beneath the aged tree fighting his
battle between harsh duty and yearning desire till,
roused by Sarah's comely, cheerful presence he checked
a sigh and glanced round with a smile.

"Lork, Mr. Dallas, this be the first time as I've
caught 'ee idling."

"Because I'm just about through," he answered,
his smile fading.

"Then tak' a rest, sir. I never nowhen see nobody
work s'constant an' quick as you works, nowheer.
I've brought ee a piece o' pie, veal 'n dam an' a jug
o' beer as I fetched across from the 'Duck,' so set
down, Mr. Dallas an' swaller 'em like a Christian."

"You're mighty good to me, Sarah."

"Which be only nat'ral seein' as you've proved
purty good to them two lorn orphants o' mine—specially Miss Patience—but . . . !" And here she shook
her handsome head in frowning reproof.

"But what, Sarah?" he inquired, seating himself
on the grass nearby.

"Why are you tryin' t'commit sooicide?"

"Gee!" he exclaimed opening his grey eyes. "That's some thought, Sarah, and—it never occurred to me. But just how d'you mean?"

"Which I mean sir, and 'eed my words, Mr. Dallas, why are you a-tempting o' Providence? Why are you tryin' to die afore your time?"

"Am I, Sarah? Please explain, let's hear?"

"Well, aren't you very determined to ride 'The Thunderbolt'—aren't that right, now?"

"Why that's impossible——"

"Oh I know as the beast's gone an' sprained 'is leg or tendon or summat, but ain't you a-going to have a try so soon as 'e be fit again?"

"But, how d'you know all this?"

"Last night, sir, I . . . 'appened to walk down the lane and . . . just 'long by Drunbrell's farm 'twould be, I . . . 'appened to meet . . . that Lomax and 'e telled me."

"I'm wondering what else he told you, Sarah?"

"Which now I ax you," quoth Sarah, becoming slightly pink, "wot should 'e tell me?"

"Well, that he thinks you're a mighty handsome girl and would make him a splendid wife and a cosy home and——"

"Lorks!" exclaimed Sarah, becoming rosy. "And that's just wot 'e did say!"

"Fine!" nodded Dallas. "Bully for Ben!"

"I do bleeve 'twas you as put 'im up to it! The boldness of 'im! The things 'e said!"

"And what did you say, Sarah?"

"Me? I boxed 'is owdacious years!"

"Lucky Ben!"

"Which I ax you—whyfore lucky, sir?"

"Because I guess you'll be kissing him one day maybe. I hope so."

"Oh, the very idea!" gasped Sarah, becoming

crimson; wherefore Dallas nodded up at her with
his quick, boyish smile:

"Blushing sure becomes you, Sarah." At this she
turned her shapely back, took two or three paces and
stopped:

"Hows'ever," said she over her shoulder, "Ben
telled me as you'm set on ridin' that 'Thunderbolt.'
Now, Mr. Dallas, sir—why do such a fool thing?"

"Well, maybe just because I am a fool."

"Which if you do," said she, turning to shake
admonishing head at him, "I warns you, sir, and
mark these words o' mine, you'll be flyin' straight
into the very face o' Providence, which nowise shouldn't
be, Mr. Dallas!"

"It sounds pretty irreverent!" he admitted.

"And, sir, you'll need a deal o' very 'ard prayin'
for, that y'will!"

"I do, Sarah, I sure do!" he answered fervently.
"Nobody more so, I guess!"

"Which then, sir, it may comfort ee to know as
there's one as prays for ee regular. Miss Patience
have took to prayin' for ee every night—ah, prays
for ee very 'ard, she do!"

"Prays? For me? Does she, Sarah?" said he
very tenderly.

"Very persistent, sir."

"And, Sarah, sure such prayers—cannot go un-
answered."

"Well," said Sarah, rubbing her dimpled chin a
little dubiously, "prays about such queer things she
do, got it into 'er little head as you'm goin' to be awful
rich an' marry her someday: 'Please, Lord, bless
my Dal and make 'im rich enough to be my husbant,'
says she—which is fullishness yet don't, somehow,
sound fullish when she prays it. Prays about everything she do, lately—prayed for 'er noo kitten last
night . . . a queer child she be—and so's my other

orphant, Miss Jo. I can't nowise understand 'er no more o' late, I can't."

"Why so?"

"Well, here be you an' me, sir, a-workin' and a-striving to get 'er well an' dooly married, 'ere be us doin' our best to fit her with a lord, a gen'leman and a rich man arl at once, ain't us? Well, here's her wastin' of her opportunities shockin' an' shameful!"

"But, Sarah—how?"

"Which here's 'er and 'im been a-riding out together reglar for a week an' more, ain't they?"

"Sure!" sighed Dallas, viewing what remained of the pasty with lack-lustre eyes. "Every day!"

"Ar!" nodded Sarah, "and sometimes twice a day—Miss Jo allus loved 'osses. But this here very morning when she 'ears him and the 'osses jingling up the lane—and she, mind ye, in the very act o' getting into her 'abit as I've kep' laid by in camphor balls so long—when, 'Sairey,' says she, suddent-like, 'I've got an 'eadache,' says she. 'Which, Miss Jo,' I answers, bold and straight, 'you 'ave not!' 'Well,' she says, 'I'll not go ridin' to-day,' she says. 'Why not?' I axes. 'Becos I think,' says she, beginnin' to frown, 'becos I know that he means to be fullish again.' 'Ah, but 'ow fullish, Miss Jo?' I asks. 'Very fullish,' says she, frownin' 'eavensard. 'Miss Jo,' I says, serious-like, 'wedlock beant fullish,' I says, 'no mam, not with a lord, it beant,' says I. 'Sairey,' says she, growin' 'aughty, 'please go down and tell Lord Withymore I shan't ride to-day.' 'Miss Jo,' says I, very gentle but determined, ''eaven forbid!' I says, and leaves 'er."

"And she . . . went!" murmured Dallas, watching the airy gambols of a butterfly, "she went, Sarah!"

"She did, sir—thanks be! And I only 'opes as she comes back a lord's promised bride—which mind ye, if she do, she'll only 'ave me an' you to thank for it and—Lork!" cried Sarah as upon the air afar, yet coming nearer was a sound of voices and slow-pacing hoofs. "'Tis them surely, and 'alf an hour afore their regular time too! Now—I wonder?" And catching up empty glass and platter Sarah sped away into the cottage.

Josepha's voice. Dallas stared blindly before him, found an odd difficulty in breathing, then, scrambling to his feet, crossed to that shady corner where was the little summer-house, and there busied himself with nails and hammer. . . .

CHAPTER XIII

IN WHICH JOSEPHA ASKS ADVICE

. . . AND after he had thus hammered very pertinaciously for some time, he knew that she was standing close behind him and, being so extremely conscious of this, he hammered away harder than ever.

"Oh, for heaven's sake stop—do!" she cried at last in sudden, and somewhat unusual petulance.

Dallas obeyed instantly, and turned with expression of surprise so patently assumed that her red nether-lip curled itself for very scorn:

"You're a frightfully bad actor!" said she.

"Am I?" he inquired, keeping his gaze upon the hammer he was twisting and turning in restless fingers.

"Pitifully rotten!"

"Oh?" he murmured.

"Beyond description!" said Josepha, seating herself upon that wooden anomaly (her own construction) that she called a ' brooder,' and tapping her boot with the riding-switch she carried.

"And will you—please, stop fidgeting with that hammer?"

"Sorry!" he muttered, with a humility that was abject.

"Why," demanded she, staring up at his so persistently averted face, and tapping her boot a little more quickly, "why have you avoided me lately?"

For answer he gestured round about towards the result of his labours.

"Yes, you've done nothing but work and smoke your pipe and hammer in corners——"

"That's why I'm here," he ventured to remind her.

"And hardly a word to—to throw at a dog! Is that friendly, Keith, Dallas, Chisholm? No! Is it even courteous? Certainly not! I call it . . . absolutely—boorish . . . ! And will you be good enough to put down that hammer?"

Dallas forthwith laid by the hammer and, folding his arms, fixed his sombre gaze on the ancient apple-tree.

"Are you really and truly my friend?"

"You can be sure of that always . . . always!" he answered with a certain breathless fervour.

"Then I want you to advise me."

"I'll do my best."

"Well then, to-day . . . ! Are you listening?"

"Why surely!"

"Then suppose you condescend to look at me, now and then! Suppose you come a little nearer and try to appear a little less wooden! More sympathetic! And I think you'd better sit down, the grass is perfectly dry. And you can smoke your pipe if you wish."

Murmuring his thanks, Dallas seated himself upon the grass in the exact spot indicated and began to fill his pipe.

"Now—are you listening?"

"With both ears."

"Well then first, what kind of a man is Lord Withymore?"

"One of the very best!" answered Dallas promptly, looking at her at last with eyes aglow. "I can tell you George is—well he's my friend!"

"Is he a—good man?"

"Good, Miss Josepha? Well now say, old George is what you call in England a true-blue gentleman, and we, in America, a white man, which I guess means about the same. Why old George is clean—through and through! He's a man any woman . . . might trust herself to . . . always."

"Strange!" murmured Josepha musingly.

"Now please what might you mean by 'strange'?"

"Well, you say about him almost exactly what he is for ever saying about you."

"About . . . me?" Dallas almost gasped.

"Yes—you! He's always telling me how very magnificent and splendid you are."

"What . . . old George is? He must be crazy!"

"Oh, why?"

"Well to do . . . to say such a fool thing."

"And yet he talks almost rationally at times. For instance to-day—he was talking about you, of course, trying to impress me with your heroical perfections, and he said it something like this: 'Old Kay, Miss Dare, is—if you know what I mean, about the top-holest sportsman that ever—I mean he's absolutely sound, d'you see, very stout fla and so forth, a trusty old sportsman and what not, absolutely! What I mean to say he's a man, absolutely! Quite!' . . . So you see, I come from hearing him sing your praises only to hear you singing his. Which strikes me as strange. Don't you think so?"

"Surely!" answered Dallas, flushing beneath her serene gaze. "But as it happens, old George and I have been pretty hard up against it once or twice and he's apt to . . . to over-rate things, I guess."

"That's what I told him!" nodded Josepha. "And then he became so vehement in your praise that I couldn't understand him at all except that he called the heavens to witness that you were 'stout'—which you are not, 'sound'—which you appear to be, and 'solid gold from head to foot'—which is extravagantly impossible and altogether ridiculous—now isn't it?"

"Sure!" murmured Dallas.

"And yet," she continued, "whenever you have condescended speech with me lately, you have done nothing but praise him to the skies. Why?"

"Well, you see—old George saved my life."

"Where?"

"In France."

"He says you saved his." Here Dallas muttered unintelligibly and gave all his attention to charging his pipe.

"Well anyhow," said Josepha, "to-day, after he had praised and glorified you until I could have prodded him with a pin, Lord Withymore asked me to marry him." Here Dallas dropped his tobacco-pouch:

"Oh?" he murmured picking it up rather awkwardly. "Yes?"

"Good heavens!" cried Josepha, cutting at the grass with her riding-switch. "Is that all you have to say?"

"I . . . guess so," he nodded. "What should I say?" She merely looked at him: Dallas went on filling his pipe.

"Well," said she at last, "you might be ordinarily polite, at least."

"I beg pardon . . . yes," he stammered. "I . . . I hope you will be happy . . . very. . . ."

"Do you indeed?" quoth she, bitterly.

"Why yes . . . yes indeed——"

"Why should I be happy?"

"Well, as . . . old George's . . . wife—you'll surely be happy."

"Oh, thank you!" said she more bitterly than before. "Thank you, but I shan't."

"But——" said Dallas.

"No!" she answered. "I shan't be happy as 'old George's' wife because I shall never marry 'old George.'"

"But," said Dallas again, "you . . . you say he asked you?"

"Certainly he asked me . . . and you, you of course imagine that I instantly snapped at him!"

"No, no, not snap——"

"Threw myself into his arms and snapped out: 'Yes, old George!' Isn't that what you expected me to do?"

"Well no . . . no, not . . . not exactly," stammered Dallas, "but I . . . I hoped——"

"What, pray?"

"That you . . . that for George's sake you'd——"

"Well, I didn't!" said Josepha rising suddenly, the switch quivering in her grasp, rather as if she yearned to use it on Dallas. "Poor as I am I withstood his gilded fascinations. Lord Withymore knows I shall never marry him." So saying, she nodded resolutely, caught up the folds of her habit and turned towards the cottage, little dreaming how very nearly she had been seized, swung aloft in two yearning arms to be there fast prisoned and kissed, sighed over, worshipped. . . . And yet, perhaps she sensed something of this, for the face of Dallas was very eloquent just then, and her woman's eyes were very quick and wise; howbeit she walked slowly, and reaching the cottage door, glanced back—and saw him standing where she had left him, but now his comely head was bowed, his shoulders drooped, he looked indeed the very picture of dejection, wherefore Josepha knit her brows in puzzled frown; then she made to enter the cottage, hesitated and finally retracing her steps, stood a moment viewing his unconscious yet so eloquent back and, being more puzzled than ever, touched him gently with her riding-switch. The very softest

of touches, yet he started round upon her so violently
that she recoiled; and now, seeing his face her bewil-
derment grew.

"I hope," said she lightly, "that my refusal to
marry Lord Withymore hasn't upset you very much."

"No . . . no," said he, in his nervous, halting
manner. "Oh no . . . on the contrary!"

"Is that why you look so frightfully wretched?"

"No, I . . . I was . . . thinking," he muttered.

"Then give it up," she laughed, "it seems to dis-
agree with you." And so she turned to leave him
—but—caught her foot in a fold of her long riding-
habit, tripped and—was seized, swung aloft in two
fierce, yearning arms and, there fast imprisoned, was
kissed, sighed over, worshipped . . . and freed—
all in a moment.

Leaning against the old apple-tree she closed her
eyes, clasped hand to tempestuous bosom and so
stood a breathing space, then, opening her eyes, she
looked at him.

"Well!" she murmured. "Oh . . . Keith . . .
Dallas . . . Chisholm——" the words ended in a gasp,
and she shrank back against the gnarled old tree (as
well she might) for with sudden, wild gesture and
uttering a broken, inarticulate cry, he turned and
hurried across the garden—out and away.

CHAPTER XIV

OF REMORSE AND THE SUB-CONSCIOUS MIND

AWAY he went, striding down the lane, blind, deaf, his every sense and faculty whelmed by this stupendous, amazing, wonderful fact—her lips had quivered responsive to his own! Josepha had kissed him! And, therefore, because she was Josepha, this meant. . . . Oh marvel of marvels, this could only mean the one supreme and mighty truth, for Josepha (being herself) was not one to kiss lightly, nay stoop to kiss any man—unless she truly loved . . . !

And his hands were bloody.

Dallas gasped and stood suddenly appalled as before his mental vision rose the pale, dead face of Red Rory. . . . And straightway from the pinnacle of Joy Triumphant he was plunged to the black deeps of passionate despair. Now, sinking down upon the grassy bank that bordered the way, he crouched with bowed head between clenched hands while wave after wave of bitter remorse swept over him. He had glimpsed the Vision of Beatitude that must remain a vision only, a dream never to be realized; he had seen the Promised Land, beheld the very Garden of Life that must be a garden shut and for ever barred against him by his own mad folly. . . . Love such as hers, a passion so pure and ennobling was not for such stained wretch as he! . . . Oh fool most sorry and most accursed! . . . His least touch would be contamination, his caresses worse than death . . .

she was not for him. . . . Yet in her love lay his salvation, her white arms might lift him up from shame and black despair. . . . And yet Red Rory had groaned and bled and died—and by his act, so must he know himself blood-guilty wretch even with her arms about him . . . a murderer still!

. . . And then indeed arms were about him, small, tender arms that clasped and clung; a smooth cheek pressed his own, wayward curls tickled him and a voice murmured consolation:

"Never mind, Dal, oh never mind—I'm here!"

"Honey!" he whispered. "My little honey girl!" and drawing the childish body close he hid his face against her small shoulder lest she see the agony that wrung him; when at last he looked up, it was with a smile.

"Oh, Dal," said she viewing him anxiously and cherishing him like the small mother-creature she was. "I thought you were crying!"

"Why no," he answered, kissing her nearest curl. "I'm not crying, Honey."

"But your eyes look a bit weepy, you know."

"Do they, Hon? I guess it's just a cold, or dust in them—anyway I'm fine and dandy now you're here, so let's——"

"Was it a pain, Dal?"

"Something of the sort, Hon, but——"

"And did it 'ketch you in the j'ints' like old Jesse's pain does, or was it 'innards' like Tom Merry's?"

"Innards I guess, Honey."

"Why then, I'll tell you what, Dal! You must always carry a potato in your pocket like Tom Merry does. Tom says there's nothing like a 'pitater for the axey'. . . . An' now, if you're quite better again, I'll tell you something."

"What is it, Hon?"

"You are quite, quite better—reely?"

"Really and truly!"

"Why then, Dal, I've been wondering and wondering all day. I was wondering all the while I did my lessons. I was wondering all the way home, and—I'm wondering now!"

"And what are you wondering, I wonder?"

"Well, I'm wondering if you'll take me to the fair at Lewes on Saturday. Oh, Dal, they've got bears an' tigers an' clowns an' a woman frightfully fat— Oh triffic! And there's swings an' roundabouts an' tents with flags on to them, an' drums an' trumpets— so will you, Dal, please—just to please me?"

"Why sure I'll take you, Honey—I mean if . . . if your sister will let me. . . ."

"Oh she will, she will, 'course she will!" cried the Small Person, clapping hands for very joy. "I asked her an' she said yes if you wouldn't mind the trouble."

"Trouble?" repeated Dallas, kissing her bright hair. "Trouble doesn't live near you, Honey—not for me, at least. I'll take you, and we'll see just all there is to see."

"What—everything?"

"Every blessed thing, Hon."

"How . . . triffickly . . . splendid!" whispered Patience in a sort of awful pleasure. "But it will be frightfully 'spensive for a notrich man! Are you sure you can manage it, Dal?"

"Oh we'll manage it somehow, I guess."

"Why . . . then——!" said she, and kissed him. "Now I'll tell you something else, something that'll 'sprise you. I met Ben in Alfriston an' so he took off his cap to me. Ben's frightfully plite sometimes —an' he asked me how you were, so I told him. Then he asked how my Jo was, so I told him. Then he asked how our Sarah was, so I told him that. Then he asked if I'd mind taking a parcel an' I said 'no.' So he gave me the teeniest, weeniest little parcel you

ever saw—it's here in my satchel. I'll show it you—
an' then he said 'for her,' and went. And, Oh, Dal,
it ticks! I mean the parcel does. I can hear it an'
so shall you—here it is . . . now listen!"

And opening her satchel the Small Personage drew
forth divers .ink-splashed copy-books and dog's-eared
primers and with these the parcel in question which
she handed to Dallas, a small, neat package tied with
pink string, adorned here and there with splotches
of purple sealing-wax and inscribed in carefully printed
capitals, thus:

TO SARAH (THE ONE AND ONLY)
FROM
U KNOW WITH LOVE

"Listen to it, Dal! It's ticking away! I believe
it must be a wrist-watch!" said Patience, in hushed
voice.

"I guess it is, Hon."

"Ooh! Won't Sarah be pleased!"

"She ought to be."

"Ben must be a rich man to go buying wrist-
watches!" sighed the Personage. "And yet I don't
think I'd want him for a husbant, even if he is
rich."

"Why not, Honey?"

"Well, I don't seem to have that kind of taste for
him."

"I wonder if Sarah has?" said he smiling as he
watched the Small Person stow Ben's gift back among
her school-books with extremest care. "What d'you
think, Hon?"

"'Course not, Dal, she'd rather eat worms, I heard
her say so. . . . An' now take my hand an' we'll
go 'long to tea."

"Why, sure," said he, rising. "I'll take your hand, dear, and go along as far as the cottage but I can't come in for tea to-day."

"Oh, but why not? Jo'll be so frightfully dis-'pointed and so shall I—so do come, please!"

"I'm sorry but—not to-day, Honey."

"Business, I s'pose, Dal?"

"Why yes," he nodded.

"Yes, it always is!" she sighed. "Business spoils lots of things."

"It sure does!" he answered, sighing also.

After this they went in silence until they came in sight of the cottage, its steep, thatched roof, peeping through its screen of leaves; and here Dallas halted.

"Not . . . just one cup, Dal?" she pleaded.

"Not to-day, Honey," he answered and stooping, kissed her.

"I hate business!" quoth the Small Personage; then she pouted, sighed, and, reaching the little wicket gate, waved her hand to him and was gone.

So Dallas trudged on again, still harassed by his unhappy thoughts, on and on until, pausing at last, he looked up and found that golden afternoon had changed to roseate evening.

Before him upreared in stately grandeur was that particular eminence whose every gentle curve he had come to know so well, upon whose grassy steep, boldly outlined in the green, stood the solitary Giant of Wilmington, that Thing of Mystery, his mighty feet just now bathed in amethystine shadow, his lofty head crowned in rosy haze; there stood this Shape of Wonder seeming to watch and brood over that fair, wide country-side as he has done for so many countless generations.

Pausing at a stile, Dallas leaned there and, gazing upon this marvel, nodded and spoke as to a friend:

"So, there you are, old Thing, and there you'll be I guess, long after I've ceased to worry and am through with all my troubles. Life's a pretty rotten sort of game anyway, as you found out long ago, I bet— it sure is, for me at least. My own fault? Why, yes, I blame only my fool self. I've made an unholy mess of my life, and now it seems I've blundered into Arcadia and that's no place for me. I spoil the pic- ture—Arcadia and Murder don't exactly suit each other. So here's good-bye, old Sport, it must be the road again for me until——"

"Oh you ass!" cried a voice at no great distance, "you detestable donkey! You hateful moke! Will you gee-up? Get along with you! Oh you odious animal, you beast! Will you go on? Well then— damn you! There! Oh dear . . . you've made me say it again!"

Now, looking about Dallas saw the road made a sharp bend nearby and, rounding this corner, he beheld a lean lady of uncertain age, seated in a small governess-cart, tapping with inadequate whip at an exceeding plump, extremely shaggy donkey, which animal stood with stumpy fore-legs in the ditch, cropping ravenously at any and everything that grew within reach.

The lady, now perceiving Dallas, elevated her tiny whip and therewith summoned him imperiously:

"Assistance, if you please!" said she in accents of command, and fixing him with a pair of piercing black eyes. "Be good enough to take Felix by the bridle and lead him out of the ditch, he is so naughty, so wayward and wilful."

So Dallas touched his hat respectfully, after the manner of country hind, and urged the reluctant Felix back upon the road, where he stood, ears woe- fully a-dangle, eyes half-closed—meek but motion- less.

"Many thanks!" said the lady, nodding to Dallas, then: "Gee-up!" she cried, rapping the donkey's broad back with her very small whip. "Go along, you obstinate beast!" Felix merely breathed gustily and closed his eyes altogether.

"Oh well, never mind!" said his mistress, philosophically, "I daresay he'll go on presently if I don't notice him, and I'm not in any hurry. . . . But I'm afraid you heard me use an evil word, just now. I frequently do when driving Felix, which grieves me. Though Mr. Merry, who grooms him for me, declares all donkeys need swearing at, especially our Felix. But bad language is so unladylike, though everybody swears nowadays, especially in novels and on the stage! An odious era this, thanks to modern woman and the emancipated miss—coyness is quite out of fashion, this is the age of legs and lawlessness. To-day Woman's 'crowning glory' is a bob or shingle, her whispering robes and draperies have ceased to flow and become a kilt, a flaunting impudence! And everyone not a male is a 'girl'—there isn't a woman left unless it's the charwoman—and she calls herself a lady! And you are Mr. Dallas, aren't you, the young gentleman from America?"

"Why, yes," he answered in no little surprise, and off came his hat. "But how——?"

"Oh you needn't look so amazed, sir, and pray put on your hat. I've heard all about you from my niece."

"Your . . . niece, madam?"

"My adopted niece, then, little Patience Dare. A truly strange child."

"Yes," said he, gently, "I think she's just wonderful!"

"But quite too old, too terribly grown up for her age, don't you think?"

"Why no," he answered, shaking his head with

very tender smile. "I sure wouldn't have her changed any."

"And what of her sister, what of Josepha, with her shingled hair and bobbed skirts and head-strong wilfulness, what of her?"

"Well, I guess I . . . wouldn't have her any different either."

"Oh, indeed? Can it be that you—whoa, Felix, you contrary creature! Can it be that you don't—stand still, Felix, I bid you! Is it possible, Mr. Dallas that—Felix . . . Oh dear——" Here, with scurry of hoofs, Felix was off and away, ears cocked, stumpy legs twinkling until he, lady and governess-cart had vanished round the corner. And then, almost in that instant, a motor horn hooted wildly, brakes screamed; and presently round that same corner shot a long, low racing car that jerked to sudden stop beside Dallas and, leaning back from the steering-wheel, Lord Withymore fanned himself feebly with fluttering handkerchief:

"Phew!" he exclaimed, removing hat to dab at his curly head. "Near shave! Elderly bird in donkey-chaise asking for death! Absolutely! Comes round corner on her wrong side, of course. I save her from destruction by a sheer miracle and she threatens to take my number, slangs me like a confounded pick-pocket—what I mean is—such base ingratitude and driving a donkey hell-for-leather! A bad world, my masters! But Kay, old son, I was on my way to dig thee forth—you see I'm off, as a matter of fact, I'm hopping it, tottering hence, if you know what I mean."

"Oh?" inquired Dallas. "Leaving, are you?"

"Absolutely, my bright lad. I'm hencing forthwith."

"Rather sudden, isn't it, George?"

"You see, Keith, old bean, I mean to say the country's frightfully jolly and that, rural and so forth, picturesque and what not—but, I'm somewhat fed. What I mean is London beckons . . . fleshpots, laddie, the 'Dilly Grill'—a theatre—a club or so. Pop in and let us flit forthright. We'll be bathed and togged in a couple of hours and the vast Metropolis before us."

"Not for mine, George."

"No?"

"No, thanks. Rather sudden, isn't it?"

"Sudden?" repeated his lordship, opening blue eyes of innocence. "How d'you mean—sudden?"

"Just sudden, George."

"Sudden?" murmured his lordship, pondering the question. "Well, yes, perhaps it might appear a bit suddenish. But what of it?"

"Well, I was thinking of Miss Josepha," answered Dallas, his sombre gaze on the long bonnet of the powerful car.

"Old bean, will you gasp?" inquired his lordship, tendering open cigarette case.

"Thanks!" said Dallas. And after they had smoked together in silence for perhaps half a minute, his lordship spoke:

"Old lad, I'm the prize goof!"

"Oh?" murmured Dallas. "How so?"

"She wouldn't, Kay, of course—no, absolutely not! And I'm not surprised. . . . I'm not her sort, what I mean is, I don't appeal, fascinate or—or so forth. I'm minus the personal magnetism and what not. I mean to say—briefly, in a word, if you know what I mean—it's no go—abso-lutely!"

"Meaning she's refused you? "

"Quite!"

"So you're bolting?"

"Well . . . er . . . quite!"

"That's no way to win out, George."

"Well, but, Keith, old man, there's no sense hanging round—sheep's eyes and what not. I'm done, old bean, she said 'no'—three times——"

"Only because you weren't quite personal enough, I guess, George."

"Eh, but my good ass, a fellow's entirely personal on such personal occasions, he has to be."

"You, George, should talk more in the first person, singular number and less in the third."

"Meaning, laddie, just what?"

"More of yourself, George and less of—other folks."

"What folks?"

"Well . . . me."

"You? Good lord! Now what," quoth his lordship, "I mean to say, what the dickens should I talk about you——"

"She told me, George, that you were eternally singing my praises, heaven forgive you!"

"My very dear, good blitherer," answered his lordship, a little red in the face, "whatever I said about you, confound you, was merely in answer to her questions and because she seemed so dashed confoundedly interested in you!"

"In me?" quoth Dallas, also somewhat red-faced. "Oh tosh, George!"

"Quite!" nodded his lordship. "And moreover, my doting lad, she told me, this very day, that you actually called me a . . . oh dash it all . . . a gentleman!"

"Sorry!" murmured Dallas, wincing. "It sounds pretty rotten, I know—but she . . . she asked me, and I had to say something, George."

"Quite!" nodded his lordship, and they smoked a while in silence again.

"Is it so . . . entirely hopeless, George?"

"Abso-lutely!"

"George, I'll tell you," said Dallas, frowning at him, "if I didn't know you so all-fired well, I'd say you'd got no backbone."

"Eh?" quoth his lordship, starting. "No backbone? What d'you mean—no back-b——"

"Why, to give in so almighty quick."

"But, my dear old Kay, it's been a hopeless business from the first—I see it now."

"Why?"

"Well, because—and more particularly these last few days, I believe there's—someone else. And if you ask 'who'—I'll curse you!" Here again ensued an interval of silence, then said Dallas suddenly:

"George, I shan't try out your 'Thunderbolt' after all."

"Good man! Glad of it! But why?"

"Because I shan't be around. I'm going to light out for parts unknown . . . so I guess this is . . . Good-bye, George."

"Eh?" cried his lordship, hurling away his cigarette-end with passionate gesture. "Good-bye? Why? When? Where to? What the devil, Keith?"

"I'm going to-night—now. And—listen, George! She . . . she's working and slaving to save that old Manor House over at Southdene—the old home that's belonged to her folk for generations—and she can't, George, a man named Jessam has a lien or mort-gage on it or something—he's getting it from her this month . . . and only a miserable three hundred and fifty pounds! We've dropped more than that on a fool bet, before now. . . . And this means a whole lot to her . . . this old house, George, it sure does."

Round the corner whirred another car towards which Dallas glanced instinctively—an open touring car that carried one, beside the chauffeur, a pallid, lank-faced narrow-eyed man with lint-coloured hair, brows and lashes. . . .

"Good God!" exclaimed his lordship in sudden alarm. "Keith . . . what is it?"

"Nothing . . . I . . . I'm all right, George," answered Dallas, staring wide-eyed after that vanishing car. "I must have been dreaming, I guess . . .

dreaming. . . . I thought I saw one of that New York gang. . . . I've been worrying over that ghastly business again lately and just now I . . . thought I saw . . . Whitey Neeves in that car. I . . . pshaw! I was surely dreaming. The sub-conscious mind again, George!"

E

CHAPTER XV

OF A SMALL INVALID AND A PARABLE

"I be main sorry as you be a-goin', sir!' sighed Mrs. Weldon, placidly regretful.

"Thanks, but I guess I'm sorrier," answered Dallas, sighing also, as he took up his knapsack.

"I do 'ope as I've made you comfortable, sir?"

"Mrs. Weldon, you surely did—so comfortable that I'm asking you to accept this——"

"Why bless us!" murmured Mrs. Weldon, pointing suddenly. "If there beant Sairey . . . and actooally running! I wonder whatever can the matter be, for——"

"Good-bye, Mrs. Weldon, my hearty thanks!" And, thrusting divers crumpled notes into his landlady's grasp, Dallas turned and hasted to be gone; but, even as he strode down the darkening land, Sarah's voice reached him, high-pitched in agonised supplication:

"Mr. Dallas . . .! Oh, Mr. Dallas . . .! Wait, oh wait!"

Unwillingly he stopped and, glancing back, saw hands beckoning desperately, eyes wide in a pale face, and heard Sarah's voice louder yet and unnaturally shrill, gasping with a sound of tears:

"Oh, sir, come back wi' me. . . . She wants ye . . . come back, she'm cryin' for ee . . . little Miss Patience . . . knocked down by a car . . . in bed an' cryin' for ee!"

Down went stick and knapsack, and, grasping Sarah's unsteady hands, he stared into her wide, tearful eyes.

"Is she hurt . . . badly, Sarah? Is it much? Is it . . . serious?"

"We don't know . . . doctor aren't come yet——"

"How . . . how did it happen?" he inquired as they hurried along, side by side.

"One o' them motey-cars . . . come round the corner . . . knocked the poor lamb into the ditch . . . an' never stopped—the murderin' brutes! 'Twere John, the waggoner, found her—and John were cryin' like a babby when 'e brought her in—thought she were dead, e' did . . . an' so did I, she were so pale and still. . . . But Miss Jo brought 'er to, and the first thing she says when she opens 'er pretty eyes is: 'I want my Dal. . . . Oh, where's my Dal?' over an' over again. So, seein' Miss Jo knowed wot to do I came runnin'—lookin' for you, sir. . . ."

Reaching the cottage, Sarah ushered him in and stood listening at the narrow stair-foot.

"'Bide a minute," she whispered, "set ee down whiles I goes up to see . . . to tell 'em as you'm here." So saying, she crept away, and left Dallas staring miserably out of the open lattice at the gathering dusk.

Presently the stairs creaked beneath a heavy tread and a bass voice rumbled:

"Shaken and shocked, Miss Josepha! Bruised— bad enough! Shaken—worse! Shocked—worst of all! Shock's always bad for Youth or Age. . . ." so saying, appeared a large, red-faced man, whose vital personality seemed to fill and overflow the little room.

"Er—are you 'Dal'?" he demanded, staring at Dallas beneath a pair of large, twitching eyebrows.

"Yes, doctor," answered Josepha, "this is Mr. Dallas—Doctor Treeby."

"Why then, young man, you're her medicine, I shall prescribe you often—large doses!" nodded the doctor. "Miss Jo, your little sister must be soothed, m'dear, gentled——"

"Is she badly hurt?" inquired Dallas, glancing from the doctor's large, rubicund visage to Josepha's pale face. "Is she . . . in pain?"

"No, sir, and yes," answered Doctor Treeby, with a gusty cheeriness. "She's a mass of contusions—but then no bones are broken! A few abrasions but no internal injuries, and she is a remarkably healthy child! She has escaped lightly. Miraculous! And the dam scoundrels ran away—never stopped! Two men, John tells me. I'd like to be in their rear with a dog-whip! Now!"

"Yes!" murmured Dallas. "May I see her?"

"Certainly! Certainly!" boomed the doctor. "Take him up, Miss Jo, my dear. Don't worry! Don't grieve! And see she takes the medicine I send! Bye-bye!" And Doctor Treeby was gone.

"Come!" said Josepha and forthwith led Dallas upstairs to a small, dainty chamber where Sarah sat beside the bed, though all he saw was the little pale face upon the pillow.

"Oh, Dal, they've found you at last!" cried the damaged Small Personage in tones fretful though faint. "I've waited an' waited an' you never came —you'd have been sorry if I'd died, I know! Some frightful beasts in a car knocked me over an' I thought I was dead only Jo 'vived me. And now I've got a pain, Dal, lots an' lots, all over me like old Jesse Blee, only his pain isn't so big as mine else they'd have put him to bed too. So now won't you kiss me, please Dal, 'cause I'm a ninvalid."

Then he was on his knees, and somehow she was nestling in his arms.

"Oh, take care of her poor bad side!" exclaimed Sarah.

"Don't be so silly!" retorted the Personage indignantly. "Dal won't hurt me, he's so big an' strong like my Giant. . . . Why Dal, your eyes look all weepy again! Is it 'cause you're sorry for my pains?"

"Yes, Honey."

"That's triffickly nice. I love you to be sorry for me, Dal. So if you want to cry some real tears, jest one or two, I'll look at them quick an' wipe them away for you—though I've only got one hand now— the other's all tied up."

"Is it, Hon?"

"Oh yes! You see I bled some blood, Dal, all over my nice new frock. An' then Doctor Treeby came an' pinched me an' poked me with his thumb jest where my pains were, Doctors are frightful beasts—mine is!"

"But he's going to help make you well again, dear."

"Oh? Is he?" cried Patience, her eyes very bright, her speech quick and feverish. "Well, he didn't do Jesse Blee a bit of good, not a scrinch, and Tom Merry says he's a duck—no, a quack an' his pills don't do no manner o' good so he sticks to a potato. So if he can't cure them how's he going to do me? 'Sides when my pain's not bad I don't mind being a ninvalid if you stay an' talk to me, an' people to see me with grapes an' jelly an' no lessons an' everybody so very p'lite to me, only Jo will get so awful worried, so triffickly frightfully—you do, Jo, you do, don't you an'——"

"Yes, dear," answered Josepha laying her hand upon the flushed and restless brow. "But aren't you talking a little too much?"

"No, Jo. No—oh no. I want to talk, I never seem 'llowed to talk enough. 'Sides Dal likes me to tell him things, don't you, Dal?"

"Yes, Honey girl," he answered tenderly, "but just now I'd like more for you to sleep a little. Can't

you, Hon? Just lay your head on my shoulder—so!
Now try! Close your eyes, dear, just to please me."

"But I don't want to sleep, I'm frightfully awake,
that's the best of being a ninvalid, you can sleep all
day an' wake up all night an' no bother of going to
bed 'cause you're always there already, you see,
so——"

"But girlie you might try to sleep now—just a little
nap—come!"

"No, Dal, no! An' don't sigh an' shake your head
over me or p'raps you'll make my pain catch me sudden
like Jesse Blee's does an' that'll be frightfully cruel
of you."

"But you see, Hon, if you go to sleep a while, I'll
still be here, still holding you just so. I . . . I
guess I'll never leave you now until . . . I have
to." His voice had hushed to such deep, unexpectedly
tender note that the child nestled to him a little
closer, and the anxious woman glanced at him in
quick surprise; and seeing how tenderly his long
arms cradled that little, bruised body (and having
so recently experienced the power of those same arms)
Josepha wondered; and beholding the infinite tenderness of his comely face bowed above that small, bright
head, Josepha sighed, and knowing wherefore she
sighed, began to flush, and aware of this, frowned,
and, crossing to the open window, stood gazing down
into the dusky, fragrant garden.

"Well then," sighed the Small Personage, after
due deliberation, "if you'll promise, 'cross your heart
not to go away, an' hold me nice an' comfy all the
time like this, I'll close my eyes an' try to sleep, if—
you'll tell me a story."

"But I . . . I'm afraid I don't know any, Hon."

"Make one up like Jo does. My Jo tells me lots
of stories sometimes—'bout ogres with green, gobbling
teeth—oh spiffing! An' fairies and princesses in

towers, an' she just makes them all up out of odds and ends. So now, you make one, for me, Dal."

"Well close your eyes, Honey."

"I have—tight, Dal—look! So now begin—'once upon a time'—go on!"

"Once upon a time, Honey, there was a man——"

"Was he a prince in disguise?"

"No, but he had everything in the world except one thing——"

"What was that?"

"A key, Honey."

"Oh! Only a key?"

"Yes, but it was the key to the Garden of Life. So he went about looking for this key——"

"With a lantern, Dal?"

"Why yes, and without. Well, he found lots of keys but none of them would do, so he grew mighty sad and disappointed at last and being a silly, foolish kind of man he gave up searching for this wonderful key and went down and down—clear out of the good, clean sunlight, down where everything was dark and evil——"

"Was it a cavern, Dal, with wicked gnomes an' bats an' frightful things that crawled an' crept—was it?"

"I guess it was, Hon. And while he was down there he . . . did a terrible thing . . . a wicked, awful thing——"

"Oh! What?"

"He . . . killed a man."

"Do you mean a gnome?"

"No, I mean a man."

"Was the man a beast?"

"Yes, he sure was——"

"Oh then that's all right. It served the beast right for being a beast. It's quite right to kill beasts —'specially in stories."

"But, little Honey, they . . . they said he . . . murdered him!"

"Who did? Who said so?"

"Everybody."

"Well everybody was wrong, Dal, 'cause you see ogres are all frightful beasts an' ogres are always getting killed. . . . But go on—what happened, next?"

"Why then he somehow found his way up and out into the good sunlight again and then . . . because he'd given up all hope of finding the wonderful key . . . he did find it . . . by accident——"

"So then, Dal, did he open the gate an' go into the Garden of Life, did he?"

"No, Hon, he couldn't! You see the moment he tried to fit the key to the lock it just—vanished away."

"Oh but why did it vanish away, Dal?"

"Because that key can never be turned by a guilty hand."

"Well, an' what happened next?"

"That's all, Honey."

"All? You mean that's the end of the story?"

"Yes."

"But . . . why?"

"Because, I just guess it has to be . . . it must be!" said Dallas, very conscious that the silent figure at the window had turned, that Josepha was looking at him, wherefore he kept his head down-bent.

"But what happened to the man?"

"He just went . . . wandering on, Honey."

"Where to?"

"Anywhere . . . following the wind. . . ."

"An' didn't he die of a broken heart or marry somebody an' live happy ever after?"

"No."

"An' that's reely all?"

"That's all, Hon."

"Well," sighed the Small Personage judicially, "I like you, Dal, triffickly much, but I don't like your stories—he doesn't tell nice ones, does he, Jodear?"

"No!" answered Josepha, staring out of the latticed window again; and Dallas, glancing at her shapely back, wondered just what the expression of her face might be. "Had she understood?" he wondered. "Well, he had made confession at last—after a fashion." . . . And anyway all that mattered, just now, was this small head upon his shoulder, this little, bruised body lying so snugly in his arms, so close against his heart. . . . And glory be, she was asleep!

CHAPTER XVI

JEDIDIAH WOLLET SITS IN LUCK

BRIGHTON sea-front was athrong; cars hummed and hooted, folk pushed and jostled, the sunny air was full of stir and bustle, with a babblement of voices, laughter and the ceaseless trampling of feet. And remote above it all, throned astride mighty steed like some demi-god, sat the burly, rosy-faced traffic policeman at whose portentous nod, the mere gesture of white-gloved hand, cars and wagons, motor-lorries and omnibuses rumbled or were hushed, moved or were still; the which blue-coated superman, feeling his stirrup grasped in arresting hand, started in snorting amaze and turned to glare down into the small, lean, bronzed face of a trim little man whose sombre garments, white choker and soft wideawake hat suggested pulpit and tabernacle, but whose keen eyes, fiercely direct, held such expression of coldly calculating world-wisdom as gave his attire the lie direct; quoth he, small, bony hand fast gripped upon the large policeman's stirrup:

"Hey bud! Say Cap, how do I getta Loo-es?"

"You mean Loois!" quoth the demi-god. "That's wot you means."

"Well how do I get there, colonel?"

"First, sir, you lets go 'o my sturrup and then you ketches a Loois bus—over yonder, along where the Aquarium used to be and now ain't."

"Thankee bud!" said the little man with quick, cheery nod, "Good-day, Cap, s'long, Colonel!" And, obedient to the demi-god's guiding finger and oral directions, threaded his way very nimbly through traffic and trippers until he beheld an omnibus that bore the legend: Lewes, Firle, Eastbourne.

This ponderous vehicle was on the very point of departure and its conductor—that attendant sprite —was chanting forth divers exhortations to sundry would-be travellers, passionately urging them to:

"Step aboard lively, please! Move forward please! Take your seats please!" Which monotonous intoning changed suddenly to:

"Now then, lady, please! If you're comin' along get in please! Step in, missus, lively please, or keep out, mam, only make up your mind please and hurry up if you please——"

"Not me!" piped a little, bustling, rosy-cheeked old woman who grasped one large bundle, a basket and three small packages. "I aren't a-goin' t'be 'urried by nobody at my time o' life an' arl me parcels too, so ketch old o' my trug, young man!" Here she thrust her basket into the conductor's unwilling arms. "An' now will some kind soul gi'e me an 'elping 'and?" Here she glanced, pathetically helpless, at a small, trim, clerical-seeming person standing beside her, who instantly took off his wideawake hat:

"Shorely, mam!" said he and possessing himself of the bundle, set small yet powerful arm about her and had gently urged the old creature up into the bus, piloted her to a seat, and placed her numerous burdens on and around her, all in a moment.

"Lordy!" gasped the ancient dame, settling herself and voluminous garments. "This be the second time in a week as I've 'ad a gen'leman's arm round me waist!"

"Which don't surprise me none whatever, mam!" answered the small gentleman, gallantly, whereat she smiled and nodded at him and he at her while the motorbus rumbled away with them. And after they had lurched side by side for some time, the bright-eyed old dame ventured a question:

"Be you a church gen'leman, sir—a minister?"

"A . . . minister?" repeated the little man taking off his clerical hat and looking at it thoughtfully, thus discovering a silky thatch of close-cropped, silvery hair. "Meaning a gospel-sharp, mam?" he inquired.

"No, sir, I means a preacher, a parson."

"Well, hardly so, mam," he answered, shaking his head at the hat somewhat doubtfully and putting it on a little diffidently, "hardly so, mam, and yet——"

"Meaning, sir, as you aren't tied to no church nor chapel, praps?"

"I betcha!" he nodded, then glancing at his questioner askance, shook his head again. "That's to say, mam," he added, "you-all shore called the turn first crack out o' the box, by heck!"

"And yet you talks so strange, sir."

"Do I, mam? Doggone it and I'm forgetting the lamps!" And from bosom of long-skirted, black coat he drew forth a pair of large, round, horn-rimmed spectacles, and perching them astride his small, fierce, hooked nose, surveyed his aged questioner with the utmost benevolence.

"I know!" she exclaimed brightly. "You be a preacher from furrin parts, a missionary!"

"Mam, you've said it!" quoth he, nodding such vehement assent that his large spectacles stood peri-lously awry. "You've said a whole mouthful, I guesso! A missionary—that's me! It sure is, yes'm. And I'm here to wise-up on your British institoo-tions, so anything you can tell me 'll be all to the good. . . . A missionary! Well, well!"

"Fares please!" chanted the conductor, mournfully. "All fares ready, if you please!"

"Oh deary me!" moaned the old creature, distressfully. "An' me wi' arl these bundles, an' me purse so 'ard to come at——"

"Fare mam, if you please!" droned the conductor.

"Arl right, young man, jest wait till I finds me pocket!" so saying, the old person having disposed her impediments here and there, undid her cloak; she pulled aside a snowy apron, she lifted a spotless, print skirt, she felt and she fumbled amid the mysterious folds beneath and looking at the small "missionary" she sighed heavily, fumbling still.

"All fares, missis, if you please!" intoned the conductor.

"I don't please—not me, young man, but I be a-searchin', beant I?"

"Mam," said her small neighbour, taking off his hat again, "lemme get into this. I'll ante up for ya, yes'm with j'y. I gotta pocketful o' chicken-feed here," and from sombre nether garments he drew a handful of silver and copper which he held forth to the conductor.

"Take it outa that, bud," quoth he, jingling the coins, "grab a holt, son, this lady's ride's on me, yessir."

"Oh thank ye kindly, sir!" sighed the old body, instantly ceasing to fumble and adjusting her numerous garments. "You be the second kind gen'leman as paid for me this week—only tother gen'leman were young, an' 'e were a furriner, too, come arl the way from America, 'e did, an' 'im so sad because——"

"Eh, America, d'ya tell me? And young? Jumpin' snakes! Say now was he tall, brown, curly hair, grey eyes?"

"Oh yes, sir, that were 'im to a tee! Tall, nicelookin', curly 'air an' grey eyes—sad eyes they was

—and very strong, sir, picked me up so easy as a feather."

"Attaboy! Mam, I'm sure settin' in luck, by heck, I'll say so! And where, mam, where did ya first stack up against him. . . . I mean, well, where did ya see him?"

"'Twere in the bus, sir—paid me fare, 'e did."

"Where did he get in—at Looes?"

"No, sir, 'twere just outside Alfriston."

"Where's that, mam?"

"Well, sir, this here bus'll take ee there, this be ⅓ the Alfriston bus. Oh, an' there be our prison——"

"Hells bells, mam! Prison, d'ya say?"

"Lewes jail, sir. Here it be! Aren't it a duck of a place, wi' that gurt, big door an' arl them little winders s'neat an' reglar?"

"It's shore some spacious mam, considerin' the size o' this island."

"Ah, it be nice and roomy, sir. I never sees it, but I thinks o' the pore critters waitin' so patient to be took out an' 'ung. Yet if murderers wasn't took an' 'ung they'd mebbe marry an' 'ave little murderers —I dunno! But wot be bred in the bone comes out in the flesh. And there be the 'White Hart' an' I gets out 'ere, sir. So if ye don't mind givin' me a 'and wi' me parcels——"

"Shore thing, mam!" And in a moment he was up and out upon the pavement, hat in one hand the other reached up to her assistance.

"Oh, thankee kindly, sir!" she beamed, dropping him an old-world curtsey. "If you should 'appen to be preachin' anywheres in Lewes, 'vivalist or mission, I'll come along an' drink in the 'Word'. . . . Mother Parsloe, sir, yarbs an' simples, roots, barks an' berries, that's me—get ee back into the bus or 'twill go without ee."

So the little man flourished his hat in gallant farewell, clambered nimbly aboard and perched upon a seat marked "smoking" drew out a long, thin cigar and lit it.

"Jed," quoth he, watching the fragrant, blue smoke-wreaths with joyous eyes, "Jed, y'doggone ole son-of-a-gun, you-all are shore settin' in a beginner's, blind-fool luck—flushes an' straights are a-comin' pat, y-draw four to a kicker an' fill! For ef this tall, nice-lookin' gink with his grey eyes an' curly hair ain't my boy, Keith, well . . . may I never cock leg over hoss or see God's own Country again, that's all!"

CHAPTER XVII

WHEREIN YOU SHALL READ OF COMFORT AND SORROW

THUS it befell upon this same afternoon that a small gentleman clad in near-clerical garb, wandering haphazard along a certain leafy by-way, beheld a tallish, extremely shapely young woman who plodded wearily up hill, pushing at a bicycle that jolted heavily on flattened tyre, and one who, despite dust, perspiration, freckled nose and tears, struck him as remarkably attractive; moreover she was a woman in bitter distress, and he a Westerner and chivalrous as any steel-clad knight-errant, so off came his hat and standing thus reverently uncovered, his silvery hair bright in the sun, he spoke in his smoothest, softest tones:

"Mam, excuse me, but I guess you-all are in trouble, how may I help ya?"

Josepha stopped and leaning wearily on her useless and cumberous machine, glanced at this very small, slim gentleman who stood hat in hand, beaming at her through a pair of large, round, horn-rimmed glasses; and now he spoke again his voice gentle as his look:

"Lady it shore hurts me to see yore tears. I allow it just breaks my heart, so . . . say, lemme help you, now do!" And he was so altogether natural, so utterly sincere, his small, thin face seemed so ineffably kind, and, moreover, despite small stature, there was about him an air of such vital, indomitable spirit

that Josepha instinctively reached out her hand,
sobbed and told him her grief:

"My little sister is . . . so ill! . . . I had no
sleep last night . . . and this afternoon I had to go
to Lewes. . . . I had to . . . yet all for nothing
it seems! And coming back my . . . my bicycle
punctured. I'd have left the beastly thing in a ditch
but . . . I can still ride it . . . down-hill quicker
than walking. . . . But Patience is worse to-day
and I'm so worried . . . so dreadfully worried . . .
and so terribly . . . tired! And I must get home
to my little Patience, but . . . it's such a long way
and I'm . . . so tired!"

"That's hard, daughter, that's shore mighty hard.
But we'll fix it somehow, I guess. Jest you-all set
down a minute an' rest a mite . . . here on the
grass."

"Oh no, I mustn't! I can't, she—she may be
worse! She may be crying for me now . . . needing
me! Though she has Sarah and . . . Dallas. . . ."

"Eh? Dallas?"

"Yes, a friend. Patience adores him . . . hardly
notices me when he's with her. And yet she may
want me now perhaps . . . she may be crying for
me! Oh I must go on. . . . I must!"

"No now! Jest set right there an' rest, daughter.
You're all tuckered out and no wonder! Set right
down, girlie, and don't worry any. I'll flag the next
auto. You-all shore need a friend and I'm your friend
if you'll have me—well, I guesso! Say, lemme dry
your eyes now—shall I?" And drawing out a large,
snowy handkerchief, he wiped away her tears so
gently, so naturally but with such anxious solicitude
that Josepha, choking upon a sob, laughed.

"You're so . . . so strangely kind!" she explained.
"And I . . . I'm afraid I'm a bit hysterical."

"That's worry, I guess, and lack of sleep, daughter."

"You're an American, aren't you?" she inquired, glancing up at him with eyes of grateful wonderment.

"Youbetcha!" he answered with quick, bright nod, "you-all can gamble a blue stack on that . . . , I mean," he explained in answer to her puzzled look "I shore am American from y-ears to hocks, daughter! The U.S.A., the Woolly West, Uncle Sam, that's me, yessir—I guesso!"

"He's an American, too!" murmured Josepha absently, gazing across at the opposite hedge with troubled eyes that saw it not.

"That so, daughter?" What might his name be?"

"Keith . . . Dallas . . . Chisholm," she murmured, in the same absent manner.

"That so?" said Jedidiah again and also gazing at the opposite hedge but with eyes wonderfully glad. "And a friend of yours, is he, daughter?"

"Yes . . . he—was!" she answered, and now the trouble was in her voice also.

"Well?" inquired Jedidiah in gentle question.

"Look, there's a car coming at last!"

"I know, daughter. I been watchin' it. But you-all was tellin' me about your friend. . . . Well, go ahead, daughter, I'm listening good with both my y-ears."

But, bowing head on hands, Josepha sat mute, nor did she look up until the motor car was close upon them—a large, powerful touring car driven at reckless speed.

"Do you think it will stop for us?" inquired Josepha, watching its rapid approach.

"I guesso!" nodded Jedidiah and, taking off his owlish spectacles, he stepped into the middle of the road. The driver, a plumpish, red-face gentleman in dashing Savoyard cap, tooted again; Jedidiah never stirred; the young man shouted—Jedidiah merely

raised one hand, but he did it like one to whom obedi-
ence was a foregone conclusion; the young man howled,
ground on his brakes viciously and stopped within
a yard:

"What the devil——" he began furiously. Jedidiah
shook small finger at him:

"Son," said he; the plumpish young man spluttered
inarticulate indignation. "Son," repeated Jedidiah
taking off clerical hat politely albeit with air of cold
determination, "here's a lady has busted her wheel
and wantsta get home to her little sister who lays
sick. We need a lift . . . what about it?"

"I . . . I'm in a dev'lish hurry!" said the young
man ungraciously.

"So's the lady!" quoth Jedidiah and, reaching out
suddenly, opened the car door. "Will you-all please
to get in, daughter?"

"Oh no, thank you," sighed Josepha wearily. "I'd
rather walk . . . or wait for some other car."

"Son," said Jedidiah in sibilant whisper, "say
something!" The young man goggled into the small
fierce visage so unpleasantly near his own, glanced
at Josepha and off came his cap.

"It . . . it would be a pleasure!" he mumbled.

"Shore!" nodded Jedidiah, taking Josepha's arm
and gently urging her into the car. "Now, daughter,
jest tell him where you wanta get while I grab a holt
of your wheel."

"'Fraid I've no room for any bicycle——" began
the young man in drawling remonstrance; but even
as he spoke Jedidiah was in the car, had closed the
door and lifted bicycle to running-board in so many
moments.

"She'll ride easy so, buddy!" he nodded in gentle
determined assurance. "Now step on the gas, willya?"
The young man uttered a sort of stifled moan, muttered
something about "his paint and enamel,"—but meeting

the little man's suddenly malevolent eyes, grasped gear lever and off they went.

And now, being filled with sense of wrong, the young man drove furiously, swooping down-hill, whirling up-hill, braking fiercely at corners with nerve-racking suddenness, though Josepha seemed quite oblivious, staring before her with that same grief-stricken look: while Jedidiah, grasping the bicycle so insecurely perched, found little chance for speech—nevertheless, and more than once, he seemed about to question her, yet seeing her in evident distress, checked the eager words upon his lips.

"Stop here, please!" said she suddenly. . . . They jerked to immediate standstill and in that same moment while Jedidiah sat grasping the bicycle, Josepha was out of the car, had thrown open a small, wicket-gate set in high hedge and vanished without a word or so much as one backward glance.

"Well, I'm jiggered!" exclaimed the young man, goggling after her.

"That's whatever!" nodded Jedidiah, and lifting the bicycle to earth, descended after it; scarcely had he done so than the young man, swearing peevishly, clashed into gear and shot away.

Bicycle in hand Jedidiah looked about him—at steep, thatched roof and square chimney rising above the tall hedge, at the narrow, leafy by-way beyond this hedge whence had come a vague murmur of talk. Softly, almost stealthily, he advanced, and leaning the bicycle carefully against the hedge, peered over the wicket-gate at this so secluded, age-mellowed cottage, its bright lattices twinkling beneath deep thatch; then leaves rustled faintly and glancing towards that shady by-way, he espied two men who also peered at this lonely cottage, the one pallid-faced and pale of hair —but beholding the other man, Jedidiah's keen eyes narrowed suddenly and his right hand vanishing,

patted a certain object that lay snugged beneath left
armpit, then adjusting his large horn-rimmed spectacles,
he strolled slowly along that narrow, leafy by-way
to all seeming a small, clerical person lost in dreaming
contemplation of leafy Nature.

Meanwhile, Josepha, hastening softly upstairs, found
there blessed relief from her anxious fears, for the
child lay fast asleep with Sarah, the devoted, in close
attendance who, seeing her mistress's questioning
glance, spoke in barely audible whisper:

"He be gone to lay down in the parlour . . . 'bout
an hour ago . . . wouldn't go afore. You better
take a nap, too, Miss Jo, you be arl wore out." Josepha
looked searchingly at the little sleeper, nodded and
crept silently away to rest herself for the long night
vigil. Being in her bedroom she tossed off her hat
and then stood hesitant, turning a folded newspaper
clipping over and over in nervous fingers and staring
at it with that same troubled, stricken look . . . then
creeping downstairs she softly opened the parlour door.

Dallas was staring haggardly out of the window,
but at her entrance he turned swiftly.

"I heard you come in," said he, viewing her with
eyes quick to heed her sick weariness. "You're very
pale—what is it? Is she worse?"

"Patience is asleep," murmured Josepha dully—
leaning her two hands upon the table as if for support.
"She looks a little better, thank God. . . . But
I . . . I think I know the meaning of your story—
now!"

"Yes," said he, meeting her level gaze unflinchingly,
"I hoped you would."

"A man followed me in Lewes," she went on in the
same toneless voice, "a strange, furtive, horrible man
with ash-coloured eye-lashes and hair."

"Whitey Neeves!" murmured Dallas, as she paused.
"So I wasn't dreaming, after all!"

"And this evil creature seemed to know I was acquainted with you, for . . . he mentioned your full name, Keith . . . Dallas . . . Chisholm, and he . . . gave me this!"

Mechanically Dallas took the slip of newspaper she proffered and unfolding it saw these words:

WANTED FOR MURDER

Beneath this the picture of his own face. And, under this again, his name

KEITH, DALLAS, CHISHOLM

FOR THE KILLING OF RORY M'GUIRE

"Yes," he murmured, staring wide-eyed at the paper, "yes, this makes it quite plain at last, doesn't it? This is why I ought never to have cast my guilty shadow on you. . . . Oh I know, I know! . . . Then I ought to have confessed . . . everything and gone away. . . . I meant to tell you, Josepha, I . . . tried to tell you, because . . . outlaw as I am, I . . . dared to love you . . . for that—forgive me if you can. But I loved you from the first. . . . I just couldn't help it, I guess—and shall go on loving you now, so long as I am I, because it's just part of me, you see, my dear. Perhaps you guessed how I worshipped you, and I only tell you now because it's surely the last thing I ever shall tell you. . . . I shall go on loving you to the end, whatever that may be . . . always, Josepha, always . . . just worshipping you. . . ."

Soft-treading and without haste he crossed to the door . . . then, with the same slow, deliberate stride, reached the little wicket-gate, opened it and was gone.

For a long while she stood there, staring blindly across the garden all glorious with sunset, and heard a blackbird piping mournfully. . . .

At last her fixed gaze faltered, she moved, drew a long, shuddering breath and saw he had left his hat behind . . . so she came to it, took it up, clasped and clenched the weather-beaten thing to her deep bosom, let it fall, and yet remained looking down at it, head bowed, motionless, scarce breathing. Then she uttered a small, soft sound, her slim body shrank . . . crumpled. . . .

The setting sun cast a level beam that, creeping across the floor, reached a bronze-gold head, at last, hair bobbed and shining like a golden helmet . . . a head that was pillowed on a man's shabby, much-worn hat.

CHAPTER XVIII

WHICH TELLETH NOTHING IN PARTICULAR

"The Thunderbolt," eyes rolling, nostrils flaring, ears flattened, stamped mighty hoof, tossed lofty crest and snorted defiance. And glancing from this incarnation of malevolence, to its would-be rider, Mr. Meredith stroked his small, blonde moustache and smiled a little superciliously.

"Not exactly a lady's pet, eh, Mr. Dallas?" he inquired.

"Well, no," answered Dallas, his quick, grey eyes following the great, fierce animal's every quivering movement, "no, not yet."

"Oho?" exclaimed Mr. Meredith, opening his eyes rather wider. "D'you suggest any mortal agency could tame this devil?"

"Sure!" nodded Dallas, still watching the horse.

"Ah? Indeed? Well now, Mr. Dallas, I've handled a good few horses in my time, and I tell you the proper place for this infernal brute is the knacker's yard. The only cure for his cursed vice is a poleaxe!"

"Oh, I don't know," murmured Dallas.

"Don't you? Well—look at him!"

"I am."

"Well, I should think one look is enough for—anyone who knows anything about horses, he's got all the earmarks of a savaging man-killer—look at him now!"

"That's not all vice, I guess."

"No?"

"No."

"Ah? Then pray what is your diagnosis?"

"Nerves."

"Really now!" said Mr. Meredith, and caressing his neat moustache, smiled so very indulgently that Dallas, studying the horse, frowned at the man. "You—ah—you do know something of horses, I presume?" inquired Mr. Meredith, still fondling his moustache.

"Oh, I guess!"nodded Dallas. "And I'll need spurs."

"Spurs? Good God, then you positively intend to—er—ride him—or make the attempt?"

"That's why I'm here. Has Lord Withymore arrived yet?"

"His lordship is in London," answered Mr. Meredith with air of smiling finality, "and not expected back."

"Yes, I know all that," sighed Dallas, a little wearily, "but I got him on the long-distance last night and he promised to be here by mid-day."

"Oh?" exclaimed Mr. Meredith, forgetting his moustache for the moment. "I was not aware——"

"Yes, I know that too," murmured Dallas.

"I—er—I beg your pardon——"

"Not at all. And with short necks."

"Pray, sir, what the——"

"Spurs!" repeated Dallas patiently. "The shortest you can find, I mean."

But at this moment Ben Lomax appeared bearing a telegram.

"Ah, for me!" said Mr. Meredith, extending imperious hand.

"No, sir," answered Ben, touching an eyebrow, "for this gentleman," and he gave the missive to Dallas who tore open the envelope and read as follows:

"Delayed old bean with you three certain await arrival wouldn't miss it for a thousand good luck.— GEORGE."

Dallas pocketed this telegram and sighed again.

"His lordship can't be here till three o'clock, and I'd hoped to be miles away by then! However!" And turning, he wandered aimlessly out of the stable-yard and presently found himself upon that grassy level called the Tye, where stands the hoary ancient church. Now against the aged churchyard wall some kindly hand had set up a stout bench for the comfort of weary or thoughtful; and hereon, Dallas, being very full of thought seated himself, back to wall, long legs outstretched, and, staring down at the velvety, green turf, seemed to see therein Josepha's lovely face, pale and stricken, as he had seen it last. . . .

"Anyway," he said within himself, "he would save her old house for her—if the 'Thunderbolt' didn't break his neck—and if he did—why so much the better! For Josepha knew him at last for what he was—had shrunk from him even as she gave him that damning news-clipping to read . . . had shrunk from him! Yes, he were better dead . . . !"

"I sent her a watch, sir!" said a hoarse voice at this juncture, and glancing up he beheld Ben, smiling at him a little sheepishly.

"Oh? Did you, Ben?"

"Ar, I did, sir—one o' them little uns on a bracelet. Cost a sight more'n I expected, too! An' she's kep it all right, she 'as, which is a good sign, eh, sir?"

"Sure, Ben! That's fine, old sport! And what did she say?"

"Not a word, sir, she—couldn't very well, ye see I ain't been over to see 'er yet! Thought I'd wait a bit—give it time to sort o' soak in, d'yer see. Besides, lil' Miss Patience bein' so sick, pore kid, I didn't like —though she's better to-day, I 'ear."

"How d'you know that, Ben?"

"Well I—I 'appened to call in an' see Doctor Treeby, ye see, sir, I 'appened to be passing-like, so knocked

at the door an' arst him, and he says as she'll be up
an' about again soon, but cripes, sir, 'e didn't 'alf let
you 'ave it, lumme not 'alf 'e didn't! Told me as
you'd run away an' deserted your post—an' I dunno
wot more."

"Well, I guess he's right, Ben. I sure ran away
and I'm . . . going farther. . . . But—by God,
Ben, I'd give something for just one peep at my little
Honey-girl." Dallas's head drooped suddenly, wherefore Ben instantly averted his own, and taking out
the straw he happened to be chewing stared at it very
hard until Dallas spoke again.

"So Sarah kept the watch, old sport?"

"She did, sir—not 'alf!" answered Ben, replacing
his straw and turning. "Leastways it ain't come
back—yet. And so, sir, seein' as 'ow . . . I'm
'oping as things 'll be all right again, eh, Mr. Dallas?"

"Undoubtedly, Ben!"

"Though, mind ye, women be queer creatures and
no error—allus ready to jib, or shy, or ditch a pore
cove afore that cove can—crikey, there's 'is lordship!
Ex-cuse me, sir!" And away went Ben at the double.

"All hail, old Blossom!" quoth Lord Withymore
grasping Dallas by the hand. "Why the gloom, the
furrowed brow and whatnot—here am I an hour before
my time—that's the new Bentley, I mean to say, she's
a bird, absolutely! Averaged fifty-eight and a fraction
all the way! Was that Ben Lomax talking to you,
my beefy, bashful Ben?"

"Yes, George, but——"

"A good lad, a right doughty lad, not to say a truly
stout lad, a veritable basher—though he bashed vainly
in thy case, old lad? Woe and alas that I should have
missed that Homeric combat!"

"See here, George, old man, I want to get across that
'Thunderbolt' of yours, now—at once——"

"Exactly! But why, my poor, old fish?"

"You know why, George."

"Precisely, my sorry-seeming gazoo, but—fact is there's no need, the little matter you mentioned touching three-fifty John B's is already O.K. I placed the matter in the hands of my agent this very morn as ever was."

"Why then, George, he won't have had time to muss it all up."

"Aha? Meaning you wish to do it off your own bat?"

"I want to do it, George, so it can't possibly hurt her pride any——"

"Quite!" murmured his lordship, glancing at Dallas with sudden intentness.

"And I've a scheme, old son, such as it is—always supposing I win our bet, of course."

"Old bean," said his lordship, whole-heartedly, "I . . . God knows I hope you do."

CHAPTER XIX

GIVETH SOME DESCRIPTION OF A RIDE

"STAND away!"

Ben and his assistants leapt nimbly aside, and "The Thunderbolt" thus freed, all fierce protest and stark defiance from muzzle to tail, shook his great head, snorted, kicked, and reared in passionate endeavour to rid himself of this puny, two-legged beast that dared bestride him. So he reared and plunged, leapt and sidled, filling the air with the wild clatter of his mighty hoofs that smote fire right and left with each resounding stroke, but these legs that gripped him, gripping the tighter, seemed like bands of steel. . . . Very well—he would bite this human beast! So round came great, fierce head with lips set back —curling from cruel, white teeth that snapped viciously at foot, at leg, at knee that moved always just beyond his reach. . . . Why very well again, he would dash this vile human from him against some wall, shatter him against some sharp corner! But even as this thought took shape, the chafing bit between his champing, foam-flecked jaws was jerked, wrenched tight . . . tighter yet, checking his forward leap; so perforce he backed instead—back went he and back, snorting rage and defiance until. . . . Ha, ten thousand devils! What was this sudden, sharp tingling on his flanks? In his right flank, in his left—again, and there again! Spurs! By the god of all thunderbolts this presuming, tormenting pigmy astride him

should pay dearly for this—oh dearly! He would
brain the detestable human with sudden stroke of
mighty, up-flung head. Now for it—so . . .! Ha,
confusion! What was this stunning shock between
his sensitive ears? A blow? This to him? The pain
itself was no matter, but the indignity—this shook
him to the very depths of his proud soul—this called
for instant and desperate retort . . .! Whirling hoofs
that smote the air before, that lashed out behind, that
struck fire anew from the resounding earth! Again
that sharp tingling . . . in ribs, in flanks, more painful now than ever. . . . How then, did this besotted
human think to cow one of his high breed by such
dastardly means? Then, by the blood of his proud
ancestors, he would away like elemental whirlwind to
the horizon's edge and hurl this vile human thing
from the rim of the world even though he plunged
thence himself to fall, perchance for ever but—for
ever unconquered . . .!

So "The Thunderbolt" gathered himself, smote
all four hoofs to earth and—was away. Walls, trees,
houses, barns, flashed and flickered by—hedges swished
beneath him, vanished and were not. . . . And what
was this? Turf! Green, springy turf! By Bellero-
phon, now for it! By Bucephalus, now he'd show
'em! . . . Some fool somewhere was shouting in
his fool, human voice:

"Hold him, Keith . . . old bean . . . hold him
. . . for God's sake . . . !"

What pitiful folly! As though anything human
might hope to check or hold the proud son of his proud
sire! Aha, the rush of wind! Ho, the wild, mad
ecstasy of smiting the reeling earth beneath him . . .
faster . . . faster . . . Bridle him, would they? Dare
inflict on him the base indignity of galling saddle and
girth? Well, he'd teach 'em! He'd show 'em . . .!
Ha, jerk away at the rein, you poor two-legged Futility!

But your thrice-accursed bit is held fast, clamped between teeth that shall never let go—so jerk away, poor mannikin—twist, wrench till your puny arms fail!

Ho, for the pride of blood! Ha, for the speeding glory of four mighty legs! For the proud, untamed spirit that no two-legged creature shall ever conquer!

Hey, for the open spaces, this rolling, wind-swept countryside . . .! And yet—this same rolling country-side begins to roll confoundedly—and always up-hill, an ascent that becomes steeper with every yard. . . .

Well, what of it, is not the turf as seducingly soft as ever . . . ? And yet this never-ending steep grows ever steeper, so—wherefore such passionate speed? Suppose we ease up a little, a very little? So . . .! That is better, distinctly better! We will amble thus a while but, once the ascent is achieved, then ho, for a swoop, for a plunge down and down into the valley! But until then, moderation is the word. . . . Ha! what is this? A tickling in the flanks again! A sharp tingling! A painful stabbing! Ten million fiends! Can this straddling creature be urging to faster gait? Absurd! We have already travelled at speed beyond anything human, and yet . . . ha, again! By the hoofs of his sire, this detestable man-thing, still crouched and clinging upon his back, is indeed at it again . . . is actually paining him! Very well, then . . . ! A muffled thunder of mighty hoofs deep-smiting into the soft ling . . . a straining of mighty legs against the precipitous slope and—up they go . . . at trot . . . at desperate gallop . . . faster . . . faster yet. . . .

Oh, Beelzebub! Will this smooth, grassy steep never end? By Zeus, his hind-hoof slipped then! And his breathing—something was wrong there!

Very wrong! Extremely so! There was no joy in
this . . . ! Intolerable . . . ! Not to be endured
. . . ! He would halt a brief moment—Ah . . . !

Gasping, stumbling, dazed, half-blind, he reached
the summit at last . . . glimpsed a wide, grassy
level, shook proud head, essayed a gallop, groaned,
dropped to ambling walk, stopped altogether and
sucked in great gulps of sweet life-giving air . . .
and—Oh wonder, those torments gored his sides no
more! Well then, here and now, he would take
his ease a while and presently go on at pace moderate,
distinctly moderate until—Ha, confusion! His jaws
relaxing a moment, the bit was snatched from his
teeth, jerked back into the corners of his sensitive
mouth . . . he must regain it somehow . . . anyhow! And then he winced to the sharp dig of those
tormentors, leapt to sudden gallop, was checked by
the bit, pulled to stand-still by powerful hand. . . .

Now as he stood thus, blown, lathered, quivering,
something sore of body but much more so in his pride, a
voice spoke to him in accents soft and unexpectedly,
strangely soothing to his ruffled feelings—a hand caressed
his drooping neck.

"So ho now, old lad! Easy now, easy!"

And "The Thunderbolt" astonished, bewildered,
his proud spirit over-borne by the first doubt he had
ever known, hung his great head, sighed gustily and,
obedient to that persuasive hand, to that gently-
urgent knee, moved forward, swung about, and began
to amble down the long, grassy slope toward where,
far below and small with distance, a horseman galloped
to meet them.

"Bravo, old Iron-legs!" cried his lordship, reining
up beside Keith, his bright eyes even brighter than
usual, "Loud cheers, congratulations and what not.
Wouldn't have missed it for double the money and
more—what I mean to say is—sound the trumpets,

beat the bally drums and so forth. . . . And herewith please receive cheque for five hundred of the best and my blessings therewith, old chap."

"But . . . gee-whiz!" exclaimed Dallas, taking the slip of paper and his lordship's hand therewith, "you're almighty prompt, George."

"Oh," sighed Lord Withymore, shaking his head. "I knew how it would be—you bet you'd ride the brute and well, I mean to say—there you are! I scribbled your cheque before I left London, to save time."

"I was lucky to turn him up-hill, George, otherwise, I guess——"

"Quite!" said his lordship.

"You see, old son, if the ground hadn't been so good and steep——"

"Oh, quite!" nodded his lordship.

"He was pretty blown by the time we got to the top and after that it was easy and——"

"Absolutely!" murmured his lordship fishing out cigarette case. "You see, Keith, old bird, if—I repeat 'if' you'd been anyone else you'd be lying back there in the stable-yard considerably dead, I fancy, generally crumpled, beat and what not, and that four-legged demon would have been shot or poleaxed. As it is, the demon's a meek saint—look at him! He knows you're his master."

"I had to punish him rather," said Dallas glancing down at his spurred heels.

"What—with those short-necked ticklers? And a snaffle-bit? By gad, Kay, I'd have worn real spurs and used a curb, a jaw-breaking bridoon."

"Anyway, George, I guess he's had his lesson, and now——"

"Now, Keith, old boy, I make you a present of him."

"Oh rot!" exclaimed Dallas, though his eyes glistened. "My dear old son—he's magnificent——"

F

"Quite!" nodded his lordship. "Another reason why you'll accept him."

"But I can't, George. I . . . I'm going away——"

"He'll be waiting when you come back. Meantime, will you gasp?"

"No, thanks. He'd make you a real splendid hunter, George——"

"Not," sighed his lordship, lighting his cigarette, "no—not in these nether-garments, old bean! 'The Thunderbolt' is thine henceforth and for ever, amen! And jolly good luck to the pair of you. . . . He carries you dashed well . . . and a pretty action! Can you jump him?"

"Sure!" nodded Dallas. They had descended the hill and were traversing a broad meadow screened from the road by a lofty hedge and in this hedge a five-barred gate with good, clean take-off—a perfect and most inviting jump. So thither Dallas swung his "Thunderbolt," urged him to a canter, to a gallop, touched him with spur, lifted him with hand steady and sure—and up rose the great animal to the leap . . . but in that moment a man darted out and back from the hedge, a pallid man with pale eyes and hair, and the horse, suddenly affrighted, tried to turn in mid air, crossed his fore-legs and came down in a kicking, floundering heap. . . .

Came sound of thudding hoof-strokes, jingling spurs, and Lord Withymore, running forward, stumbled breathless into the ditch where Dallas lay, to gather that inert body in his arms, to lift that drooping head and peer into that ghastly face with eyes of dreadful expectancy:

"Keith . . . !" he gasped. "Keith, old man . . . open your eyes . . . speak! Good God . . . not this way, old boy, not this way . . . after all we've been through together . . . not this way, it's too dashed silly, old boy . . . silly . . .!"

CHAPTER XX

WHICH CONCERNS ITSELF WITH KNOTS
AND SHADOWS

"How," murmured Dallas faintly and making feeble effort to sit up, "how is . . . the horse, George?"

Lord Withymore propped the rolling head with ready shoulder and swore softly.

"Mr. Dallas, sir, th'oss ain't took no 'arm, only shook up a bit, so don't worry, sir."

"That . . . you, Ben?"

"Yessir."

"How are you, Keith, old fellow?"

"Fine, George . . . " the gasping voice whispered, "but . . . Josepha, don't . . . let her know . . . that I . . . " the faint words ended in a tremulous sigh and Dallas closed his eyes.

"God . . . he's gone!" exclaimed Lord Withymore staring down into that ghastly face.

"No, sir," quoth Ben, peering also, "'e's only swoondin' again, fair knocked aht, my lord."

"Have they got a hurdle yet . . . a gate . . . oh, damme—anything that'll carry him?"

"They're comin' with it now, my lord. . . ."

. . . Rising up from deeps of troubled darkness, Dallas opened his eyes again, stared, blinked, and stared once more at slim, neat young person in large white apron and starched cap, who sat nearby within reach of the bed, sewing busily. And having watched her a while in growing perplexity, he spoke:

"So, it was all a dream, eh, Nurse? I'm still in Number Three base hospital . . . ! And—little Patience, my little Honey-girl, and . . . she—only a dream, eh, Nurse? No, please don't get up, sit right there, only tell me, please . . . are they going to operate again?"

"Sir," said the Nurse, folding up her sewing very precisely, "you've had a shock, but——"

"Shock?" he repeated. "Shell-shock? Why, no, it was a bullet got me. . . . And I've just lain here ever since and . . . dreamed it all!"

"Sir, your horse fell and threw you and you've been here in bed just five days. Concussion——"

"Five days? Gee-whiz! Where am I, then?"

"In Miss Hardwicke's house."

"Never heard of her. I don't know any Miss Hardwicke——"

"Sir, if you'll be quite still and not excite yourself, I'll call her." Saying which, the nurse smiled and moved silently away, leaving him to stare up at the ancient beamed ceiling that he now recognised as part of his much and wild dreaming—so many knots to a beam, and every knot a hateful little eye that watched him so persistently. Then the door opened and a lady entered; she was tall, she was bony, with Roman nose and sharp eyes, yet when she spoke, her voice was unexpectedly gentle and deep:

"So, Mr. Dallas, you are truly better. Gracious goodness be praised!"

"Thanks, but I'm very well, except for my head."

"Aches, does it, my poor soul?"

"Well, yes, but what's worse I . . . it hurts me to . . . think and my mind's kind of muzzy."

"And no wonder!" answered Miss Hardwicke, seating herself beside the bed. "We thought you'd die, you know—we were convinced of it. Poor Lord Withymore seemed quite distracted—had all sorts of doctors

—specialists, you know! Sat beside you all through the crisis, he and the doctors and nurses—wouldn't leave you for a moment—most devoted! He'll be over to see you presently, he's always here at six o'clock—so regular!"

"And how," inquired Dallas, knitting painful brow, "how's Felix?"

"Oh, quite a wretch, as usual—so wilfully wayward! There never was such a naughty creature. But all donkeys are perverse, they say. Now won't you close your eyes again like a dear, good man?"

"Why I'd rather . . . keep them open a while, if you don't mind. I'm sure beginning to feel pretty fit and snappy."

"Thanks be to the Father of Mercies!" murmured Miss Hardwicke, closing her own very sharp eyes for a moment. "For oh, Mr. Dallas, when they carried you in on that gate, you looked . . . ah, dreadfully dead, so thoroughly killed and utterly slain! And now, to see you awake again, to hear you speaking it seems a miracle. Though the specialist—a Sir Somebody or other from London—said you had passed the crisis last night and prophesied you'd be conscious this evening. Doctors are wonderful creatures —in spite of their sex."

"I've been dreaming," sighed Dallas, lifting hand to bandaged head. "I guess I've dreamed so much that my thoughts are all kind of snarled-up. I don't seem to know what's real and what isn't."

"You poor, dear soul, I'm not surprised—not a bit, considering—hush! I think Lord Withymore has just come. I'll go and see."

So, and looking very kind despite sharp eyes and Roman nose, Miss Hardwicke glided softly from the room leaving Dallas to stare up at the beamed ceiling again and to puzzle over his dreaming—what was false and what true. Then the door was gently opened

and Lord Withymore stood on the threshold survey-
ing the invalid with expression of grave anxiety
until, meeting Dallas's glance, he smiled suddenly
with extreme cheeriness and stepped lightly to the
bed.

"Why, Keith . . . old bean," said he, a little
unsteadily, "you . . . you old scoundrel, if you
know what I mean, you confounded——" his soft,
cheery voice failed suddenly, but in that moment
his hand found Dallas's and clasped it firmly.

"Old son," said Dallas, looking up into the face
bent over him, "say, George, I'm all mixed up, dreams
and realities in . . . dev'lish tangle! For instance
I guess you are real and I'm real?"

"Quite, old thingumbob!"

"And we're in England,—that right?"

"Absolutely."

"Well then, George, I seem to think I met . . .
or didn't I . . . little Patience . . . my little Honey-
girl. Is . . . is she real, George?"

"Yes, Kay."

"Oh, that's fine!" sighed Dallas, smiling tenderly.
"That's bully . . .! And . . . her sister, red-gold
hair . . . Josepha—is she real?"

"Yes, old boy, as real as we are."

"Holy smoke!" murmured Dallas, shaking the hand
he still clasped. "Then I . . . I guess I'll have
another nap. . . ." And, even as he spoke, he
slept. But in that ceiling-beam was one particular
knot like a great, bulbous eye that watched him in
his slumber, that winked and leered and troubled him
so greatly that he started and awoke suddenly and
was instantly comforted to see Lord Withymore still
seated beside his bed, to feel his lordship's cool, firm
hand still grasping his.

"And she doesn't know about my . . . accident,
I hope, George?"

"Not a word. You see she's always with little Patience lately."

"My little, good angel! How is she now, George?"

"O.K., so far as her injuries are concerned. A1 —absolutely!"

"Out and about again?"

"Well . . . hardly, what I mean to say is—not altogether."

"George," exclaimed Dallas, sitting up with an effort, "the money! That three hundred and fifty pounds! It must be paid this month . . . the man Jessam."

"All settled, old thing—so lie down again, prithee."

"George . . . you mean . . .?"

"Abso-bally-lutely!"

"The old house is hers again?"

"Quite!"

"But how——?"

"Lie down, old man, and I'll tell you." And Lord Withymore settled him back again upon the pillows with touch gentle as any woman's and, sitting down again, quoth he:

"Now it so befell, oh my friend, that while sick and a-fevered you became extreme chatty concerning many and divers things and amongst them this matter re the three hundred and——"

"Oh curse!"

"Quite!" nodded his lordship brightly. "Yet worry not, me lad, for it was all so infernally mixed up with horses, chickens, newspaper clippings, wrist-watches, brooders, pale kittens, festive cakes and what not that nobody could possibly make head or tail of it—the great central idea—except yours faithfully. And so, thereupon, incontinent and forthright I unto Jessam person aforesaid said sum in banknotes duly per post despatch-ed."

"But in whose name, George?"

"The old familiar 'a friend esq.' And got a receipt in due season addressed to: Mr. A. Friend, Poste Restante, Petworth, Sussex . . . I mean to say—a brain-wave, old bean, absolutely, what?"

"It sure was, George, and I'm mighty gratef——"

"Quite!" nodded his lordship. "So your identity is inviolate, hidden beyond faintest possibility of discovery. . . . I bow to your passionate applause, and humbly present—your medicine, one table-spoon-ful——"

"But, George, hell, it isn't time for it."

"Five minutes past, my pert and vulgar lad. So neck it—so . . . with a will . . . suck it down! Right ho!"

CHAPTER XXI

WHICH IS MORE IMPORTANT THAN IT SEEMS

WAKING from a refreshing doze in the big arm-chair, Dallas glanced instinctively towards a part of the ceiling at a certain knot in a certain beam and smiled to see it for a very ordinary kind of knot after all, and wondered why it should have haunted his dreams so persistently; from this he turned towards the window radiant with morning sunlight where sat one absorbed and very impatient over a game of patience, for she glared at the cards with eyes that reminded him of the knot of his dreaming and her Roman nose looked fiercer than usual.

"Good morning!" said he. "Won't it come out?"

Miss Hardwicke jumped, dropped a card and instantly stamped on it vindictively then, turning, smiled at Dallas in the gentlest manner.

"Oh, Mr. Dallas, I declare!" she exclaimed. "To see you sitting up like that, actually dressed—or nearly so,—how wonderful! And you look so much better!"

"Thank you, I'm quite all right to-day."

"That's nonsense, of course, and the instant you try to move about you'll know it."

"I want to try a little walk."

"Ridiculous!"

"Still, I should like to have a try at it."

"Impossible! The moment you walk you won't! I mean you'll reel and stagger—probably swoon. You

mustn't dream of leaving the house yet—no, most
certainly not!"

"Well, anyway I want to thank you. I'd like you
just to know how mighty grateful I am——"

"But my dear, good man—whatever for?"

"All your goodness. Taking me into your home——"

"Good gracious! Am I a savage? Do I strike
the casual beholder as a wild heathen? Though
savages have often been kind and showered hospitality
on the shipwrecked mariner. . . . All sea-faring men
are so romantic, at least—some . . . especially in
the Royal Navy."

"But I'm not a sailor, Miss Hardwicke. And yet
you have surely been very kind to me. I fear I've
been a lot of trouble."

"Trouble? Oh dear yes, of course you have—
being a man! All men are troublesome beings, that's
why women are so patient, so long-suffering, so—
so very womanly. And though you aren't a sailor
you have eyes like . . . him, grey-blue like stormy
seas! And you are tall like . . . him, and he was
a sailor—in the Royal Navy. He sailed away thirty
years ago and was lost 'with all hands.' The storm
that wrecked his ship, wrecked our lives . . . for
the time. And I say 'our' because sister Agnes—
poor, dear soul thinks she was his choice, though his
heart, his affections were pledged—to me! See, Mr.
Dallas, you that are so strangely like him—here is
proof!" And from lank bosom she drew a small
gold locket on a black ribbon and, opening it, showed
the tiny photograph of a comely, square-jawed young
sailor in blue coat and epaulettes, on the one side
and upon the other, a lock of curly brown hair and
round this, the legend:

> Richard to Rosa
> Loving for Ever.

"Thirty-one years ago!" she sighed, nodding at the pictured face. "How very much alive he was— thirty-one years ago! And now—poor Dick . . . so dead! And Agnes thinks, dreams it was she . . . and since he can never come back, I let her cherish the dream. Dear me, how I chatter!"

"I don't think I've met Miss Agnes, have I?"

"Oh no, she's so timid—like a mouse, like a bird! But she's peeped at you often and been struck by your likeness to—him."

"Why then I should like to see her sometime, just to express my gratitude."

"Impossible! She'd swoon—on the spot! Agnes is so shy of strangers—always was, always will be. If she goes to heaven, which is exceedingly probable, she'll be so terribly shy that she'll flit, flit away into the shadiest corner, if there are any, and hide behind her own wings. Good gracious, heavens above! Well, I never——" For the door had opened very softly and a little lady of uncertain age had crept in—a gentle-eyed, meek-faced, soft-treading, small creature who glanced at Dallas with great, wistful eyes and spoke in soft, little, panting voice:

"Oh, sir . . . Mr. Dallas . . . so sudden . . . excuse me . . . this intrusion. . . . But I had to see you . . . give it, I mean the letter . . . into your own hand. . . . I promised . . . and a promise is always sacred . . . especially to the young. Isn't it? And so——"

"Agnes," cried her sister, bony finger raised in fashion admonishing, "for heaven's sake don't gasp so, my bird! Take a breath, you poor, fluttering little thing . . . sit down, mouse—perch somewhere, my pet, and get your breath, do! And don't look so terrified. Mr. Dallas though a man is a gentleman and will never eat you. Now who gave you what, and what are you trying to tell us?"

"Little Patience, Rosa . . . a letter . . . for Mr. Dallas and——"

"Gracious heavenly powers above!" exclaimed Miss Hardwicke the elder. "You never told the child he was ill—or Josepha—or Sarah—or anyone?"

"No, Rosa! Oh no, no, no! Not a word! Not to a soul! Never! Although Sarah knows. But Josepha hasn't heard . . . and she so pale and drawn, my dear! Nor does the child, and so fractious, Rosa, so restless, so——"

"Then she's certainly on the mend. But how came she to write to Mr. Dallas?"

"Well . . . I confess it . . . it was my fault. The dear child is grieving for him so—oh so grieving, Rosa, so pitiful indeed, Mr. Dallas, that I told her . . . if she wrote, I might be able to post it where . . . where it would reach him, and—here it is!" And darting at Dallas in soft, desperate manner, she thrust the letter into his hand. Murmuring an apology and with fingers somewhat tremulous he tore open the envelope and read this:

"Dear Dal,

"They say you have gon awai and nobbodi seems to know where only I hop you will com back, and Aunty Aggi says mabe she can poast this where you can get it so I rite this to say I do luv you so and so pleas com back I am better now a bit and hope you will please come back son or els i may die of greefing and my hart will brak so be quik corse I want you so yore

loving Honi I am.
"P.S. My teny kiti scrached me so do com quick to me dier Dal."

When at last he lifted his troubled gaze from this supplication he found himself alone, and folding this ill-spelled, blotted letter between his hands, sat a great while staring out at the sunshine with eyes of bitter yearning. . . . Then the door opened and little Miss Agnes came running in again, more like a frightened mouse than ever.

"Sister Rosa's gone marketing," she explained breathlessly, "and says I must take care of you till she returns! Oh dear, why did you get rid of your nurses? I don't know how to care for a . . . a male invalid, but Rosa says I mustn't leave you alone, so here I am. What must I do? Shall I read to you? Oh dear! Fan you? Feed you? Are you thirsty? Oh dear, dear me!"

"Why, Miss Agnes, now pray don't get yourself all worked up. Please don't bother about me, I'm quite all right. Honest to goodness, I feel so fine and dandy I guess I'll go for a little stroll."

"No, oh no! You can't! You mustn't! She'd never forgive me. Besides it's only my foolish nerves. Please, please don't get out of your chair, don't try to walk anywhere or I shall become desperate. Shall I read the paper to you? A book?"

"Why no. Please don't trouble, I'll be quite well alone here."

"No, I promised I'd stay with you. Besides you're our guest. . . . Oh dear, I shall have to talk, I suppose. Shall I tell you about the child . . . little Patience?"

"No, please!" he answered, shaking his head, "I . . . I've just read her letter and I guess I can't stand any more just now. You see, she asks me to go back to her, and I . . . I just . . . never can —never!"

"Oh, but why not?"

"Because . . . circumstances forbid me. So please talk of anything else, if you don't mind."

At this, Miss Agnes gasped and was mute and Dallas, gazing wistfully at the sunny garden became lost in such unhappy musing that she ventured to touch his hand very gently and timidly:

"Oh, Mr. Dallas," she murmured, "why so sad? And your eyes so grey! Such curly, brown hair! If you only had a blue coat, gold buttons and epaulettes. . . . I was a girl then, so many, many years ago. . . . And he, well he sailed away and was drowned and my heart with him. And so like you, Mr. Dallas—so very like! Rosa thought then . . . thinks now that his heart was hers, ah poor Rosa! But it was to me he pledged his troth. He gave me a little ring that I wear only at night when all eyes are closed and . . . he gave me—this! I will show you."

She turned away for a moment, then with quick, shy, little movement, was beside his chair and had placed in his hand an open locket upon a black ribbon, a locket that showed the tiny photograph of a comely, square-jawed young sailor in blue coat and epaulettes on the one side and upon the other a crisp curl of brown hair.

"And see," she whispered, tremulously, "see his dear message, here round the edge."

Now bending above this locket so pitifully similar to one he had seen before, Dallas read this inscription:

Richard to Agnes
Forever loving.

"And Rosa thinks, Rosa dreams his love was hers and I . . . poor Rosa . . . I would not shatter her dream for the world, I wouldn't! I couldn't! It would be so cruel, wouldn't it?"

"Very cruel!" said Dallas, frowning down at that smiling, pictured face so strangely like his own.

"So I shall let her imagine, let her dream on to the end. For to imagine happiness is to be happy—almost. Isn't it?"

"Yes, I guess it is," he answered very gently.

"For you see," she continued, having closed the precious relic and hidden it away again, "by the power of Imagination the absent are brought back to us, the dead may live again. In Imagination we may hear once more the dear, hushed voice, may feel the very touch of their hands. Oh, Mr. Dallas, surely Imagination is a blessed, blessed thing!"

"Yes," he murmured, gazing into the small, radiant face. "Yes, I guess it surely is."

"Oh yes," she repeated, bowing reverent head. "Imagination must be of God, for, like God, it is the resurrection and the life."

After this was silence, each rapt in an abstraction of thought; when at last Dallas spoke he kept his face averted:

"Miss Agnes, a while back you spoke of her . . . of Miss Josepha. . . . Is she well, please? How is she?"

"Oh ye-e-s," answered the little lady dubiously, "she seems—pretty well, but . . . so pale, so listless! The child's illness, the care and anxiety are accountable, I suppose, and yet she is so strangely despondent, though Patience is quite out of all danger now. I walked over yesterday afternoon . . . the cottage . . . a cup of tea. And dear Josepha so very silent, and the only time I saw her smile was when their new friend called—with flowers for her—hot house! And a huge box of chocolates—so expensive! And grapes for the child—hothouse too!"

"A new friend?" inquired Dallas glancing up quickly. "Do you mean Lord Withymore?"

"Oh no no, this is a strange gentleman, so handsome, so kind, so very attentive—an American, I think——"

"Yes, but who is he? I mean what's his name?"

"Well, Josepha told me he is a friend of yours, a . . . a Mr. Derek Rogerson—no Ryerson and . . . Merciful heavens . . . ! Oh, dear God . . .! What is it . . . ? Mr. Dallas—what is it?"

For he was up out of the arm-chair and stood swaying, staring at the terrified speaker, his pale features dreadfully convulsed; then, uttering a broken, inarticulate cry, he leapt towards the door, staggered, tripped and fell heavily. . . . Now glancing at his face, Miss Agnes saw blood there, and screamed faintly.

CHAPTER XXII

DESCRIBETH SOME EVILS OF IMAGINATION

"Your poor . . . poor head!" panted Miss Agnes, tenderly busy with moist, cool sponge.

Somehow (endued with what desperate strength who shall say?) she had got him back into the arm-chair and Dallas sat there shivering—though now, seeing her tremulous anxiety, he contrived to smile up into her so troubled eyes.

"Did I startle you?" he murmured. "Please forgive me!" And taking her small, quivering hand he pressed it reassuringly. "I . . . I'm all right now, Miss Agnes, I'm fine . . . bully!"

"Oh . . . what was it?" she gasped.

"A kind of—spasm, I guess," he answered lightly, "a sort of brain-storm."

"But it was dreadful! So terrible! Are you really better?"

"Surest thing!" he nodded, smiling again, rather wanly. "So please don't worry on my account."

"But you—you cut your poor head . . . here, above the temple."

"Why that's nothing at all!"

"Yet your eyes look, oh—hunted! And you are so dreadfully pale! Shall I . . . may I give you some brandy?"

"Brandy? Ha—yes, yes!" he nodded, with strange eagerness. "Brandy or—whisky, if you have it?"

"Oh, we haven't! I'm so sorry! But here is the brandy—shall I——?"

"Thank you, I will," said he and taking the bottle in unsteady hand he poured out and instantly swallowed so stiff a dose that little Miss Agnes opened her innocent eyes and, waiting for him to choke, gasped in sympathy.

"Now, please," said Dallas, leaning back in the chair and sighing gratefully, "please tell me about this Mr. . . . Ryerson. I mean, has he been acquainted with her, with Miss Josepha long? No—that's impossible! And yet, please, how long?"

"But Mr. Dallas . . . oh dear! Are you truly feeling better?"

"Yes—yes thanks! I'm quite all right, so tell me please."

"But you were so . . . so dreadfully pale, and now so flushed, so hectic——"

"That's only the brandy. Does he visit her . . . them—often? Is he often at the cottage . . . Ryerson, I mean—is he?"

"Oh yes, every day, Sarah tells me. It seems he first dropped in to inquire about you the very afternoon you were hurt . . . he said you were an old friend."

"And has . . . visited the cottage every day, since?"

"Oh yes, every day, and always brings flowers and boxes of chocolates, Sarah says—huge! Sarah says she's never seen so many chocolates in all her life! Grapes too! Says they'll never be able to eat them all."

"And he . . . he is made welcome? Is he?"

"Well, chocolates are always welcome, and all nice girls love flowers."

"And . . . does he stay long? To tea ever?"

"Sometimes, I believe. He is such a wonderful talker, Sarah says."

"And what does she say—Miss Josepha?"

"Very little. When I was there, yesterday, she hardly spoke—so distrait! I believe she'd been weeping! Tears in secret, you know, some hidden grief! The dear girl needs a change, a complete rest, I'm sure."

"And is this 'friend' of mine—Mr. Ryerson, living in the neighbourhood?"

"No, in Lewes at the 'White Hart,' so Sarah told me. And I don't think Sarah likes him, but then she never likes anyone much unless—Oh Gracious! Are you going to faint?"

"No, oh no," answered Dallas in slumberous tone and opening drowsy eyes, "only sleepy, I guess."

"Oh, then perhaps you could take a nap? If you could only sleep a little! Could you?"

"Why yes," he murmured, shutting his eyes again. "Yes."

"Oh, I'm so glad!" exclaimed little Miss Agnes, clasping her hands. "Suffer me to settle the pillow under your poor head—there! Now sleep, I'll leave you and no one shall disturb you." So with a final soft, little pat to his pillow and the lightest, shyest touch to his curly, brown hair that was so very like what another's had been, Miss Agnes stole away, closing the door very softly behind her.

For perhaps two minutes, after she had gone, Dallas lay back in the arm-chair utterly motionless, in attitude of one deep-plunged in slumber, then very suddenly he sat up, glanced furtively about and rose to his feet, his cheeks flushed, his eyes bright with desperate purpose, and stood awhile as if testing his strength. Upon small table nearby stood the brandy bottle and taking it up in shaking hand he poured a stiff peg and swallowed it and thereafter, yet another. Then, putting off his shoes, he began to walk softly up and down the airy chamber, his hands clenched, his brows close-knit—

up and down, to and fro. And as with this exercise his limbs strengthened somewhat, so the purpose that fired his brain strengthened also.

Up and down, to and fro—just six paces from window to wall and back again. And as he walked, his harassed mind in a sick frenzy of fearful apprehensions too hateful for spoken word, he counted his footsteps with a singular care, whispering to himself: "One, two, three, four"—Ryerson, that insatiable libertine! "Five, six—one, two"—past master of every nameless evil, vile as Red Rory and far more dangerous! "Three, four, five, six—one"—Ryerson, this cold cynic to whom nothing was sacred! This merciless hunter of Innocence, with his strangely handsome presence, winning tongue, and veneer of social polish! Well, he was out of place here, a menace, corruption was on his tongue, pollution in the touch of him! "One, two, three, four"—And she in her innocence, used only to sweet, simple things, to clean, honest country-folk! The arts of the underworld of New York, the dens and dives of Chicago—the simplicity of Sussex.

Here Dallas clasped his throbbing head between fierce-griping hands, closing his eyes vainly against the obscene and frightful visions conjured up by his sick and fevered imagination. . . .

. . . Then up and down again, to and fro, counting, tramping, haunted, racked and plagued by unspeakable visions of—what might be, while with every step, with every quick-drawn breath, the fierce and dreadful purpose within him waxed and grew . . . Ryerson was a threat to more than her mere life! "One, two, three, four"—pollution breathed around him! Well, there was a way and he would take it—this very night!

And so, within this pleasant room and the joyous sunshine bright about him, Dallas walked the very deeps of hell.

And yet when Miss Hardwicke returned from her marketing and the two sisters peeped in at their invalid they beheld him, outstretched in the big arm-chair, to all seeming deep, deep in balmy slumber and, stealing noiselessly away, left a haggard wretch who, starting up from his chair, groped for the brandy bottle, gulped the fiery liquor thirstily, and opening the window with the caution of any thief, crept out and away into the sunset.

CHAPTER XXIII

TELLS HOW DALLAS BOUGHT A STICK

On he trudged though pausing often to rest but, driven by fierce purpose, on he tramped again until at last he sank trembling beside the way and, head bowed between clasping hands, cursed his bodily weakness. Thus sat he some while until, the faintness passing, he rose and struggled on again through this early summer's evening, his sick mind harassed by dreadful fancies, his trembling body threatening to fail him at every faltering stride; but he trudged resolutely forward, hands clenched, brows knit above fever-bright eyes, failing body upborne by determined will, relentless purpose in every line of him.

Reaching a shady stile he paused there to fetch his breath; and leaning thus, glanced round about upon this gentle country-side glorious with sunset, at radiant heaven, and shivered violently for, in earth and sky, his fevered eyes saw only Ryerson's face gloating in triumphant lust. . . .

A menace to her—body and soul! Well, if there was indeed a just and merciful God let that God endue his weakened muscles with sufficient strength—enough for the purpose only . . . if there was a God indeed. And yet did that God ever look down upon the underworld of great cities . . . all the unspeakable shame and misery. . . ?

Heavy footsteps upon the road and, looking round, he saw a rough-clad man approaching; a mean, peak-faced, shambling fellow who, espying Dallas, paused to stare, made to touch his hat, changed his mind and nodded:

"Gud evenin', mate!" said he, leering. "Waitin' for y'r donah, y'r sweet-eart—eh?"

Dallas shook his head, staring fixedly at the stick the fellow carried, a stout, knotted cudgel shod with a wicked-looking iron spike.

"No more ain't I," growled the man, "sweet-'eartin' ain't wot it's cracked up t'be—not unless a chap 'as plenty t'eat an' drink—'specially drink—woman an' wine—eh? 'Ere's me on th' tramp from the Smoke and ain't ate reg'lar for a month an' as for drink— blimy! So, chum, spare a few coppers to a chap as is da'n on 'is luck, will yer?"

"No," answered Dallas. "I'll buy your stick."

"Stick, mate? Wot this 'ere? No, it ain't for sale."

"Five shillings!" said Dallas.

"Six, matey—say six!"

"Six then."

"Show us!" Dallas held out the money.

"Lumme!" exclaimed the man. "She's yourn!" And he thrust the unlovely thing into Dallas's ready hand. "Now give us the dibs, mate!" Hardly was the money paid than the man spat on it for luck and hurried off lest the purchaser might repent his bargain.

Being alone, Dallas stared again at sunny earth and radiant heaven.

"Now!" said he aloud, "if there be truly a living God——" And raising the heavy weapon he twirled it and struck with gesture and look inexpressibly terrible, and so went trudging on again.

. . . The cross-roads at last and after some while, the omnibus into which he clambered and, sinking upon the nearest seat, sat huddled in a kind of waking dream wholly unconscious of jolting racket or the

curious glances of his fellow-travellers, nor did he lift
his drooping head until aroused by the stir and bustle
of traffic he glanced up to find himself in the narrow
High Street of ancient Lewes town.

So down he got and, remembering his head was bare,
turned in at the first haberdasher's, selected a soft
hat of inconspicuous colour, clapped it on, pulling it
low, paid for it and went his way, head bent, shoulders
drooping wearily, but right hand fast clenched upon
that knotted, iron-shod stick.

"Good evenin' dearie!" said a voice, while a hand
clawed his arm, and, glancing round, he beheld a small,
bright-eyed old woman smiling up at him.

"You hain't forgot Mother Parsloe, sir? Yarbs,
roots, barks an' berries, that's me. But lor, dearie,
'ow bad you'm lookin', s' pale an' thin, dearie. Been
sick, sir? Not for love, dearie—no that ain't arl for
love, I'll lay a pound."

"Why, no . . . no," he stammered in his most
nervous, halting manner. "No, I . . . I had an
accident, but I . . . oh I'm better now."

"Are ye, dearie? Well, you looks like you 'ad the
'orrors. But if y'are sick—don't let no doctors get
'old of ee—don't ee. Most ailments is bowils only
they gives it different names. The Stummick, dearie,
that's where most folks' troubles lays. So if you'm
feelin' so bad as ye looks, keep away from them murderin'
doctors and come to one as knows a thing or two—
an' that's me, along by the bridge and through the
twitten, anybody'll tell ee." So saying, the old
creature nodded and trotted off, leaving him to stare
after her vague-eyed, ere he wandered on up the steep
hill.

Reaching the "White Hart," he paused to glance about
on the busy street and from this, to the formidable
cudgel in his fist, then he entered the ancient inn and
made his way through its cheery bustle to a certain

corner where, behind a sort of small counter, sat a neat,
trim, young person.

"Yes, sir?" she inquired, for Dallas was looking at
her in the same vague fashion. "I'm afraid you can't
have a room, sir, you see the fair's here and we're quite
full."

"A room?" he repeated, his gaze roving, "why no
. . . no, I don't want a room, thank you."

"Then what is it, sir?"

"Let me . . . think," he murmured; but his
wandering glance coming upon the stick in his hand
he glanced up and smiled brightly: "Of course . . .
Ryerson! I wish to see Mr. Derek Ryerson who is
staying here, I think?"

"Yes, sir, the gentleman has rooms here, but you
can't see him because he's away at present and won't
be back to-night."

"Oh?" murmured Dallas. "Gone away . . . has
he?"

"We expect him back to-morrow, sir, or the day
after."

"Oh?" murmured Dallas again. "Can you please
. . . tell me just . . . where he is gone?"

"No, sir, I can't."

"But he is expected back . . . to-morrow?"

"Yes, sir, or next day."

"Or . . . next day!" repeated Dallas, in the same
dull tone. "I see . . . thank you!" And, lifting
his hat, he turned and moved away, walking a little
unsteadily, noting which, the neat, capable young
person shook reproving head.

"And so early in the evening too!" she murmured. . . .

. . . Dallas wandered into the bar and was presently
crouched in remote corner behind a small table whereon
stood a bottle of whisky and a glass. . . .

"Crikey!" exclaimed a hoarse voice, vaguely familiar,
and looking up beneath painfully contracted brows

he saw Ben Lomax staring down at him over a foaming tankard. "Crumbs!" gasped Ben, "whisky! A whole bottle! Love-a-duck, sir!"

"Hello, Ben, how are you, friend?"

"As-tonished, sir—fair a-mazed, not 'arf I ain't!"

"Oh? Why Ben?"

"Well, sir, first to see you aht and abaht again, and second, to see the way you're a-goin' of it at that bottle—and w'isky too! Lumme!"

"Sure, Ben, I need it."

"Well, sir, I thought as I did the last time as we met here—and look wot you says to me! 'W'isky,' says you to me, 'w'isky ain't no good to anybody!' you says. 'Pizen!' you says, and likewise—'we'd all be better without it!' you says. And now, blimy sir, 'ere's you fair a-lappin' of it up like I dunno wot!"

"I sure am, Ben!" murmured Dallas, refilling his glass. "I'm at a loose end to-night, need a drink, and when I drink—I drink!"

"Sir," quoth Ben, setting down his ale untasted and viewing Dallas with anxious eyes, "you didn't ought to be aht and abaht so soon, and you didn't ought to be drinking w'isky so 'olesale. So, sir, Mr. Dallis will you come back 'ome along o' me?"

"Hell—no!" snarled Dallas. "I've been shut up too dam long. . . . Haven't had a real drink for months—so now I'm off on a bat . . . do me good."

"Mr. Dallis, sir, you look terrible bad——"

"And I'm feeling mighty good—better than I've been since . . . since I struck this dam country."

"Mr. Dallis, sir, you ain't yourself, sir, and if you drink any more o' that cursed stuff you'll be worse."

"Oh shut your head!" muttered Dallas, a sudden glare in his wild, bright eyes. "And keep it shut!"

"Mr. Dallis, sir, please lemme speak for speak I must—seein' as 'ow you're one o' the few men as I trooly respex—because you're a gentleman true blue,

sir, and a sportsman, and seein' as 'ow you licked me
fair and square, I'm standin' by you now, sir, and so
here's me a-beggin' you to come along o' me——"

"And that'll be about all!" said Dallas, clenching
passionate fist, his voice harsh and stammering oddly.
"Y-you annoy me, so q-quit right now! B-be on your
way——"

"Sir, f' the love o' Gawd lemme get you out o' this,
back to your friends . . . to his lordship. Come
wi' me—do, Mr. Dallis, sir!" And in his growing
anxiety, Ben laid a hand on Dallas's quivering shoulder.
But this pleading, friendly hand was smitten fiercely
away and Dallas glared up at him with look so murderous
that sturdy Ben recoiled and, backing away, stood
gaping in amazement and speechless while with sudden,
febrile gesture Dallas corked the whisky bottle, thrust
it into his pocket and catching up his stick, rose and
strode out of the bar. Yet, even so, Ben ventured
to follow him:

"Sir," he began, but Dallas turned on him, the heavy
stick quivering in his grasp.

"Get on your way!" he muttered thickly. "Out
of it, d-d'ye hear and mind your d dam business!"

And thus at last the faithful Ben, shaking his bullet
head in very evident distress, turned and left him.

CHAPTER XXIV

CONCERNS ITSELF WITH THE GLORY OF UNREASON

HEDGES and trees and winding road that led through a vague country dim-seen beneath a rising moon that swam in a mist, a strange eddying vapour that seemed within him also, clouding his faculties as he trudged his slow, uncertain way. Sometimes he paused, muttering hoarsely, to stare away at the moon rising in large splendour, once or twice he turned suddenly about and smote savagely with his heavy stick at some fancied shape conjured up of the mists, that fogged his brain, swift, murderous blows—so that such few wayfarers as chanced abroad, gave the drunkard a wide berth.

Up-hill and down, through a night stillness troubled only by the sound of his own unsteady footsteps, until at last came a winding, narrow, well-remembered lane . . . a thick, high hedge . . . a little wicket-gate. And, leaning wearily across this gate, he blinked at the thatched cottage beyond, its lattices glinting to the moon.

Thus stood he some while, breathing an air redolent of dewy earth, of herb and flower, which sweet, clean fragrance, sweeping the evil from his brain, filled him with a yearning so deep and passionate that, fumbling with awkward fingers, he unlatched the gate and stepping into the garden peered round about him at this little plot of ground which, hallowed by her labour, was for him the most sacred spot on earth. . . .

These trim flower-beds where weeds had begun to spring. . . . The unsightly chicken-coop he had once mistaken for a dog-kennel. Crossing the garden to view this nearer he saw it only vaguely through a sudden blur of smarting tears and therefore touched it with caressing fingers, this the work of her hands, and bowing his head, laid his cheek against its rough timbering and so remained until, roused by the squawk of startled chicken, he stumbled across to the little summer-house and, sinking upon the bench within its dim interior, closed his eyes.

Suddenly he rose, had caught up the stick and was out in the moonlight, all in a moment; then the heavy stick fell and, snatching off his hat, he stood blinking down into Josepha's pale, set face.

"What is it?" she questioned, quick-breathing. "I heard the gate click . . . I saw you . . . Oh what is it . . . ? What is the matter . . . ? Can't you speak to me?"

"S-sorry!" he muttered. "Mighty sorry if . . . if I startled you."

She drew a quick step nearer, viewing him with widening stare—his loose lips, blinking eyes, the sway of his slouched shoulders.

"Oh . . . my heavens!" she whispered, "you are drunk!"

"That's so!" he answered thickly. "Better drunk than mad."

"So you . . . are a drunkard as well as a. . . ."

"Murderer!" said Dallas as she hesitated at the word. "Go ahead—say it! Yes, that's me I guess —a drunkard for to-night, but a murderer always. Yet—say . . . !" Here he clenched his hands and strove desperately for clearer speech. "Oh girl— listen! There are worse things even than I am . . . devils that look like men. . . . I'm here to warn you against one . . . Ryerson."

"And you are drunk—you!"

"Yes, but I know what I'm saying, and I tell you
. . . Ryerson's a devil . . . a vile menace——"

"And you—are a drunkard!" she repeated in the same
hushed tone of horrified conviction, and turned to leave
him.

"Yes, yes," he answered, staying her with a wild,
imploring gesture. "I know . . . I admit I'm pretty
well everything that's rotten—I admit all that, but
I'm no menace to you . . . to your happiness . . .
to little Patience, God knows I'm not! I was going
away, but when I heard Ryerson was around here
. . . so often . . . on the hunt . . . I came to
warn you, I had to—I just simply had to, for you
see I knew him in America . . . his beastly vileness——"

"I've never seen him drunk!" she retorted and again
she turned to be gone—but, gasping a broken, inarticulate cry, Dallas caught a fold of her gown. And
then he was on his knees before her, his haggard face
uplift to the bright moon, his eyes full of agonized
entreaty:

"Josepha, I know I'm down and out for good . . .
down in the mud and sinking lower. . . . Yet I
can't help loving you, so how—how can I stand by
and see you in such peril, threatened with worse than
death? Josepha for God's sake be warned . . .
he's out to hunt you down . . . a brute beast . . .
a smooth-tongued, merciless devil up to every vile trick
—and you in your confiding innocence. . . . No
no, don't shrink from me, I'm not drunk now, and
I'm not mad—yet. Josepha, dear angel of innocence,
won't you . . . Ah, God . . . ! won't you believe
when I tell you——"

"There . . . there . . . hush!" she murmured,
laying a cool, firm hand on his burning lips. "Don't
distress yourself with such wild fancies, for I'm no

angel, and only a fool could be as innocent as you think me. Oh you poor miserable creature to bring yourself to this, to madden yourself with—why . . . you're hurt!" she exclaimed, bending above him in swift compassion. "Hurt . . . here, above the temple. Did you fall?"

"Yes. But Derek Ryerson is such a . . . sly devil, so I want you to promise that when he . . . if you should need a friend when I'm gone . . . as you will . . . you'll go to George, to Withymore . . . promise me this, Josepha, promise and I'll go . . . only promise . . . George will take care of you, so——"

"I promise!" said she obediently, and began to smooth the damp curls from his painfully contracted brow. "How ill you look . . . so thin and pale! Come indoors and let me bathe your head."

"No!" he muttered, shrinking from her touch. "No, I . . . I'm quite all right, now. I'll get on my way."

"Where to?"

"Does it matter?" sighed he wearily, and would have risen but her hands upon his shoulders stayed him.

"Why are you going?" she demanded in the same gently compelling manner.

"It's about the only decent thing I can do—being what I am."

"Well, what are you?"

"A murderer."

"Who says so?"

"I know it."

"How?"

"Oh, does it matter?" sighed he again.

"No!" she answered, gazing deep into the tired eyes upraised to hers. "No, it doesn't matter a scrap because I don't believe it. I never really believed you

a murderer—I couldn't. . . . And to-night you came
here drunk . . . and yet, in spite of this, I know,
I'm sure . . . sure and certain that you are good
. . . and clean really!"

"Josepha!   Oh girl . . . you—you . . . believe
in me?   But—how can you?"

"Because, being a Dare, I dare have faith in you
despite everything! Because your face is not wicked!
Because Patience loves you so! And—because my
heart tells me you are good and clean and honourable. . . ."

"Why?" he questioned breathlessly, looking up at
her with eyes of adoration.   "Why?"

"Perhaps because of the motto of my house," she
answered.   "Perhaps—just because——"

"Of what—what?" he whispered eagerly, for she had
paused and turned to look up at the moon's radiant
splendour.   "Josepha . . . why?" he repeated.

For a moment she neither spoke nor moved, then,
all at once, she sank to her knees before him and thus,
kneeling even as he knelt, she looked at him, eye to
eye:

"Perhaps because I love you," she answered.

Dallas caught her hands and bowing his face upon
them, was dumb a while, then:

"Josepha . . ." he whispered, "my dear!"—and
the word was a sob.

"You see," she murmured. "I don't think I could
love a wicked man so greatly, no—not even you."

"Oh, girl," said he, not daring to look at her, "if
you knew how I'm just . . . yearning to—kiss
you!"

"I think I do," she answered gently.   "I hope you
are!   Why don't you?"

"No!" said he, grim-lipped.   "Not while I know
myself a—so unworthy.   I couldn't!   I mustn't!"

"Still, I'm glad you want to, dear!" she sighed.

"But I'm gladder you don't, because it helps my belief in you. And so, my honourable man, I——" she swayed to him, sighed and kissed him on the lips: "My dear murderer!" she whispered, "that couldn't ever murder anyone—and never did! My drunkard that will never do so any more!"

"Never!" said he, brokenly. "Never again, Beloved! But . . . oh Josepha, if . . . if only I dared hope . . . believe . . . if only you could help me to prove myself innocent—to myself! Anyway your glorious faith, your belief in my innocence just fills me with a new hope, a new life . . . And now—I'll go!"

"You won't!" she answered softly, yet speaking with a new authority. "You look too ill, too fagged —and besides you—belong to me now, Keith Dallas. So you must stop here for little Pat's sake, and your own sake, and mine! Come indoors, you shall sleep on the couch in the parlour as you did before. Come!" And, rising nimbly, she reached him her two hands. "Come!" she repeated. But, kneeling still, he lifted these gentle hands to his lips and held them there, clinging to them desperately as a child might have done, lost in the dreadful dark.

"Josepha," he gasped, "I never knew—the real horror of my guilt until now . . . it is between us. —parting us—even now—yes, even now—God help me!"

"He will, dear, oh he will!" she repeated, stooping to kiss that head in its abasement. "For who but God put this certainty of your innocence into my heart, or this undying belief in your goodness? Look up, my dear, look up—into my eyes and see how sure, how very sure I am."

"Ah, girl," he whispered, "how I worship you . . . these beloved hands . . . perhaps the hands of my salvation to lift me up out of the dark . . . back to honour and self-respect."

G

"And now," said she, touching the hurt above his temple very tenderly, "they shall bathe and bandage you, and you'll come indoors."

"No!" he answered miserably, "thank you but— no, I couldn't. My head's perfectly right now, and if I may stop around I . . . I'd rather stay right here."

"But," said she, shaking reproachful head at him, "heavens, child, don't be wilful, you can't stay out here all night!"

"I've camped in many a worse place, dear."

"But, my Dallas—Keith, why won't you come into the house, like a sensible creature?"

"Because . . . oh well—I'm not fit!"

"Silly boy! You certainly can't sleep out here among the spiders and earwigs and things, so come and——"

"Josepha . . . dear . . ." he stammered, "I . . . guess I'm worse . . . much worse than you . . . you ever thought. . . . To-night I went out to kill a man!"

"You . . . mean . . .?" she whispered.

"Ryerson. Oh I guess I was half crazy but . . . I surely meant to. . . . The stick there . . . I bought it . . . for murder! So here's why I won't come into your home, here's why I'm not worthy to touch you."

She had lifted his head so that he must needs look up into her anxious face:

"Dear," said she, holding his gaze with hers, "do you ever pray?"

"Not now," he sighed. "Not for years."

"But you believe in God?"

"I . . . don't know——"

"My poor child. Then to-night I'll pray for you, but first I'll bring you some rugs and a pillow."

"Anyway," said Dallas fervently, "thank God for making you!"

CHAPTER XXV

TOUCHETH UPON THE COLD REASON OF ONE JEDIDIAH

A SHARP stabbing pain in the back of his hand roused him from a refreshing, dreamless sleep, and glancing down he beheld the cause of this so sudden awaking to be the obtrusive beak of Catherine, that one-eyed, scrawny, limping hen.

"Why old lady, so there you are—eh?" said Dallas cheerily. "And here am I back again and mighty glad to be! Glad? Well, I should say! And—listen, Kate! She loves me—me, mind you! In spite of everything! And it's no pipe-dream, old lady, she told me so, last night. And what d'you say to that, Katie?"

Catherine ruffled her scanty plumage, viewed him coldly with her single bright orb and clucked hoarse disparagement.

"Eh? You don't believe me? Well I don't blame you, I can hardly believe it either. But then you see, Kate, when she told me of her love it was in her dear voice, it looked at me from her eyes, it was in all the trembling sweetness of her when she kissed me. Yes she kissed me, old lady, she sure did! And of her own will! So what does anything else matter in all this blessed universe? I don't care two hoots for anything or anyone else from now on. . . . Only it's up to me to get busy for her sake . . . to square myself . . . prove my worthiness somehow—though I never shall be worthy of her, I know that of course! I guess the only way for me now is to get back to New

York . . . give myself up and . . . take what's
coming. . . . Imprisonment . . .? The chair? I
wonder . . . ! Anyway, she loves me and . . .
she believes in prayer . . . ! Both mighty strange
things—yes, and mighty comforting, especially when
you're up against it good and hard as—why what now
—what the——?" For at this moment Catherine
uttered a loud squawk, spread her scraggy wings and
scuttered away into the early sunshine.

So, tossing off his blankets, Dallas sat up and glancing
round expectantly, beheld the reason of Catherine's
sudden departure: A face was peering in at him
through the creeper-clad trellis—a head adorned with
silky white hair and crowned by a soft, clerical hat
whose austere brim shaded a lean, small face lit by a
pair of deep-set, exceedingly bright, sharp eyes and
surrounded by a fringe of grizzled whisker and beard.

Dallas stared hard at this apparition, drew a deep
breath, rose slowly to his feet and spoke in whispering
amazement:

"Jed . . . by the Eternal . . . it's Uncle Jed!"

"Then gol darn these yere doggone whiskers!"
snarled the little man snatching off his hat and casting
it to earth with the utmost ferocity. . . .

And then Dallas was upon him, had caught him
in full-armed hug, had squeezed him, shaken him,
patted that silvery head in a very ecstasy of welcome:

"Uncle Jedidiah!" he exclaimed, laughing a little
uncertainly and keeping his face averted. "Good
old Jed! Well, for the love of Pete!"

"'S me, Keithy-boy!" nodded the little man sharply,
though his look was anything but ferocious now. "'S'
me, y'long-legged maverick, yessir, I guesso!"

Then, still clutching each other, they drew back to
stare at each other speechlessly awhile and the eyes
of both unwontedly dim; thus when Jedidiah spoke
at last, his voice sounded harsher than ever:

"Hell's bells!" he snarled. "A pretty, dam kinda boob y' are! I guesso! A helluva mess you got yourself inta, yessir."

"I sure have, Uncle Jed, but——"

"Plum locoed, boy—that's whatever, y' young t'rant'ler."

"Admitted, Jed, I was mad, sure enough. I've been every kind of fool——"

"Shore y' have!" nodded Jedidiah in heartiest agreement. "And, by heck, Keithy, ya look like a two-spot in a dirty deck!"

"And I feel worse, Jed. But, God bless you, it does me mighty good to see your old dial, it sure does! But what's dragged you from your woolly West? What are you doing in England, and this particular little corner of it—and, for heaven's sake, why the whiskers?"

"Whiskers?" snarled Jedidiah, giving them a scornful tug. "Doggone 'em! I've growed 'em and trained 'em and now they've let me down! Here's me all set from y-ears to hocks like a sky-scout, a shore-nuff gospel-sharp—and you-all calls the turn on me first crack-out o' the box! 'Uncle Jed' says you, quick as gun-play! You un-disguises me in a wink, gol-darn ya!"

"Why sure!" nodded Dallas, smiling down at the fierce, little man and cuddling an arm about him. "It was your eyes, Jed, I'd know them any time, anywhere. But how did you find me here?"

"Daughter sent me."

"Eh? Daughter?"

"Well, Josepha, then!"

"So you—know her?"

"Oh shore! But now, Keith, come into the wickings . . . set right down, for I'm aimin' to know all I can about the shootin' of Red Rory M'Guire—so open up!"

"First, Jed—did you see my . . . father before you left New York?"

"Yessir, I sure did."

"Then you know, maybe, that . . . that he . . . that I, well—that we've agreed to . . . drop the— all relationship?"

"That's why I'm here . . . son!"

"Son, Jed?"

"Ibetcha!"

"This means a whole lot to me, Jed . . .! You were always a mighty big little man . . . I'm grateful——"

"Pisah!" exclaimed Jedidiah fiercely. "Let's hear about Red Rory—shoot, son, shoot!"

And so, after he had seized and shaken his companion's hand by main force, Dallas told his story, every too-well remembered ghastly detail. Perched opposite, bearded chin on small, bony fist, Jedidiah hearkened with never a word or sign, yet his eyes were quick to heed each changing expression of face, or eloquent gesture, his ears as quick to notice every change and inflection of voice; thus sat he, silent and motionless until the tale was ended, even then he stared and sat silent so long that Dallas questioned him at last:

"What are you thinking, Jed?"

"That yore fancy stampedes an' gets away with ya . . . Keith, you-all shore makes a crazy-hoss play and these yere coyotes, these slick Alecs stacks the cyards agin ya—that's whatever, son!"

"You think they framed me?" sighed Dallas, shaking his head despondently. "I wish to God they had! But no, Jed, no—I did it sure enough. Rory was a vile—oh well, I threatened to shoot him, I meant to shoot him, and——"

"You-all didn't shoot him, boy—not you! No, never in this yere world—which is a fact as I'm willin'

to back with my money, arguments or guns—yessir!
Well, I guesso! You-all—and mind I'm tellin' ya—
never killed Red M'Guire, son, not you—no!"

"Ah, Jed, how . . . how can you, how dare you
be so sure when I myself remember——"

"Well, first—you never shot a man in the back,
no sir—not you! And that was their first mistake!"

"But how if I shot him accidentally . . . as we
struggled?"

"Ya didn't!"

"Why are you so positive?"

"Because there was no burnin'—no powder-marks.
And that was their second mistake! M'Guire was
shot from a distance."

"How do you know all this?" said Dallas, eagerly,
his pale face flushing.

"I examined M'Guire's clothes, son, I saw noomerous
photos. D'you-all ferget I'm United States Marshal
of Pikes Ferry, Montanny . . .? And daughter,
does she think you a murderer?"

"No!" cried Dallas, his eyes glistening. "That's
the everlasting wonder of it—she doesn't, Jed, she
won't!"

"Good for her!"

"But, Uncle Jed, she only believes in my innocence
because, well, I guess just because she—wants to.
A woman's faith in a man is often misplaced and
generally illogical, unreasonable."

"Son," quoth Jedidiah, solemnly, "I hain't never
had the luck to be married, or love a woman that a
way—except one, but—now mind I'm tellin' ya—
you can shore gamble a blue stack that a woman's
gift of intooition is some surer than any man's reason,
yessir! And a good woman has faith in a man because
she's a darn sight nearer the angels than anything
in pants, with all his doggone logic—and that's whatever!
I guesso! And what's more—now mind I'm tellin'

ya this too—if a fine, clean-bred, dainty-steppin'
creetur like daughter has faith in ya, why then, son,
you-all oughta be feelin' and lookin' more like a real
he-man than a pieca chewed string, yessir!"

"Why so I am, Jed, so I am surely! For you see I
. . . well I just worship the shoes on her pretty feet!"

"And, son, I ain't wonderin' none at that, no sir.
But does she reciproocate said kind sentiments?"

"She made me think so—last night."

"Eh? D'ya mean that she actooally . . .? No?"

"Yes, by heaven!" answered Dallas softly. "Yes!
And, oh Jed, this is the greatest miracle of all—that
knowing me for what I am——

"No, for what you think you are!"

"That she can love me anyway—in spite of all—
me, Jed! Oh, marvellous!"

"Son," quoth Jedidiah, reaching out his hand,
"this bein' so—shake! And now then, whyever are
ya lookin' so undooly chastened, so unboisterous and
doggone meek?"

"Meek am I? Well, I've been a bit off-colour lately
and then last night, you may as well know, I went
on a jag . . . got pretty full . . . whisky, damn
it! And then I . . . started out to kill a man."

"Oh? Why?" murmured Jedidiah in gentle
inquiry.

"Because I thought him a deadly menace. I thought
him my friend once, fool that I was . . . a fellow
vile as Red Rory but infinitely more dangerous!"

"Meanin' Mr. Derek Ryerson?"

"What—you know him?"

"Son, I've got his number pretty accurate, yessir!
I been ridin' herd on him since he come pirootin'
around hyere—which explains these yere doggone
face-bushes and gospel-sharp's outfit."

"Just what are you up to, Jed?" inquired Dallas
in sudden anxiety.

"I'm settin' in a small game with this gent, Ryerson, and Keith, I'm playin' a lone hand."

"But he's not alone, Jed, there's a thing with him called Whitey Neeves, a gunman——"

"Shore! I've seen the hoss-thief, and three or four others of his outfit too. So, look a here, son! If it comes to any gun-play, or if there's any killin' to be done, there's only one man can do it an' that's me! Now mind, I'm tellin' ya, you sits out of this! Look!" and opening his sober, clerical garments, he showed a silver star pinned on the inside thereof. "I'm Marshal of Pikes Ferry, Montanny—if I shoots, I shoots to kill and sonny—I kills within the law. So you're keepin' out of this and leaving it to your Uncle Jed. . . . And there's daughter, at last, fresh as a dooey flower and clean-goin' as any blooded cayuse!" Even as he spoke, Jedidiah was afoot, had picked up his hat, dusted it, put it on, only that he might take it off again to greet Josepha as she came towards them through the sunny garden.

"Well, here he is, daughter," quoth Jedidiah, motioning towards Dallas with his hat, "himself, my dear, the very same Keith as I remember him, though at present needin' a wash! But the same straight-lookin' feller, with truth in his eyes—though, just now, a heap out of condition."

"Why, Dallas," she exclaimed, struck by the alteration in him, now so very apparent in the kindly sunlight, "you're frightfully pale . . . and thin! Oh, Keith, my dear, why are you so changed?"

"Only a little accident," he answered, smiling as he clasped the hand outstretched to him. "I'm well enough now, though, thanks to the Misses Hardwicke —and good, old George."

"But what accident?"

"'The Thunderbolt,' Miss Jo!" quoth Sarah at this moment, leaning forth of the kitchen window

G I

to answer. "'Thunderbolt' mam, as Mister Dallis
rid an' tamed, too, so Ben do tell me, but fell at an
'edge, Miss Jo—which I means 'Thunderbolt,' mam
and very nigh killed 'im, which I means Mr. Dallis,
miss, for Miss Rose said as nobody thought as 'e'd
ever get over it, 'is death were expected hourly at one
time, which I means Mr. Dallis again, mam, and glad
I am to see you again, Mr. Dallis. Good morning,
sir—and breakfast's a-waiting, if you please, Miss Jo,"
—with which Sarah vanished sudden as she had
appeared.

"So near death!" said Josepha. "And I never
knew. Why didn't they tell me?" And she gave
him her quick, vital hand again. "Why wasn't I
told?"

"Well, I guess you had worries enough!" answered
Dallis, looking down at that slim hand as if he yearned
to kiss it.

"Breakfast!" cried Sarah. "Breakfast be's a-waiting, miss!"

"Come!" said Josepha, turning to go indoors.

"Why . . . thank you," said Dallis, hesitating and
awkward, "but I . . . please . . . I'd rather not!"

"Come!" she repeated.

"But, Josepha . . . dear——"

"Take his other hand, Uncle Jed."

"'Uncle'?" repeated Dallis, glancing from one to
other.

"By adoption," explained Josepha, smiling at
Jedidiah.

"A mootual agreement," quoth Jedidiah, smiling at
Josepha.

"But when did you meet . . . how?"

"Come to breakfast and you shall hear, sir."

"Why then, please, soap and water first."

"I'll have him up to my room, daughter."

"Eh—your room?" exclaimed Dallis.

"Shore!" nodded Jedidiah. "Son, I live here."

"And pay me a lot too much!" said Josepha.

"Why then," said Dallas thankfully. "Oh Jed
. . . I . . . Ryerson—he can't——"

"Ibetcha!" nodded Jedidiah, and so they went in
to breakfast.

CHAPTER XXVI

DESCRIBETH A BREAKFAST PARTY

"But where," said Dallas, glancing round the bright, cosy little breakfast-room, "where is she—where's Patience?"

"In bed!" answered Josepha, throwing open the wide casement. "Oh don't look so frightfully anxious —you see, being nearly well she's more of an invalid than ever, and insists on breakfasting in bed—she doesn't know you're here, yet. But indeed, Keith, I'm afraid you'll be jealous, she's growing so fond of Uncle Jed."

"I'm not surprised," he answered smiling. "All children love old Jed, I know I did—and do!"

"I expect he's sitting with her now," nodded Josepha. "I wonder what it is about you American men that children seem to love so?"

"Oh, I guess it's just because we love them and— let them know it."

"Anyhow," said she, smiling, "Uncle Jed is the dearest thing—only I feel that I want to take care of him, to mother him, you know—he's so little and seems so very frail."

"Seems?" murmured Dallas, hiding a smile. "Why, yes!"

"Well, he's so small, and so quaintly simple, so tender and gentle."

"Tender?" murmured Dallas again. "Oh surely!"

But this time she saw his covert smile and, setting down the jug of flowers she had been arranging, demanded instant explanation.

"Why you see, Josepha, Jed, though born east, has lived west all his life in places pretty wild and tough, and consequently though he seems so gentle he's not always as tender as——" But here was a bumping at the door and a large, well-laden tray entered, followed closely by Sarah herself, whose comely face, flushed from the kitchen stove, smiled cheery greeting as Dallas hastened to relieve her of her burden.

"Which, sir," said she, turning up her eyes, "if you beant a young gen'leman come back out o' the Valley o' the Shadder, Mr. Dallis, I never seen one, and glad I am this day so to do, sir!"

"Thank you, Sarah!" he answered, heartily. "How is the watch?" At this Sarah blushed, laughed and beat a somewhat precipitate retreat. . . . Then was a patter of small, quick feet upon the stair, the door swung wide and in bounded little Patience with Jedidiah in close attendance.

"Dal!" she cried, "Oh, Dal!" Next moment she was in his arms, on his knees, her bright head pillowed on his breast. "So you've come back to me—Uncle Jed told me. He said Jo found you for me, and so I love her more'n ever. . . . But, oh, Dal, you do look so poorly! Have you been a ninvalid, too, have you?"

"Why, yes, Honey," he answered, kissing her soft hair, "just a bit that way."

"Then you must eat lots an' lots—I do! So give him his breakfus, Jodear. We must feed him. But first, Dal—please—have you come back to stay this time, have you?"

"Well——" said he, hesitating.

"Yes!" said Josepha, busied with the coffee-pot.

"Oh!" murmured the Small Personage, clasping her hands in an ecstasy. "How scrumptious! And

Uncle Jed, too! What a spiffink large family we're
growing! But, Dal, dear, you won't mind if I like
Uncle Jed rather a lot, will you?"

"No, Honey, I'll love you all the better—if that's
possible."

"You see, Dal, Uncle Jed is so nice an' small an'
cuddly, an' makes me whistles that blow, you know,
an' he's going to teach me to ride horseback like Jo
so soon as I'm quite well again, an' he's always saying
such funny words, so you're not s'prised I love him,
are you?"

"Surely not, Hon," answered Dallas, kissing that
little eager face, while Jedidiah, hiding his lean visage
behind large coffee-cup, choked—and not altogether
by reason of coffee perhaps.

"Oh, Jodear," sighed the Small Personage rap-
turously, "we are going to be most frightfully happy,
aren't we?"

And surely never was there meal more wholly joyous
than this breakfast; what wonder the Small Personage
was so radiant, or that Jedidiah chuckled so often,
or that Josepha, forgetting past cares, laughed so
gaily, or that Dallas's haggard face was radiant too.
And so they laughed, and thus they talked:

THE SMALL PERSON: You know, Dal, Uncle
Jed's most triffickly clever! The other day Mrs.
Stacy's great, big pig ran away, so he took Sarah's
clothes line and throwed it at Mrs. Stacy's pig and
there it was—caught by the hind leg while it was
running frightfully fast, an' Tom Merry said he was
blowed if it wasn't a ruddy marvel——

JOSEPHA: (*In tones of horrified reproach—from
behind the coffee-pot*): Oh, P-Patience!

THE SMALL PERSON: But that's what Tom Merry
said, didn't he, Uncle Jed? An' I like Tom, don't
you, Uncle Jed?

JEDIDIAH: Shore, Babe. Tom's got p'ints.

THE SMALL PERSON: Yes, he's frightfully fond of beer. But wasn't that awfully clever of Uncle Jed an' the pig, Dal?

DALLAS: Why, yes—Uncle Jed can do anything with a rope.

JEDIDIAH: (*Self-consciously*) Huh! You're no such slouch either, son.

THE SMALL PERSON: Ooh! Are you Uncle Jed's son, Dal?

DALLAS: Yes, Hon, sort of—by adoption.

THE SMALL PERSON: Then I spose that's why he calls you such funny names, you see when I told him 'bout you, Dal, he said when you were a little boy you were a rip-snorter—didn't you, Uncle Jed?

JEDIDIAH: (*chuckling*) Shore! And so you were, son. D'ya mind the time you-all uncorralled and stampeded them unbroke Injun ponies?

DALLAS: (*cheerily*) And you locked me up for it, Jed.

JEDIDIAH: Ay, I tanned you good.

DALLAS: And then gave me a twenty-two rifle.

JEDIDIAH: Because ya took yore medicine and nary a yelp. (*Smiling at Josepha*) Pretty good times they was, daughter—yes'm!

THE SMALL PERSON: Now isn't it funny, Dal, how he will 'sist on calling Jo his daughter? But she isn't really you know else he'd be my father, wouldn't he? An' sometimes he calls me "Babe," an' I don't like it you know, Uncle Jed, cause I'm getting growder-up every day, soon I shall be eight and no baby was ever eight years old.

JEDIDIAH: (*nodding*) And that's whatever. Nearly eight? My, my—"Babe" 'll never do, I guess I'll have to call you-all Heart's-Delight. How'll that soot now?

THE SMALL PERSON: (*gravely considering*) I think that's an awful, frightfully pretty name. Yes,

I like Heart's-Delight, it sounds like the name of a
princess in a fairy-tale, doesn't it, Jo?

JOSEPHA: (*glancing up, very conscious of Dallas's
adoring gaze*) Yes dear, I—oh yes, very.

THE SMALL PERSON: (*staring, egg-spoon at lip*)
Why, Jodear, how bright your eyes are to-day! And
now you're getting frightfully red! And . . . oh,
Jodear, you've got your nearliest-best dress on. . . .
I do hope you're not thinking of wedding any-
one——"

JOSEPHA: Why what . . . whatever do you
mean?

THE SMALL PERSON: Well, I do hope you won't
ever go marrying Mr. Ryerson or anything of that
sort, will you, Jodear?

JOSEPHA: (*breathlessly aghast*) Patience . . .!
Oh . . . ! What are you saying?

THE SMALL PERSON: (*serenely*) Well, the other
day when he brought me that 'normous box of chocolates that you hid away cause you said I'd be sick
only I shouldn't, he asked me to kiss him but I wouldn't
'cause somehow I don't like his mus-tarsh, an' he said
I must learn to because he was going to be my brother,
so I said how, an' he said you'd marry him, only I
shouldn't if I was you, Jodear, and——"

JOSEPHA: (*angrily*) How dared he! I hope you
told him I'd die first!

THE SMALL PERSON: Well, no, I didn't say that
'xactly, Jodear, you see I didn't quite know what to
say, so I said what Uncle Jed says when he's a bit
'sprised, I said "Hell's bells!"

JEDIDIAH: (*chuckling and thumping the table,
ecstatic*) Didya by heck! Now jest for that you gotta
kiss *me*—yes'm, I guess. (*They kiss.*) Though mind
ya, and I'm tellin' ya, my Heart's-Delight, little ladies
an' princesses don't talk that a way—no'm, I guess
not.

THE SMALL PERSON: (*self-reproachful but sedate*)
'Fraid my mouth was a bit eggy—and, Jodear, there's
George!

"Absolutely!" said a cheery voice, and in at the
open lattice came Lord Withymore's curly head. "Yes,
here I am, Pat, old chap, bright as a new half-crown
and early as—well, dash me! what I mean to say is—
er—well, well, if you know what I mean, Miss Josepha!"

"Yes," she answered, smiling in glad welcome.
"You mean," here she hesitated for the fraction of
a second and her voice sank to softer, tenderer note,
"you mean . . . Keith-Dallas."

"Eh? Oh?" quoth his lordship, blinking. "Er
. . . yes . . . oh abso-lutely . . . good, old Kay!
Yes, I mean him, a creature o' stealth, Miss Jo! For
here am I roused from my innocent slumbers—and
no breakfast—by two distracted ladies, the Misses
Hardwicke, with harrowing tale of deserted couch, of
sick-bed vacant and deserted, of poor, errant invalid,
lost, rambling abroad to die in ditches and what not.
So forth incontinent hop I and into car—and still
no breakfast—to seek the wanderer and find him . . .
gulping coffee, absolutely! And wolfing bacon and
eggs, or are they kidneys? So what I mean to say is,
if you know what I mean—tush, and so forth!"

"They're eggs, sir," laughed Josepha, "so come and
partake. Patience dear, run and ask Sarah for another
cup. Oh, George, does your lordship know Uncle
Jed, I mean—Mr. Jedidiah Wollet—Lord Withymore—
and now, come in at once, do!"

"Like a bird!" said his lordship, and came in through
the window, head first, to grip Jedidiah's outstretched
hand.

"Then you haven't forgotten me, Mr. Wollet—the
time Keith and I visited you out West?"

"No, siree, shorely not, though you-all named me
different, out there."

"To be sure, I had the cheek to call you 'Uncle Jed'."

"Do it again—won't ya?" inquired the little man wistfully.

"Ab-solutely!" quoth his lordship heartily. "Uncle Jed it is! As for you, Keith, you old lead-swinging scrounger, what I mean to say is—naughty, naughty! Oh, fie . . . And by Gad old lad I—I'm rejoiced—absolutely!"

And now, his lordship being usually as pleasant as his looks, the little breakfast room became so full of cheery good-fellowship that the very sunbeams shining in upon them all, seemed to gather a new glory, while out in the dewy garden butterflies danced more gaily, bees hummed and birds chirped and piped a sweeter, gladder note.

CHAPTER XXVII

CONCERNING UNCLE JED, HIS POINT OF VIEW

LORD WITHYMORE glanced from Josepha's radiant loveliness to where Dallas sat in shady summer-house, the Small Personage perched upon his knee, and turned away with something very like a sigh.

"Well?" demanded Josepha.

"Absolutely!" answered his lordship cheerily. "You look topping this morning. . . . Happiness, if you know what I mean, is better than all the face-creams and what not! Old Keith has a way with horses and children and w——especially children. I remember in France behind the lines the French kids used to follow him about for no apparent reason, and his French was rotten. . . . I'm fond of children, too, but they don't——" his lordship sighed again but, catching himself in the act as it were, laughed instead, and became more cheery than ever: "Keith's rather a wonderful chap . . . . deserves all the very best in life, and so forth—what I mean is, I'm glad, absolutely——" here, meeting Josepha's bright, direct gaze, he flushed and instantly floundered. "I mean you know—er—what I mean to say is—quite!"

"Did he . . . has Keith told you?"

"No, not yet—I guessed . . . the light in your eyes, Josepha, the old lad's adoring phiz . . . and I'm glad . . . rejoiced . . . very! Keith's all true Yank, the best type of American, and there are no better men in this world. . . . So I should like . . .

that is, I mean I want . . . what I'm trying to
say is—I wish you, both of you, every joy and—er—
what not, if you know what I mean—absolutely!"

"Dear George," she murmured, "what a friend,
what a man you are!"

"Oh I don't know," he answered, fishing out his
cigarette-case rather awkwardly. "Shall we gasp a
while? No? Why then, talking of horses, old Kay
has promised to give an eye to my stables, which is
a top-hole stroke of luck for your very obedient, humble
George."

"But—Mr. Meredith?"

"We parted last week. Keith can move in and
take over as soon as he will."

"How splendid!" she murmured, giving him her
hand.

"And now I'm off to the Misses Hardwicke—allay
their anxiety about their—I mean your—invalid,
sooth their perturbation and so forth. Which reminds
me, I promised to take your small invalid to visit 'em
if you'd permit—little Pat. I'd like to give her a
spin in the car—if she'd go. Do you think she would?"
he inquired rather wistfully.

"She'd love it! And it will do her lots of good,
so come and tell her."

"Pat, old chap," called his lordship cheerily as they
crossed towards the summer-house, "how about a
visit to your aunt's and a ride in the car, a jolly old
teedle round?"

"Ooh!" cried the Small Personage. "How triffickly
fine!" Then checking her transport suddenly she
turned to Dallas. "You won't mind if I go for jest
a little, teeny ride, Dal—or p'raps George'll take you
too?"

"No, no, Hon, you go—two's company, you know.
But be sure you give my love to your aunts, bless
em! Say I'll be around to thank them soon."

"Then first, George, please—is it your great, big magnif'cent car or only the little one?"

"The big one, Pat."

"Then, Jodear, I'd better wear my best hat an' coat, don't you s'pose? And my new gloves?"

"Oh, of course!" smiled Josepha. "So come and put them on."

"Old boy," said Dallas as soon as they were alone, glancing askance at his lordship and filling a well-seasoned, somewhat battered briar-pipe, "George, old fellow——"

"Hallo?" quoth his lordship, lighting cigarette.

"I . . . . I want—I've got something to tell you."

"Oh?" inquired his lordship staring up hard at the cloudless sky.

"Why yes, George, and I . . . well, I find it a bit awkward . . . under the circumstances."

"Oh? What circumstances?" said his lordship, still gazing skyward.

"Well, you see, I think—no, I'm very sure that . . . that you . . . dammit man, what are you staring at?"

"Lark!" answered his lordship, pointing. "Yon feathered warbler a-warbling so gaily and what not."

"Well, listen to me, will you?"

"Good fellow, mine ears attend you—say on! Take a slow, deep breath, count nine and—let it come!"

"George . . . old man, I . . . I guess you understand . . . you surely know me well enough to know, I mean I . . . well, I'd just hate to . . . oh hell!"

"How true!" murmured his lordship. "How very, very true! Old Thing I find your eloquence so affecting that——"

"George . . . George be serious! I want you to know, I . . . I want to tell you that she . . . I . . . that we——"

"Old bean, shut up! These stammering confessions stint, cease—enough, go to—I know all!"

"You mean . . . about . . . Josepha . . . me?"

"E'en so, forsooth. Thou art the man!"

"Did . . . she tell you?"

"Not so, old bird. Being of an average intelligence—I guessed. 'Twas in that speaking visage. 'Twas sticking out all over you—feet, yards! 'Twas impossible to miss. Wherefore I spoke the sweet soul, bestowed on her my blessing, and now—the same to you . . . happiness, old boy, good luck, the best in the world and . . . so on!"

Laying aside his unlighted pipe, Dallas rose, glanced into his friend's face and beholding it so untroubled, so pleasantly serene, thereafter lifted his gaze also to the soaring lark.

"George . . . " said he at last, his own face not at all serene, "old sportsman . . . !" Then, turning suddenly, he took up his pipe and set himself to light it, and broke three matches ere he had it going. Then the Small Personage hailed them, and side by side they crossed the sunny garden to the wicket-gate beyond which stood the great car, all gleam and glitter from bonnet to tail-light.

"Ooh—magnif'cent!" sighed the Small Personage dancing ecstatic.

"She's a beauty!" said Josepha, opening the door.

"Moreover, she—goes!" nodded Lord Withymore, lifting his small passenger to the luxurious seat beside him and starting the engine; then he waved his hand cheerily and the long, silent car glided away round the bend and was gone. But Dallas remained staring after it so long that at last Josepha's hand came creeping within his arm:

"Dear, why so thoughtful?" she inquired, a little anxiously.

"I'm just wondering," he answered, looking down

at her with eyes of reverent adoration, "how you could ever have chosen me . . . such as I—with old George around."

"Just because you happen to be—you."

"And yet there are very few like George—old England can never be anything but great while she breeds such men. . . . But as for me, ah, Josepha . . . oh my dear . . . what am I?"

"The man I love!" she murmured. "Oh, silly boy, don't you know, can't you see? Even if you were vile, the guiltiest wretch—it would break my heart but—I should love you still, love you always until perhaps—somewhere, at some time my love should win forgiveness and we together expiate your sin——"

"Expiate!" he repeated. "Expiation—yes, that's the word! Listen, girl—the thing I've done is between us still and always must be until I have atoned. I know myself not worthy to even touch you—this hand of mine was once red with blood . . . sticky . . . God, I can feel it now! And . . . Josepha . . . last night you touched it with your sweet, pure lips . . . a thing so foul! And I can't come to you clean or anyways worthy until I've made atonement somehow—anyhow! Can't you see—can't you see?"

She had led him back to the summer-house and now, seated within its shade, she strove to comfort him:

"I don't believe—I won't—I can't! I know you are no murderer!"

"But I threatened his life. . . . I saw him dead. . . . I felt his blood, it was on this hand that held the gun—this hand you kissed! I must atone, I can't be worthy of you unless—how can I—how can I?"

"Hush, dear, hush! You are not well yet——"

"I'm well enough to long for you in my arms, to yearn to kiss you and not dare, because I'm vile! I meant to go away, Josepha dear, but now—now instead . . . to let you love me, a guilty fugitive! I wonder what old George would say—what he's thinking—I meant to ask him, but hadn't the courage. I'm turning coward! So there's only one way for me, I must go back and face it out, I must stand my trial and take what's coming."

"No!" she cried. "No—that would be madness!"

"It's the only atonement I can make and—whatever happened, I should feel myself clean again and . . . and be worthy of your kisses then . . . maybe?" For answer she folded him in quick, protecting arms, pillowed his drooping head upon her shoulder, kissing his hair, his brow, his tired eyes.

"Oh, my dear, how you suffer!" she whispered. "But how silly to harrow yourself with such bitter self-reproaching when I am so sure of you, so very, very sure that you never knew a really murderous thought in all your life."

"I threatened to shoot him, Josepha!"

"You threatened!" she repeated in tender scorn, "and what of that? Everybody's always threatening to do perfectly frightful things to somebody some time or other, and of course never does. I do myself, I know, I threaten fearfully when I'm in a rage. . . . Oh there's Uncle Jed, thank heaven—No, lie still, sir, don't be so ridiculously shy just because you happen to be in my arms—so absurdly prudish—for shame! Uncle Jed!" she called in her clear, rich contralto. "Come here at once, come to your silly, adopted son, I'm afraid he's a fool."

"Eh, a fool?" repeated Jedidiah, opening his sharp eyes rather wide. "Why now seein' him so, I mean jest where he is and how you got him, I hain't so sure, daughter. You-all haint the kinda woman to be grabbin' a holt of any fool—not so lovin' and affectionate, no'm!"

"But, Uncle Jed, he talks of going back to America and standing his trial as a murderer."

"My whiskers!" exclaimed the little man fiercely and stepping into the summer-house, seated himself beside Josepha. "Said that, did he, daughter?"

"Yes, Uncle Jed, and a lot more, he's wild to make atonement for——"

"Atonement, eh?" snarled Jedidiah. "Oh, he's a fool all right—atonement, psha!"

"And for a crime we know him guiltless of, Uncle Jed."

"Ah—tone—ment!" quoth Jedidiah, rolling the word sonorously. "Sounds fine, don't it, daughter?"

"Oh but he means it!" cried Josepha indignantly.

"Shore he means it!" nodded Jedidiah, with expression of the utmost ferocity. "And he'll do it, too —if we-all let him. But that's jest Keith—oh, that's him—full of his gol-darn, high-minded, crazy-hoss notions, yes'm—he allus was, even as a rip-snortin' galoot of a varmint boy, I guesso!"

"But, Jed," cried Dallas passionately, "can't you see I—love her, man, worship her and she, God bless her for it, she loves me and yet . . . I can hardly bear to touch her because I know myself so foul."

"Daughter," inquired Jedidiah, "do you-all ever feed your chickens?"

"Why, of course! But what on earth——?"

"Daughter—go feed 'em and leave this yere crazy galoot to me, I gotta swear at him good."

"But—oh, Uncle Jed, he's been so ill and he isn't well even yet. You'll be your dearest self, you'll be kind to him, very gentle?"

"Daughter, I'll shore curse the fool kid as tender as any bleatin' lamb, yes'm. And no man can say fairer than that, I reckon. This yere Keith o' yourn's gotta be brung to reason—if that thing as looks like his head acts any."

"Yes, dear Uncle Jed, he is mine now as surely as I am his. . . . And, Keith, I like Keith better than Dallas so I'll call you Keith, Keith. . . . And now I'll leave him to you, Uncle Jed—remember he's still an invalid so—be gentle." And so, she turned and left them together.

"Now ef," said Jedidiah, gazing after her, "ef there's many like her in England, then, by heck, this is sure some country! And now as for you-all, Keith, Dallas, Chisholm listen here to me . . .!"

So Dallas perforce listened, and listened, and listened yet again until Jedidiah, having somewhat exhausted his vocabulary, sat back, whipped a thin, black cigar from his pocket, stuck it fiercely into a corner of his grim mouth and nodded:

"And that's whatever!" said he and striking a match on his black, clerical-seeming nether garments, lit his cigar, puffed violently and spoke again:

"Now look a here, son—and mind I'm tellin' ya —so jest git this inta that dome o' yours if it hain't solid ivory: First off—you-all didn't do this yere murder! Second—there's folks as knows ya didn't! Third—there's folks as knows who did! Fourth— there's folks has trailed and watched ya—oh they've kept tabs on ya all along——"

"Yes, I've seen Whitey Neeves once or twice, Jed—but just what are they after, what's their game?"

"I'll tell ya presently. But now you tell me— you-all hain't met up with this Derek Ryerson over here yet, have ya?"

"No, I . . . I tried to!" Dallas admitted, flushing guiltily. "But I didn't—thank God! Why is he over here anyway?"

"Well, son, I guess there's three purty good reasons and one of 'em's Hank Finlay. You'll shore remember Fin?"

"Why, of course, he was your ranch foreman."

"And deppity marshal. Well, sir, Fin's shore stirred things up around Noo York, he cert'nly has, well I guesso! Next, there's me—I hain't done a whole lot—yet, though I've give 'em a jolt or so. And then—there's that young fe-male . . . Olive."

"Olive Lemay?" exclaimed Dallas, starting. "Good heavens, Jed, is she over here?"

"Keith boy, she sot out for Eu-rope jest about three weeks after you-all."

"Olive over here too? Good Lord! Does Josepha know—have you told her?"

"Not me, no, sir. If anyone tells her it's gotta be you."

"Not I, Jed—where's the need? And I hate talking about women anyway."

"Why, son, I'll allow it's a bit orkard sometimes to tell one gell about another gell!"

"Oh dammit! Why are they all haunting me like this—Ryerson and his crowd and now Olive? Why on earth is she here?"

"Son, you can search me! All I know is, she does so, and this yere Derek Ryerson chases after her on the next boat—with four of his bunch."

"But damn it all, Jed, why should she quit New York—was she afraid of them—Ryerson's gang?"

"Well, son, I guess she is to-day, anyway! Now tell me, gimme it straight, boy—wasn't you-all kinda sweet on her?"

"No! No, Jed, I swear. I . . . I liked her, yes I liked her a whole lot because she seemed, well —so mighty different to the rest of that crowd . . . this was why I took her part against Red Rory, yes and Ryerson himself once . . . you see she seemed too good for—that kind of thing. But I never loved her, Jed. Good Lord, man, I didn't know the meaning of the word—then."

"Well, wasn't she some sweet on you-all, hey?"

"Oh, I don't know . . . not properly . . . surely not."

"Ha—and that's why!" nodded Jedidiah. "So she comes py-rootin' over here after you-all, son, a purpose to make good with ya, and Ryerson's out to prevent her gettin' word with ya and tellin' the truth o' that murder."

"Good Lord, Jed!" exclaimed Dallas, his eyes brightening. "And yet—no! I found the pistol in my hand when I came to."

"Was Miss Olive anywhere's around—was she?"

"No . . . not that I remember. I was too dazed."

"Dazed, shore you was—that was dope or a sand-bag. And then Ryerson and the bunch hustled you out of it—eh?"

"Yes . . . I guess they must have done, anyway, I woke up in my own flat next evening . . . and thought it all a horrible dream until Ryerson came around and told me . . . what I'd done."

"Shore! And, son, d'ya know where M'Guire's body was found?"

"Well at Hetzel's place I suppose."

"Heck no—on the railroad tracks at Thirty-fourth street and Eleventh Avnoo. The police hain't a cloo, nary a suspicion o' the killer in consequence."

"You're out there, Jed. Yes, you're all wrong. I'm known, the newspapers have my portrait . . . my name . . . the poor, old dad——"

"Pore old nothing!" quoth Jedidiah fiercely. "A father that turns and quits on his own son deserves all that's comin' to him—and then some more——"

"He's still my father, Jed!"

"He was my partner first, boy—my side-kick in Montanny 'fore you was foaled."

"Well, anyway, the newspapers have my picture and——"

"Well and I'm tellin' ya they hain't."

"But I've seen it, Josepha showed me a——"

"Shore, she showed it me, an' I'm tellin' ya that news-clippin' was a fake."

"A fake? Good Lord! Are you sure?"

"As a pair of six-guns, boy!"

"But why . . . what's it all mean?"

"It means blackmail for one thing, son—and that you're a plum locoed, crazy fool fer another. Anyways I'm bettin' a blue stack this Olive dame is jest oozin' info'mation. And, Keith, we gotta find her before Ryerson does, and, most important, we gotta find her—alive!"

"Alive? Jed—what do you mean?"

"Well we can't expect her to tell us a whole lot ef she's dead, it hain't reasonable, no, sir."

"Jed, what are you telling me?"

"That it'll depend purty much on daughter, I reckon."

"On Josepha? Good heavens! How?"

"Well, this Ryerson I figger to be a mighty slick proposition, a purty ornery cuss."

"I know it—he's a devil. But how is Josepha concerned?"

"She's gotta rope him, son, corral him, hold him——"

"How d'you mean, hold him?" demanded Dallas starting.

"Get onta this, son: Ryerson trails you here, sees daughter and falls for her—on sight."

"Well, damn him!"

"Shore! But lemme explain—now get this! Josepha's simply gotta act upta him a mite, string him along until——"

"No!" cried Dallas frowning.

"Yes!" quoth Jedidiah, scowling. "She's shore a-going to keep him millin' around wastin' his time while me and Fin ropes in this yere Olive and——"

"No!" cried Dallas again, his pale cheek flushing suddenly. "Never on your life, Jed—I say no!"

"Yes!" snarled Jedidiah, his every whisker bristling. "We've talked it over, daughter and me, and she's a heap sot on the idea, she's shore burnin' with zeal, she's aimin' ter keep Mister Ryerson on a——"

"And I tell you I'll not allow it, Jed—that beast!"

"Now look a here, son!"

"See here, Jed! I know this fellow better than you do. I'm on to all his cursed trickery and crookedness, I know him for a merciless——"

"Shore, so do I, Keithy boy, I got his number, and you don't haveta worry none."

"Anyway," said Dallas, between his teeth, "I just won't have him meeting Josepha or hanging around——"

"Hell! Can't you trust her then?"

"Dammit! You know I don't mean that—but Ryerson's too vile to breathe the same air. Besides it would be degrading for——"

"Son, some women can't be degraded, and daughter's one."

"Well, anyway I won't stand for it, not for a moment and that's final."

"Well, anyway—you jest gotta stand for it! Daughter's all sot to go through with the scheme for your sake, and I guess she hain't to be turned, no, sir, not daughter—some woman, that!"

"Then by God, I'll give myself up!" cried Dallas, leaping to his feet.

"Shucks!" snarled Jedidiah. "Set down an' behave! No harm can come ta daughter, y' bone-head—hain't you-all around and, doggone it, hain't I watchin' over her when you hain't—constant? Well, I guesso!"

"Now, Jed, see here—and for the last time!" said Dallas, speaking with a deliberate finality that set Jedidiah scowling fiercer than ever, "in half an hour

or so I am going over Alfriston way to take up my
new job in Withymore's stables—but, unless you
cut out all idea of this damned scheme of yours——"

"'Tisn't all mine, ding-bust ya!"

"Yours and hers, then—I go instead to Will Bridger,
the policeman, proclaim myself M'Guire's murderer,
and give myself into custody."

"Yore plum locoed, crazy!"

"Sure! But that's exactly what'll happen, Jed.
This rotten scheme doesn't go! Ryerson's a dog—
and Josepha is . . . well, she's just Josepha, and
she surely isn't going to . . . to have to pretend
any kindness for Ryerson on my account. And there's
my last word, so——"

"Silly boy!" said Josepha, and parting the vines
at the trellis, she peeped through and made a face
at him. "Uncle Jed is quite right and you, of course,
are quite wrong—absolutely, what I mean to say is
—quite! as your 'old George' would say."

"But, Josepha—my dear, just what are you and
old Jed up to?"

"Well, in about five minutes we are off to Lewes—
marketing."

"No. I mean about—Ryerson?"

"Oh, Uncle Jed," she laughed, "I do believe he's
jealous already!"

"Not of Ryerson—only I want to know——"

"That's it!" she cried. "We want you to know,
we mean you to be sure and certain that you are innocent, because you are such a——"

"Gol darn bone-head!" snarled Jedidiah.

"Yes, I suppose you are," she admitted: then in
quick tenderness stretched out her hands to him,
"but dear, I love you for it! So we are scheming to
prove your innocence to you beyond even your doubt-
ing so that you may learn to honour yourself almost
as much as I honour you."

"Dearest girl!" he murmured, catching her hands to his eager lips. "But . . . what about Ryerson?"

"This!" she answered, very solemnly. "Should you happen to meet him here—or anywhere, you must promise me—on your word of honour, dear—that you will be friendly."

"No, I can't promise that, dear."

"Then . . . Oh, Keith . . . promise, promise faithfully you won't quarrel or give him any cause to quarrel with you—promise me, this moment, on your word of honour!"

"Very well, you angel, I promise, but——"

"No 'buts'!" she cried. "Sit here in the sunshine and think of me and your sacred promise. Now, Uncle Jed, hurry or we shall miss the bus."

"Go ahead, daughter, I'll be right along! Son," said Jedidiah, looking after her, "you called her 'angel' and yore dead right! I knowed another angel once as—went aloft twenty odd years ago, yore mother, boy, and she's been watchin' over ya ever since . . . and now here's another to work for ya, and so here's old Jed willin' to risk a blue stack as you-all shore wins out for, son, you're shore settin' in luck at last. . . . Comin', daughter, comin'!"

The wicket-gate creaked open, Josepha waved her hand cheerily and Dallas was alone in the quiet garden.

It was a hot morning, very slumbersome and still; birds chirped drowsily, butterflies hovered, ducks quacked drowsily ever and anon from their pond in remote and shady corner, hens clucked and Dallas, basking in the kindly sunshine, felt in his body, a waxing health and vigour, and in his mind, an ever-growing certainty that Josepha's inspiring faith and old Jedidiah's unwavering loyalty must, somehow and at some time, be justified, and this haunting knowledge of guilt be changed, by some miracle, to a blessed assurance of innocence.

And as, in the worst of those bad, old days in France, he had once or twice cried within his shaken soul, a prayer to the All-Father, that merciful God of his long-dead mother, so now, dumb of tongue yet eloquent of mind, he made passionate supplication that he might, indeed, somehow—at some time, prove worthy of this white-souled woman's love, this true-hearted man's unchanging friendship. . . .

The clump of heavy boots aroused him and, glancing up, he beheld Tom Merry drooping despondent upon a spade; meeting Dallas's glance he sighed, groaned, shook his head and spoke:

"Lord, sir, lord love me, theer you be a-settin' up so 'earty an' free an' lookin' so bright as a noo arf-crown! A deceivin' world it be sure-ly!"

"How so, Tom?"

"Well, why ain't you in your coffin, sir, nice an' dead and buried so comfortable—eh?"

"Buried, Tom?"

"Ar."

"Well perhaps, because I'm pretty much alive."

"Ar—so I see! And 'ere's folks been tellin' me as you was dyin'—repeated they 'ave and now—theer you sits, givin' everybody the lie—leastways if everybody's right and you'm dead I never see sich a lively corpse. Not as I 'olds it agin you, sir, for keepin' alive—only it be a deceivin' world sure-ly! And now, sir, since you ain't dead, I got a bit o' noos for ye, it aren't much, but—why Lord love us, wot ails ye, sir?" he exclaimed, startled by the sudden change in Dallas; for at that moment the little wicket-gate clicked sharply, swung wide open and Derek Ryerson stepped into the garden; now at sight of him Tom Merry whistled softly, shouldered his spade and clumped heavily away.

H

CHAPTER XXVIII

WHICH IS SHORT AND TO THE POINT

DALLAS rose to his feet, fists clenched, eyes bright and keen, staring at that well-remembered, arresting figure, this man so sleekly handsome and superciliously self-assured who had entered the quiet garden like master coming home rather than visitor making a call. And suddenly, as if he sensed this fierce scrutiny Ryerson halted in his leisured, easy stride, glanced round about and, espying Dallas, flourished his smart walking-cane in jovial greeting and strolled across to him.

"Hello, Keith, old sport!" said he, extending neatly-gloved hand. "Glad to see you around again, heard of your accident. How's the game?"

Dallas glanced at the out-thrust hand, scowled into the long-lashed eyes behind it and neither moved nor spoke.

"Oh? What's this?" demanded Ryerson in voice gentle as his sleepy-seeming eyes. "Won't shake—eh?"

"No!" answered Dallas, thrusting fists into pockets. "I cut you out and all you stand for, months ago."

"Is that so?" murmured Ryerson.

"Yes!" nodded Dallas, grimly.

"Well, well!" sighed Ryerson, bending gracefully to survey his own neatly-trousered legs. "Bit risky, isn't it? Considering—what we know!"

"I'll chance that!"

"My, my!" said Ryerson in the same soft tone. "Going to kick, eh? Going to shake us are you, old man, after all the good times we've had together?"

Dallas merely looked at him.

"So?" nodded Ryerson. "You mean it, do you? Why then let me tell you something—it's not so easy as it sounds, old sport, not by a jug-full! We shall continue to take quite a lively interest in you if only for the sake of your old man, your respected dad, your revered sire. Now what's it to be. Keith, friends or—the other thing?"

"I've said it once—not friends."

"No?"

"No."

"Well, you've called the game, remember! As for me, Kay old man, I shall still be as much your friend as ever I was."

"Sure!" nodded Dallas, more grimly than ever. "And what might you be after around here?"

"The same as you, I guess, old top—admiring the peaches, or say—one! Watching it grow ripe enough to pluck, and—then!"

Dallas jerked quivering fists from his pockets, Ryerson lounging upon his cane, sighed and nodded:

"Some baby—oh boy!" he murmured. "Yes, Josepha is sure a dream of bliss, and with more soul than Olive, eh, old man?"

"That's enough!" said Dallas, so fiercely that Ryerson fell back a pace and surveyed him in smiling wonder.

"What? Are you jealous, old top? Have you fallen for Josepha too? For the love of Mike! What'll Olive say, poor kid?"

Restraining the fury that threatened to choke him, that was urging him to wild and desperate action, Dallas folded his arms, smiling on his tormentor, and spoke at a venture:

"Olive?" he repeated. "Well, I guess you'd best ask her opinion, ask her to-night when you get back to Lewes."

The mocking smile on Ryerson's shapely mouth remained, but his sleepy eyes grew suddenly keen.

"Say, what are you handing me?" he demanded sharply and now his sleepy languor had given place to a watchful ferocity. "She's found—you've seen her? Has she——?" his snapping white teeth cut the question short. "Hell! You know she's way off in N'York."

Now staring into those fierce, eagerly-questioning eyes, Dallas smiled, laughed suddenly and nodded: "She has!" said he, answering that unfinished question. "And I see now that I've been even a bigger fool than I thought—your miserable, self-accusing scapegoat. But I'm on to it all at last, I surely am!"

Mute stood Derek Ryerson, gloved hands griping upon his elegant cane, viewing the speaker with smouldering eyes, his ready tongue failing him for once, as, laughing still, Dallas stepped out of the summer-house, and, taking up that heavy iron-shod staff from where it had lain all night in the grass, twirled it joyously.

"Look at this, Ryerson!" said he, a new, glad ring in his voice. "I bought it for you. Attempt any of your devil's games around here and they'll be your last—so help me God!"

"Ah!" cried Ryerson, his voice now as altered as his looks, "you'd murder me, eh?"

"Would it be murder?" said Dallas, smiling happily. "Seems a hard name for it."

"You'd murder me as you did Rory! You're getting a regular killer, aren't you—developing a thirst for blood, eh?"

"Oh I don't know," demurred Dallas, as he tucked the formidable stick beneath his arm, "I've never tried it yet. I didn't kill Red Rory—I know it, at last!"

Derek Ryerson fell back a pace and, for the fraction of a second, his fierce gaze wavered, was averted . . . then his rigid pose relaxed and he laughed:

"You're crazy!" said he, shaking indolent head, "you know and I know and others know you're for Sing Sing and the chair if——"

"Tut, tut!" quoth Dallas cheerily, "that poor stuff doesn't go with me any more, I'm through with doing the conscious guilt act!" So saying he turned to be gone but a touch from the smart walking-cane arrested him.

"Hold on a minute!" said Ryerson softly. "I've seen your bludgeon, now—look at this!" A lightning movement of those gloved hands—the elegant cane snapped asunder and Dallas was staring into the grim muzzle of a derringer.

"Rather neat, eh, old sport?" inquired Ryerson, keeping the deadly thing in line with Dallas's head. "But its main charm lies in the fact that it's silent, old man, silent— as death!"

"Pretty useful, I guess, for your line of business!" nodded Dallas and turning, strode off across the sunny garden; now, remarkable fact, before he reached the wicket-gate he was whistling, clear and blythe as any thrush or blackbird!

CHAPTER XXIX

TOUCHES UPON THE WOES OF BEN

"Good morning Mr. Dallas, sir, and glad I am to see you up and about again, I'm sure."

"Thank you, Mrs. Weldon. You're looking fine . . . and the old 'Duck' so bright and cosy. It seems ages since I was here."

"Why yes, sir, time do seem long when you'm ill."

"And how's everyone?"

"All pretty well, sir."

"And 'The Festive Cake,' the picture of those nice, plump . . . kittens, I think you said—hangs it where it did?"

"Oh yes, sir, 'tis never moved, except Fridays when I dusts it. And Mr. Lomax is inside—Ben, sir, though it ain't 'ardly time to open. Still, if you was wantin' anything, sir."

"I surely am!" nodded Dallas, cheerily. "Beer, Mrs. Weldon, and Ben." Following this smiling, placid landlady into the taproom, he there found Ben seated alone and glooming above a half-empty glass, who rose to touch hat respectfully, albeit gloomy still:

"Good mornin' sir!" said he, sounding a little hoarser than usual. "I hear as you're a goin' to take charge o' the stables in place o' Mr. Meredith, sir!"

"Why yes—but right now I want to apologise, Ben, old scout."

"Apologise . . . to me, sir?" quoth Ben, becoming instantly flushed and uneasy. "Crumbs, sir, there ain't no need!"

"There's every need. Last time we met you acted by me like a real friend and I—well, like a drunken fool. You see I was completely soused, Ben, perfectly pie-eyed, that's my only excuse . . . damn whisky anyway! So now if you'll shake hands, Ben, why— shake!"

"Sir—love a duck!" exclaimed Ben as their fingers gripped. "You're lookin' prime, I never see you so full o' beans!"

"I haven't felt so full of beans for a goodish while," laughed Dallas. "By heaven, it's a great, old world, Ben, it sure is!"

"Is it, sir?" sighed Ben, sinking to the very deeps of gloom.

"Well, but isn't it?"

"Why, sir, I dunno. I useter think so, sometimes, now an' then, but to-day—wot wi' this and that— I dunno!"

"Just what's your trouble, Ben?"

"First of all—this, sir!" sighed Ben, and from his right-hand waistcoat pocket he fished a sapphire bangle, and from his left, a small, gold wrist-watch. "Sir, I give her this—the bracelet, last March the twenty-third, bein' her birthday. I give her that— the watch, June the nineteenth, bein' my birthday. And, sir, she give 'em me back last night—and she says, says she, layin' of 'em atop the stile because I wouldn't take 'em: 'All,' says she, very sark-astic, 'All,' says she, 'is now over betwixt us!' she says. And, sir, wot I now says is—that ain't no way for no woman to treat no man—no!"

"But she's said the same before, hasn't she, Ben?"

"Sir, she 'as—frequent. But she never give me back the bracelet afore—that's wot makes it so serious."

"Well, now, just how have you annoyed her this time?"

"Lord, sir, it ain't me—it's Sairey."

"Tell me, Ben."

"Why then, sir, in the first place it's all along of a bloke as talks through 'is boko, with light 'air and a mug like a sick cow, named Mr. Neeves."

"Oh?" inquired Dallas, setting down his glass. "What about him?"

"Well I've caught this bloke talkin' to her, more than once."

"But there's no harm in that, Ben, surely?"

"That's wot she told me. But, sir, there's 'arm in 'im—and that's wot I told her. 'And wot's more,' I says, 'if I find 'im 'anging abaht you again, I'll bash 'is ugly mug uglier,' I says, and sir, she ups and——"

"Hold on, Ben! I happen to know this fellow's dangerous——"

"Crikey, sir, that's wot she said!"

"He's armed most likely—a gun——"

"Then I'll cop 'im in the dark and dahn 'im afore 'e can use it."

"No, no, Ben, don't try any fool trick like that—besides there's no need, I'm sure, mighty sure, you've no real cause for jealousy, not a scrap."

"Sir," growled Ben, shaking bullet-head, "if say you was—say took up with a girl—say a lady and another bloke come crawlin' around—wot would you do—wot?"

"Why . . . I guess . . . it would all depend."

"Wot on, sir?"

"Well . . . circumstances, Ben."

"Sir, if you was took with any girl—say, lady—she'd be all the circumstances as mattered."

"And I guess that's so!" Dallas admitted. "Now see here, Ben, before you try any rough stuff, will you let me have a word with Sarah, will you wait and see if I can't fix the matter, as I'm pretty sure I can. How about it?"

"Thankee, sir. I was hoping as you would. But, sir, if she agrees, you'll please to say—if she takes this bracelet and that watch back again, she takes 'em for good—and the giver along wi' 'em, world without end, amen, in a manner o' speakin', Mr. Dallis, sir."

"Meaning—marriage, Ben?"

"Ar!" growled Ben, very red in the face. "Summat o' that sort, sir. You can say, please, as I've got a bit o' money put by. Been savin' up for it, I 'ave, ever since me an' Sairey met."

"Have you ever told her all this?"

"Crumbs—no sir! I ain't got the face to—if she ever laughed at me—oh crikey!"

"I'm pretty sure she wouldn't laugh, Ben."

A motor horn tooted without, at which sound up started Ben, emptying his glass at a gulp.

"Blimy, sir—the governor!" he exclaimed and reached for his cap.

"Good egg!" quoth Dallas, rising also. "Sit still, Ben, and order another pint, this is an occasion."

Opening the window he beheld the long bonnet of Lord Withymore's car within a yard of him, with that young gentleman himself behind the wheel who, becoming suddenly aware of Dallas, his beaming face and joyous eyes, opened his own eyes rather wide.

"What ho, within there!" cried he. "If that's really you, Keith, old bean, order me eftsoons a foaming beaker."

"Old son, it foams already. Come right in, I want to talk." Entered then his lordship forthwith, nodded to Ben, raised aloft his tankard of beer and nodded at Dallas.

"To our new boss!" quoth he, and drank.

HI

"And now," said Dallas, "here's to our friendship in particular, George, and this good, old world
in general."

"Dashed astounding!" exclaimed his lordship, setting down half-emptied tankard.

"What is?" inquired Dallas.

"You are! I leave you with a phiz like a grave-
yard . . . 'the heart bowed down' and what not,
and find you cheery as a dashed cricket, merry as a
confounded lark and so forth—what's it all mean?"

"Just that I've been every kind of a fool, old
lad."

"Quite—quite!" murmured his lordship. "But how
now? And wherefore rejoice therefore?"

"Let's get along and I'll explain."

"Right ho—we'll toddle . . . Ben—oh, where are
you?"

"Here, me lord!" answered Ben rising from seat
in remote corner.

"Well, just collect Mr. Dallas's traps and so on,
will you? Bring 'em along in the car, we're walking."

So away they strode together forthwith, but uttering
never a word between them until Dallas chuckled
suddenly, laughed and halted, laughing still.

"Dashed astounding!" exclaimed his lordship staring.
"I mean to say I haven't heard you laugh like that
since——" Dallas turned, caught him by the shoulders
and looked at him radiant-eyed.

"George," said he, solemn now, a little breathlessly,
"George old fellow—I didn't kill Red Rory after
all!"

"Quite!" nodded his lordship. "I never thought
you had, of course. But how did you find it all out,
my bright lad?"

"Well, have you met this man—Derek Ryerson?"

"I have."

"How do you reckon him up?"

' Too much in every way for simple soul like me, old bean—absolutely!"

"Yes, he's a superlative proposition, in every way. However, George, I pulled a big bluff on him all the same and he fell for it—hard!"

"Quite! Yes—oh quite! Now try to tell me all about it—in English."

"Well, it seems he came to England after Olive who is on her way right now, to tell me the truth about M'Guire's death—at least so Jed thinks, and by heavens, I'm thinking so too!"

"Olive?" murmured his lordship. "She is, or was, the lady in the case, eh, old chap, the girl you fought for?"

"Yes. Now, George, it's reasonable to suppose that, expecting Ryerson to follow her, she'd keep out of his way until she'd located me, and that consequently Ryerson hasn't found her yet. Anyway I bluffed him into thinking she'd seen me already and told me everything. . . . And old lad, it worked like a charm—struck him speechless—yes, for once he had no lie ready. 'I didn't kill Rory,' said I—and he was dumb! And in that moment I—just knew . . . God—to be free of it all at last, free of this ghastly incubus, this haunting knowledge of blood-guiltiness that has paralized me! Ah, George, can you guess just what this means to me?"

"Oh yes . . . I think so, Kay," murmured his lordship as they strolled on across the sunny meadows. "Yes . . . it means . . . Josepha . . . marriage. and . . . er . . . what not. Well . . . you've a house all ready for her—look, you can see its chimneys from here—above the treetops, there! Quite decently comfy and so forth, though I'll have it re-decorated for you, of course."

"George," said Dallas suddenly after they had gone some way in silence, "right now, old fellow,

there's only one thing hurts—that there aren't two
of her."

"Old bean, thanks! Certainly—oh quite!" answered
his lordship, fishing out his cigarette-case. "Gasp,
will you?"

Then, having lit their cigarettes, they walked on
together in a silence so profound that it was eloquent
of a friendship tried and trusty.

CHAPTER XXX

IN WHICH A ROMAN PARENT BECOMES AMERICAN

NEW YORK, the mighty, roared and rattled, clanged
and hooted; Broadway, palpitant with scurrying
life, flamed and flashed its myriad lights against the
gathering dusk and Wilbur Chisholm's great limousine,
caught in a block of traffic, slid to a standstill; but
the solitary man who leaned so wearily against its
luxurious cushions, his long arms folded and massive
head bared, sat wholly oblivious of the stir of the
great thoroughfare and the wonder of its ever-changing
sky-signs. And now, since he sat alone, his grimly-
handsome features relaxed, the harsh lines of mouth
and chin softened and he uttered a sigh very like a
groan. Now as he sat thus bitterly remorseful and
grieving as, surely, no thorough-going Roman parent
should, a sudden, harsh whisper reached him, uttering
two words that smote to the very heart of his
trouble:

"Boy Keith!"

Wilbur Chisholm caught his breath, started violently,
peered hastily out of either window but saw only the
serried ranks of motor traffic. . . . Then his own
car moved on and, sinking back, he shivered even
while he wiped brow suddenly moist. . . .

"Was this an omen? Was it a warning to tell
him the boy was, even then, lying dead?" With
fingers strangely awkward and unsteady he drew

a wallet from breastpocket and thence, a cablegram of yesterday's date, bearing this curt yet eloquent message:

"Son injured. Fear seriously."

Having stared haggardly at these words for some while he refolded the paper and set it away again with a certain painful care, he sat with his brooding gaze upon the small leathern satchel that lay beside him upon the broad cushioned seat.

If this dreadful thing should prove true and Keith be dead indeed, nothing else mattered! Of what avail the power of all his millions? Life would be a black emptiness henceforth . . . if Keith indeed lay dead!

"Son injured. Fear seriously."

The words seemed to start forth wherever he looked, in characters of flame. If the boy lay dead and himself left . . . to drag out a solitary old age! And yet he had been a solitary man always since that black hour had snatched from him the wife he had so loved. . . . And Success had crowned him! Hard-fought battles had been won because he walked alone, confiding in no man. Victory upon victory . . . riches and power! To these he had devoted himself, bent all his indomitable energies, until they had obsessed him utterly at last—while his little son, all unnoticed, grew from child to youth, from youth to manhood, almost a stranger. . . . Now if he might recall but one hour of boyish love, of youthful affection and confidence . . .? But no, not one! He had left the care of his child to others, to servants, tutors, and, last of all, to Jedidiah.

. . . Well, the iron Vespasian, marching to the wars, had left his son to the charge of others beyond all doubt . . . but young Titus had been spared to know his father, to fight beside him and rule after him, but . . .

"Son injured. Fear seriously."

And now this hoarse whisper out of the air! Well, supposing the boy dead, of what avail now this profitless repining? It was too late and remorse could do no good, let him rather get busy somehow—anyhow. . . . To think was to act, and taking the speaking tube Wilbur Chisholm spoke to his chauffeur. Presently, obedient to instructions, the big car swung out from the main stream of traffic and halted before a tall office building where at sight of Wilbur Chisholm men nodded, touched hats or stared, and uniformed officials hasted to serve him. So came he to certain lofty, swing doors and passing through, beheld divers people, clerks and employees, who stood about idly, talking together in excited undertones, but espying his tall figure and grim visage, they gave way before him mute with a surprised dismay, while some there were who frowned.

"Merwin here?"

"Yes, sir, but he . . . he refuses to see anyone, he——"

"Say I want a word. Don't stare, man—move!"

The clerk moved, hastily, and presently came hurrying back:

"This way sir!"

A door opened, closed, and a man rose from behind a great desk littered with papers, a haggard man who glared:

"Come to gloat, have you, Chisholm?" he demanded in high, unnatural tones, lifting nervous hand to his disordered hair with strange, wild gesture. "Come to see the bits and pieces? Well, go ahead, damn you. You've got me at last! I'm down and out for good! You've smashed me . . . another of your triumphs, eh?"

"Why, yes!" nodded Chisholm, watching the speaker's pallid face, beneath bent brows, "I've got you, Merwin, precisely where I wanted you, so I'm here to say you can have the time you pleaded for——"

"Eh . . . time . . . time, but you refused it yesterday!"

"I've changed my mind."

"God . . . Chisholm, d'you mean this or is it some ghastly . . . some devilish joke?"

"I'll put it in writing," said Wilbur Chisholm, taking out his fountain-pen.

"But man . . . you . . . you know just what this means to me . . . ?"

"I know," nodded Wilbur, scribbling the needful words. "You'll be back in the fight, stronger than ever. . . . Well, there's your release . . . good luck to you." A shaking hand caught up the sheet of paper with its message of salvation, haggard eyes looked their amazement into other eyes just as haggard.

"Chisholm, I've no words. I . . . I can't thank you!"

"Don't!" said Chisholm, and crossed to the door, his great shoulders bowed as though beneath some burden.

"But how . . . why . . .? Chisholm has anything happened? You look——"

"Boy injured. Fear seriously!" answered Wilbur Chisholm like one repeating a lesson, and, opening the door, went his way, leaving wonderment and a great joy behind him.

On again through broad streets and across shadowy park his car bore him until it stopped at last at his own house.

"Sir," said the chauffeur, hastening after him as he ascended the wide, stone steps, "you're forgetting this satchel."

"Thanks!" he muttered and with it in lax fingers stood to watch the car swing away; then sighing, he turned and approached the massive front-door, but halted suddenly as from the deep and shadowy portico stepped a tall man.

"All right, Mis' Chisholm!" said a soft voice, "ye'll no juist be disrememberin' me, I reckon. Finlay and Hank, whateffer."

"Finlay?" he repeated, peering, "sounds kind of familiar."

"Shore it is—familiar as hell if ye'll juist carry your mind back West to the old O bar O."

"Why, yes, you're Jed's partner, of course."

"Ranche foreman and deepooty marshal. An' I'm shore muckle re lieved to see as ye've still gotten your money along!"

"Eh—money?" repeated Wilbur sharply and glancing instinctively at the satchel in his hand. "What the devil d'you know about it?"

"Aweel," said Finlay in sudden, hoarse whisper. 'Five hundred thousand dollars is an unco' lot o' money toe be totin' around."

"Well," growled Wilbur, "and how d'you happen to know of it?"

"Sir, 'tis ma business tae get wise tae certain matters y'ken, and by hookey, I've been on the jump tae see as nobody got that dough awa' frae ye, and that's a fac'."

"What's this? D'you mean you've been shadowing me?"

"Ay, I've been ridin' herd on ye, Mis' Chisholm. Mebbe I'm a wee bittie o'er cautious, but ma mither, God bless her, was Scots, d'ye see. Hows'ever I shore kep' my eye on ye——"

"The hell you have!"

"Ay, sir, indeedy! And—so have others, they
shore have. I tried to get in touch wi' ye in a traffic
block way down-town, but——"

"Ha, so it was you! You whispered—you
said——"

"Mis' Chisholm, I said two words as only you and
me and Jed kens, whateffer—I whispers to you frae
the winda o' my gas-buggy. 'Boy Keith' I whispers,
and Mis' Chisholm you shore jumped, like you was
bit by a t'rant'ler—yeh!"

"What do you know of Keith, have you any
news?"

"Not a hull lot. 'Tis these rum-sharps I been
keepin' tabs on—these gangsters, y'ken."

"Just what d'you mean, Finlay?"

"Invite me inta yore wigwam, sir, and I'll wise
ya up muckle good and plenty."

Without another word, Wilbur Chisholm took out
his latchkey, opened the house door, closed it softly,
and beckoning Finlay to follow, led the way to his
library.

"Now," said he, switching on the lights and motioning his visitor to deep armchair, "sit down and let's
hear." But in that moment Hank Finlay crossed
swiftly to the door, opened it suddenly and without
a sound, closed it as silently, peeped behind the heavy
curtains into each window recess, glanced up keenly
at the gallery above and shook his head.

"Sir, I'm a body mebbe a wee suspeecious but 'tis
me nature."

"Sit down, Hank. Now tell me what brings you
in New York and what's all the mystery? Out with
it, man. And stop mistering me—I was Wilbur to
you and Jed in the old days and I am now."

"Why then, Wilbur, bend closer," said Finlay
leaning forward and whispering, "there's four sharps,

four slick ducks out for your wad! Man, it's gospel truth I'm tellin' ye, they mean tae hae your siller, it's a' framed up for 'em tae be awa' wi' it the nicht."

"So?" murmured Wilbur Chisholm smiling grimly at the grim head of Vespasian. "Robbery, eh? Are you sure?"

"As shootin', Wilbur."

"Then have a cigar. What more d'you know?"

"Plenty. F'instance, four days ago you wrote Derek Ryerson at his N'York ad-dress agreein' you'd hand over the million bucks he demands in the matter o' your boy Keith, didn't ya?"

"I did!" answered Chisholm a little defiantly.

"Yesterday you drew the mazuma, half of it, but then you gets a letter an-nonimous tellin' you as Ryerson was way off in England. That right?"

"Yes, but how do you know?"

"I wrote the letter, Wilb. So you jest nachurally held onta the dough." Here Finlay pointed sinewy finger at the satchel lying on the desk beside them. "But, oh man, why keep it layin' around 'stead o' cloppin' it back intae the bank, whateffer?"

"I forgot it. You see I . . . received a cable-gram——"

"Not from Jed?"

"No, from an agent I sent out there to—to keep track of . . . the boy. It was a short message, Hank, only these four words: 'Son injured. Fear seriously.' Well, old-timer, this just drove everything else out of my mind."

"Shore it would, Wilb. And I'm no blamin' ye."

"You see, Hank, it occurred to me that he might be . . . dead."

"Hell—no, Bud, not him! Keith hain't the kind as dies young. Hoot man, dinna fash! Keith's a'

richt the noo, I'm tellin' ye . . . ! Keith deid—
my grief, it'll no bear thinkin' on, whateffer!"

"No, Hank, it surely doesn't. And yet who knows,
he's injured, you see, and seriously, and this may
mean—oh well, that's why I forgot this cursed money."

"Aweel, aweel, there's these four stick-up birds
vera determined tae get awa' wi' it the nicht—ay,
to-night, Wilbur, and so——"

"They'll surely have to be pretty quick about it
then," said Wilbur, glancing at his watch, "because
in an hour I'm sailing for England."

"The hell y'are! What boat?"

"My yacht, *Albatross*, she's lying in the river off
Twenty-third street with steam up, at this minute."

"Good f'you! Does anyone know you're leavin'?"

"No one except Hedges, the captain. I only decided
to go this afternoon."

"And what," whispered Finlay, "what o' this
money?"

"Oh I'll hike it along."

"Then, Wilbur, the sooner you're safe on the water
the easier I'll be. Are ye heeled?"

"I don't carry any such hardware these days,
Hank."

"No gun? Losh man, I'm fair astonished at ye—
sic wild and waefu' recklessness is juist plumb ornery
foolishness! Will ye hae one o' mine?"

"No, no, I lost the knack. But see here, Hank'
I'm wondering if you'd care for a trip over with me."

"Eh? Me? To England? In a yacht? Gosh no!
And yet hold on, bide a wee—it's no sic a bad proposition. I'm pretty well through wi' the bunch over
hyar—what ain't been rounded-up and jailed. And
Ryerson's in England. So's Neeves, and . . . and
. . . not forgettin' Miss Olive, forbye——"

"She was the first cause of all the . . . trouble,
wasn't she, Hank?"

"I reckon."

"Do you think he . . . Keith—did it?"

"No, siree! An' we're a-goin' to prove it, you bet, Jed and me."

"Tell me how?" said Wilbur, with an eagerness he didn't trouble to conceal.

"Well, sir, Jed an' me 's been playin' some game wi' these yere short-horn sharps, him in England and me over here and—oh man, I'm juist sayin' it looks unco like we're agoin' to fill a top royal flush agin 'em—ay, it shore does, whateffer! Leastways the last hand'll be played out in England and Wilbur, I'm juist ditherin' tae be there. Ye see I hain't flashed a gun since I dunno when—and it may, yes, I'm riskin' a small stack as the end o' this game will call for gun-play."

"Not in England, Hank. Anyway, if you've a mind to come along I'll be mighty glad to have you."

"Say nae mair, Wilbur man, I'm sticking right with ya."

"Why, then," said Wilbur Chisholm, rising, "I guess we'll be starting."

CHAPTER XXXI

WHICH SUGGESTS TROUBLE AHEAD

DALLAS was whistling cheerily; his eye was quick and bright, his step firm and assured, himself all blithe, vigorous young manhood from neat spurred riding boots to neat, peaked cap; for the blasting shadow was lifted from him, and thus, as he strode Josepha-wards, he was himself again, indeed—thanks to her unshakeable faith and love, he knew himself for better man, in every sense, than he had ever been.

In one hand he bore a prodigious bunch of roses whose fragrance perfumed the sunny air all about him, hidden in the burberry across his arm, was a large box of chocolates, for his way to Josepha's thatched cottage led past the Misses Hardwickes' little villa and it had become his custom of late, to pause here for a chat with the sisters.

Coming in sight of the villa he espied Miss Rosamond, gauntletted to the somewhat osseous elbows and armed with vasty pair of shears, daintily snipping at wayward leaf and twig of the somewhat riotous hedge that formed a green barrier between tiny front garden and tarmacked highway.

Dallas waved his cap, Miss Rosamond smiled and nodded, snapped violently at an errant twig, missed it and depositing the very large shears upon small, rustic seat conveniently situate to afford unobstructed view of a very diminutive sundial, hasted to welcome her visitor.

"Dear me, Mr. Dallas," she exclaimed, removing the gauntlets, "how very smart you look to-day, positively—quite handsome—ah, my heart, and more painfully like—Him, than ever! Do sit down, sister will presently appear with the tea equipage, an early afternoon cup of tea is so refreshing! What beautiful roses! How sweetly fragrant! Oh, Mr. Dallas—for me?"

"If you'll please accept them with my very best, truest, affectionate gratitude and esteem!"

"Why, Mr. Dallas, how very gallant! And how reminiscent of an earlier and far, far better era, before short skirts, bobs and shingles—odious words—had reft from woman her dignity."

"Yes, but," ventured Dallas, "don't you think that modern dress is—well, healthier and more——"

"Shocking? Indeed I do. I declare the modern miss has no reticence in skirts or speech. Only this morning a pert young hoyden just unloaded upon the village, with several others, from one of those detested charabanc horrors, this young person, observing the modest length of my own draperies, had the effrontery to tell me that I but no matter! Such things are best forgot. But talking of skirts, Mr. Dallas, I grieve to say Josepha's are already far, far too brief, and I greatly fear, becoming ever more so! That last new costume she purchased see—when would it be? Yes, in April—was very decidedly too short—just below the knee, Mr. Dallas—so revealing!"

"But then, Miss Hardwicke, since it reveals such very beautifu——"

"Oh, Mr. Dallas, pray silence! Do not mention them. Limbs should ever be nameless—and forgotten. However, I felt called upon to voice a remonstrance to Josepha and—pray believe me—she positively snapped at me! Quite fiercely! So unusual in the dear girl. But then, she'd been weeping and——"

"Weeping?" exclaimed Dallas and was afoot instantly. "Great heavens—weeping—Josepha——"

"Gracious me, Keith Dallas, don't look so shocked and shaken, don't reel and stagger as beneath some fearful blow! A woman's tears are sometimes her solace, her comfort and blessed relief. I frequently indulge in tears, and am always better, calmer, more serene."

"But, Miss Rosamond, she—Josepha isn't the weeping sort—that is—I mean——"

"Sir, Josepha is by nature feminine, is she not?"

"Yes, thank heaven!"

"But why this fervour of gratitude? Ha, is it . . . can it be . . . is it possible . . . you—she . . . wedlock?"

"Yes," answered Dallas softly, " she has actually promised to . . . to be my wife. Sounds wonderful to say and seems too good to be true, but she has promised at last——"

"Oh, when—when is it to be?"

"In about a month, I guess."

"How positively thrilling!" exclaimed Miss Hardwicke, her sharp features beaming with a quick tenderness. "And how romantic! Dear Josepha—the artful, secretive minx, she never breathed a word of it to me! And when you've wed you'll still live at Lord Withymore's stables, I suppose? Such a charming old house yet so large for two young people!"

"It's much larger for one," smiled Dallas. "But——"

"And Mrs. Webb your housekeeper, such a good soul, you'll keep her on, of course?"

"I guess so. But what should make her cry?"

"Heavens! Don't tell me Martha Webb——"

"No no, I mean Josepha. Why in the world——?"

"Just because, being a woman, she felt like it of course. And now, if you'll excuse me, I'll just put

my beautiful roses into water—besides I would steal
them unto my chamber before sister Agnes sees them,
the dear thing might perhaps be a little jealous. But
pray don't go, tea will be out in a moment and I shall
be back directly."

So saying, Miss Rosamond hastening across the
tiny lawn, slipped in at the front door of the little
villa just as Miss Agnes appeared from the side door,
urging before her a wheeled table whereon, surrounded
by cups and saucers and snug beneath ornate cosy, stood
that most welcome object to English eyes, a tea-pot.

"Let me help," said Dallas, rising, whereat Miss
Agnes emitted a small scream:

"Gracious!" she ejaculated. "So sudden! No thank
you—oh no—don't trouble! Oh thank you, Mr.
Dallas! . . . Oh goodness me! Chocolates! Such
an enormous box! Oh dear! I really couldn't!
Such a vast quantity! Ah no . . . no really! Oh
dear, Mr. Dallas, how very good, how very, very kind
of you. But, oh dear! If you don't mind, I'll hide
them away in the arbour—if Rosa should see—she
might feel . . . well. . . . Oh you'll understand,
I'm sure."

"Miss Agnes, have you seen Josepha to-day?"

"Oh yes. We drove over and Felix got into a
ditch, he generally does—so provoking! It took
two men and a boy quite a time to get him out."

"How was she, Miss Agnes, how did she seem?"

"Dreadfully stupid and so very wilful—though
Felix is a male, at least I—oh dear me, I've always
thought so, but——"

"No, Miss Agnes, I meant——"

"Oh forgive me, how silly I am! Of course! So
sad! Josepha, I mean—she'd been crying."

"Are you sure? I wonder why?"

"Quite sure, her sweet eyes were so mournful.
She's in some trouble, I know she is, some hidden

grief, I'm sure—though she called it a headache, of course. . . . Why, Mr. Dallas, what . . . where . . . you're not going?"

"Forgive me—I must."

"And without one spot of tea! Oh dear, what will Rosa say?"

"Please make my excuses. I'll try and step in on my way back."

CHAPTER XXXII

IN WHICH TROUBLE DEVELOPES

AWAY strode Dallas faster than ever, but now he whistled no more.

He had just vaulted a stile beyond which lay the water-meadows when he espied the object of his anxious thoughts coming to meet him, and in that moment forgot all but her dear loveliness—the sweet, proud carriage of her head, the lithe, free grace of her every movement, her high-bred air . . . and her skirts were not a bit too short since they did, indeed, reveal only loveliness.

As they approached each other he scanned her face for any sign of grief or trouble but saw it gently serene as usual, only it seemed, she carried herself in fashion rather stately, perhaps.

"My own dear!" said he, reaching out eager hands, and would have kissed her, but flushing, she shook head at him reprovingly.

"Not here!" she murmured gently; and yet, yes to be sure, there was an indefinable air of stately aloofness about her, also she was silent and, moreover, kept her gaze studiously averted.

"Anything wrong?" he inquired, lightly, yet viewing her somewhat askance.

Josepha, glancing at the line of pollard willows bordering the stream, merely sighed.

"I've been kind of hoping," said he, "that you'd have been up to the stables since I took over. Everything's pretty fine. Besides I want you to see the house, look it over—considering it's going to be your home—soon, I hope, just as soon as you will, dear."

"It looks very large—from the outside!" said she.

"But it's mighty comfortable. And, Lord, Josepha, what a home you'll make it. When are you coming to take charge of it—and me? A month—three weeks!"

"Good heavens, no!"

"But, girl, since you're sure going to marry me soon, why not make it sooner? Why dally, with a house and husband waiting for you?"

"Talking of houses, Keith, I went to Lewes the other day and happened to meet Mr. Jessam."

"Tough luck!" murmured Dallas.

"So naturally I thanked him for not worrying me for his money—the interest of that mortgage on my old house, and—he simply stared at me like a fool."

"Naturally!" nodded Dallas.

"Then he told me the money had all been paid for me by a Mr. Friend."

"Oh?" said Dallas.

"Yes. I was so amazed that I blurted out that I didn't know anyone named Friend, and I don't think he believed me—but he showed me a letter!"

"Oh?" said Dallas again, and now, being very conscious of her scrutiny, glanced at the pollard-willows in his turn.

"A letter—yes!" she repeated, "a letter written on my behalf enclosing the whole Three hundred and fifty pounds and signed: A Friend."

"Oh?" said Dallas for the third time, his gaze still abstracted.

"Yes. It was in Lord Withymore's writing. And for goodness sake stop oh-ing!"

"Withymore's writing, eh?" quoth Dallas breezily. "Well now that's fine—good old George!"

"Fine?" cried Josepha in sudden anger. "How can you say so? Can't you see how utterly impossible it is?"

"Well . . . no!"

"Won't you see how beastly and altogether frightful it is for . . . for a girl to be so indebted to a—a man she has refused—frequently!"

"Frequently? Poor, old George, but I guess——"

"It wouldn't be so . . . so painfully humiliating if—if it had been done by—by any other blundering person."

"Wouldn't it, dear?"

"Of course not."

"Well, then—it isn't, dear."

"Isn't what?"

"So humiliating as you seem to think."

"You mean it wasn't George?"

"Why, no, it wasn't old George."

"No!" said she softly. "But I thought you were so frightfully hard-up."

"Me?" repeated Dallas, turning at last to stare at her.

"Of course. I suspected it was your doing all along."

"My heavens but you're clever!" said he with the utmost admiration.

"No! I'm indignant. I'm frightfully angry. I'm mortified. . . . And it was just like you to sign it 'a friend!' So silly!"

"Then you're not so bright!" he sighed. "No, not so clever, because that was old George's idea."

"And did you borrow the money from him?"

"No, dear, I—oh well. . . ."

"Tell me."

"I just won it."

"Playing cards?"

"Riding a horse."

"Ah!—you mean 'The Thunderbolt'! You mean you risked your life for that . . . that miserable, old ruin!"

"But you loved it, dear, and I just couldn't bear that you should lose it and——"

"Well, I have lost it."

"Good Lord! How?"

"Because it's yours now. You bought it with your money—your life almost, and you shall keep it."

"Sure I will—for you. It shall be a wedding-present which brings us back to the question of the hour—when will you marry me? Because, dear, now that I know myself innocent of——"

"That reminds me!" said Josepha, pausing beside a little bridge that spanned the stream. "There is another matter."

"What now, dear?" he inquired, glancing at her averted face with sudden, and growing apprehension.

"Do you know a girl called Olive Lemay?"

Dallas caught his breath, and, turning, stared down at the smooth flowing stream below.

"Olive . . . Lemay," he repeated slowly. "Why yes, but——"

"Was it for her you fought with the man Red Rory?"

"Well . . . yes, but only to——"

"You never told me."

"Didn't I?"

"You know you didn't. You never so much as mentioned her name. Why?"

"Well only because I didn't want to drag her into the miserable story, and then——"

"Why not?"

"Well, I . . . I was—yes, I guess I was afraid you might . . . misunderstand—as you are ready to do now, it seems."

"You would have been wiser to explain, instead of hiding it from me so very carefully. She was the real cause of all your trouble, wasn't she?"

"Oh I don't know. I was sure out hunting trouble just then. As for Olive, I only tried to . . . to protect her from a beast's brutality, as any man—her own brother might have done."

"But you weren't her brother!"

"What does that matter?"

"She's a very beautiful . . . a captivating person, isn't she?"

"Oh I guess so . . . in a way . . . some may think so, but I——"

"Dark or fair?"

"Eh?" he inquired, staring, "what do you——?"

"Is she a blonde or brunette?" demanded Josepha softly, but with expression of such extreme aloofness that he suddenly felt as if oceans and continents divided them.

"Dark . . . I think so!"

"Think!" said Josepha, and curled red lip at him.

"She's . . . yes, dark. But my . . . oh my dear," he stammered, "why . . . why bother about——"

"I hate dark women!" murmured Josepha, staring up at him beneath puckered brows. "And of course she was frightfully grateful and kissed you, or you her—or——"

"Great heavens, Josepha, what——"

"Did she? Did she?"

"But what . . . what in the name of——"

"Are you afraid to answer? Did she?"

"I . . . forget. Maybe . . . once or twice. But——"

"That means frightfully often. Yes—I know, I know—don't touch me!"

"Now for heaven's sake! Why are you trembling? And I swear you're wrong. Oh, my dear, why distress yourself so unnecessarily, why make all this troub——"

"You should have told me yourself! Why didn't you tell me? Why did you leave me to find it all out——"

"From Ryerson, damn him!"

"Well, it's the truth, isn't it?"

"No, it's only partly true. I——"

"It would be a hateful dark creature, of course!"

"Say now, Josepha . . . dear, try to have a little reason . . . let me explain!"

"You can't . . . explain . . . those—kisses!"

"But I can. Be fair and let me——"

"Fair?" she cried, a little wildly. "So I am— in every sense, and you go—kissing this dark creature!"

"Oh con-found it!" he exclaimed, also a little wildly, "you know I don't mean that! I'm only asking you to be a little just and let me——"

"You kissed her—you admitted it!"

"Well, what of it? That's all forgotten long ago. I never loved her and as for——"

"That makes it worse!"

"Won't you please," said he murmurous with desperation, "please allow me——"

"No!" said Josepha, her eyes very bright, her rounded chin so very nearly grim that now he felt the whole universe divided them.

"Girl," said he, between white teeth, "are you going to let this . . . this dog Ryerson come between us then, with his——"

"It isn't Mr. Ryerson, it's this—oh, this Olive woman."

"But this," said Dallas, glancing round about in

helpless fashion, "this is just sheer, absolute, dam nonsense——"

"Thank you!" sighed Josepha plaintively and, turning her back, moved away.

"You're not . . . not going?" he stammered, beginning to follow.

"And, please, I prefer to go alone."

"Oh surely," he answered, and taking off his cap, halted instantly. "Gee—whiz!" he exclaimed with the utmost bitterness. "And I came here dreaming of—our marriage, poor fool that I was!"

"Fool indeed!" she murmured, and so went from him, her head held high and never one backward glance. Once he made to follow her again, but checked the impulse and stood watching until, having crossed the sunny meadow, she vanished into the lane beyond; then, resting elbows on the coping of the bridge, and squared chin upon clenched fists, he scowled down at the placid, smooth-flowing waters.

"Oh hell!" he exclaimed savagely.

"That's wot they all say!" croaked a voice at his very feet, and out from beneath the arch of the little bridge came the dejected face of Tom Merry.

"What the devil d'you mean?" demanded Dallas angrily.

"No 'arm, sir, an' no offence. Only there never was no man as was so desprit in love as didn't and don't find 'isself cussin' 'isself for bein' sech a fool, sooner or later—it be only nat'ral."

"What, have you been listening?"

"Ar! I 'ad to—couldn't nowise 'elp. There was you and Miss Jo and 'ere was me under bridge awaitin' for ye to walk on an' you didn't walk on, so 'ere I stood and, 'aving y-ears, 'ow could I 'elp? Why nohow and——"

"Oh, hush up!" cried Dallas. "Get moving—leave me!"

I

"Well then, no offence, sir, but——"

"Oh all right—all right!"

"Well, sir, seein' you'm so crossed in love and all, I shouldn't go for to 'ang 'ereabouts if——"

"What d'you mean?"

"S'near the water, pretty deep it be—chap drowned 'isself 'ere once, yards o' rope onto 'im and eight flat-irons, my mistus uses one o' they irons to-day, reglar. So I shouldn't stay so near, sir, no—you might be tempted to drowndin' likewise, and that 'ud be a pity, praps."

"I'm not such a darn fool, Tom."

"Glad to 'ear it, sir, though I can't 'ardly bleeve it seein' as all men in love is fools else they'd never be in love!"

"I guess maybe that's right, too!" Dallas admitted.

"'Course it's right, sir! Not as I wunt agree as Miss Jo's a fine, 'andsome creetur—to look at—but Lord—wot's looks? Looks don't last, 'ere to-day an' gone t'morrer. And woman's been man's biggest trouble ever since Eve ate that theer apple, and well I knows it! For 'ere was me like me name once, so cheery and 'appy-'earted as I dunno wot, then a woman married me and—well, look at me now!"

"Yes, you're a dismal dog, Tom."

"So I am, sir, ar that I am—as a tumb-stone. That's woman, that is! So don't you go a-grievin' for Miss Jo, sir, it'll be all the same when you're both nice an' dead, and besides it wunt do no manner o' good to worrit."

"And that's true enough, Tom."

"'Course it is, sir. So you stick t'your 'osses."

"That's sure sound advice. I will, by George!"

"Ar, stick to your 'osses, sir, an' leave Miss Jo to tother fellow and you'll be——"

"Eh?" cried Dallas, starting, "What? What other fellow?"

"Why 'im as be arter 'er so constant an' keen as
mustard—the gen'leman as meets you over to th'
cottage, to'ther day——"

"What—Ryerson?"

"Ar—'im! And, sir, from wot my y-ears an' eyes
is a-tellin' me so constant, I'm betting any man a quart
as afore the moon changes she's off an' away wi' 'im—
'e be a fine-lookin' chap an' rich and she's only——"
The words ended in a choking gasp, as, pinning the
lugubrious speaker by the collar, Dallas shook him
to and fro. . . .

. . . Came the patter of little feet; small hands
that tugged desperately at his coat; a childish voice
that cried upon his name in terrified entreaty:

"Dal . . . Oh Dal, please . . . please don't . . .
that's our Tom . . .!"

The man staggered free, and Dallas, turning upon
the child, beholding the fear of him in her wide eyes,
felt abashed, and lifting her to his breast, cuddled
her there, bowing his face upon her bright curls.

"Oh, Dal!" sighed the Small Personage, reproach-
fully, "I didn't think you could be so triffickly awful!"

"There, there, Honey!" he murmured soothingly.
"Forgive me . . . kiss me."

"Well, please let me look at your face first, Dal,
'cause it looked so fright-flee fierce and frocious, you
know." So Dallas raised his head obediently and,
looking into these grave, eagerly-questioning eyes,
smiled to reassure her, his quick, boyish smile. Then,
smiling also, she nodded, clasped soft arms about
his neck and kissed him; in which moment of forgiveness a doleful voice spoke:

"Mr. Dallis, sir, I never meant no offence, sir, no.
Nor I wudn't speak no 'arm agin—'er, for nothin nor
nobody, sir, strike me deaf, dumb an' blind!"

"All right," growled Dallas. "All right. Get on
your way—be off."

"Oh no—no!" cried the Small Personage imperiously. "Wait a minute, Tom!" Then nestling to Dallas, her rosy lips tickling his ear, she whispered: "Please, Dal, I like our Tom, so won't you be a teeny bit p'lite to him and say—'excuse you'—jest to please me?"

"Why surely, Hon. Tom, excuse me. I'm sorry if I was rough, but I thought—well, I guess you know what I thought."

"Ar," sighed Tom mournfully, "but you was almighty, everlasting wrong, sir. I couldn't speak no disrespeck of—'er, an' I never would, dog bite me—for ever and ever, amen, sir!"

"Right ho, Tom—shake hands. And here—take this and go and drink—her health at the first opportunity."

So Tom shook hands, pocketed the coin, moaned his thanks, and trudged dejectedly on his way.

CHAPTER XXXIII

INTRODUCING A LADY

"Aren't you going to put me down, Dal?"

"Surely!" he answered and having kissed her again, did as she suggested.

"Please," said she, smoothing her brief petticoats so soon as her small shoes touched earth, "please do you love me as much as you did long ago?"

"More, Honey girl, much more."

"Well, I don't seem to see you so much, and when I do you're with my Jo."

"But you've got Uncle Jed now, Hon, and old George."

"Yes, I know, but I didn't find them for my husband—and George is always going away and Uncle Jed's a bit old, 'sides I'd rather do without a beard, that's why I'm growing myself up for you so fast as ever I can. Only you must wait for me, Dal, it would be so triffickly awful if I growed myself into a lovely lady and—no husbant. So you won't go marrying without me, will you, Dal?"

"No," he sighed, "if ever I marry, you shall be there, Honey. But I begin to think I'll die an old bachelor."

"Oh but do old bachelors all have to die?"

"Well yes, but——"

"Then why be an old bachelor and die? Why not marry an' live happy ever after?"

"God bless you, Honey!" said he stooping to kiss her very tenderly. "I'd just love to, only I guess I'm not that sort."

"Now that's exac'ly what Sarah said to Mr. Neeves yesterday evening out of the kitchen window."

"Mr. Neeves?" repeated Dallas, frowning. "Was he there yesterday?"

"Oh yes, he often is, he drives Mr. Ryerson's car, only I don't think I like him much 'cause he's got such funny eyes—all washed-out, you know, like my old blue frock an' eye-lashes just like Mrs. Stacy's pig's eye-lashes—short an' white an' stiff, you know. And our Sarah was triffickly angry with him an' said: 'I'm not that sort,' she said 'and if you come any more of it, I know a man as'll tell you so with both fist-es,' she said. And you know, Dal, I've told her lots of times, it's fists an' not fist-es. And she will 'sist on saying ghostesses for ghosts!"

"And what said Mr. Neeves, Hon?"

"Oh, he said: 'Hello cutie!' 'cause he saw me watching—he's got awful quick eyes. So then I just said gol-darn him, and walked away."

Dallas chuckled, yet they had not gone a dozen yards before he was sighing, his gloomy gaze on the distance, forgetful of the bright eyes that watched him.

"Aren't you quite happy, Dal?"

"Well, no—not quite, Honey."

"But the sun's nice and sunny an' I'm here, an' the dear, old Giant's over there watching over you 'cause he's your friend now as well as mine, an' he doesn't like his friends to be sad. That's what I told my Jo yesterday when I found her crying into the duck's food."

"Was she, Hon?"

"Oh yes. I saw a great, big tear roll right down her nose an' fall slap into the pan with the duck's food in it."

"I hope you tried to comfort her, Honey."

"'Course I did. I said 'hell's-bells' like Uncle Jed does and then she tried to frown an' laughed an' choked and so I kissed her like you did the other evenin, saying good night at the gate an' I was peeping out of my bedroom window. An' you know, Dal, I don't think it was quite nice of you to kiss my Jo 'cause Jo says nice, gentlemanly men never kiss ladies unless they mean to marry them, an' you can't marry my Jo, you know, and me growing myself up for you— now can you?"

"No—it seems not!" he sighed.

"Well then, why did you, Dal?"

"Oh, I guess, just because she happened to be your Jo, dear. But where are you taking me?"

"Home to tea, of course."

"Say now, Hon, why not come to tea with me at my home? I'll show you the horses and——"

"Ooh! How spiffing!" cried the Small Personage, dancing for very joy. "But I'll have to go an' tell my Jo else she'll only worry an' worry."

"That's all right, Honey. I'll send one of the stablemen."

So, hand in hand, they went, across sunny meadow and by shady path, the child and the man; and, hearkening to her merry chatter, looking into her joyous eyes, the sun seemed brighter, the world a better place to him by reason of this pure, childish presence, so that, little by little, his sombre thoughts lightened, he smiled, laughed and soon was chatting merrily as she.

Thus Dallas went his way, little dreaming (as indeed how should he?) the strange trick Destiny was to play him.

Reaching the wide stable-yard, a place as clean, as neat and orderly as twelve pairs of hands could make it, they beheld Ben Lomax, seated in shady corner, busied upon some mysterious operation to a light, racing-saddle, but who, espying them, rose respectfully, albeit gloomy of visage, and touched his cap to them.

"Oh, Ben, just ride over to the cottage," said Dallas, "and tell Miss Josepha—or Sarah, that Miss Patience has been good enough to come and pour out a lonely bachelor's tea for him."

"Ooh—Dal! Can I pour out?"

"You surely can, Hon. . . . And Ben, cheer up old sport, I guess you'll find, maybe, a kinder welcome than you expect. . . . Come on, Hon. Come and see my new home."

In the hall there met them a rosy-faced, motherly person who rustled pleasantly—who wore an old-fashioned lace-cap and who curtseyed.

"Your tea will be ready in a few minutes, sir," said she, smiling at the Personage.

"Thank you, Mrs. Webb. Please tell Martin to let me know when the horses are in from the gallop."

"Yes, sir," beamed Mrs. Webb and, having greeted the Small Personage like the old acquaintance she was, rustled pleasantly away about her household duties.

"Is this your home now, Dal—all this?" inquired the Personage, laying by her hat and glancing, round-eyed, about the spacious sunny room with French windows that opened upon a wide terrace.

"Yes, Honey."

"Is it all your very own?"

"No, it all belongs to old George."

"I 'spose he's triffickly rich isn't he, Dal?"

"Yes, I believe he is."

"Why then if I hadn't found you, I'd have choose i him for a husband 'cause he's so fright-flee nice an always looks so—so clean!"

"And that's surely gospel-true, Honey."

"Is he living here with you, Dal?"

"Oh no, only now and then. You see he's got bags of other houses—castles and halls and things all over the place."

"Ooh—how spiffingly fine! And does he live in them all—I mean one after another?"

"I guess he does, though he's mostly in London. He's there now. . . . And here's the tea! Thank you, Mrs. Webb. You needn't bother about us, we'll wait on ourselves."

And now—with what an air the Small Personage seated herself before the tea-tray! With what tremulous joy she addressed herself to the serious business of—pouring out! First the milk, then the sugar, lastly (eyes wide and very grave, silky brows contracted, small hands somewhat quivery) the tea. And Dallas, seated beside her, watched it all with such smiling yet profound attention that he saw nothing of the shape leaning in at the open window—a slim, comely figure dressed, from coquettish hat to dainty shoe, with that super-elegance that seems an attribute of modern American womanhood—a pale, beautiful face, dark-eyed, black-haired, a face just now rather sad and very wistful.

"'Fraid I've made yours a bit too full, Dal," said the Small Personage anxiously, "so please mind you don't slop it."

"Never fear, Honey!" he answered, reaching out for the brimming teacup; and then from the window a soft, caressing voice spoke:

"Well now say—if that isn't just the cutest picture!"

And Dallas slopped his tea, after all, as, starting round, he rose hastily to his feet, staring at the speaker in blank amazement.

"Olive!" said he in shaken voice. "Olive . . . Lemay!"

CHAPTER XXXIV

WHICH IS A CHAPTER OF CONTRASTS

"You're right both times, Keith. I'm Olive and I'm still Lemay," said she in her soft, husky voice. "But you're not so wild with joy as I could wish. Aren't you even going to ask me in?"

"Why yes—yes surely . . . but you were a bit sudden, unexpected as usual and . . . have some tea."

"I'm just dying for a cup!" she answered crossing the wide room with graceful, gliding, close-kneed walk. "But won't you please introduce me to your li'l lady friend?"

"Of course," said Dallas, ringing the bell with unnecessary violence, "this is little Patience Dare— Honey, this is . . . Miss Olive Lemay . . . Oh Kitty," said he, turning to the trim servant maid who answered the bell, "another cup and saucer, please."

Olive Lemay had drawn off her gloves and now reached out a slim, delicately-manicured hand to touch the Small Person's bright hair, a touch so light that it seemed almost timid, while her great, dark eyes became more sadly wistful than ever.

"How old are you, child?" she inquired gently.

"Oh, I'm almost nine an' getting growder-up every minute, as fast as ever I can."

"Almost nine!" murmured Olive, bending above that bright head. "If only I were—almost nine!"

"And now, please, may I pour you some tea," quoth the Small Personage reaching eagerly towards the pot.

"Thanks, dear . . . but . . . say, girlie, will you, . . . would you kiss me first—just once?"

The Small Personage glanced up at the beautiful face bent above her, the delicate features, great, pleading eyes, the quiver of full-lipped, ruddy mouth and, lifting small fist that chanced to be grasping the sugar-tongs, drew this so wistful stranger down to be kissed.

"There!" she nodded. "And so now please how many lumps of sugar?"

"Just one, dearest," and sitting down, rounded elbows on table and chin on hands, Olive devoted all her attention to their small hostess; thus Dallas, burning to ask so many vital questions, asked none, while the child who had seen so little of life, and the woman who had seen so much, talked and laughed together in strange good-fellowship—yet always in the woman's eyes that same expression of wistful sadness.

"Olive," quoth the Small Personage, "I do like the way you laugh."

"Do you, dearie?"

"Yes, it's so soft an' coo-cy. Only I wish you'd look happier. I think you must be in love—are you?" Olive's beautiful eyes opened wider, her slender fingers clenched suddenly.

"For . . . heavens . . . sake!" she murmured in gentle astonishment, "what makes you think that of me?"

"Well—you, you know. But please drink your tea before it's cold."

"But, li'l honey girl, what do you know about love?"

"Lots!" nodded the small Personage solemnly. "Heaps! Our Sarah's in love an' knows all about it an' tells me. She says any woman as loves a man's always miserable, an deserves it for not loving summat

better. . . . Oh Dal, poor Olive hasn't got a scrap
to eat yet."

"Eh?" exclaimed Dallas, starting. "By George,
no! I beg pardon, Olive! Cake? Jam? Bread and
butter?"

"And please pass her cup, Dal, it's nearly empty
an' I've plenty in the pot."

"That's right, Hon, get busy. We must look after
our guest." And, now seeing the child quite engrossed
with the business of milk-jug, sugar-basin and tea-
pot, he leaned nearer and spoke to the woman:

"Olive I . . . it's good to see you again."

"Is it?" she questioned, softly.

"Why surely! I . . . I want . . . are you staying over here long?"

"It all depends, Keith."

"On what?"

"Can't you guess?"

"No."

"Well, make a try."

"Have you . . . seen Ryerson yet?"

"No."

"Do you intend to?"

"Not if I'm lucky."

"Why not?"

"It all depends."

"You're not afraid of him, are you?"

"Not yet."

"Olive, just why did you come to England, anyway?"

"Can't you guess?"

Dallas picked up his tea-spoon, looked at it, put
it down and asked the question he had been leading
up to:

"I think . . . I hope I can. Is it because you
know the truth of . . . what happened to Rory
M'Guire? You do, don't you?"

"Yes, I know."

"And now because you are my friend, will you tell me the fact of it . . . good or bad? Will you?"

"I was always your friend, Keith," she murmured, leaning towards him in turn. "Yes, always that and . . . more if you'd wished." Here Dallas shrank a little and glancing instinctively towards the Small Personage saw she was holding forth her plate to him.

"What is it, Hon?" he inquired, glad of the diversion.

"Well, I've ate three pieces of bread'n'butter, but no toast, Dal, an' not a scrinch of cake! So cake now, please, an' please pass Olive's tea—and why doesn't she eat something? An' you haven't drank a spot of your tea——"

"Here goes, then!" nodded Dallas and emptied his cup at a draught. "I'll have some more if you please, mam."

"Have you known each other long?" inquired Olive glancing from man to child.

"Fairly," answered the man.

"Ages an' ages!" nodded the child. "I went out one day, Olive, long—long ago and found him for a husband. Oh please, Dal, now I've dropped the sugar-tongs—gol darn it!" Olive stared and broke out into her soft, rippling laughter.

"Oh, girlie," said she, leaning to kiss the small speaker. "Did Keith teach you 'gol darn'?"

"No, that was Uncle Jed, he says 'hell's bells' too an' lots o' funny things."

"Are there any more at home like you, dearie? I mean sisters?"

"Only one and she's growed up and——"

"Here are the sugar-tongs!" said Dallas rather hastily.

"Only one sister?" repeated Olive, gently. "And grown up, is she?"

"Yes, an' her name's Jo and——"

"Three lumps of sugar for me, please!" Dallas admonished, somewhat impressively.

"And is she cute and pretty like you, Honey girl?" inquired Olive.

"Oh lots and lots prettier than me."

"No! Is she so, Honey? Tell me what's she like," persisted Olive, while Dallas leaning back in his chair, stared resignedly out of the window, albeit he fumbled restlessly with his teaspoon. "Is she anything like me?" continued Olive, glancing swiftly at Dallas's averted face.

"Oh no, not a bit only she's as tall. But her hair's gold, almost carroty only nicer, and she hasn't such spiffing clothes or shoes or hands as you."

"But she's mighty pretty, eh girlie?"

"Well—yes, I think so—so does George, that's Lord Withymore, you know, an' wanted to marry her, an' I saw Dal kiss her once, so he thinks so too —don't you, Dal?"

"Yes," answered Dallas, still gazing at the trees swaying gently beyond the open window, "I think she's just the loveliest thing that ever happened."

Here fell an interlude of silence, for the Small Personage was much occupied with cake, Dallas appeared quite lost in contemplation of those rustling trees, while Olive, head a little bowed, was gazing down into her teacup, thus her long, silky lashes drooping upon rounded cheek, quite hid the expression of her eyes, yet every supple line and curve of her shapely form was eloquent . . . in her sudden, breathless immobility was something almost terrible.

So by reason of cake, trees and a teacup ensued a silence that, to Dallas at least, grew more and more irksome, being pregnant of so very much; and when it had endured some while the Small Personage sighed deeply and spoke:

" 'Fraid I'm eating quite too much cake!"

"Then go easy, Hon!" said Dallas, sighing as with sudden relief.

"Why then, please, can I pour somebody another cup of tea—I do so love pouring out tea!"

"Then bless your little heart, so you shall!" cried Olive gently, and now her cheeks were flushed, her eyes strangely bright. "Give me some more, dearest, and Keith shall have more too."

But at this juncture, knuckles sounded on the door, a grizzled head projected itself into the room only to vanish again instantly and a hoarse voice was heard to say:

"Th' 'osses is in, sir."

"Good!" exclaimed Dallas, rising forthwith. "We'll be right along, Martin."

"Ooh!" cried the Personage, setting down tea-pot with a clatter. "Let's go, Dal—now!"

"Won't you take me with you, girlie? May I come too?" said Olive so pleadingly that the Person, turning in the doorway, came running back to nod and smile and clasp her hand.

"Yes, a course!" she laughed. "I love horses, don't you? So come along, Olive. I'll take care of you."

So forth went they all three, across terrace and paddock, to the stables, where horses stamped and snorted, tossed shapely heads, backed and sidled, while grooms hissed and rubbed, cried "so ho now," and "stand over"—and all was cheery stir and bustle, to the Small Person's keen delight. They watched the beautiful animals watered, fed and littered down; they visited the saddle room, with its neat rows of gleaming stirrups and bits, they peered into mysterious corners, they sniffed the spicy fragrant air. And who so bright, so gay, so full of gracious and gentle inquiry as this handsome, elegant American lady whom divers of these shy-smiling young jockeys and grooms were to remember and speak of in time to come.

"Think I'd better go now," said the Small Personage at last, sighing regretfully for evening had begun to fall. "But oh Dal it's all been so triffickly lovely, so you'll let me come to tea again—soon?"

"As often as you will, Honey."

"Why then, please take me home."

"Yes, dear, but—our other guest?" Here, being at a loss he turned to Olive who, sinking upon her knees to settle the Small Person's hat with deft hands, answered without glancing up:

"Don't worry about me, Keith. I'll just stay around here a while."

"Good!" he nodded. "That's fine! Ask Mrs. Webb for anything you happen to want. I shan't be long. Come on, Hon."

CHAPTER XXXV

WHEREIN A QUESTION IS ASKED

"So Olive, it seemed, had indeed seen the fatal shot fired and knew the facts of that ghastly night! Then in a little while he would know—ah, but what?" This was the question that plagued him, for now, as he sped homewards through the gathering dusk, giving little thought to the woman but much to the news she bore, Hope like a kindly angel went beside him, only to pale little by little, and vanish before the demon of sickening Doubt, a demon that was at his elbow as he reached the terrace, as he stepped into the room—then his senses were smitten by the heavy scent of Turkish tobacco, a smell that whirled him back in thought to New York . . . days and nights of reckless folly all leading up to, and culminating in, that one fatal evening.

"Why Keith Chisholm—for heaven's sake! Don't look so terribly scared—I'm no ghost—yet!" said Olive, looking up at him through the blue wreaths of her cigarette. She wore a dainty silken wrap, and was throned upon the broad chesterfield, combing her black curls by the aid of a small hand-mirror.

"My land!" she exclaimed. "Why such gawping amaze?"

"Because I am—rather amazed."

"Oh why?"

"Well that . . . that robe——"

"This? Don't you like it?"

267

"But how . . . where on earth?"

"Out of my suit-case."

"But you hadn't one."

"Yes. I left it outside on the stoop. But please shut the window and come and talk. I'm off to bed in half an hour."

"Bed?" he echoed. "You mean . . . you're staying the night?"

"Surely—unless you throw me out."

"But . . . does Mrs. Webb know?"

"If you mean the early-English exhibit in bombazine and mob-cap—yes. It's all fixed, she's given me the gable-room—furthest from yours."

"Mine?" repeated Dallas. "But how——"

"I peered and pried and poked around in all the rooms, just naturally gave them the once-over until I found yours—clothes all around. So I tidied it some and left a kiss for you on the pillow. . . . Oh, Keith boy—you can still blush! Now make yourself at home—sit down—smoke, drink, do anything only be sociable and talk to me."

"Why, yes," said Dallas, sinking into the nearest lounge-chair and viewing the speaker's vivid beauty with eyes a little troubled, "let's talk, tell me just how Red Rory was—put out."

"No, Keith, let's not talk of that beast to-night."

"But, Olive, I must. See here, girl, when I left New York I was sure, from what Ryerson told me, that I had killed Rory—murdered an unarmed man! But lately I've known better—to-day I'm almost certain of my innocence, and now it only needs you to tell me so and my last doubt will be gone!"

"Why me, Keith?"

"Because you've always been straight and good. Because you're my friend—I hope."

"Yes, I've gone straight," she answered with slow nod, "it's been mighty hard sometimes, but I did

it because there's—there was—just one thing made
it worth while . . . just one thing, Keith, and I
guess you know what!"

Here Dallas took out his battered briar pipe and
began loading it rather clumsily.

"Yes," she repeated, "I guess you know."

"And that's why," said he, without glancing up,
"I'll just have to believe whatever you say, whatever
you tell me goes because you are Olive and I know
you couldn't lie to me—about this."

"What do you want me to tell you?"

"If I really shot Rory—yes or no. I don't ask who
fired the shot, all I want you to say is—if it was my work."

"Keith," she murmured, "I'd say—I'd swear to most
anything to please you."

"I want only the truth. You saw him killed?"

"Yes, Keith."

"You know who fired the shot?"

"Yes, Keith."

"Well, I just want the truth of it."

"No!" she retorted. "I guess what you really want
is for me to swear you didn't do it."

"God knows I do!" he exclaimed vehemently. "But
only if it's the truth."

"And she's not a bit like me—your Jo—eh, Keith?"

"No!" he answered, somewhat perturbed by the
sudden question. "But I'm not asking you about——"

"No, she wouldn't be like me. She's the real thing,
I guess . . . quite the English lady . . . regular,
sure-enough high-bred dame, eh, Keith?"

Dallas reached for a match-box and frowned at it.

"Let's talk of Red Rory and——"

"It's a queer name—Jo, but kind of cute. What's
it mean exactly?"

"Josepha. But I want you to answer me——"

"Keith, I'm just wondering what she'll think of me."

"How d'you mean?" he inquired, a little sharply.

"Well, you're surely going to introduce me, aren't you?"

"Am I?"

"Why yes. I'd rather meet her—through you."

"Well anyway just now I want you to talk of Red Rory—to tell me——"

"Not a thing, Kay."

"You mean you won't say just——"

"No!"

Here Dallas lit his pipe and smoked a while in frowning perplexity, what time Olive studied her reflection in the mirror again.

"But," he inquired at last, "didn't you come from New York to tell me the——"

"No!"

"Then, dash it all, why did you come here?"

"My, my!" she sighed, "aren't you growing English, by Jove! And since you want to know, though I guess you do know or should know, I came to this country just to be nearer you, because I've hoped you might have gotten, maybe, to like me enough to let me stay around and——"

"Olive . . . my dear girl," said he greatly troubled, "you know——"

"Yes . . . yes I know it was only just a fool pipe-dream—but some of us, I guess, couldn't live without our dreams! Anyway I'm awake now all right. . . . And you've fallen at last, Mr. Iceberg! And—for a blonde! It takes red hair to melt you, it seems—and look at mine, will you! Oh well, I was never lucky. But—a blonde! So I just naturally want to look her over."

"And you won't answer my question about Rory and——"

"Sure I'll answer it—when I've met her! Say now, Keith, how d'you like being in love? Is it all candy and violets . . . roses red and white—I wonder? Mine's so bitter—well I'll tell the world! But I drank it all the same. And my roses all withered and left only the thorns, but I wear them next my heart still, and always shall . . . and if my heart bleeds, nobody sees or cares—I don't—much, a bit hardened, I guess —so what's it matter? But a blonde! Oh, well, I guess blondes can love—in a blonde sort of way! She'd be sure to hate my black fuzz—yes she'll detest me right away—just like that!" Here a slim finger and thumb snapped sharply. "And she'll hate me because —she'll know. . . . Oh all right, Mr. Volcano, I'll close up and beat it in a jiff. I'm hitting the hay right now . . . you never liked slang, did you Keithy? I guess she doesn't know the meaning of the word— surely not! But, say kid, did you wise her up, put her next—did you tell her about you and—Rory?"

"Of course!"

"Well, and then what?"

"She doesn't believe."

"Did you tell her about . . . me?"

"There was nothing to tell."

"Surely not, Mr. Grundy! But does she know I'm alive?"

"Ryerson told her that much."

"What! Is Derek nosing around? Say, Keith, do you surely love her, honest to goodness, really and truly?"

"Ryerson's going to behave!" muttered Dallas.

"Or else," she murmured, glancing at his fierce-clenching hands, "you'll send him the same road as Rory——"

Even as she spoke, Dallas was out of his chair, had stooped and caught her rounded arms and was peering down into the fathomless deeps of those strange, dark eyes.

"Olive," said he, breathlessly, "for God's sake . . . what are you suggesting . . .? Do you mean I did shoot M'Guire? Do you . . . do you?"

Leaning back in his grasp Olive sighed, shivered and closed her eyes.

"Speak . . . speak!" he urged, his grasp tightening. "Tell me! Say something——!"

"Oh, Keith," she whispered, red lips curving to very tender smile. "I sure just love you to hold me so!"

Loosing her suddenly, Dallas recoiled and, turning, frowned down at the empty fireplace, yet when he spoke his voice was soft and kindly.

"Don't you think it might be a bright idea to get a little shut-eye?" Olive laughed a little drearily.

"Oh all right, if that's how I make you feel!" she nodded and yawned at him behind white finger. "I'll go right now Mr. Chisholm, if you'll please to show me how to get there."

So upstairs they went, and reaching the door of that room Mrs. Webb had hastily prepared for her, she smiled and gave him her hand.

"Good-night, Keithy boy!" she murmured. "Sweet dreams!"

Shut within his own room Dallas sat down, eased off his boots and swore; then, crossing to the open window, stared out upon the cool, fragrant night in troubled perplexity.

At last, prompted by sudden impulse, he caught up a pair of shoes, opened the door, switched off the light and creeping with the utmost care, stole silently downstairs; with the same elaborate caution he opened a window and stepped out upon the terrace. Here he donned his shoes and had tip-toed perhaps four paces when he was startled by a soft ripple of laughter in the air above and, glancing up, saw Olive looking down at him from her casement.

"Poor boy!" she murmured. "Am I driving you from hearth and home? What a shame . . .! Oh big coward to run away!"

"Good night, my dear!" said Dallas and strode off stablewards, but the ripple of her soft mocking laughter went with him.

CHAPTER XXXVI

CONCERNETH THE DARK AND THE FAIR

JOSEPHA was uncomfortably hot, rather breathless, somewhat dishevelled and extremely thirsty, for the afternoon was warm and she had been digging; thus, ceasing her labour, she leaned upon the five-pronged fork she had been using, and hailed the kitchen:

"Sarah! Sarah, is it tea-time yet?"

"'Land of hope and glory . . . '" sang Sarah, full-throated and quite deafened by her vocal efforts.

"Oh dash it!" panted Josepha, drooping upon her fork, and hailed, thereafter, louder than ever until forth of kitchen lattice popped Sarah's comely face and Sarah's mellow voice hailed in answer:

" Yes, Miss Jo—what now, 'm?"

"Blow you, Sarah, how you sing! You sing and sing while I——"

"Yes, Miss Jo, when I sings I sings. You'll mind as my old feyther be a songster too——"

"Well, is tea ready yet?"

"No, miss, it beant nowise time for it."

"Well make it now! At once! I'm simply parched with thirst."

"And no wonder, miss—such diggin'! Why not leave it to that Tom Merry as be——"

"Tea, Sarah! Tea—at once!"

"Very well, Miss Josepha, mam. Kittle be on the b'ile."

"Bring me a cup out here," said Josepha, and went back to her digging. But she had not turned a foot of soil when a strangely soft, husky voice spoke behind her:

"Good afternoon."

Turning hastily, Josepha beheld an arresting vision —an elegant, shapely creature, deliciously cool who smiled at overheated, dishevelled Josepha and looked at her with long-lashed, wistful eyes.

"I'm Olive Lemay," said the vision in tone wistful as her look—and Josepha instantly frowned. For this vision besides being Olive, a brunette, perfectly attired, and so aggravatingly cool—was even more beautiful than Josepha had dreamed. Thus and therefore Josepha frowned; and now, leaning upon her fork, she shook the damp, red-gold curls from perspiring forehead and elevating her dark brows with expression slightly supercilious and wholly well-bred, murmured:

"Oh, really?"

"Yes," said the visitor gently. "I'm Olive."

And so was silence while eyes of blue gazed steadfastly and with scarce-veiled hostility into eyes of velvety blackness that seemed more wistful than ever.

"Indeed?" quoth Josepha, and though her brow was still moist and cheeks and self so distressingly hot, she contrived to sound frigidly cold, perishingly bleak, and astoundingly icy. "Indeed? You are a friend of Mr. Ryerson's, I think?"

"No, of Keith's," sighed Olive in soft answer.

"Then I'm afraid you won't find him . . . your friend, Mr. Chisholm . . . here."

"No. But he's coming. He'll be right along, I guess. I left word he'd find me here."

"Very thoughtful of you. But I'm not receiving visitors to-day, I'm too frightfully busy." So saying,

Josepha turned and grasped the fork again, but in that moment a cool, slender hand touched hers and a soft voice spoke in accents almost humble and pleading:

"Say now, Miss Josepha, please don't freeze me up like that, won't you be just a li'l kind to me? Maybe I'm a whole lot better than I seem."

So Josepha, loosing the fork, turned round again and again eyes of blue questioned eyes of black.

"Would you like a cup of tea?" said Josepha suddenly.

"Well say now, I'd just love it."

"Come then, we'll have it in the orchard. Though, heavens, I'm not fit to entertain a guest—look at me!"

"I sure am!" said Olive, gravely. "And I never thought blonde hair could be so beautiful . . . all cute and crinkly."

Behind the cottage was a small grass plot shaded by aged, nobbly fruit trees, where stood rustic seats and a table.

"This," said Josepha, motioning her guest to be seated, "is my orchard, five apple-trees, a plum and two pears the apples are quite good, so are the pears but the plum generally refuses to plum, still he's old and nice and shady—and thank goodness I can hear the tea-things!"

"I guess you've heard of me from your li'l sister, haven't you?" inquired Olive sinking gracefully upon one end of the rustic bench while Josepha flopped down upon the other.

"Oh yes," she nodded, shaking earth from her frock. "Patience mentioned you."

"Bless her li'l heart! Is she around?"

"No, she's away shopping in Lewes with Uncle Jed. . . . Glory—here comes tea! We shall want more bread and butter, Sarah, and cakes and things."

"Yes, Miss Jo, sure-ly!" answered Sarah, setting down the tray and eyeing their visitor furtively the while, who, meeting this sharp scrutiny, smiled— whereupon Sarah flushed, bobbed a curtsey and sped away indoors.

"Milk and sugar?" inquired Josepha.

"Thanks. Your li'l sister poured my tea yester- day."

"So I understand!" said Josepha, gulping her own tea thirstily.

"Quite some home Keith's gotten there," murmured Olive, sipping hers daintily.

"So I believe" nodded Josepha, refilling her cup while Olive watched her beneath languorous-drooping lashes.

"I guess you've been there often?"

"Oh no," answered Josepha lightly. "Do I under- stand you expect him . . . Mr. Chisholm, to—follow you here—to tea?"

"Well, I left a note telling him I was coming to see you."

"A note? At his house?"

"On his desk."

"Oh? Really?" murmured Josepha glancing quickly at the speaker who chanced, just then, to be gazing dreamily at the cottage.

"You've gotten a mighty pretty home here, Miss Josepha!"

"It's cosy enough," said Josepha absently.

"I guess you're one of the happy ones."

"Do you?" said Josepha, folding a piece of bread and butter rather violently and frowning at it.

"You sure ought to be."

"Indeed!" said Josepha and bit into her bread and butter with snapping, white teeth.

"With such a home and sweet, li'l sister . . . with friends all about you. . . . Never to be lonely, never to be afraid . . . or hate yourself, or—want what you can never have . . . yes, you ought to be mighty happy."

Josepha merely raised her eyebrows and sipped her tea.

"Say now, tell me," murmured Olive, "just why don't you like me?"

Setting down her cup Josepha glanced at the beautiful speaker, the shapely figure and exquisite attire and shook her head.

"Miss Lemay," she answered. "I don't know you well enough to dislike you."

"And you don't want to know me, I guess."

"Let me give you some more tea."

"No thanks! We sure live in different worlds, you and I."

"That is quite evident," nodded Josepha.

"Yes! And yours is a better, kinder world than mine."

"We make our own worlds, don't we?"

"No!" answered Olive, her dark eyes smouldering. "No,—the world makes us what we are. Look at me. I've always wanted the simple life—a li'l farm and some quiet corner like this, and me in a gingham gown shooing chickens——"

"Instead of which you live in cities and—dress like a princess!" added Josepha. "Are you visiting . . . staying in the neighbourhood?"

"Why yes."

"Where?"

"With Keith. He put me up last night."

"Good of him!" said Josepha, smiling brightly. "You and he are quite old friends, I understand."

"Yes," answered Olive, smiling also. "He told you about me, did he then?"

"Not a word. Mr. Ryerson did."

"Derek? Just what did he say?"

"Oh—well . . . does it matter?"

"Not a whole lot, but I'd like to hear."

"He said that you and Ke—Mr. Chisholm were . . . had been . . . he insinuated that you were rather intimate . . . lovers, in fact."

"He would!" murmured Olive, glancing towards a certain shady corner of the tall, thick hedge. "Say now, what d'you think of Derek, anyway?"

"I seldom do think of him."

"No?"

"No!"

"Well do you trust him?"

"I've no reason to do otherwise."

"I mean—do you swallow all he feeds you or are you hep?"

"Hep?" inquired Josepha, and up went her eyebrows again.

"Are you wise to him being just a smarmy liar?"

"Really!" murmured Josepha, opening her blue eyes rather wide.

"Do I shock you—vurry much?" inquired Olive, half-closing her black eyes as she spoke.

"Oh no, but I'm afraid you're a little beyond me. The word 'smarmy' means what?"

"Smooth's another word for it. Oh, Derek's smooth all right, but he can be mighty rough, too! And say, he's a whale for blondes—eats 'em alive, pretty well. And sister, when Derek has a girl set, she's just got to kiss and be friends or sure go some, if she won't."

"He sounds quite interesting," murmured Josepha.

"About as inter-esting as a whip snake, and I guess as quick and deadly."

"You seem to know him rather well."

"Oh yes, I know Derek!" said Olive, her sleepy gaze travelling to that dense corner of the hedge again, but now she started, leaned quickly forward and seemed about to rise.

"What is it?" inquired Josepha, glancing thither also.

"Eyes!" whispered Olive, her gaze still fixed. "I thought I saw eyes watching—peeping at us through those bushes."

"I don't see anything," said Josepha, and rising quickly she crossed to the hedge. "There's no one here."

"No? Why then it was my nerves—a bit jumpy, I guess."

"Won't you have another cup of tea?" inquired Josepha, seating herself at the table again. "Some bread and butter? Cake?"

"No thank you."

"I'm wondering," said Josepha, "yes, I'm quite puzzled to know why you called on me."

"It's vurry simple—I was lonesome and I hoped that maybe you might like me—a little. You see I never had a girl friend."

"But plenty of the—other sex, perhaps?" murmured Josepha.

"Ah yes," sighed Olive, tenderly, "there was Keith!"

"Was?" questioned Josepha, "You mean 'is,' don't you? He's still your friend, isn't he?"

"Yes—oh surely. Keith isn't the changeable sort."

And then the wicket-gate clicked sharply and, as if conjured up by the mere repetition of his name, Dallas himself was standing before them; and it was to be noticed that his eager glance passed over Olive's dark beauty to fix itself on Josepha's impassive face.

"I'm afraid the tea is nearly cold," said she, nodding in welcome, "but if you'll ask Sarah for another cup . . ."

CHAPTER XXXVII

IN WHICH THE QUESTION IS ANSWERED

So Dallas, sipping lukewarm tea (which might have changed to any other liquid without his noticing in the least), glanced from Olive's drooping lashes to Josepha's too serene face and began heartily to wish himself anywhere else; thus he glanced around somewhat wildly, yearning for the Small Person's joyous chatter, for old Jedidiah, for anyone or anything to break this most irksome and ominous silence; at last, in sheer desperation, he essayed to do so himself:

"I've had a wire from old George."

"Oh?" murmured Josepha.

"Who's George?" inquired Olive.

"Lord Withymore, a . . . an old friend. He means to stay a week at least, Josepha."

"How nice!" she murmured, "you'll be quite a jolly little party, won't you?"

"Party?" repeated Dallas.

"Yes—he and Miss Lemay and yourself."

"I've never met an English lord," said Olive. "I knew a German baron and an Italian Count, but I guess that's not the same?"

"No," smiled Josepha, "an English lord is like nothing on land or sea except an English lord—especially this one!"

"Why then I'll sure be glad to meet him."

Silence again, Josepha gazing dreamily at the nearest apple-tree, Olive apparently lost in pleasing thought;

as for Dallas he glanced uneasily from one lovely face to the other, gulped the last of his tea (quite unconsciously) and setting down cup and saucer with a rattle, frowned and spoke:

"Josepha, has Ryerson been around here to-day?"

"Mr. Ryerson? Oh no."

"Marvellous!" exclaimed Dallas, bitterly.

"He couldn't," murmured Olive. "I fixed he should go to London. I sent him a fake message. You see I didn't want him to meet me around here. Yes, I got rid of Derek all right—but oh, what's the use! Your Josepha's been doing her best to freeze my very soul out because she's so jealous of me——"

"Jealous?" cried Josepha indignantly, "I jealous —of you?"

"Why, surely!" nodded Olive gently. "And no wonder after listening to Derek. You're just crazy with jealousy—it's sticking out all over you. Well, I don't mind. But you wouldn't even try to like me and that hurts kind of, somehow. Oh well . . .! But say, Miss Josepha, and get this—you don't have to be jealous of me one li'l bit—in Keith's life I'm not even a 'has-been'. I'm a 'never was or will be.' And listen some more, sister—Keith's straight, a real, white man, so forget your fool jealousy and if he wants you, why marry him quick, and be everlastingly thankful."

"What hateful impertinence!" cried Josepha, leaping to her feet, hands clenched, eyes fiercely bright. "Do you know—do you know what you are saying?"

"Surely!" sighed Olive, rising also. "And now I'm saying that you're mad and jealous because you know that you'll never be able to love him like I do——"

"Oh, for heaven's sake!" groaned Dallas in the utmost misery but quite unheeded, while eyes blue and black flashed and glared bitter scorn and searing contempt. . . .

"And now," said Josepha, a little shakily, "if you —have quite done, I bid you ' Good afternoon'."

"Ah yes," murmured Olive, "you win! But I'm so used to losing that I can take it better than you could, I guess. Good-bye, Miss Josepha, forget your jealousy and be as happy as—you'll let yourself."

"Wait!" said Dallas; but still unheeding him, they turned their backs upon each other and took a step in opposite directions. Then Dallas was afoot and grasping Josepha by the wrist and Olive by the arm, swung them back to face each other; and Josepha frowned while Olive smiled.

"Josepha—listen!" said he, frowning back at her. "Olive Lemay, this good friend, came here to-day to tell us the truth of Red Rory's death——"

"I've no wish to hear her!" said Josepha, endeavouring to free her wrist.

"It is my wish that you should!" said Dallas, tightening his grip.

"Oh," cried Josepha, finding herself helpless, "I wonder how I could ever dream I loved you!"

"You'll wake up yet and find it true," he retorted. "Now, please, Olive—speak!"

"Well then, sister, Red Rory M'Guire was the kind of wild beast that you, safe in your cunning li'l home and friends all around you, have never seen, never had to battle with—but I was all alone and desperate with fear till Keith happened along and to save me from his vileness—bumped him off—yes, killed him —shot him stone dead! He loved me enough for that! . . . And now will you believe it?"

A moment's dreadful stillness, and then:

"No!" cried Josepha. "No! Ah, never. It's a ghastly, wicked lie!"

"It's truth!" cried Olive, in sudden, fierce passion,

tossing shapely arm aloft towards heaven with swift, wild gesture. "It's true or—if there is a God—may God smite me!" And with the awful words upon her lip, she turned and sped away.

Presently, aware that her wrist was freed, Josepha glanced round and saw Dallas had sunk down upon the rustic bench, his head between clenched fists:

"Dallas!" said she. "Oh . . . Keith!" Then, seeing he neither moved nor heeded, she came and laid her hand upon his bowed head, but shrinking from her touch, he spoke in dreadful, broken voice:

"I'm . . . done! This . . . ends . . . everything! There's blood between us—still!"

And now she was beside him on her knees, her arms fast about him, whispering, pleading, weeping—looking up with awful eyes into his distorted face.

"It isn't true! No . . . no, I can't believe it . . . I won't! Or if . . . if . . . why then, my darling, I'll only love you more . . . you said I should wake and find my love was true and it is, beloved, oh it is—it is indeed!"

"Guilty!" he whispered. "Guilty . . . oh my God! After all my hopes! I must go back— yes, I'll go back . . . face it out and pay my debt . . . I'll go back!"

"Then, Keith . . . dear love—husband, you shall take me with you . . ."

And Olive, hastening through the gathering dusk, took with her a vision of blue eyes, fiercely scornful, widening in sudden horror, smitten with agonized dismay—and Olive smiled . . . and in that moment was seized in cruel arms while hands, skilled in brutality, choked her to awful silence, and she was whirled up and borne away to a wild, and wind-swept desolation where, half-swooning, she beheld the vulpine leer of Whitey Neeves, the scowling vindictiveness of Dago Sam, the cold, more terrible ferocity of Derek Ryerson.

K

"Damned traitress!"

The veneer of social polish riven asunder, showed only the merciless gang-chief—the elemental beast. . . . Fists drove into that pale, beautiful face . . . there were also feet. . . . And now, to her failing senses it seemed there was a God indeed.

CHAPTER XXXVIII

TELLETH HOW CONVICTION CAME

"Uncle Jed," quoth his lordship swinging his great racing-car deftly through the traffic of Lewes's narrow High Street, "bit of luck spotting you in the crowd like that, eh?"

"Yessir! And this is sure better than the old bus, eh, Heart's-Delight?" inquired Jedidiah, tightening his arm about the Small Personage.

"Heaps!" she answered, lolling back against the luxurious cushions. "I love riding in George's big cars, I always feel so triffickly ladylike. You know, George, that's why if you're reely going to marry my Jo, I do wish you'd hurry up an' do it."

"Eh?" exclaimed Lord Withymore, glancing down at the small speaker rather aghast, "but, I say, what do you know about such things, Pat, old chap?"

"Everything! You see Sarah knows all 'bout you falling in love with Jo, an' Sarah says it was a act of Providence, because she says we need somebody to bring money back into the fam'ly again. An' I thinks Jo needs a husbant."

"Well, but," said his lordship, "I mean to say she's going to marry a much richer man than I am, old chap."

"Ooh, how spiffing! Who?"

"Why your Dal, of course—old Keith."

"But she can't, George, that'd be triffickly awful an' awfully frightful—oh no, she can't do that!"

"Why not, old chap?"

"Because I went an' found him for my own self. Besides she's got you, George, and you're frightflee

285

rich with cars an' houses an' castles an' things all over the place, an' that ought to be 'nuff for my lady. Don't you think so, Uncle Jed?"

"Shore!" wheezed Jedidiah, averting his face.

"George'll make her a spiffink husbant if she'll only let him—won't you, George?"

"Abso-lutely!" murmured Lord Withymore, averting his face, also.

"Yes, I'll tell her you said so——"

"Well, no, Pat, old chap, don't do that."

"Oh, why not? It's all for her good."

"Well, I fancy—what I mean is, I'm pretty sure she wants old Keith——"

"Well, she can't have him!"

"By heck!" chuckled Jedidiah, "and that's what-ever!"

"But suppose she . . . loves him, old chap?"

"That would be frightflee wrong of her."

"But how if he loves her, what I mean is, suppose they both love each other?"

"That'd be worse—so frightflee selfish, you know—'sides what should I do then? I'd be so dreffle lonely."

"Well but you've sure got me, Heart's-Delight," said Jedidiah, squeezing her again. "I guesso!"

"Yes, I know," she answered, nestling closer, "you're jest right for an uncle, Uncle Jed, but I was talking of husbants."

"Well, how about me?" inquired his lordship, "I look like being rather lonely, too."

"I like you a frightful lot, George, but I didn't find you, and I'd 'ranged for Dal. But I do like you."

"Well, think it over, old chap, I'm going cheap at present."

Thus they talked together as the powerful car hummed upon its speedy course, by winding road and crooked lanes with evening shadows deepening about them, until at last they turned from the highway into a familiar leafy lane beyond which lay the open down sweeping away and up to the noble heights of Windover upon whose steepy side stands out that gigantic shape of mystery.

"Oh, there he is!" cried the Small Personage. "There's my giant—see how fine and grand he looks. Please, George, do you mind stopping a minute, so I can say Good-night to him?"

"Why, certainly, old chap!" answered his lordship and checked the car obediently. Then the Personage, supported by Jedidiah, stood upon the seat and reached out her frail arms towards that strange, titanic thing to whom, in ages long forgotten, countless other arms were raised, mayhap . . . so now this child reached forth her arms and stood—rigid—listening. . . .

"Hark!" she whispered in sudden awe. "Do you hear a sound . . . like . . . a little lamb . . . bleating? Do you hear it?"

"Yes, old chap, but—that isn't a lamb—eh, Jed?"

"No, siree!" answered Jedidiah and was up and out of the car in an instant. "Stay right there, Heart's Delight," said he.

"Yes, Pat, wait there while we peer around a bit."

They had stopped almost opposite an old chalk-quarry cut deep into the upland, where riotous bushes grew in mazy tangle and where night gloomed already.

"Somebody hurt—I thought so!" muttered his lordship.

"Shore as you're . . . by the E-tarnal—a woman!" gasped Jedidiah. "Look a hyere!"

Together they bent above the dim, moaning shape and now his lordship gasped in turn while Jedidiah swore savagely.

"God! the child mustn't see this, Jed!" whispered Lord Withymore.

"Ibetcha!" snarled Jedidiah. "I'll send her 'long home, it's only a step, thank God!" So back he sped to the Small Personage who seemed very small indeed seated in the big car. "My Heart's-Delight," said he smiling, "jest you get 'long home, run on dearie and tell daughter a lady's had an accident and we're bringin' her along. Don't stop to talk, babe—run!" So saying, he lifted Patience from the car, watched her dart away up the lane and hastened back to where Lord Withymore crouched upon his knees.

"Think she's cashin' in, George?" he inquired.

"God knows, Jed. But if so—it's murder—this is the work of brutal fists!"

"Shore—it would be!" nodded Jedidiah as together they stooped and lifted that inert form. So, gently as might be, they bore it to the car.

"Can you hold her while I drive, Jed?"

"Ibetcha! Let her go, George, the cottage lays right handy. My, my, they've shore beat her up!"

"Eh?" exclaimed his lordship, reaching for the gear-lever. "They? Who? D'you know who she is?"

"Well no, George, but I'm willin' to risk a blue stack as I could tell her name?"

"Then who is she, Jed? She seems a lady and . . . very beautiful!"

"She'll look a whole lot better when she's washed, I guess, George. And yon's the cottage, glory be! And there's daughter ready and waitin' for us—Lord bless her!"

"What's the matter?" called Josepha, hurrying forward as the car stopped. "Who is it?"

"Hold on a minute!" answered Jedidiah, busied with his handkerchief upon that bruised face. "Now take a peek, daughter, and see if——"

"Oh!" gasped Josepha. "It's Olive Lemay!"

"And that's whatever!" nodded Jedidiah. "I shore called the turn again, by Heck!"

"Bring her in," said Josepha, opening the wicket-gate. "Sarah—quick, get warm water, a sponge, clean linen—run!"

"Give her to me, Jed," said his lordship, holding out his arms. Very tenderly he raised that limp form, and thus with Olive upon his breast, followed Josepha into the cottage.

"Upstairs, George, into my bedroom. Can you manage alone?"

"Oh yes."

Up the narrow stair, across the small landing and into dainty, oak-raftered chamber he bore her and laid her gently upon Josepha's bed.

"Poor girl!" murmured Josepha, bending above her with quick, cherishing hands.

Then the long dark lashes quivered, lifted, and from bruised lips came a gasping murmur:

"Oh . . . I guess there's . . . a God—all right!"

CHAPTER XXXIX

WHICH IS A CHAPTER OF ACTION

DALLAS trudged homewards despairing, for Hope, that bright angel was dead, his life wrecked, his future a grim horror; even the memory of Josepha was an agony, her undying faith no more now than a loving woman's unreasoning prejudice. He was guilty beyond all possibility of doubt, and come what might, shame, prison, death itself—nothing mattered any more.

It was as he turned in amid the dense shade of trees fumbling for the stile, for there was no ray of moon or star, that the shadowy earth reeled violently beneath him, swung giddily up and up to meet the lowering heaven in roaring thunder-clap, flames shot athwart his dazzled vision with sense of sudden pain and he was down among the dewy grass, his troubles all forgotten.

Little by little he became aware of light, of immaculate, patent leather shoes, trim silken socks, elegantly trousered legs, be-ringed hands that held an open newspaper. Beyond this lounging figure his aching eyes beheld a floor thick-strewn with litter of windborne twigs and leaves, a panelled wall, warped and mildewed, a great carved fireplace whereon five candles guttered whose mellow light struck upon an ancient escutcheon deep-graven in the stone above, with the two words:

"I dare."

So here then was the ancient home of the Dares. . . . Josepha's old house! And, struck by the fantastic irony of it all, Dallas laughed harshly, whereat the newspaper was instantly lowered.

"Greetings, old top!" said Ryerson cheerily, his handsome face smiling and debonair as usual. "Feeling better?"

"So it was you," said Dallas, leaning back against the panelled wall and bowing painful head upon his hand, "it was you slugged me?"

"No, no, Sam's black-jack," answered Ryerson. "Just one tap—in the right place, of course. Sorry, old man, but had to for your own good. Fact is, your presence here is urgently desired by one you should be glad to meet." Here Ryerson paused expectant of eager question, but Dallas merely stared at the littered floor, beneath pain-wrinkled brow.

"Say now, Keith, if you're wishing to know——"

"Nothing," said Dallas dully, "nothing matters any more."

"What—is that the way you feel? Well anyway seeing Olive has spilt the beans pretty considerably, we'll just have to gag you until——"

"Go ahead!" murmured Dallas.

"Oh we'll do it all right, old man. Only first, aren't you interested any, or wondering what——"

"Hell—no!" said Dallas, in the same toneless voice. "Nothing will ever matter any more. . . . I killed Rory and I'm through caring about anything else."

"So!" exclaimed Ryerson, leaning down swiftly to peer into the speaker's impassive face, "you believe me at last, eh?"

"No! I believe Olive—she saw me kill him."

"Olive . . . why . . . sure she did! But did she tell you so?"

"Yes, and her word goes with me."

"So Olive . . . told you. Yes, Whitey saw her chinning with you and Josepha at the cottage this afternoon, and I naturally thought . . . oh well— the poor kid!"

"So nothing matters now!" repeated Dallas, "the sooner I'm jailed the better."

"You poor fish!" laughed Ryerson, gently. "There'll be no jail stuff coming to you if your old man acts right—yes, if your millionaire pop comes across and squares the deal, as I'm betting he will."

"That would make no difference," said Dallas, picking up a handful of dead leaves. "I'm starting for New York and the Tombs right away."

"The hell you are? Well, first" . . . Ryerson whistled softly, whereupon a pale head glimmered amid the shadows of a yawning doorway.

"Do I shoo in the boid, boss?" inquired Whitey Neeves, hoarsely, and receiving affirmative nod vanished again, while Dallas fingered the dead leaves and Ryerson watched him curiously. And after some while was a heavy, deliberate tread, a tall form loomed in the doorway, at sight of which Dallas dropped the leaves and, scrambling to his feet, stood staring.

"Father?" he exclaimed doubtfully, at last.

Then Wilbur Chisholm stepped into the candlelight and halted; his lips moved, yet no word came, his square chin quivered oddly and, in that moment, the iron Roman was whelmed and lost in the American father, than whom breathes no kindlier creature; yet when at last he spoke, all he said was:

"Hello, Keith!" But all he left unuttered was in the grip of his hand.

"Well," said Ryerson pleasantly, "here's your jail-bird, Mr. Chisholm, delivered sound and well as per contract."

"Father," muttered Dallas, very conscious of that eager clasp. "I'm . . . not worthy——"

"You're my son, anyway."

Now beholding his father so strangely altered, quick to heed the new kindliness in his every look and word, Dallas turned away, and happening to glance at the coat of arms above the mantel, saw the words "I dare" show suddenly blurred. And now it was that Derek Ryerson made a mistake, for he laughed mockingly and next moment was looking into glaring eyes, tearful yet fiercely bright, and recoiling, snatched up his cane; but as he whipped out the concealed weapon a powerful fist staggered him and Dallas had wrenched the weapon from his grasp.

"Now . . . damn you . . ." panted Dallas—then a hand gripped his shoulder and Wilbur Chisholm spoke:

"Son, give me that!" said he, and taking the pistol tossed it into a corner. "There's no need for this sort of thing—my word goes. I stand by my deal, Ryerson—you will collect your bribe aboard my yacht—*Albatross* lying off Newhaven!"

"Father—wait!" said Dallas, interposing. "Because I am surely convinced of my guilt at last, I'm going back to—to take what's coming and no money you can pay this blackmailer shall stop me."

"Son," said Wilbur, his eyes kindling, "that's why! You're going back to take your medicine and of your own free will rather than let this fellow have you arrested and—I'm coming with you, we'll fight through it together."

"Sir," said Dallas, in choking voice. "Oh, father . . . I——"

"My word goes," growled Wilbur, unscrewing fountain-pen. "And what's the money, after all—a button off my shirt! And then, Keith, I've only just found out I have a son and—well, I guess that's worth more than any money." So saying he scribbled a line in his notebook, tore out the page and gave it to Ryerson.

"Show that to Captain Hedges, my skipper and he'll give you the money."

"Good enough!" nodded Ryerson, scanning the hastily scribbled lines. "Your dam son is perfectly safe now, so far as the boys and I are concerned, indeed we're out to boost his game from now on. Well, I guess you want to be off—I do. And I'm sorry you must walk, but we need the car and we're pressed for time, so I'll say good-night and so long, gentlemen."

Then Derek Ryerson reached his elegant cane from adjacent corner, flourished it, turned to be gone and recoiled suddenly as forth of that shadowy doorway stepped a small person, or rather a little man in clerical attire, for the eyes beneath his soft-brimmed hat were bright and fierce and in one sinewy fist he grasped a large revolver.

"Why . . . great snakes! Hello—Jed!" exclaimed Wilbur Chisholm in joyous greeting.

"Howdy—Mr. Chisholm, sir!" snarled Jedidiah, scowling. "Hold on—you!" he barked, gesturing at Ryerson with his pistol.

"Oh!" inquired Derek, lounging against panelled walls, "who'n hell are you, then?"

"Hey *Mister* Chisholm," growled Jedidiah, his fierce gaze never leaving Ryerson's lounging figure, "hain't ya got nothin' better to do with ya dam money than hand it to this yere doggone coyote—hey?"

"No, Jed. Keith's my son and——"

"Hell's bells! You—all ha' found that out have ya?"

"Say, Grandpa," murmured Ryerson edging towards the scowling little man, "watch out you don't hurt yourself with that gun! What are you around here for, anyway?"

"You!" snarled Jedidiah. "Do I git ya?"

"What for?"

"Blackmail!"

"Oh?"

"Assault and battery!"

"Is that so?"

"Murder! That enough?"

"Whose murder?"

"I'm holdin' you-all, Derek Ryerson for the murder of Red Rory M'Guire——"

"So ho!" laughed Ryerson. "Then say, Fluffy-face, you look a fool and——"

"Shore!" nodded Jedidiah, grimly, giving a tug at his hated whiskers, "but they helped the game an' I'm quit of 'em to-night——"

"And," continued Ryerson, "you're a bigger fool than you look!"

"Mebbe! But lemme tellya it hain't no good lookin' or waitin' fer ya confed'rates, they're handcuffed in the cyar awaitin' fer you-all. Now, d'ya come good 'n'quiet?"

"Oh I guess so!" nodded Ryerson and straightening lazily he leapt suddenly towards a certain corner but, in that same instant was a stunning report, a jet of red flame, and he was lying a gasping, crumpled heap.

"Resistin' arrest!" quoth Jedidiah, glancing down into his convulsed features.

"God! Have you killed him, Jed?" cried Wilbur, hurrying towards the fallen man.

"No siree! jest his hind laig. Stand away ef ya please. I've jest handed out enough to keep him good 'n' quiet a while. I know this gol-darned cane!" And he tossed it into dim corner.

"Who—damn you . . . who are you?" groaned Ryerson.

"Wollet, that's me—U-nited States marshal, yessir! Look a here!" And opening his clerical waistcoat Jedidiah discovered the familiar silver star.

"Can we help you any?" inquired Wilbur with look and tone almost humble—for him.

"Yessir!" snarled Jedidiah, "you and—yore son, Mister Chisholm, sir, can leave me an' Fin to our job o' work."

"One minute, Jed! If you are arresting this man for the murder it stands to reason my son must be innocent?"

"So you've found that out now, have ya? Well, Mister Chisholm, sir, ef you-all and yore son'll git I'll be——"

"It's a lie!" gasped Ryerson. "I didn't shoot Rory . . . I couldn't . . . I wasn't there! Keith knows . . . ask Keith!"

"He's right, Uncle Jed," said Dallas, "yes, he's right, I remember enough to swear Ryerson was not in the room—I'm afraid you're making a big mistake."

"Well, anyway—I got him!" quoth Jedidiah. "And as you go out tell Fin to hog-tie his pris'ners and come here to gimme a hand wi' this pizen-toad, will ya, Keith?"

"Hold on!" panted Ryerson painfully. "Keith . . . old sport, listen . . . I——"

"Shut-up, you!" snarled Jedidiah. And Ryerson did so for, gasping a curse, he groaned and fainted.

CHAPTER XL

IN WHICH THE QUESTION IS ANSWERED—ALMOST

So father and son, like comrades, went forth together across the silent downs, leagued together in a new understanding, a growing sympathy, a community of spirit that was to endure. Thus, as they walked, Dallas talked from his very heart, speaking of Josepha, her loneliness, her brave struggle against poverty, her old ruined house; he told of the abiding wonder of her love for him, her passionate faith, and of his own shattered dreams. And as he hearkened, this new Wilbur Chisholm blinked often, in fashion most un-Roman, and was glad of the dark.

Reaching home at last, they found Lord Withymore's car at the gate and himself in the billiard room tramping nervously to and fro, who, beholding Dallas, came hurrying forward, but espying Wilbur Chisholm, halted to look his speechless surprise.

"George, what's up?" demanded Dallas. "Anything wrong?"

"Why yes, old lad . . . how do, Mr. Chisholm! They think she's dying . . . absolutely!"

"Who . . . who?" cried Dallas, seizing his friend's arm. "Not Josepha? You don't——"

"No, no! Miss Lemay . . . Miss Olive. She's had an accident . . . wants to see you . . . doctorman says she won't rest properly till she does . . . my car's ready——"

"Father . . . will you come, sir?"

"Yes do, sir!" said his lordship as they hurried out to the car. "We can sit together, sir . . . be company and—what not—absolutely . . . Keith, she must have been a . . . er . . . howling beauty once, old lad . . . Miss Lemay?"

"She is!" said Dallas, ushering his father into the roomy tonneau and leaping in after. "Is she badly injured, George?"

"'Fraid so!" sighed his lordship; then off they went, speeding along shady lanes, hooting round sudden corners until they pulled up at that small, so familiar wicket-gate.

"I think you'd better go up at once," said Lord Withymore, motioning towards the stairs as they entered the cosy sitting-room. "Mr. Chisholm and I will hang about down here. Will you gasp, sir?"

So upstairs sped Dallas, forthwith, treading very softly yet, even so, as he reached a certain door he heard a strangely soft, husky voice crying upon his name. Knocking gently, he opened the door and stood upon the threshold.

He saw Josepha bending above the bed, the doctor's burly form in the window-recess, and upon the pillow a head and face so bandaged that little was visible except two great dark eyes that stared up at him, more tenderly wistful than ever.

"I knew . . . your step," said the husky voice, speaking with painful effort. "I'd sure know it . . . in a thousand. . . . Listen boy. I'm just a liar . . . and with a lie on my lips . . . I called to God to smite me . . . and he's sure . . . done so, hasn't he? And, Kay dear, I . . . lied to hurt your Josepha because she was . . . kind of mean to me . . . proud and cold as an icebox. So . . . I got catty, too, and . . . told her a lie . . . because . . . oh boy, you didn't kill Rory."

"I'm glad!" stammered Dallas, looking at Josepha's lovely, downbent head.

"No, Keith, no . . . Rory M'Guire was shot by . . . himself. . . ."

Dallas set his teeth, his hands clenched, his shoulders drooped with all the old, sick hopelessness, his brows twitched with sudden pain, yet when he spoke, his voice seemed gentler than ever, though his heart was wrung with utter disbelief.

"So . . . that was the way of it?" he murmured. "Well, now dear, try to sleep."

"Yes, he shot himself . . . by accident. I—was the accident."

"You?" exclaimed Dallas, and took a quick step forward.

"Yes, he had a gun . . . he meant to . . . kill you so I—ran and . . . jerked his arm."

The great wistful eyes closed wearily, and in that moment Josepha, stooping, kissed each closed lid.

CHAPTER XLI

WHICH, BEING THE LAST, IS A CHAPTER OF PARTS

PART I

"But everything should always end happily, you know!" declared the Small Personage, nodding vehement assurance at the invalid.

"Should it, Honey-girl?" sighed Olive, smiling wanly from her pillows.

"Course it should! 'Cause you see, Olive, everything was made by God an' He means us all to . . . to get married an' live happy ever after!"

"Oh, child," said Olive, between tears and laughter, "just for that you'll have to kiss me."

The Personage stooped obligingly.

"Why I bleeve you're crying!" said she, reprovingly.

"No, not really, dear."

"Well, your eyelashes wet me."

"That was just love for you, Honey, I guess."

"You know, Olive," said the Personage, shaking small head portentously, "I think you need a husbant!"

"My heavens!" gasped the invalid.

"I told George, an' he thinks so too!"

"Do you mean . . . Lord Withymore?"

"Yes. He said 'abso-lutely!' And he's promised to help me find one for you, only he thinks we'd better wait till you're well 'nough to go with us. So you'll please hurry an' get well, won't you?"

"Yes dear . . . only . . . I don't think . . . I'll ever . . . marry."

"Oh but you will, you will—you must. Sarah says you're the 'marrying sort,' an' Sarah knows! You see she's going to marry Ben as soon as my Jo's married Dal. So you must marry somebody, you know, an' then everything'll be spiffink. . . . Now I s'pose I'd better give all your flowers some fresh water—such a lot you've got! That's the best of being a ninvalid, everybody's always so much nicer to you and bring s'prises—presents, you know. I had heaps when I was a ninvalid only not such a triffick lot of flowers as you."

"Yes, folks have been mighty kind to me, Honey."

"And I know who sent them, too! This 'normous bunch of violets came from Dal's father—I like him! George brought you these red roses, and all these white and yellow ones came from Dal, and I picked you all these pansies my own self and—oh there, now you're all weepy again! Are you frightflee miserable?"

"No, dear, I'm just . . . too grateful!"

"Well, I like you to be grateful," nodded the Personage, small head bent to her task, "only please don't weep, tears aren't good for a ninvalid."

And so, having watered these many flowers that made a fragrant glory all about the bed, our Personage being summoned to her lessons, kissed that dark head very maternally, shook up a pillow or so, somewhat vigorously, and pattered softly and rather unwillingly downstairs.

Left alone, the invalid lay very still a while then, reaching out unsteady hand, chose from the many a single great bloom and inhaling its sweetness, closed her eyes. And thus presently Josepha found her fast asleep, the rose upon her pillow; and seeing its colour, Josepha smiled.

Part 2

"She's only got one eye . . . an' she's frightflee lame and . . . not any tail, so I call her . . . Catherine."

"And a mighty good name too!" said Wilbur Chisholm, glancing from the Small Person's tearful face to the unlovely hen and back again. "Why were you crying here all alone, sweetheart? Not because of Catherine, sure now?"

"N-o!" answered the Personage, striving right valiantly against her sobs. "It's . . . only . . . George!"

"What? Young Withymore? What's he been doing, girlie?"

"Nothing, only . . . 'serting me."

"Eh? Deserting you?"

"Yes, he—he's . . . doing it . . . now!"

"But, dearie, he's only at the window yonder, talking with Miss Lemay."

"Yes, but . . . he's always at the window yonder! First there was Dal—*he* 'serted me! Then I took George 'cause he said he was lonely an' going cheap —an' now . . . he's done it too! So . . . when I've growed myself into a lovely l-lady . . . I'll be all lonely an' no husbant . . . like Catherine."

Wilbur Chisholm's grim lips twitched, but, beholding the child's tear-filled eyes, the pitiful quiver of her rosy lips, he stooped and gathering her into his long arms, though a little awkwardly, to be sure, lifted her to his breast.

"Little sweetheart," he murmured, kissing her tear-wet cheek. "I've been lonesome too!"

"Have you—oh, have you reely?" said the Personage, and kissed him vehemently in each eye.

"Well," exclaimed Josepha, coming upon them suddenly at this moment, "whatever in the world——"

The Personage waved her away:

"Please, Jodear," she sighed, "we're just being nice an' lonely together so—won't you go away again?"

"Josepha . . . my dear," said Wilbur, hoisting his small comrade to his shoulder, "as I rode with Keith this morning we passed a fair—tents and round-abouts and . . . I thought maybe I'd take the child there—that is if there's no objection?" he added with strange, new diffidence.

"Oh, I simply 'dore fairs!" exclaimed the Small Personage ecstatically.

"So do I!" laughed Wilbur Chisholm, "especially the roundabouts."

Oh shadow of Wall Street!

PART 3

"A whole fortnight!" said Olive, glancing out of the open lattice across sunny garden. "I ought to be dead! Yes, it was surely up to me to die——"

"Nonsense!" said Josepha, smoothing a tress of glossy black hair. "You're nearly well, and your face won't show a mark—except where it won't be noticed."

"Thanks to you, my precious!" cried Olive, turning to kiss that caressing hand. "Oh, but you've been kind, terribly kind and good to me! And wherever I go . . . whatever happens to me, I just want you to know I'm carrying a prayer for you in my heart—for you and your Keith. . . . And I sure love your blonde hair. . . . And now . . . about Keith—he was the first real, good man I ever knew. . . ."

"But you've met another lately, dear. He always brings you—red roses. He carried you here in his arms——"

"Oh!" sighed Olive drearily, "I sure ought to have died!"

"Why, dear? What's troubling you?"

"I'm—I'm so out of place here, Josepha—right out of the picture. If I were in a book, I'm the character the author would just have to kill off some way or other——"

"The question is," said Josepha, kissing her patient's troubled brow, "what shall I give you for dinner? Let's see, I might get you——" the wicket-gate clicked sharply and Josepha nodded, "yes—red roses as usual, dear!" Olive caught her breath and would have risen, but Josepha's gentle hand stayed her. "Why run away?" she inquired softly. "Why have you avoided him lately?" Olive glanced yearningly towards the door and clasped her hands nervously; and then in at the wide-open casement came Lord Withymore's curly head.

"Glorious morning!" he beamed, laying a great sheaf of roses on the window ledge. "Topping absolutely. How's the invalid to-day?"

"Well, George—look at her!"

"I am. She sure——"

"Pink as your roses, George."

"Quite! Taking her feed regularly, I hope and——"

"Do not talk as if she were a horse, George."

"No, no—absolutely not! I mean to say she's certainly looking more robust and so forth, coming into condition and what not—what I mean is, blooming!"

"That's the sunshine, perhaps," smiled Josepha.

"No, it's . . . just you, dear, all you!" said the invalid.

"Quite!" nodded his lordship.

"And yet," said Josepha, smiling down into the dark, adoring eyes upraised to hers, "being so much better she talks of—dying, George."

"Dashed absurd!" quoth his lordship. "No, no! what I say to that is, if you know what I mean, tut, tut—absolutely!"

"Exactly!" nodded Josepha. "Bully her, George, while I go and potter in the kitchen, bully her—she needs it!"

"Rightho!" answered his lordship, cheerily. "Oh by the way, Josepha, I was to say Keith will be over later on to take you for a gallop."

"Why couldn't he bring the message himself?"

"He's out with the horses and his governor. Regular old sportsman, Mr. Chisholm, knows a horse when he sees one."

"They ride together every day, don't they?"

"Yes, they're great pals——"

"And always in the same direction towards West-dean, at least so Tom Merry tells me. Now I wonder what they're up to? I've asked them both heaps of times, but they always laugh and put me off—you could tell me, of course, George."

"Aha—smuggling perchance, girl—heave, yo-ho and so forth!"

"Anyhow I know there's something, because you are all so tremendously mysterious about it—even Mr. Chisholm."

"He's taken a dashed tremendous fancy to you, Josepha, I mean to say he has an eye, y'know——"

"For a horse, George?"

"Yes—no, I mean—what I mean is beauty and what-not, if you know what . . . absolutely!" said his lordship somewhat incoherently, for Olive's dark glance had met his at last; when they looked away again, Josepha had vanished.

"Why," inquired his lordship, seating himself on the window ledge and leaning farther into the room, "why talk of dying? So dashed—unheal—thy! I mean to say—life and what-not all before you, joy and so forth."

"I only said if I were in a book I'd have to die because the poor author just wouldn't know what to do with me."

"Why not?"

"Because I'm right out of place here."

"Oh, I don't know!" murmured his lordship leaning still farther in through the window. "If I were an author, which I'm not, of course, I'm jolly sure I could fit you in—well rather! Oh quite!"

"How?"

"I'd marry you off happily, like all the other characters—if it wasn't a modern novel."

"Don't modern novels end happily?"

"Not if they're improperly up to date and—really dashed clever—but mine wouldn't be clever, naturally! Anyhow I'd see you married happily."

"Not—the hero?"

"Rather not! Dash it—no!"

"I'm glad!" she sighed; and here, somehow, anyhow, his lordship was through the window altogether.

"Glad? Are you?" he questioned rather breathlessly. "Would you be content with one of the minor characters—a fellow who doesn't know anything much —except horses, what I mean is . . . oh my dear —could you?" Here her nearest hand was caught and held in a warm, vital clasp.

"No—ah no—please!" she whispered, brokenly and shrank from him trembling. "It wouldn't ever do . . . couldn't ever be possible . . . for me!" And now beneath her long, down-drooping lashes he saw the glitter of painful, slow-gathering tears—wherefore he took her other hand also.

"Wait . . . no . . . oh wait!" she faltered. "I'll just have to tell you . . . yes, I must tell you now——"

"Nothing at all!" said he gently. "No, not a dashed word!" And lifting her trembling hands he kissed them, one after the other, very reverently; then these tearful lashes were raised swiftly and she was looking up at him with eyes wherein he read startled wonder that changed to a great awe, and so to a radiant gladness that dazzled him. . . . And Lord Withymore stooped his curly head.

"Oh, George," wailed a plaintive voice from the garden, "don't you think you've talked to Olive long enough please, 'cause I—ooh, I bleeve you were ki——"

"Absolutely!" said his lordship, fronting the Small Personage rather self-consciously.

"Then I s'pose this means you'll be marrying each other soon?"

"Pat, old chap, I . . . it does!"

"Oh dear me!" moaned the Personage, distressfully, "that leaves me only Uncle Jed, an' he's so old . . . an' with a beard——"

"Hold on thar, Heart's-Delight!" cried a cheery voice. "Jest look a here, willya?" And up the garden path strode Jedidiah himself, but quite marvellously transfigured; true his silky locks still flowed, but beard and whiskers had vanished, his small, trim figure was brave in fashionable tweeds, in gloved hand he flourished a jaunty hat. "Gol-darn it! Who says 'beard'?" he demanded, thrusting out square, smooth-shaven chin. "Whatya gotta say now, Heart's Delight?"

The Small Personage looked, uttered a gasp of ecstatic wonder and ran at him, both arms outstretched in welcome.

"Whatya gotta say t'me now, Babe?" he chuckled.

"Hell's bells!" she cried

Then Jedidiah laughed, smote hand on knee and snatched her up to be hugged.

"Will I do then, Sweetheart? Will I soot?"

"Yes," she answered happily, "you're so nice an' smooth an' new—and you've growed so triffickly—young!"

"Shore I have, my Heart's-Delight, and growin' younger every blame' minute, yessir, I guesso!"

"Then now I'll call you jest my Jed!" sighed she, stroking his new-shaven cheek. "But, oh, Jed, you won't go marrying or kissing other ladies—like all the others, will you?"

"No *mam!* Not me—not Jed Wollet."

PART 4

"England!" snarled Jedidiah, chewing viciously at his cigar and scowling at the beam of sunlight flooding in at the open door of the little summer-house. "England! A blame, wall-eyed, on-civilized snip o' land I tell ya—yessir! It's took me a hull fortnight to tell 'em as a U-nited States marshal's gotta right to shoot a crook afore he plugs me. A fortnight! Yessir!"

"They aren't so used to gun-play over here," said Dallas. "How is Ryerson?"

"Gettin' fat, his kind takes a lot o' killin'."

"Well, say now, Jed, I do wish you'd be friends again with my father, he's grieving, I know."

"Has he told ya so?"

"Not on your life. But I just know it."

"Well let him darn-well grieve!"

"No, it's not right, Jed. Such old friends as you were. I hate to think I'm the cause."

"Well, son, you hain't. No, it's the son of yore angel mother—that's whatever! She could never ha' mothered a skunk or murderer—no, sir! And them as thought so . . . oh well! Say, when are you fixin' to marry daughter?"

"In three weeks, Jed."

"Good! But, son—George is a-lookin' wedlock at Miss Olive!"

"Well?"

"Is it? That's what I'm wonderin'. I'm allowin' as she's a fine critter—t'look at, an' mighty soft an' purty spoke—t' listen to—but!"

"Well?"

"About this tale of hern? She sees M'Guire with a gun, she runs in an' jolts his arm and the ornery cuss shoots himself. That's her statement, hain't it?"

"Yes—you believe it, don't you, Jed?"

"Son," answered Jedidiah, his keen gaze roving afar, "nobody hain't a-goin' t'tell me I don't—but——"

"Well?" said Dallas impatiently, "what, Jed—what now?"

"Nothin', son—only . . . there was no powder-marks—no burnin'! Son, Red Rory was shot—from a distance. . . ." For a moment was utter stillness, broken suddenly by a gasping sigh, and Olive was standing before them in the sunlight.

"And that's right, too!" said she in her strange husky voice. "I killed him . . . I shot him from the doorway . . . across the room. And now . . . if I must answer for it I'm ready. You're a law-officer, aren't you, Mr. . . . Uncle Jed?"

Then taking off his hat, Jedidiah rose:

"Ma'm," said he gently, "I was waitin' for this and now——"

He paused, for uttering a gasping sob, Olive turned and hurried away.

"Con-sarn me!" exclaimed Jedidiah and made as if to follow, but checked suddenly for—with dark head bowed and faltering steps, Olive, speeding cottage-wards, blundered into a pair of arms—but arms very strong and very comforting.

"My dear!" said his lordship, and led her round into the little orchard, and there the wild passion of her grief and bitter remorse broke its stubborn bonds at last.

"George . . . my dear!" she sobbed. "This must be . . . good-bye! I'm going away, back . . . to it all. . . . Oh I should have told you . . . I . . . meant to . . . it was I . . . killed Rory M'Guire!"

"Quite!" murmured his lordship and kissed her.

"You . . . know?" she breathed.

"Dear old thing," he smiled. "I guessed it weeks ago."

"Did you?" she whispered. "Did you—and loved me—in spite of it? Did you?"

"Abso . . . lutely!" he murmured, with voice and look serene no longer.

"Ah, George," she murmured brokenly, "you dear . . . stolid Englishman . . . how I worship you!" And then her arms were about his neck and she clung to him, trembling.

"Dear . . . girl," said he, clasping her fast, while his words halted strangely, "you shall . . . never . . . be afraid . . . never be . . . lonely . . . any more. I mean to say if . . . you know what I mean . . . never again!"

PART 5

Reaching the top of the long grassy ascent they paused to breathe their horses; and now, being close beside her, Dallas took her gloved left hand to feel a certain finger.

"Yes," said he, kissing that same finger, "it's still there all right."

"And will be—always!" murmured Josepha, looking at that finger, also. "How surprised they'll be! . . . And what will your father say?"

"He knows, of course."

"Why then, Keith, take me—home."

So they rode on again, speaking very seldom for some happiness is beyond words. But presently she checked her horse.

"Dear, you're going wrong," said she, "over there, hidden in the hollow is the poor old house—your house!"

"Ours, dear," he corrected.

"And all crumbling to ruin!" she sighed. "Come away, I don't want to see any ruins—to-day."

But Dallas rode on, beckoning her to follow, and she unwillingly obeyed; and then—uttered a little cry and thereafter sat dumb, staring down wide-eyed at the wonder below.

For there, in place of desolate ruin, stood a noble house set within trim gardens, an ancient manor house mellow with age, wall and gable and twisted chimneys whence (O marvel!) rose a blue haze of smoke.

"Keith," she whispered at last. "Oh, dear love, am I mad? There! The dear, old house . . . itself again, only . . . more beautiful! Is it a miracle?"

"Yes—of a sort," he answered, stealing his arm about her.

"But how . . . who . . .?"

"My father!" he answered proudly, stooping to kiss her quivering lips. "It is his wedding present. You see, dear heart, when my father takes hold, well—things happen."

"But it was a ruin . . . a few weeks ago!"

"He had an army of workmen on it."

"Money!" sighed Josepha in awed tones, "money is a wonderful power and rather—terrible!"

"It all depends," answered Dallas, kissing her again. "And now come and accept your present, dear—and yes, there's old George's car in the courtyard."

So down they rode together, through massive gates, along trim drive, into the courtyard where grooms waited to take their horses. Then forth of the open doorway strode Wilbur Chisholm, his grey head bare, to lift Josepha from the saddle and kiss her right heartily:

"Welcome home, my dear!" said he.

And now what wonder if her eyes were brighter for the rush of happy tears, or if her hands trembled in his?

"It's all like a dream come true . . . the dear old house, I can scarcely believe it's real," said she looking up into Wilbur Chisholm's kindly grey eyes."

"Daughter," said he, kissing her again, "I guess it's real as your sweet faith in my son, but not half so wonderful. Now go in, both of you and have a look at things, take her in Keith and show your wife her home."

Being alone Wilbur glanced up at this ancient house that he had made alive again, and smiled, as from within came the stir of joyous bustle, the sound of happy voices.

Thus pacing slowly, hands behind him, Wilbur smiled but became suddenly grave as out from stable-yard stalked the little, upright figure of Jedidiah, jaunty hat tilted, long, thin cigar cocked at ferocious angle; thus they approached each other until they came face to face.

"Well, Jed?" inquired Wilbur, halting. "How's it to be?"

The cigar quivered and was still.

"Old-timer," said Wilbur, and held out his hand.

The sardonic mouth twitched but uttered no word.

"Partner," said the big man, hand still outstretched, "I was in wrong and . . . I'm owning up to it, so can't you . . . won't you . . ." (Oh Spirit of Vespasian, Wilbur Chisholm was actually stammering!) "I . . . I was a fool and worse, but, but—Josepha's forgiven me."

"She may!" grunted Jedidiah, scowling at a chimney-pot.

"So has Keith——"

"He would!" snarled Jedidiah, glowering at impending gable. "Yep, he would, but—not me, no sir, not Jed Wollet. And here's why: The Lord gave you-all an angel wife, she gave ya a son to bear your name, you-all called that son a murderer and cast him off—her son! You quit an' left him cold—Lucy's son!"

"And yet, Jed, I'm daring to think that maybe she has forgiven me too."

"Mebbe!" growled Jedidiah, turning away. "But she's a holy angel and I'm only Jed Wollet."

And then from behind trim hedge hard by, stepped the Personage.

"Oh, Uncle Jed," she called softly yet imperiously as became a real personage, "please come back here a minute."

"Well?" inquired the fierce, little man, turning back reluctantly, "what is it, Heart's-Delight?"

"Did you love your angel, reely an' truly?"

"Eh? Why yes, shore."

"And do you want to see her again, someday?"

"Ibetcha! . . . Yes, dearie."

"Well, I've got an angel, too, my mother . . . but Jo says I shall only see her again if I'm good. And it's frightflee good to forgive people 'cause it says so in Our-Father-which-art, you know. So hadn't you better forgive Dal's father—I like him a lot—like he wants you to so's you can see your angel again, someday?"

Jedidiah's fiercely cocked cigar drooped suddenly, his keen eyes shifted here, shifted there—blinked:

"Gol-dar——" the little man choked suddenly and stood mute.

"Jed?" muttered Wilbur and out came his hand again.

"Gosh!" said Jedidiah hoarsely as he gripped his old partner's fingers. "Gosh, Wilbur, whatcha know about that?"

"There are angels on earth too, it seems, Jed."

"I guesso, Wilb."

"So now, please," said the Personage, giving each of them a small, yet imperious hand, "come indoors and let me show you where I'm going to sleep to-night —the dearest, teeniest little bed with silver on to it— yes, George says it's reel silver, an' lace and silky curtains—oh, spiffink! . . . And there's a cake with sugar icing—so do let's go—now!"

Then very obediently the two old friends turned and with the Small Personage walking between, went whither she led them.

THE END

Sampson Low's New Books
Autumn, 1929

ANOTHER DAY
JEFFERY FARNOL

7/6 net

GIVEN a hero bereft of memory, who was found unconscious across the dead body of the man he had threatened to murder, Mr. Jeffery Farnol has the beginning of as thrilling a mystery as ever was imagined, and one particularly suited to his own ingenious and lively methods, especially since the said hero is a romantic figure, to boot—a champion fighter with his fists and an intrepid breaker in of the most ferocious of horses. In addition to which, Keith, Dallas, Chisholm has for the Goddess of his Destiny a lissom Sussex beauty whose face is deep-eyed, vivid of mouth and framed in bronze gold hair cut close, sleek and shining like a gold helmet, whilst the rival claimant to his love is a pale and wistful beautiful American woman dark-eyed and black haired. Derek Ryerson is the villain, an altogether superlative creature, far too handsome as to face and form and garments—a wily bird of prey among women and a desperate gun-man when opposed by members of his own sex. Uncle Jed, a United States Marshal, is a lovable old man, fond of picturesque gestures, nowise the less reliable an ally in a tight corner; while Lord Withymore, Chisholm's close friend, is a typical sporting and chivalrous peer of the realm. And last but not least, there is the great small personage, little eight year old Patience, the sister of the Goddess, a wee damsel who rules it over one and all alike.

Mr. Jeffery Farnol's Romances

Pocket Edition:—Cloth, 3/6 net.   **Pocket Edition:**—Leather, 6/- net.

Popular Edition, 4/- net.

THE BROAD HIGHWAY	THE HON. MR. TAWNISH	MARTIN CONISBY'S VENGEANCE
THE AMATEUR GENTLEMAN	THE GESTE OF DUKE JOCELYN	PEREGRINE'S PROGRESS
THE MONEY MOON	THE DEFINITE OBJECT	SIR JOHN DERING
CHRONICLES OF THE IMP	OUR ADMIRABLE BETTY	THE LORING MYSTERY
BELTANE THE SMITH	BLACK BARTLEMY'S TREASURE	THE HIGH ADVENTURE
	THE QUEST OF YOUTH	

THE SHADOW AND OTHER STORIES, 7s. 6d. net.   GYFFORD OF WEARE, 7s. 6d. net.

EPICS OF THE FANCY
A Vision of old Fighters
7s. 6d. net.

1

SIR TOBY
AND THE REGENT

PAUL HERRING

Author of "Bold Bendigo"

7/6 net

THE ghosts of the Royal Pavilion at Brighton have been conjured up in *Sir Toby and the Regent;* they walk the old Steine again, this gentleman tapping his snuff-box, that gentleman raising his quizzing-glass and bowing to the first Gentleman in Europe, who, wearing a tight-fitting blue coat, rides a bay horse at a leisurely pace, hob-nobbing with fashionable acquaintance over the rails as he proceeds. And at night, with the light of many candles shining on their white cravats, the gentlemen of the Regency take their places at the Prince's mahogany, a roystering company of ghostly wine-bibbers who one by one fall silently to rest under the table.

How the last highwayman on the Brighton road offered Beau Brummel's diamond snuff-box to the Regent, and entered the Pavilion on the arm of His Royal Highness, forms an entertaining episode in the romantic story of Sir Toby, a young country baronet who incurred the displeasure of Trixie the toast of his own county, by making friends with the Fighting Tinman, a Gipsy Fiddler, and breeding gamecocks for the gentlemen of London. Yet when the main is fought at Barnet, the Regent plays a flute to the Gipsy's fiddle, and thinks him a better fiddler than any at the Pavilion.

Again the pages are perfumed by the unseen presence of My Lady Greensleeves, whose lavender and rosemary sweet memory is enshrined in the hearts of two elderly gentlemen like a portrait in a locket.

THE PATTERN OF CHANCE

GORDON GARDINER

Author of "At The House of Dree"

7/6 net

IN this book the author of *At the House of Dree* turns from "Secret Service" to a study of the workings of chance in human life. It is the story of a young man of good family, but bad up-bringing, who, while yet a youth, was convicted of theft, and, after serving a term of imprisonment, sails for South Africa to begin life anew. There, aided by friends and his own better qualities, he makes a promising start. But the shadows of the past persist: his imagination gets the upper-hand, and, finally, at a social gathering, the chance greeting of an acquaintance takes a form that produces a disastrous self-betrayal. In the ostracism and loneliness which follows he sinks into despair. But again chance intervenes. At his darkest moment he is plunged into an adventure of love and mystery.

The theme is both poignant and exciting. In the widely diverse tragedies that have marred the lives of the young people concerned is arrestingly revealed the caprice of fate. From their trials emerge alike the comprehension which draws them irresistibly together and the sense of isolation that bids them snatch their happiness in the face of the world. While the little up-country town, with its English traditions, provides a novel setting unfamiliar in South African fiction, for the mysterious events and vividly depicted characters of the tale.

THE POWER OF THE DOG
DONN BYRNE
7/6 *net*

LARGE success in more than one kind of fiction is achieved by very few writers. Most commonly it predicates versatility, and versatility is perhaps the most dangerous gift with which a fairy can endow an artist at his birth. Thus it may be taken as a proof of Donn Byrne's exceptional gifts as a writer of imaginative literature that he has produced works of first rate quality in such different kinds as " Messer Marco Polo," "Hangman's House" and "Brother Saul," the first a prose poem of singular beauty, the second a story pure and simple, so steeped in atmosphere as to suggest direct inspiration from the genius loci, and the third a biography set against a background of history, in which the beauty and fidelity of the portrait are so admirable as the accuracy of the background. " Brother Saul " was further remarkable for disclosing another aspect of the genius with which Donn Byrne must be credited ; the infinite pains he took in assimilating the actual learning accurate necessary to give him knowledge of the facts that he subsequently presented with the verisimilitude which is a prime essential of fiction.

These same qualities distinguish " The Power of the Dog," the novel to which Donn Byrne had put the finishing touches only a few days before his premature and much to be lamented death. But whereas in " Brother Saul " his novel took the form of a biography set against a background of history, in " The Power of the Dog " he essayed the much more difficult task of utilising a story as a medium for giving a vivid picture of the contemporary history, presenting real historical figures and relating real historical events as they appeared to the people during whose lifetime these respectively lived and happened. Moreover, in choosing the period between 1804 and Napoleon's death in 1821, he elected to deal with a subject almost as vast as that which Hardy treated in such masterly fashion in " The Dynasts," thereby deliberately challenging comparison of his novel with that great epic drama It was a most daring scheme, but it was accomplished with conspicuous success. Without ever forfeiting the interest of the reader in the story of the young husband and wife temporarily separated by divergence of opinions passionately cherished on political issues of the moment, he contrives to give a really remarkable conspectus of the history of those tremendous years, introducing a series of vignettes of the dominant figures of the time which are extraordinarily good as pen portraits while the series episodes in which these figures pass before the mental vision have the clarity and dramatic sequence of costume pictures thrown upon a screen.

Mr. Donn Byrne's other Novels

DESTINY BAY 7/6 *net*	THE FOOLISH MATRONS 7/6 *net*
CRUSADE 7/6 *net*	CHANGELING 7/6 *net*
BROTHER SAUL 7/6 *net*	BLIND RAFTERY
	and his wife Hilaria 5/- *net*
MESSER MARCO POLO 5/- *net*	AN UNTITLED STORY 5/- *net*
THE WIND BLOWETH 7/6 *net*	HANGMAN'S HOUSE 7/6 *net*

IRELAND, THE ROCK WHENCE I WAS HEWN 5/- *net*

BLACK BLOOD
AYLWIN MARTIN
7/6 *net*

HERE is a first novel which reveals unusually fine promise. It is a tale full of atmosphere and colour. The central figure, the Gambler, is a type that has largely vanished, but is still spoken of in terms of respect. Caxton, although he would not scruple to cheat a man at cards, still has his own code of honour. On one of the old Mississippi River steamers he bankrupts a Louisiana planter, and obtains the title to his estate of Seven Pines. It is in slave-holding days, and the new owner obtains the slaves as well as the plantation. Among them is a beautiful girl, about whom little is known except that she has been a ward of the former owner. By the old slave-holding laws, Caxton becomes her master, but gambler though he is, he will not take advantage of the law. Although he falls in love with her, he will not claim her as his own until she reciprocates his affection, which she perversely refuses to do. From this simple situation evolves a series of complicated events rising in intensity and passion until the culmination in a dramatic scene where Caxton attempts to sell the horrified girl on a slave block, but will not accept his rival's bid for her.

It is a story full of life, colour, and action, involving the primal passions, that demands reading from start to finish.

DANCING SHADOW
NANCY MORISON
7/6 *net*

TO many authors, the subject of modern youth in post-war London presents an opportunity for depicting a small corner of Chelsea or Bloomsbury, crowded by strange neurotic creatures of dubious morals and blasphemous conversation. Miss Morison, however, has little use for the easy path of generality and caricature. Young herself, she writes of youth as she sees it—eager-hearted ; impatient of the fears and suspicions of the older generation ; hesitant between stale conventions and new ideals. And of middle-age as she sees it too, in the persons a querulous mother and an eccentric lovable nurse. Her story, which has a strong plot running through it, centres round a little group of teachers in a fashionable school of ballroom dancing. Faith, the heroine, being a pupil-apprentice of that highly respectable martinet, the great Maida Collins. Her life as a dancing-teacher boarded-out with a pair of unsuccessful artists, her love affair with a young doctor, her friendship with the wholly delightful and irrepressible Ena, are darkened by the foreknowledge of sorrow to come. Wherever she goes, dancing on her light feet, a shadow goes too, dancing in rhythm—her constant companion.

How the shadow is finally exorcised, and Faith finds happiness, comes as the inevitable climax to a simple, human story.

4

ROME HAUL
WALTER D. EDMONDS
7/6 *net*

SOMETIMES a civilization, complete in itself, with its own racy native customs, speech, and types of character, springs up about some human trade or means of bread-winning in a particular locality. Sometimes also, such a civilization is handed down to immortality in literature. Such was the fortune of Nantucket whaling at the hands of Melville in his "Moby Dick," and of the old days on the Mississippi when Mark Twain shipped on a raft. Here is the reflection of still another little world, centred in its tow-ropes and sturdy teams and big-fisted bullies, the world of the Erie Canal. Picturesque and distinct in its roving characters with its special oaths and codes the canal with its romance, tragedy and comedy lives again in this pungent, humorous, ample story.

Walter Edmonds, brought up on a branch of the Erie, has talked with old boaters and their descendants, learned their speech, the turn of their trade, their habits of mind. His characters are a Dickensian cast, yet authentic in every syllable. Fortune Friendly, Mrs. Gurget, Dan Harrow, Hector Berry, Gentleman Joe Calash—to meet them and to follow their episodic adventures through the lazy days on the canal, plunging suddenly into moments of intense excitement and stress, is an experience entirely novel and utterly delightful.

GARDEN OATS
FAITH BALDWIN
Author of "Alimony," "Betty," "Three Women," etc.
7/6 *net*

IN *Garden Oats*, two young people, Dolores and her lover, Peter, come to the conclusion that marriage is a fetter and not a bond, and that love and romance flower only in the freer pastures and not in the closed garden. Eloping without the formality of marriage, they are soon driven to it by force of social convention—only to find that romance dies and glamour fades. Their youth, inexperience, poverty and a score of other factors are responsible for this disillusionment but they confuse the issues and come to the conclusion that not themselves but the institution of marriage is at fault. How they break free, how they find together a false freedom—only finally to return again to the fetters, which understanding and maturity see as bonds, concludes the story.

Garden Oats is another fearless discussion of a present-day social tendency as was the author's previous novel, *Alimony*. It is actually based on a life story which came to the attention of Judge Ben B. Lindsey to whom the novel is dedicated.

THE PAVED PATH

PHYLLIS HAMBLEDON

Author of " Jane Cray," " Autumn Fires "

7/6 net

DR. SIMON DEVENHAM left his laboratory in Newchester for the tall house in Lowmarket High Street—firstly, because making love to his neighbour's wife offended his fastidiousness —secondly, because he was weary of bacilli, and liked his own kind. The Paved Path led up to his surgery, and in his first year in general practice, three women passed along it, who were to mar and make his life : Moira, compound of air and fire, whose death was to be so cataclysmic a tragedy ; Sissie, of the streets, who took her own way of trying to console him, and nearly brought him to ruin ; Catherine who saved him at the twelfth hour, and who was eventually to lead him to happiness. These three women, and their reactions upon him, are the theme of the book.

The scene is a small country town, where medical practice is a comparatively peaceful thing. Catherine herself is a very quiet heroine. She has left school all glamorous with hope and happiness. But seven years of life in Lowmarket has changed her. It has removed a smile here, a laugh there.

When she first meets Simon, she is suffering from a Lowmarket complex. When gossip couples their names, it is she who lies bravely. But his dire necessity brings her to him again, and we leave them, after much Sturm and Drang, happy in the tall house in the High Street.

AS FATE DECREES

HENRY ST. JOHN COOPER

Author of " Sunny Ducrow," etc.

7/6 net

POSSESSION! That vast human element before which all others pall into insignificance. Possession, unadorned, unfettered by convention, dominates the fascinating and deeply romantic story from the well-known pen of Henry St. John Cooper.

Two men and one girl are cast up under thrilling circumstances on an uncharted island. On one man's head rests the supreme penalty—that of death. A crime most foul lies at his door.

The other, a peer of the realm, is the dissenting note. The girl, superbly lovely, a vivid creature, is capable of rising to great heights of courage and endurance.

And so these three, so strangely assorted a trio, work out their separate destinies on a lawless isle where death is sometimes better than life.

Following a very natural repugnance, the girl turns, when she needs protection, to the man whose future is under a cloud. Against her better judgment, she begins to love him as passionately, hopelessly as he loves her.

Once they would have welcomed a ship now it is the sight they dread most. They want to be left alone with their love.

But it is not to be. They rise one morning to find a liner on the horizon.

It is on the tiptoe of expectancy that the fascinated reader is led through chapter after chapter of this exquisite and thrilling love story.

CHICAGO MAY
HER STORY BY HERSELF

A HUMAN DOCUMENT BY
THE QUEEN OF CROOKS

12/6 *net*

CHICAGO MAY, " Queen of Crooks " was recognized by the police of three continents as the outstanding woman figure in the criminal world of the twentieth century.

Here, for the first time, she has given her complete story. Told in her own living words, and in her own untrammeled way, it is a human document without parallel.

In her lifetime, Chicago May had many emotional interludes. One of the greatest of these was her partnership with Eddie Guerin, famous international crook and the only man ever to escape from the famous Devil's Island. Chicago May engineered his escape from the monstrous French Penal Colony and she tells here, for the first time, how she put over this unique and seemingly impossible feat.

The craftiness with which she wrought her bold plan and the curious and ingenious manner in which she communicated with Guerin, her lover, while he was isolated in his tropical prison, make one of the most vivid chapters in modern criminal history.

Her many experiences in prisons both here and abroad are outlined in a remarkable chapter that is notable not only for its detail and accuracy, but also for its constructive suggestions for practical reform.

" Chicago May—Her Story " challenges the theory that an honest autobiography cannot be written.

SOME IRISH DRAMATISTS

ANDREW E. MALONE

WITH 16 HALF-TONE ILLUSTRATIONS

7/6 *net*

FEW institutions have had such a marked effect upon the drama of the early 20th century as the Abbey Theatre in Dublin. In every part of Europe and America its influence has been felt, and from it has sprung the folk-drama that is now a feature of the theatre throughout the world. In England and America its inspiration has brought into being local theatres and local schools of drama, which otherwise would probably never have existed.

In this book the author of *The Irish Drama* very vividly sketches some of the leading dramatists of that Theatre, and in addition some of the leading dramatists of the English-speaking world who are either Irish by birth or parentage. Thus Mr. Andrew E. Malone gives biographical and critical sketches of W. B. YEATS, LADY GREGORY, J. M. SYNGE, EDWARD MARTYN, PADRAIC COLUM, SEAN O'CASEY, ST. J. G. ERVINE, LENNOX ROBINSON, T. C. MURRAY, LORD DUNSANY, RUTHERFORD MAYNE, and BRINSLEY MACNAMARA, among the makers of the Irish Theatre ; and he has added chapters on " The Irishness of GEORGE BERNARD SHAW," " The Cosmopolitanism of C. K. MUNRO," and one " Annexing EUGENE O'NEILL "

The book is one that no person interested in contemporary drama will be likely to overlook. Its author is a well-known authority of the drama, whose writings on that subject have attracted considerable attention in the leading Reviews of Ireland, Great Britain, and the United States.

PEEPSHOW OF
THE PORT OF LONDON

A. G. LINNEY

7/6 *net*

THE Right Hon. John Burns once called the Thames " liquid history." The Port of London (and it extends from the Nore to Teddington) is liquid and solid romance. In it are 30 named river reaches ; docks fringed by warehouses packed with all the world's riches ; water spaces where float 30,000-ton liners ; quaint old-time draw docks and miles and miles of busy wharves.

With note-book and camera, Mr. A. G. Linney the well known editor of *The P.L.A. Monthly* has wandered along the river banks from Teddington to Tilbury and all over the docks, and his knowledge of the greatest port in the world as a veritable " peepshow " has been acquired by years of careful observation.

Two chapters provide a unique account of the best places for viewing the *va-et-vient* of the River as a spectacle of movement. There is set down the strange story of " Dagenham Breach "; an account of " The Dock that was a Fortress."

Few people remember that in summer a number of old-timers of sail continue to bring timber from the Baltic to London, and keep the romance of White Wings still alive.

Mention is made of the side-streets (creeks) and hidden rivers which enter the tideway, and Mr. Linney has amassed many curious facts regarding the past and the present in London River history

AGIN THE GOVERNMENTS

MEMORIES AND ADVENTURES OF

SIR FRANCIS FLETCHER VANE, Bart.

16/- net

A REMARK made to me by that eminent Scientist, Sir Francis Galton, who was also a traveller, a humourist and one of the earlier promotors of the study of Heredity in this country, caused me to try to describe my adventures; he said that if a man would only study the careers of his great grandparents, he would probably know a great deal more about himself than he otherwise could hope to do.

This statement came home to me when I was asked to write an account of my experiences, because these great grandparents of mine were an especially varied crew—or if you like, a mixed pack. Speaking only of the male forebears, there was a philanthropic Baronet and landowner, the friend and supporter of John Howard—a Protestant, Ulster Rebel who went out in 1798 with Lord Edward Fitzgerald and escaped to America, and fought against the English at Baltimore, a Catholic Irish landowner, who was dispossessed of his estate under the Catholic Disabilities and eventually became Colonel of the 21st North British Fusileers and fought with us against Napoleon at Malta, and before Genoa—and a stolid Cumbrian small squire who looked after his land. They had only one thing in common, they all were landowners —and their varied tastes led them far afield and to pursue very different courses. Now in this book—if there be anything in heredity—from time to time the reader may discover the influence of the philanthropist, the rebel urging their descendant and victim on to various enterprises and adventures. This is his apology for the versatility of his actions, and the reader (a hundred years ago he would have properly been called gentle reader), when as may happen he differs with the opinions expressed will indulgently excuse these, ascribing them to the influence of his forebears.

From the Preface

9

THE BOOK OF THE SHIP
G. G. JACKSON
6/- *net*

IN this book the writer has endeavoured to give something of the history of the ship, with particular stress on the wonderful advance which has been made during the past century.

When we see the splendid *Mauretania* set out on her race against time across the Atlantic, which she runs at 25 knots with ease, it seems incredible to read that 90 years ago there was not a steamship on the Atlantic.

Fifty years ago, when the magnificent clippers were in their last great days, a story is told of how the captain of a celebrated liner was awakened to be told that a sailer was coming up astern. He refused to believe it, but when he reached deck he found it was the truth. The clipper came up, passed, and went on ahead despite the efforts of the black squad.

That was the last challenge of sail to steam, and now we come once more to the point when steam, having beaten sail, is likely to succumb in turn to the motor driven craft. Nor is the position of the latter at all secure, since 1929 sees the first British electrically driven ship of any size—in active service.

BRITISH LOCOMOTIVES
THEIR EVOLUTION AND DEVELOPMENT
G. G. JACKSON
6/- *net*

JUST a century ago the directors of the Liverpool and Manchester Railway, then rapidly approaching completion, sent out conditions upon which they were prepared to allow locomotives to compete for a £500 prize on their line. Secretly they hoped there would be no entrants, for although, for four years, locomotives had been working the coal trains on the Stockton and Darlington Railway, they were not wholly successful. The alternatives to steam locomotives were horses or stationary engines with long winding ropes. Everyone knew the horse, his patience, his ills and his virtues ; a few knew the reliability of the stationary engine, but how many knew and believed in the locomotive ? The number could have been counted on the fingers of a pair of hands.

It was from those famous Rainhill Trials that the passenger locomotive really emerged ; in this book, the story of that evolution is told, simply, without too great detail. Necessarily the whole story cannot be told in such a volume, but no really outstanding type of engine produced on a British railway is omitted.

THE WORLD'S WARSHIPS
OSCAR PARKES, O.B.E., M.B., CH.B.
7/6 *net*

THERE is a large public interested in naval affairs who do not require a naval encyclopædia, such as *Fighting Ships*, as a reference book—good photos and a few essential details is all that is asked for. This little book is exactly what is wanted in every way, listing the fighting ships and auxiliaries with a few salient details (dates, tonnage, speed, armament, etc.) and illustrated with the latest photos of all the principal types. Once on the bookshelf it will prove to be a constant reference book—ships mentioned in the daily news can be looked up, understood and appreciated ; on shipboard it will fill a long felt want ; budding naval enthusiasts will at once recognise it as the sort of thing they have always wanted. The text has been compiled from *Fighting Ships* and the latest official data ; the photographs have been carefully selected and are clear, good portraits of the ships.

THE POLISH HERITAGE
OF JOSEPH CONRAD
A NEW INTERPRETATION
GUSTAV MORF
7/6 *net*

THIS is a book with a definite thesis. It is nothing less than an attempt to solve the question whether Conrad's inspiration is ultimately based on his Polish-English dualism. Much new material has been used. Although the difficulties were considerable even for one well acquainted with the three or four languages which an historian of Conrad ought to possess, the reader does not feel them. Once the road is made, it is easy to walk.

According to the nature of the subject, the treatment is partly historical, partly psychological. And, in all sincerity, both veins proved rich beyond the author's wildest hopes.

Historical investigation proves clearly to what extent Joseph Conrad's personality was based on Polish memories, hopes, and resentments. Psychological research, on the other hand, makes evident how these Polish tendencies expressed themselves in his work. Incidentally, the book shows what a useful ally modern psychology, used with discrimination, can be in solving literary problems.

Though strictly critical, the book is written in non-technical language. Its aim is to throw light on the least known (but perhaps the most important) aspect of Conrad's genius, and to assist the reader in gaining a fuller understanding of his writings.

✤✤

ABRAMS
OSCAR PARKES, O.B.E., M.B., CH.B.
3/6 *net*

IN this book the pros and cons of Abrams' methods are discussed by one who studied under the doctor himself and investigated his technique at first hand, and after its perusal readers will be in a position to consider and judge for themselves whether or not Abrams deserves the place amongst the Masters of Medicine which Sir James Barr and others consider is his due.

Since his death in 1924 E.R.A. has been developed both in America and this country along lines which suggest that it will eventually have a much wider scope than its founder anticipated, and a section of the book is devoted to a description of the research work which is being done, the problems which present themselves, and some of the results obtained.

Within recent years no system of therapy has excited such a controversy as that associated with the name of Dr. Albert Abrams, and known as " E.R.A." These initials stand for the " Electronic Reactions of Abrams " and in his book Dr. Parkes describes how the famous American doctor first observed the body reflexes and came to associate them with various diseases ; how the nature of these reflexes or reactions was investigated and their importance realised ; how their connection with the earths magnetic flow led to the gradual evolution of an entirely new form of treatment by an electro-magnetic current, and how the Oscilloclast or treatment machine works. The reader is taken to the Clinic at San Francisco and is present at a typical clinical lecture; the magical personality of Dr. Abrams is vividly portrayed and his methods of enquiry and investigation so described that it is easy to understand the veneration in which he was held by his pupils.

The diagnosis and treatment of disease is a subject which appeals to nearly everyone sooner or later. Medicine is not an Exact Science and the unorthodoxy of to-day may become the " orthodoxy " of to-morrow as has been the case with hypnosis and electrical treatment. Abrams' work may be unorthodox now, but much of the opposition to E.R.A. may be due to the fact that its origin, development, and rationale have never been properly appreciated.

In their report upon the actual Abrams reactions the Committee of Investigation presided over by Sir Thomas Horder have put it on record that " The fundamental proposition underlying in common, the original and certain other forms of apparatus devised for the purpose of eliciting the so-called Electronic Reactions of Abrams, is established to a very high degree of probability."

NEW GIRLS' AND BOYS' SCHOOL STORIES
2/6 *net*

THE FOURTH FORM
NANCY DELVES

MONA RHODES begins her life at St. Mildred's by hating the school and quarrelling with her popular cousin, Allison, but Nonie Shields the merry mad-cap of the happy Fourth Form becomes her inseparable chum and Mona enters with zest into Nonie's hilarious schemes.

Nonie is determined that the cousins shall be friends and does all she can to bring this about but it is by Mona's own brave deed that the two are at last united, much to the delight of their chums in the Fourth Form.

PRUNELLA PLAYS THE GAME
IRENE MOSSOP

PRUNELLA PRENDERGAST was quite unlike the orthodox nervous new girl, and although her elder cousin, Jacinth Corriton, welcomed her arrival at St. Prisca's, her younger cousin, Camellia Corriton, was jealous of the newcomer's immediate success at work and games. By choosing Camellia's bete noire, Thyra Hearne, a born rebel and leader in every kind of mischief, for her chum, Prunella excited considerable opposition and landed herself in several scrapes; but the way in which she played the game, both in school and on the cricket field, and her pluck in backing up quiet, diffident Jacinth as Head of her form and Captain of the second XI, won her form-mates' hearts, and at the end of her first term one and all, including Camellia, voted her a " good sport."

THE GIRLS OF ST. HILDA'S
MARY LOUISE PARKER

GENERALLY speaking, they were a delightful company of girls, with one or two exceptions, of course—by way of contrast.

When they all came back after the Easter holiday a " bombshell " awaited them for they found that their popular, admired and much loved captain was on her way to Canada with her family for good and all.

Who should take her place?

The Headmistress suggested that it should be decided by ballot and the girls loved the idea of an " election."

Some people were not pleased with the result, but the Headmistress smiled and was satisfied; she knew the quiet retiring little girl had more character than most others in the sixth and knew she would be well backed up by such staunch partisans as Drusilla and her friends.

THE HARDY BROCKDALE BOYS
R. A. H. GOODYEAR

BROCKDALE is proud of being known as one of the most robust public-schools in the country. It looks down with pitying contempt on a neighbouring school which is specially designed for the tuition of delicate boys. Boarders in this " sissy " establishment feel keenly their physical inferiority, but are dismayed when a new sporting doctor comes along and tries to mould them into better shape. How the doctor becomes friendly with a sturdy Brockdale boy, who is drawn into the task of teaching the mollycoddles games, and how a way is found by which the Brockdale boys may meet the once-despised school on level terms is told and the reader's interest is maintained at a high pitch throughout a typically merry schoolboy yarn.

THE
LAND OF THE STRANGER
A KINDLY COMEDY
DOROTHEA DONN-BYRNE
5/- net

THIS Play was first produced by the Ulster Players at the Gaiety Theatre, Dublin, and the Royalty Theatre, Belfast.

Later, in a shortened form it was presented by the Empire Players (Belfast Repertory Theatre under the direction of Mr. Richard Hayward at the Empire Theatre, Belfast.

NEW EDITIONS ENTIRELY RE-WRITTEN OF
TWO VERY SUCCESSFUL 'HOBBY' BOOKS

300 THINGS A BRIGHT BOY CAN DO
HAROLD ARMITAGE
6/- net

IN this fully illustrated book, we have unfolded before the eyes of youth a very generous choice of games, with innumerable other pastimes and occupations ; so that no boy is likely to turn away from these pages without having found something that will excite his interest, making him wish to play some game, embark upon some hobby ; or construct something that will be useful, amusing or ornamental.

A very large share of the book has been devoted to athletics ; and there are carefully written chapters on training, followed by instructions for such games as football, cricket and hockey. Swimming has been included, with walking, running, jumping, paper chasing, boxing and golf.

In our climate, we cannot always be out of doors ; so that a generous proportion of the volume has been allotted to indoor activities.

301 THINGS A BRIGHT GIRL CAN DO
JEAN STEWART
6/- net

A GIRL who has this book will be introduced to a large range of happy and profitable occupations for any period of the year ; and the work has been fully illustrated in a way to make all the instructions clear.

For clever fingers guidance is given for the shaping of a simple reading stand, for the binding of books and for many other home occupations ; and passe partout picture framing has a chapter to itself.

After a generous section of riddles and puzzles, we have advice for the making of many kinds of sweets, and recipes for drinks. There is also an article on palmistry and fortune telling.

Then we have swimming, boating, golf, hockey, tennis, croquet, badminton, basket ball, net ball, lacrosse and cricket.

Life under canvas is described, and we have much about camping, sketching, and painting ; and other subjects that occupy sections of the book are stencilling, and pyrography, leaf designs, and first steps in understanding church architecture.

THE CHINA COW
GLADYS PETO

*Who also illustrates this unique volume with examples of her art
in colour and black-and-white*

With stories from such well-known pens as
G. B. STERN, BERTA RUCK, CHRISTINE JOPE-SLADE, SEWELL STOKES

3/6 *net*

A COLLECTION of eighteen charming entirely new Fairy Stories. The first one "The China Cow" from which the book takes its name is by Sewell Stokes. They are all delightful—original little tales that children will love. No less will they love Miss Gladys Peto's illustrations, for all the drawings in the book are by her, and there are nearly eighty of them. A great many of them are whole page drawings and a number of them in colour. Miss Peto's drawings are unique in their original daintiness and these as usual, are full of charming line and colour and delicate design. The book is effectively bound in black and orange, with a group of Miss Peto's inevitable children on the front, and altogether makes an ideal present for any child who can appreciate something above the ordinary.

BEHIND THE BRASS PLATE
DR. A. T. SCHOFIELD

6/- *net*
Popular Edition

"BEHIND the Brass Plate" will be found an absolutely truthful picture of the varied life of a doctor in contact with all sorts and conditions of men. Of the acid wit and scarcely decently-veiled malice that "enlivens" too many modern books of reminiscences, not a trace will be found in Dr. Schofield's pages; they express a warm humanity and a mellow, kindly humour that are very attractive yet they are rich in personal anecdotes of well-known men and women, and withal are very amusing, containing a collection of humorous stories that will be widely enjoyed. One, about thirty thousand copies of "The Daily Mail," should not be missed; nor that about the Queen and the German Empress at Cowes. There are some hundreds of stories in the book; all are good, and all are true.

RUPERT OF THE DAILY EXPRESS

A JOYOUS SERIES OF CHILDREN'S BOOKS SELLING IN SCORES OF THOUSANDS

RUPERT
LITTLE BEAR LIBRARY
1/- net

All written and illustrated by

MARY TOURTEL

Pictures and verses on every page.

1. RUPERT AND THE ENCHANTED PRINCESS

TELLS how Rupert rescues the Princess who has been changed into a golden flower. How e tricks the dragon who guards the gate of the garden and how he eventually returns the Princess to her father.

2. RUPERT AND THE BLACK DWARF

IN this story Rupert is captured by the Black Dwarf because he has set free Binoru, the good fairy. After many adventures, Binoru is able to return the good deed, by helping Rupert to escape.

3. RUPERT AND HIS PET MONKEY

BEPPO is the most mischievous monkey that ever lived. He is always causing trouble of some kind until in the end Rupert's daddy has to send him to the Zoo, but Rupert hopes later on to have him back again.

4. RUPERT AND HIS FRIEND MARGOT

MARGOT is carried off by an air balloon and Rupert knows he must rescue her or the Queen will punish her because other children have pricked Air Balloons with pins. This book tells all the exciting adventures that happened to Rupert before he manages to get Margot safely away.

5. RUPERT IN THE WOOD OF MYSTERY

GRUNDOLF the Gnome captures Rupert when he strays into his domain. While he is trying to escape he discovers that the Gnome has a Prince and Princess as prisoners. How he frees them and escapes are told in this thrilling story.

6. FURTHER ADVENTURES OF RUPERT AND HIS PET MONKEY

IN this book Rupert has his pet Beppo back again, but he is just as playful as ever and gets into just as many scrapes. Rupert takes him to the seaside, but Beppo is so naughty that they have to come home

7. RUPERT AND THE THREE ROBBERS

RUPERT falls into the hands of Three Robbers who set him to steal the Magic Cloak which belongs to a wizard. The wizard discovers Rupert in his Castle, but being a kindly wizard, he helps Rupert to escape and finally catches the Three Robbers.

8. RUPERT, THE KNIGHT AND THE LADY

HERE is told how Rupert and his friend Edward Trunk, rescue a Lady who has been carried off by a wicked Dwarf. Rupert makes a long journey to find the Lady's brother, the White Knight. After a little difficulty he finds the Knight and they return to the Black Dwarf's underground palace and kill him, thereby freeing the Lady.

9. RUPERT AND THE CIRCUS CLOWN

RUPERT is lost, when he meets a Circus Clown who promises to direct him, but really carries him off to join the Circus. Rupert escapes only to be captured by an old woman who sends him to an underground Treasure Palace. After many more exciting adventures he again falls in with the Clown, who, in the end, is the means of getting Rupert back to his Uncle.

10. RUPERT AND THE MAGIC HAT

BARRIE:
THE STORY OF A GENIUS

J. A. HAMMERTON

Author of " Barrieland," " Memories of Books and Places " etc.

*Illustrated with a unique series of photographs,
some of which have not previously been published*

16/- *net*

FOR the first time we are put in possession of all the facts—and they are as fascinating as the fictions—of Barrie's romantic career. ·Mr. Hammerton effectively disposes of the numerous improbable stories that have so long had acceptance as Barrieana, and from his pages there emerges the true Barrie in all his authentic charm of personality, no longer a fanciful figure of the journalists' creation.

A biographical narrative rather than critical analysis has been the aim of the author in the writing of this book, but criticism is not absent. Indeed the author is frank to a degree in some of his *dicta* and has never allowed the enthusiasm of hero-worship to modify or obscure his critical perception. He states in an introductory chapter that he has discharged his task of biographer with something of the detachment that he would have shown had his subject lived out his life in another century than this. Only thus is it possible to secure that measure of impartiality which is essential if a biography is to be more than a work of mere uncritical eulogy. Mr. Hammerton may be described as a critical admirer of his literary hero, as one who is alive to his limitations as well as to his greatness.

The publishers feel that they are making no excessive claim when they say that it will not only prove the most attractive biographical work of this season, but that it will take its place among the standard literary biographies in the English language

SAMPSON LOW, MARSTON & CO., LTD.
100 SOUTHWARK STREET, LONDON